From the trackless vastnesses of the great desert of the Tahari three messages came to the stronghold of Tarl Cabot in Port Kar.

One message, conveyed on the person of a slave girl, said to beware of Abdul.

Cabot knew no one of that name.

One message, carried by a hawk-faced desert chieftain, told of a warning, found scratched on a rock in the wilderness, to beware of a steel tower.

Cabot knew of no such tower.

The last, conveyed by a fellow sea captain, was that the Priest-Kings had received an ultimatum to surrender Gor.

And Tarl Cabot, who had thought that he would no longer have to serve the inhuman Priest-Kings, realized that this time he must go again – because now not one man's fortune but a whole world was at stake.

The Gorean cycle of the Chronicles of Counter-Earth,
by John Norman

TRIBESMEN OF GOR

John Norman

A TANDEM BOOK
published by
TANDEM PUBLISHING LTD

A Tandem Book
published in 1977 by
Tandem Publishing Ltd
A Howard & Wyndham Company
123 King Street, London W6 9JG

First published in the United States by Daw Books, Inc., 1976

Made and printed in Great Britain by
Richard Clay (The Chaucer Press) Ltd,
Bungay, Suffolk

ISBN 0426 18147 6

ONE

THE HALL OF SAMOS

There were bells, three rows of them, small and golden, thonged tightly about the girl's left ankle.

The entire floor of the chamber, shining, richly mosaiced, broad, reflecting the torchlight, was a map.

I watched the girl. Her knees were slightly bent. Her weight was on her heels, freeing her hips. Her rib cage was lifted, but her shoulders, relaxed, were down.

Her abdominal muscles, too, were relaxed, loose. Her chin was lifted, haughtily. She did not deign to look at us. Dark hair flowed behind her.

'There are many things I do not understand,' said Samos to me. I reached for a slice of larma fruit, and bit through it. 'Yet,' said Samos, 'I think it is important that we come to the truth in this matter.'

I regarded the vast map on the floor of the chamber. I could see, high on the map, Ax Glacier, Torvaldsland, and Hunjer and Skjern, and Helmutsport, and, lower, Kassau and the great green forests, and the river Laurius, and Laura and Lydius, and, lower, the islands, prominent among them Cos and Tyros; I saw the delta of the Vosk, and Port Kar, and, inland, Ko-ro-ba, the Towers of the Morning, and Thentis, in the mountains of Thentis, famed for her tarn flocks; and, to the south, among many other cities, Tharna, of the vast silver mines; I saw the Voltai Range, and Glorious Ar, and the Cartius, and, far to the south, Turia, and near the shore of Thassa, the islands of Anango and Ianda, and on the coast, the free ports of Schendi and Bazi. There were, on this map, hundreds of cities, and promontories and peninsulas, and rivers and inland lakes and seas.

The left ankle of the girl, under the bells, the brown thong, the golden metal, was tanned.

'Perhaps you are mistaken,' I told him. 'Perhaps there is nothing to it.'

'Perhaps,' he smiled.

At the corners of the room, helmeted, with spears, stood men-at-arms.

The girl wore Gorean dancing silk. It hung low upon her bared hips, and fell to her ankles. It was scarlet, diaphanous. A front corner of the silk was taken behind her and thrust, loose and draped, into the rolled silk knotted about her hips; a back corner of the silk was drawn before her and thrust loosely, draped, into the rolled silk at her right hip. Low on her hips she wore a belt of small denomination, threaded, overlapping golden coins. A veil concealed her muchly from us, it thrust into the strap of the coined halter at her left shoulder, and into the coined belt at her right hip. On her arms she wore numerous armlets and bracelets. On the thumb and first finger of both her left and right hand were golden finger cymbals. On her throat was a collar.

I took another piece of larma fruit, 'I gather,' I said, 'you have information?'

'Yes,' said Samos. He clapped his hands. Immediately the girl stood beautifully, alert, before us, her arms high, wrists outward. The musicians, to one side, stirred, readying themselves. Their leader was a czehar player.

'What is the nature of your information?' I asked.

'It is nothing definite,' he said.

'Perhaps it is not important,' I suggested.

'Perhaps not,' he admitted.

'Kurii, Others,' I said, 'following the failure of the northern invasion of native Kurii, halted in Torvaldsland, have been quiet, have they not?'

'Beware of a silent enemy,' said Samos. He looked at the girl. He clapped his hands, sharply.

There was a clear note of the finger cymbals, sharp, delicate, bright, and the slave girl danced before us.

I regarded the coins threaded, overlapping, on her belt and halter. They took the firelight beautifully. They glinted, but were of small worth. One dresses such a woman in cheap coins; she is slave. Her hand moved to the veil at her right hip. Her head was turned away, as though unwilling and reluctant yet, knowing she must obey.

'Come with me,' said Samos.

I swilled down the last swallow of a goblet of paga.

He grinned at me. 'You may have her later,' he said. 'She will dance from time to time during the evening.'

Samos stepped from behind the low tables. He nodded his head to cup companions, trusted men. Two briefly clad, lovely female slaves withdrew before him, kneeling, heads down, their serving vessels in their hands.

To one side, stripped, bound tightly in black leather, hand and foot, straps crossing between her breasts and circling her thighs, to which her wrists were secured, in buckled cuffs, knelt a whitish-skinned girl, blonde, frightened. Her shoulders, like those of most females of Earth, were tight, tense. The tone of her body, like that of most Earth women, was rigid, defensive. Like most others she had been acculturated in a thousand subtle ways to minimize, to conceal and deny the natural, organic sweetnesses of her musculature and structure, conditioned into a dignified, formal physical neutership, the stiffness, reserve and tightness so much approved of in females in a mechanistic, industrial, technological society, in which machines govern and present the symbols and paradigms of movement, understood as repetition, measure, regularity, precision and function. Human beings move differently in a technological society than in a non-technological society; they hold their bodies differently; a man or woman's acculturation is visible in their demeanor. Few people understand this; most view as natural motions and body positions which are the consequences of a subconsciously conditioned, mechanistic ballet, a choreography of puppets, imitating the models, the stridencies, in which they find themselves enmeshed. Yet, somewhere beneath the conditioned behavior lies the animal, which moved naturally before there was a civilization to teach it the proprieties of mechanism. It is little wonder that the Earth human, when unobserved, even the adult, sometimes throws itself on the ground and rolls and cries out, if only to feel the joy of its own movement, the unleashing of the tensions inflicted by the rigidities of the civilized restraints. Invisible chains are those which weigh the most heavily.

I looked down at the girl. She was terrified, miserable, 'Tell her,' said Samos, 'to watch a true woman, and learn to be female.' He indicated the Gorean dancer.

The girl had not been long on Gor. Samos had purchased

7

her for four silver tarsks on Teletus, with many others, for various amounts. This was the first time out of the pens for her in his house. She wore her brand on the left thigh. A simple band of iron had been hammered about her neck by one of the metal workers in the employ of Samos. She was poor stuff, not fit for a lock collar. I probably would have sold her for a kettle girl. Yet, looking more carefully upon her, examining her with candor, as she looked away, miserable, I saw that she might not be without promise. Perhaps she could be taught. The basic characteristic expected of a Gorean woman is, interestingly, femaleness; this is, I note, certainly not the basic characteristic requested of an Earth woman; indeed, femaleness in a woman of Earth, as I recalled, was societally discouraged, it complicating the politically expedient neuterlike relationships valuable in a technologically sophisticated social structure, to which sexual relationships were irrelevant, if not inimical. Western industrialized societies on Earth optimally would be manned by metal creatures, sexless, smoothly functioning, programmed to tend, preserve, and replicate the metal society. Man, on Earth, had finally succeeded, after long centuries, in creating a society in which he had no essential place; he had, at last, built a house in which he could not live, in which he had left not one room suitable for human habitation; he called it a home; in it he was a stranger; his habitat, by his own efforts, became inhospitable to himself; his efficiencies, his machines, his institutions, in his hands, had at last succeeded in evicting himself from his own realities; women were shamed to be women; men terrified of listening to their blood, and being men; in their plastic cubicles, amidst the hum of their machineries, men at night squirmed and wept, hating themselves, castigating themselves for not meeting the standards of a world alien to their sensate truths; let robots weep for not being men, not men weep for not being robots; the strong, the fine, the mighty, is not wicked; only the vile and small, incapable of power, speak it so; but there was little hope for the men of Earth; they feared to listen, for they might hear ancient drums.

The blondish girl put down her head. I gestured to the guard behind her. He thrust his hand in her hair. She cried out. Her head was rudely jerked up and back. She looked at me.

I pointed to the dancer.

The girl looked at her, horrified, offended, scandalized. She

8

shuddered, and squirmed in the straps. Her fists were clenched at her thighs, beside which they were held in the cuff straps of her harness.

'Watch, Slave,' I told her, in English, 'a true woman.' The girl's title and name had been Miss Priscilla Blake-Allen. Her nationality had been American. Then she had been branded.

She was now only nameless property in a slaver's house, no different from hundreds of other girls in the pens below.

The dancer was now moving slowly to the music.

'She is so sensual,' whispered the blondish girl, in horror.

I turned to watch the dancer. She danced well. At the moment she writhed upon the 'slave pole,' it fixing her in place. There is no actual pole, of course, but sometimes it is difficult to believe there is not. The girl imagines that a pole, slender, supple, swaying, transfixes her body, holding her helplessly. About this imaginary pole, it constituting a hypothetical center of gravity, she moves, undulating, swaying, sometimes yielding to it in ecstasy, sometimes fighting it, it always holding her in perfect place, its captive. The control achieved by the use of the 'slave pole' is remarkable. An incredible, voluptuous tension is almost immediately generated, visible in the dancer's body, and kinetically felt by those who watch. I heard men at the table cry out with pleasure. The dancer's hands were at her thighs. She regarded them, angrily, and still she moved. Her shoulders lifted and fell; her hands touched her breasts and shoulders; her head was back, and then again she glared at the men, angrily. Her arms were high, very high. Her hips moved, swaying. Then, the music suddenly silent, she was absolutely still. Her left hand was at her thigh; her right high above her head; her eyes were on her hip; frozen into a hip sway; then there was again a bright, clear flash of the finger cymbals, and the music began again, and again she moved, helpless on the pole. Men threw coins at her feet.

I looked to the blondish girl. 'Learn to be a female,' I told her.

'Never!' she hissed, in her harness.

'You are no longer on Earth,' I told her. 'You will be taught. The lessons may be painful or pleasant, but you will learn.'

'I do not wish to do so,' she said.

'Your will, your wishes, mean nothing,' I told her. 'You will learn.'

'It is degrading,' she said.

9

'You will learn,' I told her.

'She is so sensual,' said the girl, angrily. 'How can men think of her as anything but a woman!'

'You will learn,' I told her.

'I do not want to be a woman!' she cried out. 'I want to be a man! I always wanted to be a man!'

She squirmed in the harness, fighting its restraints. The straps, the rings, held her, of course, perfectly.

'On Gor,' I told her, 'it is the men who will be men; and here, on this world, it is the women who will be women.'

'I do not wish to move like that,' she wept.

'You will learn to move as a woman,' I told her. I looked down at her. 'You, too, will learn to be sensual.'

'Never,' she wept, fighting the straps.

'Look at me, Slave,' I said.

She looked up, tears in her eyes. 'I will speak to you kindly for a moment,' I said. 'Listen carefully, for they may be the last kind words you will hear for a long time.'

She regarded me, the guard's hand in her hair.

'You are a slave,' I said. 'You are owned. You are a female. You will be forced to be a woman. If you were free, and Gorean, you might be permitted by men to remain as you are, but you are neither Gorean nor free. The Gorean man will accept no compromise on your femininity, not from a slave. She will be what he wishes, and that is a woman, fully, and his. If necessary you will be whipped or starved. You may fight your master. He will, if he wishes, permit this, to prolong the sport of your conquest, but in the end, it is you who are the slave; it is you who will lose. On Earth you had the society at your back, the result of centuries of feminization; he could not so much as speak harshly to you but you could rush away or summon magistrates; here, however, society is not at your back, but at his; it will abet him in his wishes, for you are only a slave; you will have no one to call, nowhere to run; you will be alone with him, and at his mercy. Further, he has not been conditioned with counter-instinctual value sets, programmed with guilt, taught self-hatred; he has been taught pride and has, in the very air he breathes, imbibed the mastery of females. These are different men. They are not Earthlings. They are Goreans. They are strong, and they are hard, and they will conquer you. For a man of Earth, you might never be a woman. For a man of Gor, I assure you, my dear, sooner or later you will be.'

She looked at me with misery.

The dancer moaned, crying out, as though in agony. Still she remained impaled upon the slave pole, its prisoner.

'The Gorean master,' I told the blondish girl, 'commands sensuality in his female slaves.'

She stared at the dancer, her eyes wide with misery. The hips of the dancer now moved, seemingly in isolation from the rest of her body, though her wrists and hands, ever so slightly moved to the music.

'You cannot even move like that now,' I told the blondish girl. 'Yet muscles can be trained. You will be taught to move like a woman, not a puppet of wood.' I grinned down at her. 'You will be taught to be sensual.'

Samos, with a snap of his fingers, freed the dancer from the slave pole. She moved, turning, toward us. Before us, loosening her veil at the right hip, she danced. Then she took it from her left shoulder, where it had been tucked beneath the strap of her halter. With the veil loose, covering her, holding it in her her hands, she danced before us. Then she regarded us, dark-eyed, over the veil; it turned about her body; then, to the misery of the blondish girl, she wafted the silk about her, immeshing her in its gossamer softness. I saw the parted lips, the eyes wide with horror, of the kneeling, harnessed girl, through the light, yellow veil; then the dancer had drawn it away from her, and, turning, was again in the center of the floor.

'You will learn your womanhood,' I told the blondish girl. 'And I will tell you where you will learn it.'

She looked up at me.

'At the feet of a master,' I told her.

I turned away from her and, following Samos, left the chamber.

'She will have to learn Gorean, and quickly,' said Samos, referring to the blondish girl.

'Let slaves, with switches, teach her,' I said.

'I will,' said Samos. There was no swifter way for an Earth girl to learn Gorean, providing that candies and pastries, and little favors, like a blanket in the pens, were mixed in. Learning was closely associated, even immediately, with reward and punishment. Sometimes, months later, even when not under the switch, a girl would, upon a mistake in grammar or vocabulary, wince, as though expecting a fresh sting of the switch. Goreans do not coddle their slave girls. This is one of the first lessons a girl learns.

'You learned little from her?' asked Samos.

I had interrogated the girl when she had first come to the house of Samos.

'Her story,' I said, 'is similar to those of many others. Abduction, transportation to Gor, slavery. She knows nothing. She scarcely understands, now, the meaning of her collar.'

Samos laughed unpleasantly, the laugh of a slaver.

'Yet one thing you had from her seems of interest,' said Samos, preceding me down a deep corridor. In the corridor we passed a female slave. She dropped to her knees and put her head down, her hair upon the tiles, as we passed.

'It seems a random thing, meaningless,' I said.

'In itself meaningless,' he said. 'But, with other things, it induces in me a certain apprehension.'

'The remark she overheard, in English, concerning the return of the slave ships?' I asked.

'Yes,' said Samos. When I had probed the girl in the pens, mercilessly, forcing her to recall all details, even apparently meaningless scraps of detail, or information, she had recalled one thing which had seemed puzzling, disturbing. I had not much understood it, but Samos had evinced concern. He knew more than I of the affairs of Others, the Kurii, and Priest-Kings. The girl had heard the remark drowsily, half stupified, shortly after her arrival on Gor. She, stripped, half drugged, the identification anklet of the Kurii locked on her left ankle, had lain on her stomach, with other girls, in the fresh grass of Gor. They had been removed from the slave capsules in which they had been transported. She had risen to her elbows, her head down. She had then been conscious, vaguely, of being turned about and lifted, and carried, to a different place in the line, one determined by her height. Usually the tallest girls lead the slave chain, the height decreasing gradually toward the end of the chain, where the shortest girl is placed. This was a 'common chain,' sometimes called a 'march chain' or 'trekking chain'; it was not a 'display chain'; in the 'display chain,' or 'selling chain,' the arrangement of the girls may be determined by a variety of considerations, aesthetic and psychological; for example, blondes may be alternated with brunettes, voluptuous girls with slim, vital girls, aristocratic girls with sweet, peasant wenches, and so on; sometimes a girl is placed between two who are less beautiful, to enhance her beauty; sometimes the most beautiful is saved for last on the chain; sometimes the chain is used as a ranking device, the most beautiful being placed at its head, the other girls then competing with one another constantly to move to a new wrist-ring, snaplock or collar, one higher on the chain. She had been thrown to her stomach in the grass, and her left wrist drawn to her side and down. She had heard the rustle of a looped chain, and the periodic click of the wrist-rings. She felt a length of chain dropped across the back of her thighs. Then, about her left wrist, too, closed the wrist-ring, and she, too, was a girl in a coffle. A man had stood by, making entries in a book. When her identification anklet had been removed, after she was in the wrist-ring, the man removing it had said something to the man with the book, and an entry had been made. When the girls were coffled, the man with the book had signed a paper, giving it to the captain of the slave ship. She knew it must be a receipt for merchandise received. The cargo manifests, apparently, had been correct. She had pulled weakly at the wrist-ring, but it, of course, held her. It had been then that the man with the book had asked the captain if he would return soon. The man with the book spoke in an accent, Gorean. The captain, she gathered, did not speak Gorean. The captain had said, as she remembered it, that he did not know when they would return, that he had received orders that there were to be no more voyages until further orders were received. She was conscious of the departure of the ship, and the grass beneath her body, and the chain lying across her legs, and the steel of the wrist-ring. She felt the chain move as the girl to her right stirred. Her left wrist was moved slightly behind her. They lay in the shade of trees, concealed from the air. They were not permitted to rise. When one girl had cried out, she had been beaten with a switch. Miss Priscilla Blake-Allen had not dared to cry out. After dark, they were herded to a wagon.

'Why,' asked Samos, 'should the slave ships cease their runs?'

'An invasion?' I asked.

'Unlikely,' said Samos. 'If an invasion were to be launched soon, surely the slave runs would continue. Their cessation would surely alert the defense and surveillance facilities of Priest-Kings. One would not, surely produce a state of apprehension and heightened awareness in the enemy prior to an

13

attack.'

'It does not seem so,' I admitted, 'unless the Kurii, perhaps, feel that just such a move might put the Priest-Kings off guard, that it would be too obvious to be taken as a prelude to full war.'

'But this possibility, doubtless,' smiled Samos, 'too, is one which will not fail to be considered by the rulers of the Sardar.'

I shrugged. It had been long since I had been in the Sardar.

'It may mean an invasion is being readied,' said Samos. 'But I think the Kurii, who are rational creatures, will not risk full war until reasonably assured as to its outcome. I suspect their reconnaissance is as yet incomplete. The organization of native Kurii, which would have constituted a splendid intelligence probe, and was doubtless intended primarily as such, yielded them little information.'

I smiled. The invasion of native Kurii from the north, survivors and descendants of ship Kurii, for generations, had been stopped in Torvaldsland.

'I think,' said Samos, 'it is something other than an invasion.' He looked at me grimly. 'It is, I suspect, something which would render an invasion unnecessary.'

'I do not understand,' I said.

'I have much fear,' said Samos. I regarded him. I had seldom seen him so. I looked at the heavy, squarish face, burned by the wind and salt of Thassa, the clear eyes, the white, short-cropped hair, the small golden rings in his ears. His face seemed drained of color. I knew he could stand against a hundred swords, unflinching.

'What is it,' I asked, 'which would render an invasion unnecessary?'

'I have much fear,' said Samos.

'You said you had other information,' I said.

'Two things,' said Samos. 'Follow me.' I continued to follow him through various corridors, and down stairways in his house. Soon the walls became damp, and I gathered we were beneath the levels of the canals. We passed barred doors, heavily guarded. Passwords, appropriate to different levels and portions of the house, were given and acknowledged. These are changed daily. For a portion of our way, we passed through certain sections of pens. Some of the ornately barred, crimson-draped cells, with brass bowls, and rugs, and cushions and lamps, were quite comfortable; some of the cells held more

14

than one occupant; some of the girls were permitted cosmetics and slave silk; generally, however, girls in the pen are raw, totally, save for their collars and brands, as are male slaves; the costumer, the perfumer, the hairdresser then does with them what he is instructed; most retention facilities in the pens, however, are not so comfortable; most are simply heavy cages; some are small cement kennels, tiered, with iron gates that slide upward; once we walked over iron gratings, beneath which were cages; we passed through two processing rooms; off one corridor was a medical facility, with mats and chains; we passed exercise rooms, training rooms; we passed the branding chamber; I saw heated irons within; we passed, too, the dreaded room of slave discipline; there were, in this room, suspended rings, whips, a large, heavy stone table.

As we passed the cages, male slaves glared at us sullenly; slave girls usually shrank back. One girl thrust her hands through the bars. 'I am ready to be sold to a man!' she wept. 'Sell me! Sell me!' A guard struck his leather switch against the bars before her face, and she fled back within the inclosure.

'She is not yet hot enough for the block,' I said.

'No,' said Samos.

Had she knelt at the bars, knees thrust through, her body, her face, tear-stained, pressed against them, arms extended, letting her arms be switched for the mere chance of possibly touching the guard's body, then, perhaps, she would have been hot enough. Girls are often sent trembling, burning with passion, to the block. Many times I have seen them, on their feet, shudder and tremble at the auctioneer's slightest touch. Sometimes, unseen by the buyers, they are aroused at the foot of the block, but not satisfied. They are then sent naked to the block to be sold, in this state of cruel frustration. Their attempts to interest the buyers in their flesh are sometimes fantastic. Some of them almost scream in misery, aching for the physical and psychological completion of what has been done to their bodies. I have seen girls whom the auctioneer had to beat from him with his whip, merely in order to display them adequately. These girls, of course, are slaves who have been previously owned. Women who have not been previously owned, like free women, for the most part, even if naked and collared, do not yet understand their sexuality. That can only be taught to them by a man, they helpless, in his power. An unowned girl, a free woman, thus, can never

15

experience her full sexuality. A corollary to this, of course, is that a man who has never had an owned woman in his arms does not understand the full power of his manhood. Sexual heat, it might be mentioned, is looked upon in free women with mixed feelings; it is commanded, however, in a slave girl. Passion, it is thought, deprives the free woman to some extent of her freedom and important self-control; it is frowned upon because it makes her behave, to some extent, like a degraded female slave; free women, thus, to protect their honor and dignity, their freedom and personhood, their individuality, must fight passion; the slave girl, of course, is not entitled to this privilege; it is denied to her, both by her society and her master; while the free woman must remain cool and in control of herself, even in the arms of her companion, to avoid being truly 'had,' the slave girl is permitted no such luxury; her control is in the hands of her master, and she must, upon the mere word of her master, surrender herself, writhing, to the humiliating heats of a degraded slave girl's ecstasy. Only when a woman is owned can she be fully enjoyed.

A silken urt, with wet fur, brushed against my leg.

'Here,' said Samos, at the end of the corridor, one of the lowest in the pens. He uttered the password through the beamed, metal-sheathed door. It swung open. Beyond it was another corridor, but one much shorter. It was dark and damp. Samos took a torch from the guard, and went to one of the doors. He looked through the tiny slit in the door, holding the torch up. Then he slid back the bolt and, bending over, entered the room. There was a foul stench of excrement from within.

'What do you think?' asked Samos.

He held the torch up.

The chained shape did not move. Samos took a stick from beside the door, with which the jailer thrust the pan of water or food toward the shape.

The shape was apparently either asleep, or dead. I did not hear breathing.

An urt scurried suddenly, unexpectedly, toward a crack in the wall. It disappeared within.

Samos touched the shape with the stick. Suddenly it turned and bit the stick through, eyes blazing. It hurled itself, some eight hundred pounds of weight, to the length of the six chains that fastened it, each chain to a separate ring, to the wall. The chains jerked at the rings, again and again. It bit at us. Claws

16

emerged and retracted, and emerged again, from the tentacle-like six-digited appendages of the thing. I looked at the flat, leathery snout, the black-pupiled, yellowish-corneaed eyes, the ears flat back against its head, the wide, fang-rimmed orifice of a mouth, large enough to bite the head from a man. I heard the rings groan in the stone. But they held. I removed my hand from the sword hilt.

The beast sat back against the wall, watching us. It now blinked, against the light of the torch.

'This is the first one, living, that I have seen,' said Samos.

Once before, in the ruins of a hall in Torvaldsland, surmounting a stake, he had seen the head of such a beast.

'It is a Kur, surely,' he said.

'Yes,' I said, 'it is an adult Kur.'

'It is a large one, is it not?' asked Samos.

'Yes,' I said, 'but I have seen many larger.'

'As nearly as we can determine,' said Samos, 'it is only a beast, and not rational.'

I smiled.

It was chained in six places, at the wrists and ankles, and about the waist, and again about the throat. Any of the chains might have held a bosk or a larl.

It snarled, opening its fanged mouth.

'Where did you take it?' I asked.

'I bought it from hunters,' said Samos. 'It was taken southeast of Ar, proceeding in a southeasterly direction.'

'That seems unlikely,' I said. Few Goreans would venture in that direction.

'It is true,' said Samos. 'I know the chief of the hunting pride. His declaration was clear. Six men died in its capture.'

The beast sat, somnolent, regarding us.

'But why would it, a Kur, venture to such a place?' I asked.

'Perhaps it is insane?' suggested Samos.

'What purpose would such a journey serve for a Kur?' I asked.

Samos shrugged. 'We have been unable to communicate with it,' he said to me. 'Perhaps not all Kurii are rational,' he said. 'Perhaps this one, as perhaps some of the others, is simply a dangerous beast, nothing more.'

I looked in to the beast's eyes. Its lips, slightly, drew back. I smiled.

'We have beaten it,' said Samos. 'We have whipped it, and

17

prodded it. We have denied it food.'

'Torture?' I asked.

'It did not respond to torture,' said Samos. 'I think it is irrational.'

'What was your purpose?' I asked it. 'What was your mission?'

The beast said nothing.

I rose to my feet. 'Let us return to the hall,' I said.

'Very well,' said Samos. We left the chamber.

The belled left ankle of the dancer moved in a small circle on the mosaiced floor, to the ringing of the bells, and the counterpoint of the finger cymbals.

Men lifted their cups to Samos as we re-entered the hall. We acknowledged their greetings.

Two warriors, guards, held, between them, a dark-skinned slave girl. She had long, black hair. Her arms were bound tightly to her sides, her wrists crossed and bound behind her. They thrust her forward. 'A message girl,' said one of them.

Samos looked at me, quickly. Then to one of those at the table, one who wore the garments of the physicians, he said, 'Obtain the message.'

'Kneel,' said Samos. The girl, between the guards, knelt.

Samos loomed over her. 'Whose are you?' he asked.

'Yours, Master,' she said. It is common for the girl to be given to the recipient of the message.

'Whose were you?' asked Samos.

'I was purchased anonymously from the public pens of Tor,' she said. Certain cities, like Tor, dealt in slaves, commonly buying unsold girls from caravans, and selling them at a profit to other caravan masters. The city's warriors, too, were paid a bounty on women captured from enemy cities, customarily a silver tarsk for a comely female in good health. 'You do not know who purchased you, or why?' asked Samos. 'No, Master,' she said.

She would not know the message she bore.

'What is your name?' asked Samos.

'Veema,' she said, 'if it pleases Master.'

'What was your number in the pens of Tor?' asked Samos.

'87432,' she said, 'Master.'

The member of the caste of physicians, a laver held for him in the hands of another man, put his hands on the girl's head. She

18

closed her eyes.

'Then,' said I to Samos, 'you do not know from whom this message comes.'

'No,' said he.

The physician lifted the girl's long dark hair, touching the shaving knife to the back of her neck. Her head was inclined forward.

Samos turned away from the girl. He indicated to me a man who sat at a far end of one of the low tables. He did not drink wine or paga. The man, rare in Port Kar, wore the kaffiyeh and agal. The kaffiyeh is a squarish scarf, folded over into a triangle, and placed over the head, two points at the side of the shoulders, one in the back to protect the back of the neck. It is bound to the head by several loops of cord, the agal. The cording indicates tribe and district.

We went to the man. 'This is Ibn Saran, salt merchant of the river port of Kasra,' said Samos.

The red salt of Kasra, so called from its port of embarcation, was famed on Gor. It was brought from secret pits and mines, actually, deep in the interior, bound in heavy cylinders on the backs of pack kaiila. Each cylinder, roped to others, weighed in the neighborhood of ten stone, or some forty pounds, a Gorean 'Weight.' A strong kaiila could carry sixteen such cylinders, but the normal load was ten. Even numbers are carried, of course, that the load is balanced. A poorly loaded kaiila can carry far less weight than one on whom the burden is intelligently distributed.

'Ibn Saran, in the past months, has heard an unusual thing,' said Samos. 'I learned of this from a captain, one known to him, with whom he spoke recently upon the salt wharf.' Samos was first in the Council of Captains of Port Kar, which body was sovereign in the city. There was little of interest which did not, sooner or later, come to his attention.

'The noble Samos has been most kind,' said Ibn Saran. 'His hospitality has been most generous.'

I extended my hand to Ibn Saran and he, bowing twice, brushed twice the palm of his hand against mine.

'I am pleased to make the acquaintance of he who is friend to Samos of Port Kar,' said Ibn Saran. 'May your water bags be never empty. May you have always water.'

'May your water bags be never empty,' I said. 'May you have always water.'

'If it pleases you, noble Ibn Saran,' said Samos, 'would you speak before my friend what you heard in Kasra.'

'It is a story told by a boy, a tender of kaiila. His caravan was small. It was struck by storm, and a kaiila, maddened by wind and sand, broke its hobble, plunging away into the darkness. Foolishly the boy followed it. It bore water. In the morning the storm had passed. The boy dug a shelter trench. In the camp was organized the wheel.'

A shelter trench is a narrow trench, some four or five feet deep and about eighteen inches wide. The sand, struck by the sun, can reach temperatures on its surface of more than 175 degrees Fahrenheit. Set on rocks, boards of metal some two feet in length, and six inches wide, exposed to the sun, are sometimes used by the nomad women in frying foods. Only a foot or two below the surface, these temperatures are reduced by more than fifty degrees. The trench provides, most importantly, shade from the sun. The air temperature is seldom more than 140 degrees in the shade, even in the dune country. The trench, of course, is always dug with its long axis perpendicular to the path of the sun, that it provide the maximum shade for the longest period of time.

One does not, alone, without water, move on the sands during the day. Interestingly, because of the lack of surface water, the nights, the sun gone, are cool, even chilly at times. One would, thus, if not in caravan, move at night. The conservation of body water is the crucial parameter in survival. One moves little. One sweats as little as possible.

The 'wheel' is a search pattern. Herdsmen, guards, kaiila tenders, leave the camp along a 'spoke' of a wheel, spacing themselves at intervals. The number of men in the caravan de- silent caravans, might, unknowingly, pass within yards of men from it by more than the length of the wheel's spoke, pertinent to the individual caravan. The boy, for example, presumably, if he had his wits about him, would not follow the kaiila long enough to place himself outside the 'rim' of the 'wheel.' As the 'wheel' of men turns about its axis, the camp, at intervals the men draw arrows in the dirt or sand, or, if rocks are available, make arrows, pointing to the camp. When the search is discontinued, after success or failure, these markers are destroyed, lest they be taken by travelers for water arrows, markers indicating the direction of water holes, underground cisterns or oases. The caravan kaiila, incidentally, both those which are pack animals and those used as mounts for guards and warriors, are muchly belled. This helps to keep the animals together, makes it easier to move in the darkness, and in a country where, often, one cannot see more than a hundred yards to the next dune or plateau, is an important factor in survival. If it were not for the caravan bells, the slow moving, otherwise generally silent caravans, might, unknowingly, pass within yards of men in desperate need of succor. The kaiila of raiders, incidentally, are never belled.

'By noon,' said Ibn Saran, 'the boy was found. Hearing the bells of a guard's mount, he emerged from the shelter trench, and, attracting the man's attention, was rescued. He was, of course, muchly beaten, for having left the caravan. The kaiila, of his own accord, returned later, for fodder.'

'What,' I asked, 'was the story of the boy?'

'What, in pursuing the kaiila, he found,' said Ibn Saran. 'On a rock there was scratched this message: Beware the steel tower.'

Samos looked at me. I made little sense of this.

'Near the rock, dead,' said Ibn Saran, 'blistered, blackened by the sun, dried, weighing no more than a child or woman, was a man. He had torn off his clothing and drunk sand.'

It would not have been a pleasant death. Doubtless he had died, mad, thinking he had found water.

'It, judging from discarded accoutrements,' said Ibn Saran, 'was a raider.'

'Was there no kaiila?' I asked.

'No,' said Ibn Saran.

'From how far had the man come?' I asked. 'How long had he been on the desert?'

'I do not know,' said Ibn Saran. 'How well did he know the desert? How much water had he?'

The man might have come thousands of pasangs before the kaiila had died, or fled.

'How long had he been dead?' I asked.

Ibn Saran smiled thinly. 'A month,' he said. 'A year?'

In the desert decomposition proceeds with great slowness. Bodies, well preserved, had been found which had been slain more than a century before. Skeletons, unless picked by birds or animals, are seldom found in the desert.

'Beware the steel tower,' I repeated.

'That was scratched on the rock,' said Ibn Saran.

'Was there any indication from which direction the man had come?' I asked.

'No,' said Ibn Saran.

'Beware the steel tower,' said Samos. I shrugged.

Samos rose to his feet and, touching twice the palm of the right hand of Ibn Saran, took his leave. I noted that Ibn Saran ate only with the right hand. This was the eating hand, and the scimitar hand. He would feed himself only with the hand which, wielding steel, could take blood.

The dancer whirled near us, then enveloped me in her veil. Within the secrecy of the veil, binding us together, she moved her body slowly before me, lips parted, moaning. I took her in my arms. Her head was back, her eyes closed. I pressed my lips to hers, and with my teeth cut her lip. She, and I, together, tasted the blood and rouge of her subjugation. She drew back slightly, blood on the side of her mouth. Fist by fist, my hand on the back of her small, delicious neck, preventing her from escaping, I slowly removed her veil from her, then threw it aside. Then with my right hand, the Tuchuk quiva in it, while still holding her with my left, as she continued to move to the music, I, behind her back, cut the halter she wore from her. I then thrust her from me, before the tables, that she might better please the guests of Samos, first slaver of Port Kar. She looked at me reproachfully, but, seeing my eyes, turned frightened to the men, hands over her head, to please them. Never in all this, had she lost the music in her body. The men cried out, pleased with her beauty.

'The message girl is ready,' said the man who wore the green of the physicians. He turned to the man beside him; he dropped the shaving knife into the bowl, wiped his hands on a towel.

The girl, bound, knelt between the guards. There were tears in her eyes. Her head had been shaved, completely. She had no notion what had been written there. Illiterate girls are chosen for such messages. Originally her head had been shaved, and the message tattooed into the scalp. Then, over months, her hair had been permitted to regrow. None but the girl would know she carried such a message, and she would not know what it might be. Even those for a fee delivering her to the house of Samos would have considered her only another wench, mere slave property.

I read the message. It said only 'Beware Abdul.' We did not know from whence the message came, or who had sent it.

22

'Take the girl to the pens,' said Samos to the guards. 'With needles remove the message from her scalp.'

The girl was jerked to her feet.

She looked at Samos. 'Then,' said Samos, to the guards, 'use her as a low work-slave in the pens primarily as a cleaning slave. A month before her hair is regrown, and she is fit for sale, wash her and put her in a stimulation cage and train her intensively.'

The girl looked at him, agonized.

'Then sell her,' said Samos.

A stimulation cage is an ornately barred, low-ceilinged cage; it is rather roomy, except for the low ceiling, about five feet high. The girl cannot stand erect in it without her head inclined submissively. In such a cage, and in training, when not in such a cage, the girl who is housed in the stimulation cage is not permitted to look directly into the eyes of a male, even a male slave. This is designed, psychologically, to make the girl extremely conscious of males. When she is sold, then only, if the master wishes, he may say to her: 'You may look into the eyes of your master.' When she, frightened, tenderly, timidly lifts her eyes to him, if he should deign to smile upon her, the girl then, in gratitude and joy, at last permitted to relate to another human being, often falls to her knees before him, an adoring slave. When next she looks up, his eyes will be stern, and she will look down, quickly, frightened. 'I will try to serve you well, Master,' she whispers. The accoutrements of the stimulation-cell are also calculated with respect to their effect on the slave. There are brushes, perfumes, cosmetics, slave jewelries, heavy necklaces, armlets, bracelets and bangles; there is no clothing; there are also cushions, bowls of copper and lamps of brass. Importantly, there are also surfaces of various textures, a deep-piled rug, satins, silks, coarsely woven kaiila-hair cloths, brocades, rep-cloth, a tiled corner, a sleen pelt, cloths woven of strung beads, cloaks of leather, mats of reeds, etc. The point of this is that the senses and body of the slave, stripped save for brand and collar, and whatever perfumes, cosmetics or jewelries she may wear under the instruction of her trainer, are being taught to be alive, to sense and feel with great sensitivity; the senses and skins of many human beings, in effect, are dead, instead of being alert and alive to hundreds of subtle differences in, say, atmospheres, temperatures, humidities, surfaces, etc. A girl with living senses and a living body, of course, is far more passionate than one whose senses and body sleep. The skin itself, in a trained girl, becomes an extensive, glorious, marvelously subtle organ. Every bit of the slave, if she is well trained, is alive. This is done, of course, to make her more helpless under the touch of a master. When she does yield to the master, her guts half torn out with the love of him, then, of course, she is a more satisfactory slave. These indignities, of course, are not inflicted on free women. They are permitted to go through life with their eyes half closed, so to speak. In this way they can maintain their self-respect. Sometimes inert, esteemed Gorean free women cry out in rage, not understanding why their companions have forsaken them for the evening, to go to the paga tavern; there, of course, for the price of a cup of paga, he can get his hands on a silken, belled girl, a slave; the free woman must denounce her companion, crying out, for his lusts; too busy for this, however, are the sweet, dark-eyed, sensuous sluts of the paga tavern; they do not have time to denounce the lusts of their master's customers; they are too busy serving and satisfying them. The trainer directs the girl in the cage, or in the exercises, tending, observing, and prescribing, honing her with expertness into a delicious, responsive slave animal, the Gorean girl, collared, in bondage, trained to drive a man mad with desire, and then serve that desire, vulnerably, frequently and absolutely. The girl was thrust through the door, between the guards. I wondered what the trainer would prescribe for her. Girls differ, trainers differ. I glanced at the blondish girl, kneeling to one side, the former Miss Priscilla Blake-Allen. I, if her trainer, would probably put her frequently, at least at first, and later for discipline, in a rope slave harness. After a night in such harness, her wrists braceleted behind her that she might not remove it, I expected Miss Blake-Allen would be suitably docile, and eager to attend to her lessons.

When the girl had been forced through the door leading to the pens, I turned to Samos.

'Who is Abdul?' I asked.

Samos puzzled, looked at me.

'Who is Abdul?' I repeated.

'I do not know,' said Samos. He turned and went to his place behind the low table.

Those at the table paid us little attention. All eyes were on the dark-haired dancer, the skirt of diaphanous scarlet dancing silk low upon her hips. Her hands moved as though she might be,

24

starved with desire, picking flowers from a wall in a garden. One saw almost the vines from which she plucked them, and how she held them to her lips, and, at times, seemed to press herself against the wall which confined her. Then she turned and, as though alone, danced her need before the men.

'There is much here that appears to make little sense,' said Samos. 'Yet, there must be a meaning, a pattern.' With an eating prong, of Turian design, Samos tapped the table before him. He looked at me. 'Little has of late occurred in the Wars of Priest-Kings and Others.'

'Beware of a silent enemy,' I said.

Samos smiled. 'True,' he said. Then he pointed the eating prong at the leather-harnessed American girl, on the tiles to our right, naked, two guards with spears at her side. The heavy butts of their spears rested, one to each side of her. Her fists were clenched in the leather, buckled cuffs of her harness, held to her thighs by the thigh straps. 'We learn from this slave,' he said, indicating the former Miss Blake-Allen, 'that, until further orders, slave runs from Earth to Gor have been canceled.'

'Yes,' I said.

'Why?' he asked.

'Have the runs actually been stopped?' I asked.

'Information from the Sardar,' said Samos, 'suggests that they have. There has not been a detection, let alone a pursuit, in three weeks.'

The Gorean week consists of five days. Each month consists of five such weeks. Following each month, of which there are twelve, separating them, is a five-day Passage Hand. The twelfth Passage Hand is followed by the Waiting Hand, a five-day period prior to the vernal equinox, which marks the Gorean New Year. It was currently in the late winter of Year 3 of the Sovereignty of the Council of Captains in Port Kar, the year 10,122 C.A., Contasta Ar, from the Founding of Ar. I had, two months ago, returned from Torvaldsland, where I had attended to certain matters of the sword.

'Further,' said I, 'into your keeping has come a captive beast, clearly a Kur.'

'It seems irrational,' said Samos. 'Only a beast.'

'I think it is rational,' I said. 'Its intelligence, I suspect, is the equal of ours, if not greater.'

Samos regarded me.

'It may not, of course, be able to articulate Gorean. Few of

25

the Kurii can. It is extremely difficult for them to do so.'

'You understand the direction in which it was traveling?' asked Samos.

'Yes,' said I.

'Strange,' said Samos.

The beast had been taken southeast of Ar, while moving southeast. Such a path would take it below the eastern foothills of the Voltai and to the south. It was incredible.

'Who would enter such a place?' asked Samos.

'Caravans, crossing it,' I said. 'Nomads, grazing their verr on the stubble of verr grass.'

'Who else?' asked Samos.

'The mad?' I smiled.

'Or the purposeful,' said Samos, 'someone who had business there, who knew what he was intending?'

'Perhaps,' I admitted.

'Someone who had a mission, who knew precisely for what he was searching?'

'But there is nothing there,' I said. 'And only the mad, deeper into the area, depart from marked caravan routes, proceeding from oasis to oasis.'

'A tender of kaiila, a boy, lost from his camp,' said Samos, 'found a rock. On this rock was inscribed "Beware the steel tower." '

'And the message girl,' I said. 'We do not know, I gather, whom this Abdul is of whom we are warned to beware.'

'No,' said Samos, puzzled. 'I know of no Abdul.'

'And who would send such a message, and why?'

'I do not know,' said Samos.

I idly observed the dancer. Her eyes were on me. It seemed, in her hands, she held ripe fruits for me, lush larma, fresh picked. Her wrists were close together, as though confined by the links of slave bracelets. She touched the imaginary larma to her body, caressing her swaying beauty with it, and then, eyes piteous, held her hands forth, as though begging me to accept the lush fruit. Men at the table clapped their hands on the wood, and looked at me. Others smote their left shoulders. I smiled. On Gor, the female slave, desiring her master, yet sometimes fearing to speak to him, frightened that she may be struck, has recourse upon occasion to certain devices, the meaning of which is generally established and culturally well understood. I shall mention two such devices. There is, first, the bondage knot.

26

Most Gorean slave girls have long hair. The bondage knot is a simple looped knot tied in the girl's hair and worn at the side of her right cheek or before her right shoulder. The girl approaches the master naked and kneels, the bondage knot soft, curled, fallen at the side of her right cheek or before her right shoulder. Another device, common in Port Kar, is for the girl to kneel before the master and put her head down and lift her arms, offering him fruit, usually a larma, or a yellow Gorean peach, ripe and fresh. These devices, incidentally, may be used even by a slave girl who hates her master but whose body, trained to love, cannot endure the absence of the masculine caress. Such girls, even with hatred, may offer the larma, furious with themselves, yet helpless, the captive of their slave needs, forced to beg on their knees for the touch of a harsh master, who revels in the sport of their plight? Does he satisfy them. If it is his will, yes; if it is not his will, no. They are slaves.

The girl now knelt before me, her body obedient still, trembling, throbbing, to the melodious, sensual command of the music.

I looked into the cupped hands, held toward me. They might have been linked in slave bracelets. They might have held lush larma. I reached across the table and took her in my arms, and dragged her, turning her, and threw her on her back on the table before me. I lifted her to me, and thrust my lips to hers, crushing her slave lips beneath mine. Her eyes shone. I held her from me. She lifted her lips to mine. I did not permit her to touch me. I jerked her to her feet and, half turning her, ripping her silk from her, hurled her to the map floor, where she half lay, half crouched, one leg beneath her, looking at me, stripped save for her collar, the brand, the armlets, bells, the anklets, with fury. 'Please us more,' I told her. Her eyes blazed. 'And do not rise from the floor, Slave,' I told her. The music, which had stopped, began again.

She turned furiously, yet gracefully, extending a leg, touching an ankle, moving her hands up her leg, looking at me over her shoulder, and then rolled, and writhed, as though beneath the lash of masters.

'You discipline her well,' said Samos, smiling.

I grinned.

The girl now, on her belly, yet subtly to the music, crawled towards us, lifted her hand piteously to us.

I heard a cry of dismay, of protest, from the horrified, once

27

Miss Blake-Allen.

Samos regarded her. He was not pleased. 'Free her legs of the harness,' said Samos to one of the guards.

The guard took the straps which had bound her ankles together, and, untying them, slipped them through the metal ring, glinting, sewn into the back of the leather collar of the harness, worn over the simple curved collar of iron which marked her, even should she be clothed, and her brand not visible, as slave. The straps had run from the back of the collar to her ankles, holding her in a kneeling position. Her legs were now free. The ankle straps then, sewn to the sides of the collar, and now circled about the collar and crossing in back, and now run through the ring on the front of the collar, served as leash. The harness is designed to provide a large number of ties. The girl, her legs freed, looked at Samos with horror. But he was no longer regarding her.

The dancer now lay on her back and the music was visible in her breathing, and in small movements of her head, and hands. Her hands were small and lovely.

She lay on the map floor, her head turned towards us. She was covered with sweat.

I snapped my fingers and her legs turned under her, and she was kneeling, head back, dark hair on the tiles. Her hands moved, delicate, lovely. Slowly, if permitted, she would rise to an erect kneeling position her hands, as she lifted herself, extended toward us. Four times said I 'No,' each time my command forcing her head back, her body bent, to the floor, and each time, again, to the music, she lifted her body. The fifth time I let her rise to an erect kneeling position. The last portion of her body to rise was her beautiful head. The collar was at her throat. Her dark eyes, smoldering, vulnerable, reproachful, regarded me. Still did she move to the music, which had not yet released her.

With a gesture I permitted her to rise to her feet. 'Dance your body, Slave,' I told her, 'to the guests of Samos.'

Angrily the girl, man by man, slowly, meaningfully, danced her beauty to each guest. They struck the tables, and cried out. More than one reached to clutch her but each time, swiftly, she moved back.

Samos rose from behind the table and strode to the map floor. I went with him.

He stopped at a point on the smooth, mosaiced floor. I

looked at him. 'Yes,' he said, 'somewhere here.'

I looked down at the intricately wrought mosaiced floor. Beneath our feet, smooth, polished, were hundreds of tiny, fitted bits of tile, mostly here, in this area, tan and brown. The bits of tile seemed soft, lustrous, under the torchlight. The dancer, now behind us, continued to move before the low tables. The eyes of the men gleamed. Before each man, for moments seemingly his alone, she danced her beauty.

'There is one thing more,' said Samos, 'which I have not told you.'

'What is that?' I asked.

'Kurii have delivered to the Sardar an ultimatum.'

'An ultimatum?' I asked.

'Surrender Gor, it said,' said Samos.

'Nothing more?' I asked.

'Nothing more,' said Samos.

'This makes little sense to me,' I said. 'For what reason should this world be surrendered to Kurii?'

'It seems insane,' said Samos.

'Yet Kurii are not insane,' said I. 'There was no alternative specified?' I asked.

'None,' said Samos.

'Surrender Gor –' I repeated.

'It seems a mad imperative,' said Samos.

'But if it is not?'

'I am afraid,' said Samos.

'And how has the Sardar responded to this?' I asked. 'Have they repudiated it, scoffingly, ridiculed the preposterousness of this demand?'

Samos smiled. 'Misk, a Priest-King,' said he, 'one high in the Sardar, has asked Kurii for a further specification of details.'

I smiled. 'He is buying time,' I said.

'Of course,' said Samos.

'What response, if any, was made?' I asked.

'Surrender Gor,' said Samos. 'A repetition of the original imperative. Then there was communication silence.'

'Nothing more has been heard from Kurii?' I asked.

'Nothing more,' said Samos.

'Doubtless it is a bluff on the part of Kurii,' I said. 'Priest-Kings would not well understand that sort of thing. They are quite rational generally, unusually logical. Their minds seldom

29

think in terms of unwarranted challenges, psychological strategies, false claims.'

Samos shrugged.

'Sometimes I think Priest-Kings do not well understand Kurii. They may be too remotely related a life form. They may not have the passions, the energies, the hatreds to fully comprehend Kurii.'

'Or men,' said Samos.

'Or men,' I agreed. Priest-Kings surely had energies and passions, but, I suspected, they were, on the whole, rather different from those of men, or, indeed, those of Kurii. The nature of the sensory experience of Priest-Kings was still, largely, a mystery to me. I knew their behavioral world; I did not know the world of their inner experience. Their antennae were their central organs of physical transduction. Though they had eyes, they seldom relied upon them, and were perfectly at ease in total darkness. Lights, in the Nest, were for the benefit of humans and other visually oriented creatures sharing the domicile. Their music was a rhapsody of odors, many of which were, to human olfactory organs, not even pleasant. Their decorations were largely invisible lines of scent traced with great care on the interiors of their compartments. Their most intense, pleasurable experience was perhaps to immerse their antennae in the filamented, narcotic mane of the golden beetle, which would then, piercing them with its curved, hollow, laterally moving jaw-pincers, drain them of their body fluid, feeding itself, slaying them. The social bond of the Priest-Kings is Nest Trust. Yet, in spite of their different evolutionary background and physiology, they had learned the meaning of the word 'friend'; too, I knew, they understood, if only in their own way, love.

I smiled to myself. 'Sometimes,' once had said Misk to me in the Nest, 'I suspect only men can understand Kurii.' Then he had added, 'They are so similar.'

It had been a joke. But I did not think it was false.

Unfortunate though it might be, I doubted and, I think, realistically, that Priest-Kings, those large, golden creatures, so gentle and delicate seeming, so content to mind their own affairs, truly understood their enemy, the Kurii. The persistence, the aggression, the fevers of the blood, the lust, the territoriality of such beasts would be largely unintelligible to them. There was little place in the placid, lucid categories of Priest-

Kings for comprehending the bloods and madness of either men or Kurii. They, Kurii and men, understood one another better, I suspected, than the Priest-Kings understood either. As long as the Kurii remained behind the fifth ring, that determined by the orbit of the planet called on Earth Jupiter, on Gor, Hersius, after a legendary hero of Ar, the Priest-Kings were little concerned with them. They had no objection if such ravening wolves prowled their fences, and scratched at their very gates. 'They, like men, are an interesting life form,' once had said Misk to me. But now the Kurii worlds, sensing the weakness of the Sardar, following the Nest War, damages that had destroyed their basic power source and had split the very Nest open to the sky, prowled more closely. The worlds, now, or several of them, we understood, concealed, shielded, lurked well within the asteroid belt. Contact points, bases, had been established, it seemed, on the shores of Earth itself. The major probe of Kurii, the organization of native Kurii by ship Kurii, had taken place recently. It had failed. It had been stopped in Torvaldsland. Ship Kurii, still, then, did not know the extent to which the power of Priest-Kings remained crippled. This was the major advantage which we now held. Kurii, cautious, like sharks, did not wish to commit their full attack until assured of its success. Had they known the weakness of the Sardar, and the time required to restore the power source, regenerating itself now at inexorable concentration rates determined by natural law, they would have surely launched their fleets. Most, we conjectured, they feared a ruse, a display of pretended weakness that would lure an attack, then to be decimated. Moreover, I knew there were factions among Kurii. Doubtless they had individuals who were bolder, and those who were more cautious. The failure of the Torvaldsland probe might have had great impact in their councils. Perhaps a new party had come to power among them. Perhaps now, a new strategy, a new plan, was afoot.

'Surrender Gor –' said Samos, looking down at the portion of the map beneath his feet.

I looked to the map. Was this where the new plan of Kurii, if there was such a new plan, touched this primitive world?

'The path of the captured Kur,' said Samos, pointing, 'would have taken it here.'

'Perhaps he intended to cross it?' I asked.

Samos pointed with his finger, west of Tor. 'No,' said he,

'surely one would circle the area, taking the routes west of Tora, where there is ample water.'

'One would surely need a caravan, and guides,' I said, 'to survive east of Tor?'

'Of course,' said Samos. 'Yet the beast was alone.'

'I suspect,' said Samos, 'that the beast's destination lay not on the other side of this area, but within it.'

'Incredible,' I said.

Samos shrugged.

'Why should a Kur go to such a place, and enter such a country?' I asked.

'I do not know,' said Samos.

'Strange that at this time, too,' said I, 'the slave runs should cease, and the imperative, inexplicable, to surrender Gor should be served upon the Sardar.'

'What did the Kur seek in such a country?' asked Samos.

'And what,' I asked, 'of the message on the stone, "Beware the steel tower"?'

'It is a mystery,' said Samos, 'and the answer lies here.' He pointed to that dread area of Gor.

I looked downward. Though on the map it occupied only some several feet of the floor, in actuality it was vast. It was roughly in the shape of a gigantic, lengthy trapezoid, with eastward leaning sides. At its northwestern corner lay Tor. West of Tor, on the Lower Fayeen, a sluggish, meandering tributary, like the Upper Fayeen, to the Cartius, lay the river port of Kasra, known for its export of salt. It was in this port that the warehouses of Ibn Saran, salt merchant, currently the guest of Samos of Port Kar, were to be found. This city, too, was indicated in the cording of his agal, and in the stripes of his djellaba.

The area, in extent, east of Tor, was hundreds of pasangs in depth, and perhaps thousands in length. The Gorean expression for this area simply means the Wastes, or the Emptiness. It is a vast area, and generally rocky, and hilly, save in the dune country. It is almost constantly windblown and almost waterless. In areas it has been centuries between rains. Its oases are fed from underground rivers flowing southeastward from the Voltai slopes. The water, seeping underground, eventually, in places, due to rock formations, erupts in oasis springs, or, more usually, is reached by deep wells, some of them more than two hundred feet deep. It takes more than a hundred and fifty years for some of this water to make the underground journey, seeping hundreds of feet at times beneath the dry surface, moving only a few miles a year, to reach the oases. Diurnal air temperatures in the shade are commonly in the range of 120 degrees Fahrenheit. Surface temperature, diurnally, is, of course, much higher. In the dune country, by day, if one were so unwise as to go barefoot, the bright sand would quickly cripple a man, abraiding and burning the flesh from his feet in a matter of hours.

'It is here,' said Samos, pointing to the map, 'that the secret lies.'

The dancer turned from the tables and, hands high over her head, approached me. She swayed to the music before me. 'You commanded me to dance my beauty for the guests of Samos,' said she, 'Master. You, too, are such a guest.'

I looked upon her, narrow lidded, as she strove to please me.

Then she moaned and turned away, and, as the music swirled to its maddened, frenzied climax, she spun, whirling, in a jangle of bells and clashing barbaric ornaments before the guests of Samos. Then, as the music suddenly stopped, she fell to the floor, helpless, vulnerable, a female slave. Her body, under the torchlight, shone with a sheen of sweat. She gasped for breath; her body was beautiful, her breasts lifting and falling, as she drank deeply of the air. Her lips were parted. Now that her dance was finished she could scarcely move. We had not been gentle with her. She looked up at me, and lifted her hand. It was at my feet she lay.

I gestured her to her knees, head down. She obeyed. Her hair fell to the map floor.

It touched the portion of the map which, together, Samos and I had been contemplating. I regarded the lettering, in Gorean script.

'The secret is there,' said Samos, pointing to the map, 'in the Tahari.'

Delicately, timidly, the dancer reached out, with her two hands, to touch my ankle. She looked at me, agonized.

I signaled to the guards. She cried out with misery as she was dragged by the ankle across the floor and thrown over two of the small tables.

I would let others warm her.

The men cried out with pleasure.

33

Her final yieldings I would force from her later, when it pleased me.

She who had once been Miss Priscilla Blake-Allen, a free Earth girl prior to her enslavement, struggled to her feet, her eyes wide with horror, trying to struggle backward, but the guards' hands on her arms, she now only a nameless slave, for her master had not yet given her a name, held her in place.

She looked at her master, Samos of Port Kar. He gave a sign. She screamed.

She fought the harness.

She, too, was thrown across the tables.

Ibn Saran, salt merchant of Kasra, did not rise from behind the table behind which, cross-legged, he sat. His eyes were half closed. He paid no attention to the raping of the slaves. He, too, it seemed, contemplated the map.

'Either girl's use is yours, noble Ibn Saran,' said Samos, 'if you wish.'

'My thanks,' said he, 'Noble Samos. But it will be in my own tent, on the submission mats, that I will teach a slave to be a slave.'

I turned to Samos. 'I will leave in the morning,' I said.

'Do I understand,' asked Ibn Saran, 'that your path leads you to the Tahari?'

'Yes,' I said.

'That direction, too, is mine,' said Ibn Saran. 'I, too, leave in the morning. Perhaps we might travel together?'

'Good,' I said.

Ibn Saran rose to his feet, and brushed his hand against the right palm of Samos, twice, and against my right palm, twice. 'May your water bags be never empty. May you always have water.'

'May your water bags be never empty,' I said. 'May you always have water.'

He then bowed, turned, and left the room.

'The Kur,' I said. I referred to the beast in the dungeons of Samos.

'Yes?' said Samos.

'Free it,' I said.

'Free it?' he asked.

'Yes,' I said.

'Is it your intention to follow it?'

'No,' I said. Few, if any humans, in my opinion, could long

34

follow an adult Kur. They are agile, highly intelligent beasts. Their senses are unusually keen. It would be difficult, if not impossible, to trail, perhaps for weeks, such a keen-sensed, wary, suspicious creature. It would be almost suicidal, in my opinion, to attempt it. Sooner or later the beast would become aware of the pursuit. At that point the hunter would become the hunted. The night vision of the Kur is superb.

'Do you know what you are doing?' asked Samos.

'There are factions among Kurii,' I said. 'It is my feeling that this Kur may be our ally.'

'You are mad,' said Samos.

'Perhaps,' I granted.

'I shall release the Kur,' said Samos, 'two days after you have departed Port Kar.'

'Perhaps I shall meet it in the Tahari,' I said.

'I would not look forward to the meeting,' he said.

I smiled.

'You leave in the morning?' asked Samos.

'I shall leave before morning,' I said.

'Are you not traveling with Ibn Saran?' asked Samos.

'No,' I said. 'I do not trust him.'

Samos nodded. 'Nor do I,' he said.

TWO

THE STREETS OF TOR

'Water! Water!' called the man.

'Water,' I said.

He came to me, bent over, tattered, swarthy, grinning up at me, the verrskin bag over his shoulder, the brass cups, a dozen of them, attached to shoulder straps and his belt, rattling and clinking. His shoulder on the left was damp from the bag. There were sweat marks on his torn shirt, under the straps. One of the brass cups he unhooked from his belt. Without removing the bag from his shoulder, he filled the cup. He wore a head scarf, the wrapped turban, wound about his head. It was of rep-cloth. It protects the head from the sun; its folds allow heat and perspiration to escape, evaporating, and, of course, air to enter and circulate. Among lower-class males, too, it provides a soft cushion, on which boxes, and other burdens, may be conveniently carried on the head, steadied by the right hand. The water flowed into the cup through a tiny vent-and-spigot device, which wastes little water, by reducing spillage, which was tied in and waxed into a hole left in the front left foreleg of the verr skin. The skins are carefully stripped and any rents in the skin are sewed up, the seams coated with wax. When the whole skin is thoroughly cleaned of filth and hair, straps are fastened to it, so that it may be conveniently carried on the shoulder, or over the back, the same straps serving, with adjustment, for either mode of support. The cup was dirty.

I took the water and gave the man a copper tarsk.

I smelled the spices and sweat of Tor. I drank slowly. The sun was high.

Tor, lying at the northwest corner of the Tahari, is the principal supplying point for the scattered oasis communities of that dry vastness, almost a continent of rock, and heat, and wind

36

and sand. These communities, sometimes quite large, numbering hundreds, sometimes thousands of citizens, depending on the water available, are often hundreds of pasangs apart. They depend on caravans, usually from Tor, sometimes from Kasra, sometimes even from far Turia, to supply many of their needs. In turn, of course, caravans export the products of the oases. To the oases caravans bring various goods, for example, rep-cloth, embroidered cloths, silks, rugs, silver, gold, jewelries, mirrors, kailiauk tusk, perfumes, hides, skins, feathers, precious woods, tools, needles, worked leather goods, salt, nuts and spices, jungle birds, prized as pets, weapons, rough woods, sheets of tin and copper, the tea of Bazi, wool from the bounding Hurt, decorated, beaded whips, female slaves, and many other forms of merchandise. The principal export of the oases are dates and pressed-date bricks. Some of the date palms grow to more than a hundred feet high. It takes ten years before they begin to bear fruit. They will then yield fruit for more than a century. A given tree, annually, yields between one and five Gorean weights of fruit. A weight is some ten stone, or some forty Earth pounds. A great amount of farming, or perhaps one should speak of gardening, is done at the oasis but little of this is exported. At the oasis will be grown a hybrid, brownish Sa-Tarna, adapted to the heat of the desert; most Sa-Tarna is yellow; and beans, berries, onions, tuber suls, various sorts of melons, a foliated leaf vegetable, called Katch, and various root vegetables, such as turnips, carrots, radishes, of the sphere and cylinder varieties, and korts, a large, brownish-skinned, thick-skinned, sphere-shaped vegetable, usually some six inches in width, the interior of which is yellowish, fibrous and heavily seeded. At the oasis, because of the warm climate, the farmers can grow two or more crops a year. Larma and tospits are also grown at the oases, in small orchards. Some rep is grown, for cloth, but most cloth comes to the oases from caravans. Kaiila and verr are found at the oases, but not in great numbers. The herds of these animals are found in the desert. They are kept by nomads, who move them from one area of verr grass to another, or from one water hole to another, as the holes, for the season, go dry. Smaller water sources are used in the spring, for these are the first to go dry, larger ones later in the year. No grass grows about these water holes because many animals are brought to them and graze it to the earth. They are usually muddy ponds, with some stunted trees about, centered in the midst of an extensive radius of grassless, cracked, dry earth. Meat, hides, and animal-hair cloth are furnished to the oases by the nomads. In turn, from the oases the nomads receive, most importantly, Sa-Tarna grain and the Bazi tea. They receive, as well, of course, other trade goods. Sa-Tarna is the main staple of the nomads. They, in spite of raising herds, eat very little meat. The animals are too precious for their trade value, and their hair and milk, to be often slaughtered for food. A nomad boy of fifteen will often have meat no more than a dozen times in his life. Raiders, however, feast well on meat. The animals mean little to them and come to them cheaply. Tea is extremely important to the nomads. It is served hot and heavily sugared. It gives them strength then, in virtue of the sugar, and cools them, by making them sweat, as well as stimulating them. It is drunk three small cups at a time, carefully measured.

I finished the cup of water and handed the cup back to the water carrier. He bowed, grinning, the bag, swollen and bulging, damp on his shoulder, and, hooking the cup on his belt, backed away. 'Water!' he called. 'Water!'

I blinked my eyes against the heat and glare of the sun. The buildings of Tor are of mud and brick, covered with colored, often flaking, plasters. But now, in the sun, and the dust, raised by the people in the streets, everything seemed drained of color. I would soon have to buy appropriate garments. In such a city I was too conspicuous.

I made my way to the bazaar.

I knew the light lance, and the swift, silken kaiila. I had learned these with the Wagon Peoples. But I did not know the scimitar. The short sword, now slung over my left shoulder, in the common fashion, would be of little use on kaiila back. The men of the Tahari do not fight on foot. A man on foot in the desert, in warfare, is accounted a dead man.

I looked up at the buildings. I was now in the shade, descending a narrow, steep street, toward the bazaar. The buildings in Tor are seldom more than four stories high, which is about as high as one may build safely with beams and mud brick. Because of the irregular topography of Tor, however, which is a hilly, rocky area, like most of the Tahari terrain, many of the buildings, built on shelves and rises, seemed considerably higher. These buildings, on the outside smooth and bleak, save for occasional narrow windows, high, not wide enough to admit a body, abut directly on the streets, making the streets like deep, walled alleys. In the center of the street is a gutter. It seldom rains in Tor, but the gutter serves to collect waste, which is often thrown into it, through open doors, by slaves. Within these walls, however, so pressing upon the street, I knew there were often gardens, walled, well-watered, beautiful, and cool, dark rooms, shielded from the heat and sun, many with superb appointments. Tor was, as Gorean cities went, a rich, trading city. It was headquarters for thousands of caravan merchants. In it, too, were housed many craftsmen, practicing their industries, carvers, varnishers, table makers, gem cutters, jewelers, carders, dyers of cloth, weavers of rugs, tanners, makers of slippers, toolers of leather, potters, glaziers, makers of cups and kettles, weapon smiths, and many others. Much of the city, of course, was organized to support the caravan trade. There were many walled, guarded warehouses, requiring their staffs of scribes and guards, and, in hundreds of hovels, lived kaiila tenders, drovers, and such, who would, at the caravan tables, when their moneys had been exhausted, apply, if accepted, making their mark on the roster, once more for a post with some new caravan. Guards for these caravans, incidentally, were usually known by, and retained by, caravan merchants between caravans. They were known men. Tenders and drovers, on the whole, came and went. Elaborate random selection devices, utilizing coins and sticks, and formulas, were sometimes used by merchants to assure that applying tenders and drovers were selected, if they were not known, by chance. Tenders and drovers were assured that this was to insure fairness. Actually, of course, as was well known, this was a precaution against the danger of hiring, *en bloc*, unwittingly, an organized group of men, who might, prior to their hiring, have formed a plan to slay the guards and merchants and make off with the caravan. Tenders and drovers, however, like men generally, were an honest sort. When they returned to Tor, of course, they had been long in the desert. At the end of the trip they received their wages. Sometimes, not even a hundred yards from the warehouses, these men would be met by enterprising café owners, praising the advantages of their respective establishments. The owners of these cafés, usually, would bring with them a chain of their girls, stripped, as free women in the Tahari districts may not be, purportedly a typical selection of the stock available.

39

'In my house,' he would call, indicating one or another of the girls, 'rent the key to her chains.'

But generally the men would proceed past these enticements, which were, from what I saw, far from negligible, and hurry toward their favorite cafés and hotels, whose wares, I gathered, did not need such blatant advertisement, whose worth, and capacities for total and complete satisfaction were apparently well known. Certain of these cafés I might mention. The Silken Oasis is well known, even in Ar, but it is extremely expensive; in the middle range of price are the Golden Collar and the Silver Chain, both under the same management, that of a Turian named Haran; good, relatively inexpensive cafés are the Thong, which I would recommend, the Veminium, the Pomegranate, the Red Cages and the Pleasure Garden. These various establishments, and more than forty others, from the point of view of tenders and drovers, have one thing in common. They succeed in separating, with celerity and efficiency, a fellow from his money. I do not feel this way myself. I think most of them, with the exception of the Silken Oasis, are reasonable. The drover's objection, I think, is largely a function of the fact that he does not have a great deal of money to spend. What there is, accordingly, seems rapidly diminished. Tenders and drovers often proceed from one café to the other, for several nights. The wages for a caravan trip, which often takes months, commonly will last the fellow about ten days, or, if nursed out, some fifteen days. They are, of course, a rather pleasant ten or fifteen days. At the end of this time, after a day or so of some physiological discomfort, usually violent nausea and blinding headaches, it is common to find the man again back at the tables, once more attempting to vend his services to the master of a caravan.

A fellow walked past me, carrying several vulos, alive, heads down, their feet tied together. He was followed by another fellow, carrying a basket of eggs.

I followed them as they would be going to the market streets, near which was the bazaar.

The water in an oasis is, of course, at its lowest point. Residences, at an oasis, are built on higher ground, where nothing will grow. It is the valley, naturally, which, irrigated, usually by hand, though sometimes with clumsy wooden machinery, supports the agriculture. Land, at an oasis, which will grow food, is not wasted on domiciles. Tor, rather similarly, though

40

few crops were grown within its walls, was built high, about its water, several wells in the deepest area in the city. The architecture of Tor, in concentric circles, broken by numerous, narrow, crooked streets, was a function of the radius from its wells. An advantage of this municipal organization, of course, though it is scarcely a matter of intentional design, is that the water is in the most protected portion of the city, its center. Tor's water, I might mention, was ample to her needs. Though I saw few of them, she boasted many shaded gardens. Water for these gardens, by contract with slave masters, was carried by chains of male slaves and emptied into house cisterns, whence, later, by house slaves, it would be taken in cans and sprinkled carefully, foot by foot, throughout the garden.

I was now in the lower part of the city.

'Water!' I heard. 'Water!'

Behind me, turning, I saw the water carrier, he from whom I had purchased a cup of water earlier.

A woman, veiled, passed me. She held a baby inside her cloak, nursing it.

I continued down the sloping street, toward the bazaar and market.

I had arrived in Tor four days ago, after first taking tarn to Kasra. There I had sold the bird, for I did not wish to be conspicuous in Tor, as would surely as a tarnsman. From Kasra I had taken a dhow upriver on the Lower Fayeen, until I reached the village of Kurtzal, which lies north, overland, from Tor. Goods which are to be transported from Tor to Kasra sometimes are first taken overland to Kurtzal, and thence west on the river. Kurtzal is little more than a loading and shipping point. In Kasra, descending upon my tarn, I had been a warrior. A mercenary tarnsman. As a portion of my assumed disguise, uncollared, lashed on her back across my saddle, had been the body of a naked girl. She was blonde. She was barbarian. She could not even speak Gorean. I was congratulated on my catch. I visited one of the metal workers, to purchase a collar for my prize. None, Samos and I suspected, would regard one with such a wench, so clumsy, so untaught, so obviously new to slavery, as being upon the business of Priest-Kings. She was simply a caught girl, picked up by a tarnsman with ease, simply to be used for a time and then discarded for a few tarn disks. 'I took her from a slaver's camp,' I told the metal worker. 'I see her brand is fresh,' said the metal worker.

It was true. She had not been branded in Teletus. Sometimes a girl is not branded until she is first sold. There are various brands. Sometimes it pleases the master to decide with which the girl will be marked. Within an hour, however, of her arrival at the house of Samos, the girl had been sent to the branding chamber. The standard Kajira mark, as was the house policy, was put upon her.

Masters, incidentally, seldom brand their own slaves. To brand a girl well demands a sure hand, and, usually, experience. In training a man to use the iron slavers always give him poorer women at first, sometimes having him mark them more than once, until he becomes proficient. Usually by the fifteenth woman, the man is capable of marking them deeply, precisely and cleanly. It is important for the girl's thigh to be held immobile; sometimes it is held by more than one man; sometimes it is bound to a wagon wheel; sometimes, in the house of slavers, a heavy, vise-equipped, metal branding rack is used. The girls are usually branded impersonally, perfunctorily, as cattle. Though they feel their mark intensely physically, it is felt, interestingly, even more intensely, more profoundly, psychologically; not unoften it, in itself, radically transforms their self-images, their personalities; they are then only slaves, not permitted their own wills, rightless, at the bidding of masters; the mark is an impersonal designation; this is understood by the girls; when she is marked she understands herself not to be marked by a given man for a given man, to be uniquely his, but rather, so to speak, that she is marked for all men; to all men she is a slave girl; usually, of course, only one among them, at a given time, will be her master; the brand is impersonal; the collar is intensely personal; the brand marks her property; the collar proclaims whose property she is, who it is who has either taken, or paid for, her; that the brand is an impersonal designation of an absence of status in the social structure is perhaps another reason why masters do not often brand their own girls; the brand relationship to the free man is institutional; the collar relationship, on the other hand, is an intensely personal one; it is not uncommon for masters to pride themselves on the depth with which they know their slave girls; this depth is far greater in my opinion than that with which the average husband of Earth knows his wife; the slave girl is not simply someone with whom the man lives; she is very special to him; she is a treasured possession; he owns her; he wants to

42

know, profoundly and deeply, the background, history, the mind, the intelligence, the appetites, the nature and the dispositions of his lovely article of property; this knowledge, of course, puts her more at his mercy; by making it possible for him to manipulate her feelings, exploit weaknesses, drop asides, etc., she is in the helpless condition of slavery, it gives him greater power over her. For example, it is common for a master to force his girl to speak at length and in detail to him of the secret sides of her nature, explaining and elaborating on her fantasies; if she is literate, she may be forced, naked, collared, on her knees at a small table, sometimes with her ankles shackled, to write them out; this supplies the master, of course, with abundant materials which may be used by him to make her further and more helplessly his; sometimes the girl attempts to deceive the master; it is not difficult to detect inauthenticity in such matters; she is then beaten; too, she may at times be ordered to invent fantasies, sometimes of a certain type; these, too, for she has invented them, are, to an astute master, instructive; these intellectual, emotional exercises, performed by the girl under a condition of slavery, particularly if coupled with an enforced exercised regime, posings under male surveillance, and such, can do much to sensitize her to her collar; they awaken her body and, of equal importance for the Gorean, though not for the Earthling, who sees sex with the perception of a hippopotamus, as a matter of body rubbings, her fantastic imagination and mind; she becomes curious, soon, about the deeper implications of what she is, a mere article of her master's property; then, with authority, with assurance and power, to the depth and height of her mind and imagination she is taught; the slave girl experiences a paradox of freedom; the free woman is phsically free, but miserable, fighting to be what she is not; the slave girl, physically in bondage, even to the collar, sometimes chains, is given no choice by men but to be totally and precisely what she is, slave; such women, the slave girls, interestingly, are almost always joyful and vital; they are, paradoxically, in their feelings and emotions, liberated; they are not pinched, not psychologically restrained; why this should be I do not know; to see such women, their heads high, their eyes bright, their bodies, their movements, beautiful, as no Earth woman would dare to be, is quite pleasurable; some of them are so insolent, so proud of their collars, that I have cuffed them to my feet, to remind them that they are only slaves.

It had been fortunate for us that the girl's brand had been relatively fresh, that she had been marked in the house of Samos and not on Teletus.

This made it more plausible that she was a recent prize, abducted, as I had averred to the metal worker, from the camp of a slaver. We could, of course, have taken another girl from the pens of Samos. This one, however, seemed ideal. She was obviously untrained, a clumsy wench, as stupid and raw, aside from a few rapings, as an uncooked piece of bosk meat, new to slavery. Furthermore, ideally, she could not yet speak Gorean. She could, thus, do nothing to betray or confound, inadvertently or otherwise, by word or glance, our plans. She knew nothing. She was only a part of my disguise. Nonetheless it was with pleasure that I snapped the collar, marked in the name of Hakim of Tor, as she, kneeling, naked, looked up at me in anger, on the small, lovely throat of the former Miss Priscilla Blake-Allen, of Earth.

But when I descended the narrow gangplank of the dhow which I took upstream from Kasra to the village port of Kurtzal, it was not as a tarnsman. The tarn I had sold in Kasra, for four golden tarn disks. I wore now the rags of a drover of kaiila. Bent over, carrying a grossly woven bag of kaiila-hair cloth, filled with accoutrements, I set foot on the cracked boards of the Kurtzal dock. Moments later I stood inland, ankle deep in the white dust. Following me down the gangplank, clad in a black haik, could have been only my companion, the pitiful free woman who shared my poverty. The haik, black, covers the woman from head to toe. At the eyes, there is a tiny bit of black lace, through which she may see. On her feet were soft, black, nonheeled slippers, with curled toes; they were decorated with a line of silver thread.

Beneath the haik none needed know the woman was naked and wore a collar.

We took a salt wagon, empty, to Tor from Kurtzal.

There was another reason I had brought Miss Blake-Allen, as we may perhaps speak of her for purposes of simplicity, to the Tahari districts. Cold, white-skinned women are of interest to the men of the Tahari. They enjoy putting them in servitude. They enjoy, on their submission mats, turning them into helpless, yielding slaves. Too, blue-eyed, blonde women are, statistically, rare in the Tahari districts. Those that exist there

44

have been imported as slaves. Given her complexion and coloring, I thought, and Samos concurred, we could get a good price for the wench in Tor, or in the interior, at an oasis market. We had little doubt that the men of the Tahari would pay high for the body and person of Miss Blake-Allen. It had entered my mind, too, that it might prove most profitable, under certain conceivable circumstances, to exchange her for information.

In Kasra I had learned the name, and father, of the boy who had found, in pursuing a kaiila, the rock on which had been inscribed 'Beware the steel tower'. His name was Achmed, and his father's name was Farouk, who was a Kasra merchant. I had failed to contact them in Kasra, as I had planned, but I had learned that they were in the region of Tor, purchasing kaiila, for a caravan to the kasbah, or fortress, of Suleiman, of the Aretai tribe, master of a thousand lances, Ubar of the Oasis of Nine Wells.

A merchant passed me, climbing the stones of the street. He wore a striped, hooded, sleeved, loose robe, a djellaba. The striping was that of the Teehra, a district southwest of Tor, bordering on the Tahari. Following him, in a black haik, was a woman. Suddenly I was startled. As she passed me, her stride small and measured, I heard the clink of light chain, the sound of ankle bells. She was slave. She turned her head, briefly, to look at me; I saw her eyes, dark, through the tiny opening in the haik, through the tiny, black-lace screen, about an inch in height and four inches in width. Then, with a rustle of the chain, and the tiny music of her bells, she turned swiftly, following her master. Beneath the haik, I supposed her collared, naked. The use of a light walking chain, tethering the ankles, meant to be worn abroad, accompanying the master, incidentally, is not uncommon in the regions of the Tahari. A beautifully measured gait is thought, in the Tahari, to be attractive in a woman. There is dispute as to the desirable length of the stride, and the chain may be adjusted accordingly. To me it seems obvious that one must experiment with the given girl. Height and hip structure vary. I resolved to obtain such a set of chains for Miss Blake-Allen. I was curious to see what measure of stride would best suit the slave in her. Free women, in the Tahari, incidentally, usually, when out of their houses, also measure their stride. Some fasten their own ankles together with silken thongs. Some dare even the chain, though they retain its key. Free girls, not yet companions, but of an age appropriate for the companionship, sometimes signal their availability to possible swains by belling their left ankles with a single 'virgin bell.' The note of this bell, which is bright and clear, is easily distinguished from those of the degrading, sensual bells of the slave. Sometimes free girls, two or more of them, as a girlish lark, obtain slave bells and, chaining their ankles, dress themselves in their haiks and go about the city. Sometimes their girlish amusement does not turn out as they expect. Sometimes they find themselves being sold in markets at obscure oases.

There was a great shouting, and, passing through the market gate, I had turned into the nest of market streets.

I brushed away two sellers of apricots and spices. 'Come with me to the cafe of Red Cages,' said a boy, pulling at my sleeve. They receive a copper tarsk for each patron they bring through the arched portal of the cafe. I gave the boy a copper tarsk, and he sped from me.

I made my way carefully through the crowds.

The vendors come early to the market, leaving their villages outside of Tor in the morning darkness, that they may find a yard of pavement, preferably near the market gate, to display their wares. I was jostled to one side by two men in djellabas. My ankle stung. I had nearly stepped into a basket of plums. Not even looking up, a woman had cried out, and, with a stick lashed out, protecting her merchandise. 'Buy melons!' called a fellow next to her, lifting one of the yellowish, red-striped spheres toward me. A boy passed, spitting out the seeds of a tospit. The thought of Kamchak, of the Tuchuks, passed through my mind. I smiled. Only the rare, long-stemmed tospit contained an even number of seeds. On the Plains of Turia, or in the Land of the Wagon Peoples, it was available only late in the summer. Here, in Tor, however, with its two growing seasons, they might be available much earlier. Still, if pressed, I would have guessed that the boy's tospit contained an odd number of seeds. Most tospits do. I would not, however, have been likely to wager on the matter with Kamchak of the Tuchuks. I was mildly surprised that the boy had been eating the tospit raw, for they are quite bitter, but, I knew, that people of the Tahari regions, these bright, hot regions, relished strong tastes and smells. Some of the peppers and spices, relished even by children in the Ta-

46

hari districts, were sufficient to convince an average good fellow of Thentis or Ar that the roof of his mouth, and his tongue were being torn out of his head.

I looked about myself, from time to time, as a warrior does. Seldom does he move any great distance without turning to see what is behind him. Then I continued toward the bazaar.

I passed crates of suls.

A veiled woman was hawking dates by the tefa. A handful with the five fingers closed, not open, is a tef. Six such handfuls constitutes a tefa, which is a tiny basket. Five such baskets constitute a huda.

To one side sat a fellow selling soap. It was in round, brownish cakes, sliced. It is made by boiling ashes with fat cut from meat.

When I had arrived in Tor I had, immediately, rented one of the small, hovel-like compartments in the plastered, mud-brick buildings near the street of caravan tables. Almost always, except in the greatest heat of the summer, between the fourth and sixth passage hands, when few caravans ply the wastes of the Tahari, there are many of these available. It was reached by climbing a narrow flight of wooden stairs between closely pressing walls, and opened off a narrow corridor, lit by a hanging tharlarion-oil lamp; off this corridor, too, were the doors of several similar rooms.

As soon as the wooden door was shut, the bar dropped in place, I turned to regard Miss Blake-Allen. She was standing concealed in the haik, regarding me. I strode to her and threw her to the rough boards at my feet, tearing the haik from her. She looked up at me, terrified.

'A girl,' I told her, 'on entering the compartment of her master, kneels.'

'I did not know, Master,' she said.

'Furthermore,' I said, 'commonly, in the presence of a free man, the girl kneels.'

'Yes, Master,' she said, frightened.

I looked at her. I hoped that she was not stupid.

Then I threw her on her back on the straw, and used her. When I had finished, I said to her, 'I am going to sleep now. Clean the room.'

'Yes, Master,' she said.

While I slept, on her hands and knees, with a brush and

47

cloth, and a pan of water, she cleaned the compartment. When I awakened, she knelt, trembling, while I inspected the room. It was spotless. 'It is satisfactory,' I told her. Her shoulders relaxed. She would not be beaten. I then, on the straw, again used her. I much kissed and chewed about her brand, making her acutely conscious of it. She, on her back, moaned in misery. With my fingertip I traced its incised delicacy. 'A nice brand,' I told her. 'Thank you, Master,' she whispered. When I left her I chained her ankles together, tightly, so that she could not rise to her feet. She, on her side, lifted her arms to me. 'When will you return to me, Master?' she begged. I cuffed her, and she turned, weeping, to her stomach, her head down, her tears falling in the straw.

I had then left her and gone to the cafes, to find what I might learn. In the cafes, as in the paga taverns of the north, one learns the realities of a city, what is its latest news, what is afoot in the city, what are its dangers, its pleasures, and where its power lies.

Most importantly I had gathered that there was brewing bad blood between the tribes of the Kavars and the Aretai. Raids had been becoming more frequent. If war should erupt their vassal tribes, such as the Char, the Kashani, the Ta'-Kara, the Raviri, the Tashid, the Luraz, the Bakahs, would all become involved. The Tahari would, from east to west, flame with war.

I am of the warriors.

Yet I did not look with pleasure on the prospects of a broad-scale conflict in the Tahari.

It would not, if it occurred, make my work easier.

The dancers in the cafés were spendid. In two of the cafés I paid a use-coin to the floor master and, by the hair, conducted she who had pleased me most to an alcove.

I had returned late to the compartment. Miss Blake-Allen, head to the floor, knelt when I entered. In the cafés I had feasted well. I had had verr meat, cut in chunks and threaded on a metal rod, with slices of peppers and larma, and roasted; vulo stew with raisins, nuts, onions and honey; a kort with melted cheese and nutmeg; hot Bazi tea, sugared, and, later, Turian wine. I did not forget the slave, of course. Crusts of bread did I throw to the boards before her. It was slave bread, rough and coarse-grained. The beauty ate it eagerly. She had not known if she was to be fed that day. Sometimes the slave

48

is not fed. This might occur for aesthetic reasons, as, for example, if her measurements, which are generally carefully kept, should minutely depart from her master's conception of her ideal curvatures; sometimes merely to remind her of on whom she depends, totally, for her very life, sometimes as a training or disciplinary measure; sometimes merely to startle or puzzle her. What has she done? She is not told. Has she not been sufficiently pleasing? She is not told. The girl, frightened, anxious, redoubles her efforts to please in all the thousand spheres of her slavery, intellectual, physical and imaginative; no master, it is said, who has not denied his girl food knows her; pleasant indeed are the surprises which such a fellow, who thought thitherto he knew his girl, upon the completion of the simple experiment, receives; the girl's wits are sharpened; she becomes resourceful, helpless, desperate, attentive, inventive; 'Feed me, Master,' she begs. 'Feed me!' at the conclusion of such an experiment, when she is fed, it is always, kneeling naked, from his hand. The lesson is not soon forgotten. Few things so impress the dominance of a male on a woman, and her dependence on him, as his control of her food. This dominance, provided it is absolute, thrills a woman to the core.

I had, from time to time, kept Miss Blake-Allen hungry, giving her only sparing rations. I had not, however, by means of food, truly impressed her slavery on her. I did not want to bring her to her belly at my feet. That pleasure I would deny myself, that it might be reserved for her first full, true master. I wanted to keep her, save for some refinements, a free woman of Earth, wearing a collar, until she was sold. The delights of making her a true slave girl, completely, in the full sense of the word, I would accord to the fellow to whom I would give or sell her. I could imagine her, blue-eyed, fair-skinned, angry, proud, rebellious, determined to be untamed, standing naked on his submission mat in his tent. After a week I wondered what she would be like.

I turned from the market streets into a street of shops and stalls, the bazaar, which, in Tor, is most commonly reached through the market gate.

'The Aretai will act,' I heard one man telling another.

I paused before a given stall, where light, walking chains were being sold. They were strung over racks rather like parrot perches. Without much haggling, I bought one, which seemed to me pretty. They are adjustable, with rings, from a length as small as two inches, for security, to a stride length of about twenty inches. Two keys are provided, each of which fits both ankle-ring locks. I also purchased a set of slave bells, of the thong as opposed to the lock variety. They are less expensive than the lock variety; also, they may be tied at various places on the body, about the neck, the wrist, the ankle, about the thigh, about the arm, etc.; it is delightful to bell a girl; she may not remove them, of course, without her master's permission.

I passed by the door of a slaver's house. High in the house, through one of the narrow windows, I saw a girl, looking out. She smiled, and put her arms out through the window, waving. Her face pressed against the bars. She was collared. I blew her a kiss in the Gorean fashion, brushing it upward to her with my fingers.

I looked into a shop where pottery was being turned. To one side of the wheels, along a wall, sitting among many bowls and vessels, a boy, with his finger, was carefully applying bluish pigment to a large, two-handled pitcher. When the pitcher was placed in the kiln this pigment would be burned, hardened, into the glaze. The kilns were in the back of the shop.

'The Kavars, even now, are hiring lances,' I heard.

The rugs of Tor are very beautiful. I paused to look upon several of them, hanging in stalls, many others, lying on top of one another, in great, shaded piles. It takes five girls more than a year to make certain of these rugs. The patterns memorized by the callers, some of them blind, are intricate, and passed down through families. They are made on simple looms and the pile is knotted onto the warp and weft. Some of these rugs have as many as four hundred knots per square hort. The hort is approximately an inch and a quarter in length. Each knot, by a girl, a free woman, is tied individually by hand. There are many varieties of such rugs. Almost all are incredibly beautiful. The dyes used in the making of these rugs are, on the whole, natural dyes, vegetable dyes, some made from barks and leaves, and roots and flowers, others from animal products, crushed insects, etc. At various places in the bazaar, from a latticework laid between the buildings, numerous skeins of wool hung, died in various bright colors, drying. The carders and the dyers, incidentally, are subcastes separate from the weavers. All are subcastes of the rug makers, which, itself, interestingly, perhaps surprisingly, is accounted generally as a subcaste of the cloth workers. Rug makers themselves, however, usually regard themselves, in their various subcastes, as being independent of the cloth workers. A rug maker would not care to be confused with a maker of kaftans, turbans, or djellabas.

I looked up at the skeins of wool hanging from the wooden poles between the flat roofs. They were quite colorful. The finest wool, however, is sheared in the spring from the bellies of the verr and hurt, and would, accordingly, not be available until later in the season. The wool market, as was to be expected, was now slow.

I passed the door of another slaver's house. I swung the light walking chain casually in my hand. It would look well on the slim ankles of the lovely Miss Blake-Allen.

I passed a fellow inlaying wood, and the shop of a silversmith, and stalls filled with baskets, some of which, grain baskets, were large enough to hold a man. In another place tanned, dyed leathers were hanging, purple, red, yellow. I passed a boy in a shop using a bow lathe. He spins the wood with bow and string, held in his right hand. He uses his left hand and his right foot to guide the cutting tool. Djellabas and burnooses, sleeveless, hooded desert cloaks, were being sold in another stall. The burnoose can, as the djellaba cannot, because of the sleeves, be thrown back, freeing the arms. One who rides the swift kaiila, who handles the scimitar and lance, chooses the burnoose.

I passed another stall, in which mats were being sold. These are used for various purposes, sometimes vertically for screens, more normally, horizontally, for sitting and sleeping. They can be tightly rolled and occupy little space. Among them I saw rough-fibered slave mats, and among those, the coarsest of all, submission mats, on which the female slave may be forced to perform for her master.

There were sellers of scarves and sashes, veils and haiks, chalwars and tobes, and slippers and kaftans, and cording for agals. Too, there were cloth merchants, with their silks and rolls of rep cloth. Cloth is measured in the ah-il, which is the length from the elbow to the tip of the middle finger, and the ah-ral, which is ten ah-ils. I saw sleeve daggers. I brushed a mat salesman away.

In another stall a slave girl was being vended. I watched her for a time dance before me, then I turned away.

I smelled veminium oil.

The petals of veminium, the 'Desert Veminium,' purplish, as opposed to the 'Thentis Veminium,' bluish, which flower grows at the edge of the Tahari, gathered in shallow baskets and carried to a still, are boiled in water. The vapor which boils off is condensed into oil. This oil is used to perfume water. This water is not drunk but is used in middle and upper-class homes to rinse the eating hand, before and after the evening meal.

At one place, on a stone shelf, under awnings, several girls, chained naked, were for sale, interestingly, at set prices. It was a municipal sale, under the jurisdiction of the courts of Tor. One brown-skinned girl, black-eyed, no more than fifteen, kneeling, her wrists and ankles tightly chained, looked up at me. She was being sold to pay her father's gambling debts. I purchased her, and freed her.

'Where is your father?' I asked.

'At the gaming tables of the Golden Kaiila,' she wept.

I looked at her. She was comely. I looked to the discarded chains on the stone shelf. Other girls there held out their hands to me. I looked again at the girl.

'In another year,' I told her, 'you will kneel again on the stone shelf, beneath the awnings.' I regarded her. 'Then,' I said, regarding her, 'you will be too beautiful to free.'

'I must hurry home,' she said, 'to prepare supper for my father.'

I watched her run, shamed, through the streets. She was lovely. I had little doubt that, in time, she would wear slave bells. Even if she were not to be sold by the magistracy of Tor I thought it not unlikely that she would fall to the noose of a slaver.

'Buy us! Buy us, Master!' cried the other girls on the shelf.

'Be slaves,' I laughed to them, turning away.

They wept. I heard the lash fall among them.

Here and there in the bazaar I made purchases.

Twice I was passed by pairs of guardsmen, in white robes with red sashes and scimitars, the police of Tor.

Not five paces behind them I saw a ragged cutpurse cut the wallet of a merchant, dropping its contents into his hand and, bowing and whining, twist away in the crowd. The merchant huffed away. The fellow had done it neatly. I recalled a girl named Tina, once of Lydius, now of Port Kar. She, too, had been an excellent thief. My own coins I kept in belt pockets, within my robes, save for a smaller wallet at my side. I went about Tor now as a traveler from Turia, a small merchant. I checked the wallet at my side. It was intact.

Some other thieves had not done so well in the bazaar. Several right hands, severed, were nailed to a board on which salt prices were affixed.

There were no feminine hands on the board. A female thief in Tor, even on the first offense, is immediately reduced to slavery.

I glanced behind me. For the second time I saw four men, the same four. But they were only four.

I stood aside as a chain of male slaves was herded by, with spear butts. They were bound for the brine pits of the Tahari, whence comes most of the caravan salt. I expected that less than half of them would reach the pits. Heavy collars, with rings, they wore about their necks. A heavy chain, running through the rings, linked them together by the throat. Their wrists, manacled, were behind their backs. They were naked. Men spat at them as they were herded past.

Miss Blake-Allen was no longer in my compartment. She was now in the public pens of Tor. On the morning of the second day, in the process of my work for Priest-Kings, I had entered the shaded offices of the municipal slave master of Tor.

'Stand here,' I told Miss Blake-Allen, indicating a place in the centre of the floor, before the desk of the slave master. She stood where I had indicated. 'Remove your slippers,' I told her. She slipped from the slippers, black with silver thread. She was now barefoot. The slave master came around to the front of his desk. He leaned back against it, sitting on its edge. 'Remove the haik,' I told the girl. She removed the garment. She stood between us, nude.

The slave master regarded her. Then he walked about her, slowly. She stood straight, a female examined by a man. She did not look at him. The slave master looked at me. I nodded. Her body stiffened, and she shut her eyes, as his hands, those of a Gorean flesh appraiser, informed, sensitive, professional, proficient, made swift assessment of the textures of her skin, varying at different points of the body, the tensilities of her musculature, the varying softness and firmness of her, the sweet, complex delights of her lines, the obvious exciting contours of her, the more subtle contours, too, the curve at her hip, at her shoulder, her instep, the back of her neck; he, too, made test, to her helpless, recoiling horror, of the latent pleasures of her, swiftly revealing, then passing over, it noted, the promise of an incredible responsiveness; there were tears in her eyes; how precious and beautiful, I thought, is a woman, how unsurprising that a vital man, without compromise, simply wishes to own such a fantastic, delicious creature, how unsurprising that he wishes in the full and glorious heat of his blood to overwhelm, devour, dominate and master her. On Gor, of course, men have their will, at least with lowly slaves, such as was, against her will, the lovely, unfortunate Miss Blake-Allen.

The slave master stepped back from the slave.

'Kneel,' I told her. She knelt.

'Blonde,' said he, 'apparently determined to try to remain frigid, blue-eyed, not yet tamed, an incredible potential for helpless sexual heat, an incredible potential for helpless slave submission, excellent. Do you wish to sell her?'

'Straighten your body, Slave,' I told her.

Frightened, Miss Blake-Allen straightened her back, and lifted her head. She knelt back on her heels, knees wide, hands on her thighs. It was the position of the Pleasure Slave. I had taught her the position. It is one of the first things a good-looking woman, fallen slave, is taught on Gor.

'Do you wish to sell her?' again inquired the slave master of Tor.

I knew I would not obtain the best price from this office, for the municipal pens usually buy cheaply and sell cheaply. They exist primarily as a service for caravan masters, buying unsold girls, later retailing them to other merchants, who may be short of flesh for the oasis traffic. The municipal pens exist primarily to perform a service, not to make profit.

'What would you offer?' I asked.

'Eleven silver tarsks,' he said.

I knew I could get twice that much from a private house.

'Fifteen?' he inquired.

'No,' I smiled, 'but your bids are reassuring.'

He smiled. 'I did not think you wished to sell her,' he

54

said. 'That is why I was as honest with you as I was. Now that I know you do not wish to sell her, I will tell you that, in my opinion,' he looked down at the kneeling girl, 'her potentiality is fantastic.'

'I am glad to hear it,' I said. Miss Blake-Allen, in the position of the Pleasure Slave, was looking about the room. She could not understand us, for we spoke in Gorean. It is perhaps just as well.

The usual buying price of the municipal office was two or three silver tarsks per wench. I had learned that Miss Blake-Allen was valuable in the Tahari. This pleased me.

I looked at her. She was beautiful. I agreed with the slave master. Doubtless, someday, for someone, she would make an excellent slave.

'I wish,' I said, 'to board her, and purchase her some training.'

'We cage a wench for a copper tarsk per day,' he said. 'Training is extra, but, I think, reasonable.'

'She does not speak Gorean,' I told him.

He smiled. 'She will learn swiftly,' he said.

Then the officer and I discussed details of training. He would include in her training the regime of the stimulation cage. For the first five nights, following my recommendation, she would wear the rope harness. After that it would be used, if necessary, for discipline.

'Let her, however,' I said, 'meet the eyes of her trainer, and of other males. I do not wish her to become the love slave of the first man into whose eyes she is permitted to gaze.'

'I understand,' said the man.

'Is there anything else?' I asked.

'Do we have complete food and whip rights over her?' he asked.

'Certainly,' I said.

I then turned to the girl. 'What is your name?' I asked her, in English.

'Priscilla Blake-Allen,' she said.

I looked at her. Her face went white. 'I have no name, Master,' she whispered. 'I am only a nameless slave,' she whispered.

I thought to myself. Priscilla Blake-Allen. Blake-Allen. Allen. Allen. Allena. Ah-leh-na. Then I had it. An excellent name, not unknown in the Gorean Tahari.

55

'I will give you a name,' I said.

She looked at me.

'Alyena,' I told her. The 'l' sound in this name is rolled, one of two common 'l' sounds in Gorean. An English transliteration, though not a perfect one, would be rather along the lines of 'Ahl-yieh-ain-nah,' where the 'ain' is pronounced such that it would rhyme with the English expression 'rain.' The accent falls on the first and third syllable. It is a melodic name. I thought it would improve her price. Names are often used by auctioneers. 'Here, Noble Gentlemen, for your consideration, is the slave girl called Alyena. Regard her! Does she please you? Move for the noble gentlemen, Alyena. Display your beauty. Do not such masters excite you? Do you not long to serve them? Behold, Gentlemen, Alyena dances her beauty for you! How much am I bid for the fair Alyena?'

'Alyena,' whispered the girl.

'Alyena,' I said to her.

'Yes, Master,' she said.

'I am not selling you,' I said. 'These are the public pens of Tor. You are here for boarding and training. You will begin to learn Gorean. You will learn as a child learns, without the benefit of translation. You will learn swiftly. You will also be exercised and receive slave instruction.'

'Slave instruction?' she asked.

'Yes,' I said. 'Is this clear, Alyena?'

'Yes, Master,' she whispered.

'If you are uncooperative, or slow in your lessons, you may be starved or beaten – lashed – you understand?'

'Yes, Master,' said the girl, her eyes wide.

I threw a silver tarsk to the official. He clapped his hands. Through a silver curtain, of silver strings, came a large, powerful slave girl. She wore a plain iron collar, with ring. She wore a halter of leather; she wore a belt of leather; two strips of leather girded her, falling to her knees; above her calves, crossing, leather straps bound heavy sandals on her feet. In her hand she carried a long supple kaiila quirt of leather, about a half inch in width and a yard long.

The large female slave feasted her eyes on the slender, lovely Alyena. Then she gestured with her quirt toward the threshold of silver strings. 'Hurry, Pretty One,' she said to Alyena, in Gorean, harshly.

Miserably, Alyena, understanding what was required of her, fled to the threshold.

There she turned to regard me. The quirt fell, viciously, across her shoulder. Crying out with pain, the lovely Alyena turned, and, weeping, stumbling, fled through the curtain of silver strings, to the pens of Tor.

'By the way,' I asked the officer, casually, though it was my main reason for visiting his office, 'there was a girl of interest to me who, I understand it, was named Veema, and was at one time one of your guests. I should like to discover what became of her. Would you have records on her?'

'Do you know her number in the pens?' asked the officer.

'87432,' I said.

'Information such as this is usually confidential to the municipality,' said the officer.

I placed a silver tarsk on the table.

Without taking it he went to a set of heavy, leaved books, bound in heavy, black leather, on a nearby shelf.

'She was bought for two tarsks, from a caravan master named Zad of the Oasis of Farad,' he said.

'I am more interested,' I said, 'in who purchased her.'

'She was sold for four tarsks,' said the officer.

'To whom?' I asked.

'Keep your tarsk,' said the man, wryly. 'There is no name given.'

'Do you remember the girl?' I asked.

'No,' he said.

'Why have you not recorded a name?' I asked.

'No name was given, apparently,' he said.

'Do you often sell women thusly?' I asked.

'Yes,' he said. 'It is the money in which we are interested. What is it to us what might be the name of the buyer?'

I checked the book myself. Its entries were not coded.

'Keep the tarsk,' I said to the man. Then I left the office of the slave master of Tor. I had failed to learn who it was who had purchased the girl Veema, who perhaps had sent her as a message girl to Samos of Port Kar. To me the slave master of Tor, within the normal discrepancies of the office, seemed an honest enough fellow.

I was satisfied that he did not know to whom had been sold the girl Veema, 87432, Turian Pen Number. I recalled the message which she had borne. 'Beware Abdul.'

In the bazaar I stopped, seeming to contemplate mirrors. The four men I had seen earlier, two large ones, two small ones, in white burnooses, still followed.

I had assumed the name Hakim, a Tahari name, one suitable for a merchant.

I would choose the place with some care.

I passed a stall of perfumers, and thought of Saphrar of Turia. Then I passed a shop where the high, light kaiila saddles were being made. One could also buy there saddle blankets, quirts, bells and kaiila reins. The kaiila rein is a single rein, very light, plaited of various leathers. There are often ten to a dozen strips of tanned, dyed leather in a single rein. Each individual strip, interestingly, given the strength of the rein, is little thicker than a stout thread. The strips are cut with knives, and it requires great skill to cut them. The rein, carefully plaited, is tied through a hole drilled in the right nostril of the kaiila. It passes under the animal's jaw to the left. When one wishes to guide the animal to the left one draws the rein left; when one wishes to guide it right one pulls right, drawing the rein over the animal's neck, with pressure against the left cheek. To stop the animal one draws back. To start or hasten the animal, one kicks it in the flanks, or uses the long kaiila quirt.

I passed one of the wells of Tor. There were steps, broad, flat, worn, in concentric circles, leading down to the water. At this time of year eight of the steps were uncovered by the water. Many came there for water. I saw children on their hands and knees lapping water, women filling jugs, men submerging bags, the air bubbling up as the bags filled. Like most water in the Tahari the water of Tor was slightly salty and unclear.

Casually glancing about I saw the four men. I assessed them, determining in my mind who would be the swiftest, the most dangerous, the leader; who would be the next most dangerous; and then the others.

I saw the water carrier, too, with the brass cups. It struck me suddenly strange that he should be in the area of the bazaar, which, in the lower area in the city, is in the vicinity of the wells. Surely few would care to purchase water where it lay free at hand. He descended the steps and submerged his bag, grinning at me, remembering me from earlier in the day. I smiled at him, turning away. He was a simple, poor fellow,

58

harmless, servile, slight. I felt myself a fool. Of course he would have come to the bazaar area. What would I have him do, fill his bag with the white dust of Tor's higher terraces?

I chose a side street, and another street from that, which terminated in a blind wall. There were few about.

I heard the men hurrying toward me. I swung the walking chains I had purchased lightly in my hand, not looking back, noting the shadows.

They would think I was trapped in the alley, with its blind wall. I had chosen this alley, that they might make their move swiftly, at my choosing, not truly theirs. Also, the alley was open behind them. I gave them access to flight. I had no wish to kill them. It seemed to me most probable they were simple brigands.

I saw the shadows, darting, heard the rush of robes.

Laughing, with the elation of the warrior, I turned, swiftly hurling the walking chains, spinning once, through the air. They lashed about the face of the leader. It had taken only an instant, the chain leaving my hand, to determine that he was exactly where I had expected him to be, as he would have been at any time in following me, had I earlier turned, slightly to my right. He cried out, the chains whipping about his face. I used his body to block the two men on my left. I leaped, knees bent, body turned, legs like compressed springs, toward the man on the leader's left. One foot struck him in the chest, the other snapped his head back. I slipped behind the leader, seized the small fellow to his right by the arm and hurled him headfirst into the wall. The last fellow I lifted from his feet and, turning, hurled him against the same wall as the other. He struck it, upside down, full along his back and head, and tumbling, fell beside the other fellow, who lay inert. The leader, face bleeding, wiped the blood from his forehead from his eyes, stepping back.

'You are of the warriors,' he whispered. Then he turned about, and fled.

I did not pursue him.

I returned to the bazaar, and inquired where steel might be purchased, and kaiila. I was informed by a ragged youngster, whom I rewarded with a copper tarsk. The weapon makers' street was close on the bazaar. The kaiila pens in Tor are outside her south gate.

On the way to the street of weapon makers I again passed the water carrier. His bag on his shoulder was now, again, damp, dark, bulging.

'Tal, Master,' said he to me.

'Tal,' said I to him.

I walked to the street of the weapon makers. I was anxious to make the acquaintance of the Tahari scimitar.

'There will be war between the Kavars and the Aretai,' I heard a man say.

I walked to the street of the weapon makers. Lightly, in my right hand, I swung the walking chains. They would look well on the slim ankles of the lovely Alyena, a slave girl I was having boarded and trained in the pens of Tor.

This night I thought I would have my supper at the Pomegranate. I had heard their dancers were superb.

THREE

I DO NOT PARTICIPATE IN WHAT OCCURS IN A COURTYARD; I RECOVER A SILVER TARSK

The war kaiila, rearing on its hind legs, its claws, however, sheathed, lunged at the other animal, its clawed back feet thrusting with an explosion of sand away from the ground; the long neck darted forward, the long, graceful head, its fanged jaws bound shut with leather, struck at the man astride the other beast. He thrust the jaws away with the buckler, and, rearing in the stirrups of his high saddle, slashed at me with the leather-sheathed, curved blade. I turned the stroke with my own sheathed blade, it, too, in the light, ornamented exercise sheath.

The kaiila, both of them, with the swiftness, the agility of cats, spun, half crouching, squealing in frustration, and again lunged toward one another. With the light rein I pulled my kaiila to the left as we passed, and the man, trying to reach me, was, startled, off balance. With a backward sweeping cut the sheathed blade struck him, as he hung from his saddle, on the back of the neck.

He swept past me and spun his kaiila, then jerked it up short, back on its haunches in the sand.

I readied myself for another passage.

For ten days had we trained, for ten Gorean hours a day. Of the past forty passages eight had been divided, no blood adjudged drawn. In thirty-two I had been adjudged victorious, nineteen times to the death cut.

He pulled his sand veil, yellow, from his dark face, down about his throat. He thrust his burnoose back further over his shoulders. He was Harif, said to be the finest blade in Tor.

'Bring salt,' he said to the judge.

The judge gestured to a boy, who brought him a small dish of salt.

The warrior slipped from his saddle, and, on foot, approached me.

I remain mounted.

'Cut the leather from the jaws of your kaiila,' said he. Then he gestured to the boy, that the boy should remove the claw sheaths of the beast. He did so, carefully, the beast moving, nervous, shifting in the sand.

I discarded the exercise sheath, and, with the bared blade, parted the leather that had bound the jaws of the kaiila. The leather sprang from the blade. Silk, dropped upon the scimitar of the Tahari, divided, falls free, floating, to the floor. The beast reared, its claws raking the air, and threw back its head, biting at the sun.

I lifted the curved blade of the scimitar. It flashed. I sheathed it, and slipped from the saddle, giving the rein of the mount to the boy.

I faced the warrior.

'Ride free,' he said.

'I will,' I said.

'I can teach you nothing more,' he said.

I was silent.

'Let there be salt between us,' he said.

'Let there be salt between us,' I said.

He placed salt from the small dish on the back of his right wrist. He looked at me. His eyes were narrow. 'I trust,' said he, 'you have not made jest of me.'

'No,' I said.

'In your hand,' he said, 'steel is alive, like a bird.'

The judge nodded assent. The boy's eyes shone. He stood back.

'I have never seen this, to this extent, in another man.' He looked at me. 'Who are you?' he asked.

I placed the salt on the back of my right wrist. 'One who shares salt with you,' I said.

'It is enough,' he said.

I touched my tongue to the salt in the sweat of his right wrist, and he touched his tongue to the salt on my right wrist.

'We have shared salt,' he said.

He then placed in my hand the golden tarn disk, of Ar, with which I had purchased my instruction.

'It is yours,' I said.

'How can that be?' he asked.

'I do not understand,' I said.

He smiled. 'We have shared salt,' he said.

I was returning to my compartment in Tor, from the tents of Farouk of Kasra. He was a merchant. He was camping in the vicinity of the city while purchasing kaiila for a caravan to the Oasis of Nine Wells. This oasis is held by Suleiman, master of a thousand lances, Suleiman of the Aretai.

It had been at my invitation that Farouk had consented to judge the passages at arms, constituting the final phases of the scimitar training.

It had not been inconvenient for him, for he was inspecting kaiila at the corrals near the southern gate of Tor.

The judging had not been difficult, either, fortunately, for the passages were clear. One passage, divided between us, adjudged as 'no blood drawn,' might have been disputed. Harif had wished it awarded to me. I refused to accept it, of course, for his body had not been touched. The judge had seen the matter correctly. The stroke in question was the back-handed, ascending face stroke. Even though the blade was sheathed I had held the stroke, holding it short, a hort from his face. The leather would have torn at his forehead, ascending, over the bridge of the nose. I did not wish to injure him. Unsheathed, followed through, of course, such a stroke would have taken off the top of his head, slashing upward through the hood of the burnoose.

'Would you be my guest tonight in my tents?' had asked the judge, Farouk of Kasra. It had been his son who had carried the salt, who had unsheathed the claws of my kaiila. The boy had stood by, eyes shining. His name was Achmed. It had been he who had, enroute in a caravan, months before, discovered the rock, on which had been inscribed 'Beware the steel tower.'

'I would be much pleased,' I told the merchant, 'to dine with you this night.'

That night, when our repast had been finished, and a clothed, bangled slave woman, the property of Farouk, had rinsed our right hands with veminium water, poured over our hands into a small, shallow bowl of beaten copper, I drew forth from my robes a small, flat, closed Gorean chronometer. It was squarish. I placed it in the hands of the boy, Achmed.

63

He opened it. He observed the tiny hands, moving. There are twenty hours, or Ahn, in the Gorean day. The hands of the Gorean chronometers do not move as the hands of the clocks of the Earth. They turn in the opposite direction. In that sense, they move counterclockwise. This chronometer, tooled in Ar, was a fine one, sturdy, exact. It contained, too, a sweeping Ihn hand, with which the tiny Ihn could be measured. The boy watched the hands. Such instruments were rare in the Tahari region. He looked at me.

'It is yours,' I told him. 'It is a gift.'

The boy placed the chronometer in the hand of his father, offering it to him.

Farouk, merchant of Kasra, smiled.

The boy then, carrying the chronometer, took it about the circle of the small fire, on the sand of the tent; before each of his kinsmen, he stopped; into the hands of each, he placed the chronometer. 'I give you this,' he said. Each looked at the chronometer. Then each handed it back to the boy. The boy returned and sat next to me. He looked at his father.

'You will tell the time,' said Farouk of Kasra, 'by the speed of your kaiila, by the circle and the stick, by the sun.'

'Yes, Father,' said the boy, his head down.

'But,' said his father, 'you may keep the gift.'

'Oh, Father, thank you!' he cried. 'Thank you!' He looked to all his kinsmen. 'Thank you,' he said to them.

They smiled.

'And you, swordsman,' said he to me, 'I thank you.'

'It is nothing,' I said to him.

Farouk of Kasra looked at me. 'I am pleased,' he said. Then he had asked, 'What is your business, Hakim of Tor, and may I in any way be of service to you?'

It had been on the route to the Oasis of Nine Wells that the boy had seen the rock.

'I am a humble merchant,' I said. 'I have a few small stones which I would like to sell at the Oasis of Nine Wells, to buy date bricks to return and sell in Tor.'

'You do not handle a sword like a merchant,' smiled Farouk of Kasra.

I smiled.

'I, myself,' said Farouk of Kasra, 'am soon journeying to the Oasis of Nine Wells. I should be honored if you might, with your kaiila, accompany me.'

'I should be most pleased to do so,' I told him.

'I have purchased what kaiila I need,' said Farouk.

'When will you leave?' I asked.

'At dawn,' he said.

'I must pick up a girl at the pens of Tor,' I said. 'I shall join you on the trail.'

'Do you know the desert?' asked Farouk.

'No,' I said.

'Achmed,' he said, 'will wait for you at the south gate.'

'I am pleased,' I said.

After coming from the tents of Farouk of Kasra, outside the walls of Tor, I was returning late to my compartment, which lay in the district of tenders and drovers.

Things, it seemed to me, were proceeding well. En route I would find the rock which had been discovered, some months ago, by the boy Achmed, the son of Farouk. This rock would be the place at which my search must begin. After determining this point, I would continue on to the Oasis of Nine Wells, where I would lay in supplies and water, attempt to hire a guide, and, returning to the rock, strike eastward into the Tahari. Questioning nomads, doubtless to be found here and there in the wastes, and the inhabitants of various oases, many of them off the main caravan routes, I hoped, eventually, to obtain enough data or information to make it possible to find the mysterious tower of steel. I thought it likely that there existed such a tower. I doubted that it was a figment of the imagination of the man who had made the inscription and, thereafter, had died in the desert. Towers of steel do not figure in the hallucinations, the delusions of the desert mad. Their delusions are influenced by wish-fulfillment; they involve water. Moreover, they are not likely to take the time to inscribe messages on rocks. Something had driven the man over the desert, something he had to tell. He had been, apparently a raider. But yet, for some reason, he had fought his way, presumably eventually on foot, dying, through the desert, toward civilization, to warn someone, or something, of a steel tower. I did not doubt there was such a tower. On the other hand, I would have little or no chance of finding it by striking blindly out into the desert. I would have to make contact with nomads, and others, hoping eventually to find one who had heard of, or knew of, the tower. If it were in the dune country, removed from oases and caravan trails, of course, few, if any, might have seen it. Yet, I did not doubt that at least one man had seen it, he who had made the inscription, who had died near it, whose body had been dried, blackened, by the sun.

The streets of Tor were dark. Sometimes they were steep; often they were narrow and crooked. Sometimes I felt my way by touching a wall. Some places a small lamp burned, high, near a doorway.

I thought I heard a step behind me. I threw back the burnoose, unsheathed the scimitar. I waited.

I heard nothing more.

I pressed on through the streets. No more did I hear a step behind me.

I looked back, the streets were dark.

I think I was not more than a half pasang from my compartment when, approaching an opened gate, some forty yards ahead, lit by torches in walls, I stopped.

It was a small courtyard, through which it was my intention to pass.

I saw the shadow, furtive, dart back behind one of the two halves of the gate.

At the same time I heard the movements of men behind me. There were five of them.

I felled the first. I felled the second. I caught the scimitars of three on my blade and leaped back. They separated, intelligently, and, crouching, edged toward me. I backed away, crouching. I hoped to draw the center man forward, to where he might, if I should move to the right, block the man on his own right, or if I moved to the left, block the man on his own left. But if he hung back, the two on the sides creeping forward. Whichever man I attacked need only defend himself; the other two would have a free instant, that of his defense, to make their own strokes. These men were not common street thieves.

Suddenly the three men stopped. I tensed. One man threw down his scimitar. All three of them turned and fled.

Behind me I heard the doors of the courtyard swing shut. I heard the beam, locking it, fall in place.

I turned. I could see nothing for the closed gate. The torches, high on the walls of the courtyard, flickered, casting pools of yellow light on the plaster walls.

Then I heard a human scream of horror from the other side of the gate.

I did not know at that time how many men were waiting in the courtyard. I do not think any of them escaped.

I waited, scimitar drawn, outside the closed gate of the courtyard.

High above, in a wall to my right, a light appeared. 'What is going on?' cried a man.

Lights appeared in others of the high, narrow windows. I saw men looking out. I saw one woman, holding her veil to her face, peering out.

In what could not have been more than two or three Ehn, men, carrying torches, some of them lamps, emerged into the street. We could hear, too, men on the other side of the courtyard. Within the courtyard we then heard men moving. I heard a woman scream. I could see movement, and torches, in the vertical thread of space between the two halves of the gate.

'Open the gate!' called a man, pounding from our side. We heard the heavy bar thrust up, and then creak, rotating, on its four-inch-thick pin. Four men, from our side, pushed open the gate. The crowd in the courtyard stood back, in a circle. Torches were lifted as men looked to the stones of the courtyard. My eyes examined the heights of the walls, the adjoining roofs. Then I, too, gave my attention to the stones of the courtyard.

Eleven men lay there, and parts of men.

'What could have done this,' whispered a man.

I wondered if any had escaped. I doubted it.

The heads of four of the men had been torn from them; the heads of two others had been half bitten from them; one man's throat looked as though it had been struck twice with parallel hatchets; I was familiar with the spacing of the wounds; two men had lost arms, one a leg; one of the men without an arm had been disemboweled; there was also the print of jaws in his shoulder; I was familiar with this sort of thing; I had seen it often enough in Torvaldsland; the man is seized about the neck and shoulders and held, while the squat, powerful, clawed hind feet rip at the lower abdomen; twenty feet of gut was scattered in the blood and robes, like wet, red-spattered rope; the man who had lost a leg had had his spine bitten through; I could see the stomach from the back; the other man who had had an arm torn from him, too, had been half eaten, ribs erupted from the chest cavity; the heart

67

and the left lung were missing; the eleventh man had been the most cleanly killed; about his throat, on the sides, were six black, circular bruises, like rope marks; his head hung to one side; the back of his neck had been bitten through.

I looked again to the walls, the roofs about the courtyard.

'What could have done this?' asked a man.

I turned and left the courtyard. Beside the two men in the street, who had tasted my scimitar, were gathered several townsfolk of Tor.

I looked down on the two bodies. 'Do you know them?' I asked a man.

'Yes,' he said, 'Tek and Saud, men of Zev Mahmoud.'

'They will kill no more,' said a man.

'At what place might I expect to find the noble Zev Mahmoud?' I inquired.

'He and his men are often to be found at the Café of the Six Chains,' said the man. He grinned.

'My thanks, Citizen,' said I.

I wiped my blade on the burnoose of one of the fallen men, and resheathed it.

Looking up, I saw, hurrying toward us, carrying a torch, the small water carrier I had encountered several times. He looked up at me. 'Did you see?' he asked. His face was white. 'It was horrible,' he said. He trembled.

'I saw,' I said.

I pointed to the two men in the street. 'Do you know these men?' I asked.

He peered at them closely. 'No,' he said. 'They are strangers in Tor.'

'Is it not late to carry water?' I asked him.

'I am not carrying water, Master,' he said.

'How is it that you are in this district,' I asked.

'I live but a short way from here,' he said. Then he left, bowing, carrying the torch.

I looked at the man to whom I had spoken earlier. 'Does he live near here?' I asked.

'No,' said the man, 'he lives by the east gate, near the shearing pens for verr.'

'Do you know him?' I asked.

'He is well known in Tor,' said the man.

'And who is he?' I asked.

'The water carrier Abdul,' said the man.

'My thanks, Citizen,' said I.

'Zev Mahmoud?' I asked.

The heavily built man in the kaffiyeh and agal looked up, angry, then turned white.

The point of the scimitar was at his throat.

'Into the street,' I told him. I looked at the two other men, who sat, cross-legged, about the small table, with him, I gestured with my head. 'Into the street,' I told them.

'There are three of us,' said Zev Mahmoud.

'Into the street,' I told them.

They looked at one another. Zev Mahmoud smiled. 'Very well,' he said.

One of them, who had lost his scimitar, took one from a man in the café.

'Our fees will yet be paid,' said one of the men to Zev Mahmoud.

I followed them into the street.

There I finished them.

I did not wish to leave them behind me in Tor.

It was late when I returned to the compartment in the district of tenders and drovers.

I was not surprised to find the water carrier waiting for me, sitting on the steps.

'Master,' he said.

'Yes,' I responded.

'You are new in Tor,' said he, 'and may not know the ways of the city. I know many in Tor, and might be of much help to you.'

'I do not understand,' I said.

'There will soon be war between the Kavars and the Aretai,' he said, 'Caravan routes may be closed. It may be difficult to get tenders and drovers who will, in such dangerous times, venture into the desert.'

'And how,' I asked, 'should such misfortune come to pass, might you be of assistance to me?'

'I could find you men, good men, honest, fearless fellows, who will accompany you.'

'Excellent,' I said.

'In troubled times, though,' he said, cringing, 'their fees may be higher than normal.'

'That is understandable,' I said.

He seemed relieved.

'Whither are you bound, Master?' he asked.

'Turia,' I told him.

'And when will you be prepared to leave?' he asked.

'Ten days,' said I, 'from the morrow.'

'Excellent,' he said.

'Seek then,' said I, 'such men are for me.'

'It will be difficult,' said he, 'but depend upon me.'

He put forth his palm. I put into it a silver tarsk. 'Master is generous,' said he.

'My caravan is small,' I told him, 'only a few kaiila. I doubt that I shall need more than three men.'

'I know just the men,' grinned the man.

'Oh?' asked I.

'Yes,' he said.

'And where will you find them?' I asked.

'I think,' said he, 'at the Café of the Six Chains.'

'I hope,' said I, 'you are not thinking of the noble Zev Mahmoud and his friends.'

He seemed startled.

'The word has spread through Tor,' I said. 'It seems there was a brawl, outside the cafe.'

The water carrier turned white. 'Then I must try to find you others, Master,' said he.

'Do so,' I said.

The silver tarsk slipped from his fingers. He backed away. Then, suddenly, looking over his shoulder, he turned, and fled.

I reached down and picked up the tarsk. I slipped it back in my wallet. I was weary. I did not think I would hear, soon, from the water carrier. It would be ten days, as I recalled, before I was due to leave for Turia.

Now I must rest, for I must be up at dawn. In the morning there were various preparations to be made. Among them, I must pick up a girl from the public pens of Tor. Achmed, the son of Farouk, would be waiting for me at the south gate of the city. We would join the caravan of Farouk on the trail, probably before noon.

I hoped there would not be war between the Kavars and the Aretai. It would not make my work easy.

I hoped to obtain supplies, and a guide, at the Oasis of Nine

Wells. It was held, I recalled, by Suleiman, master of a thousand lances, Suleiman of the Aretai.

I then turned and began to climb the narrow wooden stairs to my compartment. I had heard the last, I conjectured, of the water carrier, he called Abdul.

FOUR

RIDERS JOIN THE
CARAVAN OF FAROUK

The caravan moved slowly.

I turned my kaiila, and, kicking its flanks, urged it down the long line of laden animals.

With my scimitar tip I lifted aside a curtain.

The girl, startled, cried out. She sat within, her knees to the left, her ankles together, her weight partly on her hands, to the right, on the small, silk-covered cushion of the frame. It was semicircular and about a yard in width at its widest point. The superstructure of the frame rose about four feet above the frame at its highest point, inclosing, as in an open-fronted, flat-bottom, half globe, its occupant. This frame, however, was covered completely with layers of white rep-cloth, to reflect the sun, with the exception of the front, which was closed with a center-opening curtain, also of white rep-cloth. The wood of the frame is tem-wood. It is light. It is carried by a pack kaiila, strapped to the beast, and steadied on both sides by braces against the pack blankets. This frame is called, in Gorean, the kurdah. It is used to transport women, either slave or free, in the Tahari. The girl was not chained within the kurdah. There is no need for it. The desert serves as a cage.

'Veil yourself,' I laughed.

Angrily Alyena, the former Miss Priscilla Blake-Allen of Earth, took the tiny, triangular yellow veil, utterly diaphanous, and held it before her face, covering the lower portion of her face. The veil was drawn back and she held it at her ears. The light silk was held across the bridge of her nose, where, beautifully, its pourous, yellow sheen broke to the left and right. Her mouth, angry, was visible behind the veil, which, too, covered her chin. The mouth of a woman, by men of the Tahari, and by

Goreans generally, is found extremely provocative, sexually. The slave veil is a mockery, in its way. It reveals, as much as conceals, yet it adds a touch of subtlety, mystery; slave veils are made to be torn away, the lips of the master then crushing those of the slave.

Aside from her veil, and her collar, in the kurdah, she was stark naked.

She held the veil before her face. I saw her eyes, very blue, over the yellow.

'At least now,' I said to her, 'you are not face-stripped.'

Her eyes flashed.

'Shameless!' I said.

She held the veil to her face.

'Fasten it,' I said, 'and wear it in the kurdah. Should I find you again so shamelessly unveiled, without my permission, you will be lashed.'

'Yes, Master,' she said, and, holding the veil with one hand, groped on the cushion for the tiny golden string with which she might fasten it upon her. With the scimitar tip I let the curtain of the rep-cloth fall, concealing her again in the kurdah.

I laughed as I spun the kaiila, hearing her utter a tiny cry of rage inside the kurdah.

I did not doubt, however, but what the next time I opened the curtain of the kurdah it would be a veiled slave I would encounter therein.

Alyena was very lovely, though she had much to learn. She had not yet even been whipped. That detail, however, unless she displeased me, I would leave to her new master, he to whom I would eventually give or sell her.

The sand kaiila, or desert kaiila, is a kaiila, and handles similarly, but it is not identically the same animal which is indigenous, domestic, and wild, in the middle latitudes of Gor's southern hemisphere; that animal, used as a mount by the Wagon Peoples, is not found in the northern hemisphere of Gor; there is obviously a phylogenetic affinity between the two varieties, or species; I conjecture, though I do not know, that the sand kaiila is a desert-adapted mutation of the sub-equatorial stock; both animals are lofty, proud, silken creatures, long-necked and smooth-gaited; both are triply lidded, the third lid being a transparent membrane, of great utility in the blasts of the storms of the southern plains or the Tahari; both creatures are comparable in size, ranging from some twenty to twenty-

73

two hands at the shoulder; both are swift; both have incredible stamina; under ideal conditions both can range six hundred pasangs in a day; in the dune country, of course, in the heavy, sliding sands, a march of fifty pasangs is considered good; both, too, I might mention, are high-strung, vicious-tempered animals; in pelt the southern kaiila ranges from a rich gold to black; the sand kaiila, on the other hand, are almost all tawny, though I have seen black sand kaiila; differences, some of them striking and important, however, exist between the animals; most notably, perhaps, the sand kaiila suckles its young; the southern kaiila are viviparous, but the young, within hours after birth, hunt by instinct; the mother delivers the young in the vicinity of game; whereas there is game in the Tahari, birds, small mammals, an occasional sand sleen, and some species of tabuk, it is rare; the suckling of the young in the sand kaiila is a valuable trait in the survival of the animal; kaiila milk, which is used, like verr milk, by the peoples of the Tahari, is reddish, and has a strong, salty taste; it contains much ferrous sulphate; another difference between the two animals, or two sorts of kaiila, is that the sand kaiila is omnivorous, whereas the southern kaiila is strictly carnivorous; both have storage tissues; if necessary, both can go several days without water; the southern kaiila also, however, has a storage stomach, and can go several days without meat; the sand kaiila, unfortunately, must feed more frequently; some of the pack animals in a caravan are used in carrying fodder; whatever is needed, and is not available en route, must be carried; sometimes, with a mounted herdsman, caravan kaiila are released to hunt tabuk; a more trivial difference between the sand kaiila and the southern kaiila is that the paws of the sand kaiila are much broader, the digits even webbed with leathery fibers, and more heavily padded, than those of its southern counterpart.

I returned to my place in the caravan line.

In the Tahari there is an almost constant wind. It is a hot wind, but the nomads and the men who ply the Tahari welcome it. Without it, the desert would be almost unbearable, even to those with water and whose bodies are shielded from the sun.

I listened to the caravan bells, which sound is pleasing. The kaiila moved slowly.

Prevailingly, the wind in the Tahari blows from the north or northwest. There is little to fear from it, except, in the spring, should it rise and shift to the east, or, in the fall, should it blow westward.

We were moving through hilly country, with much scrub brush. There were many large rocks strewn about. Underfoot there was much dust and gravel.

On the shaded sides of some rocks, and the shaded slopes of hills, here and there, grew stubborn, brownish patches of verr grass. Occasionally we passed a water hole, and the tents of nomads. About some of these water holes there were a dozen or so small trees, flahdah trees, like flat-topped umbrellas on crooked sticks, not more than twenty feet high; they are narrow branched, with lanceolate leaves. About the water, little more than muddy, shallow ponds, save for the flahdahs, nothing grew; only dried, cracked earth, whitish and buckled, for a radius of more than a quarter of a pasang, could be found; what vegetation there might have been had been grazed off, even to the roots; one could place one's hand in the cracks in the earth; each crack adjoins others to constitute an extensive reticulated pattern; each square in this pattern is shallowly concave. The nomads, when camping at a watering place, commonly pitch their tent near a tree; this affords them shade; also they place and hang goods in the branches of the tree, using it for storage.

From time to time the caravan stopped and, boiling water over tiny fires, we made tea.

At a watering hole, from a nomad, I purchased Alyena a brief second-hand, black-and-white-striped, rep-cloth slave djellaba. It came high on her thighs. This was that she would have something in which to sleep. She was permitted to wear it only for sleep. I slept her at my feet. I taught her to pitch a tent, and cook, and perform many useful services for a man.

At night, when the caravan made camp, I would lift Alyena from the kurdah, and, sweeping her across the saddle and lowering her, drop her to her feet in the gravel.

'Find Aya,' I would tell her. 'Beg her to put you to work.' Aya was one of the slave women of Farouk.

Once she had dared to say to me, 'But Aya makes me do all her work!'

I kicked the kaiila toward her, and she was buffeted from her feet rolling in the gravel, and then lay, hands shielding her face, on her back beneath the very paws of the beast, it hissing and stamping, scratching at the gravel about her.

'Hurry!' I told her.

She scrambled to her feet, and fled to Aya. 'I hurry, Master!'

she cried. Inadvertently, she had cried in Gorean. I was pleased.

Of course Aya exploited her. It was my intention that she should. But, too, Aya, with her kaiila strap, continued her lessons in Gorean. Too, she taught her skills useful to a Tahari female, the making of ropes from kaiila hair, the cutting and plaiting of reins, the weaving of cloth and mats, the decoration and beading of leather goods, the use of the mortar and pestle, the use of grain quern, the preparation and spicing of stews, the cleaning of verr and, primarily when we camped near watering holes in the vincinity of nomads, the milking of verr and kaiila. Too, she was taught the churning of milk in skin bags.

'She is making me learn the labors of a free woman,' once had complained Alyena to me.

I had gestured her to her knees. 'You are a poor sort,' I told her. 'To a nomad I may sell you. In his tent the heavy labors of the free woman will doubtless be yours, in addition to the labors of a slave.'

'I would have to work as a free woman,' she whispered, 'and yet be also a slave?'

'Yes,' I said.

She shuddered. 'Sell me to a rich man,' she begged.

'I will sell you, or give you, or loan you, or rent you,' I said, 'to whomsoever I please.'

'Yes, Master,' she said, angrily.

At night, around the campfire, I knelt her behind me, her wrists braceleted behind her. By hand I fed her. On me she depended for her food.

I listened to the caravan bells. I pulled the burnoose down about my face, shading my eyes.

The movements of the men of the Tahari are, during the hours of heat, usually slow, almost languid or graceful. They engage in little unnecessary movement. They do not, if they can help it, overheat themselves. They sweat as little as possible, which conserves body fluid. Their garments are loose and volu-minous, yet closely woven. The outer garment when in caravan, usually the burnoose, is almost invariably white. This color re-flects the rays of the sun. The looseness of the garments acting as a bellows in movement, circulates air about the body, which air, circulating over the damp skin, cools the body by evapora-tion; the close weave of the garment is to keep the moisture and water, as much as possible, within the garment, preferably con-densing back on the skin. There are two desiderata which are crucial in these matters; the first is to minimize perspiration; the second is to retain as much moisture, lost through pespiration, as is possible on the body.

I was growing drowsy, lulled by the bells, the even gait of the kaiila.

On a rise, pushing back the burnoose, I stood in my stirrups and looked back. I saw the end of the caravan, more than a pasang away. It wound, slowly, gracefully, through the hills. At its very end came a man on a single kaiila. From time to time, he dismounted, gathering shed kaiila hair and thrusting it in bags at his saddle. The kaiila, unlike the verr and hurt, is never sheared. When it sheds its hair, however, the hair may be gathered and, depending on the hair, various cloths can be made from it. There is a soft, fine hair, the most prized, which grows on the belly of the animal; there is an undercoating of hair, soft but coarser, which is used for most cloth; and there are the long, outer hairs. These, though still soft and pliant, are, comparatively, the most coarse. The hairs of this coat are used primarily for rope and tent cloth.

I scanned the horizon. I saw nothing.

Once more I lowered myself into the saddle. Again I drew the hood of the burnoose about my face. I shut my eyes against the reflection of the sun from the dust, the gravel and rocks. I removed my slippers after a time, and thrust them under the girth strap. I put my feet against the neck of the kaiila.

I listened to the kaiila bells.

Alyena was learning Gorean quickly. This pleased me. When I had picked her up at the pens of Tor, she had been there for fourteen days, almost three Gorean weeks. I had asked, of course, for a report on her from the slave master, who had consulted his records. She had been placed, of course, as I had requested, in a stimulation chamber; the first five nights the rope harness had been used, as I had specified; it had not been used thereafter for discipline, however, as the girl had been cooperative and diligent; furthermore, her attention and efforts were such that it had not been deemed necessary either to deny her food or put her under the whip; she had not been starved; she had not been lashed.

The first Gorean words the Earth girl had been taught, and she had learned them in the pens of Samos of Port Kar, were 'La Kajira,' which means 'I am a slave girl.'

'The barbarian,' said the slave master, 'is highly intelligent, as the intelligence of females goes, but, strangely, her body is stupid; its muscles seem locked together.'

'Have you heard of Earth?' I asked.

Yes,' he said. 'I have heard of it.' He looked at me. 'Is there truly such a place?' he asked.

'Yes,' I told him.

'I had thought it might be mythical,' he said.

'No,' I told him.

'I have had girls in the pens,' he said, 'who have claimed to have been from there. Some have begged me to return them to Earth.'

'What did you do with them?' I asked.

'I whipped them,' he said, 'and they were silent. Interestingly, I have never had a girl who claimed to be from Earth, who had been fully owned, who wished to return. Indeed, it is enough merely to threaten such a girl with return to Earth to make them do anything.' He smiled. 'They love their collars.'

'Only in a collar can a woman be truly free,' I said. It was a Gorean saying. History on Earth, long ago, had taken a turning away from the body, from nature, from the needs of men and women, from genetically linked psycho-biological realities; this turning away, ultimately and inevitably, had produced an unloved, exploited, polluted planet swarming with miserable populations of unhappy, petty, self-seeking, frustrated animals; the human being of Earth had no Home Stone; this turning away had never taken place on the planet Gor.

'The girl, then,' said the slave master, referring to Alyena, 'is an Earth girl.'

'Yes,' I said, 'she is an Earth girl, brought here, like many others, by slave ship.'

'Interesting,' he said.

'Over several years,' I said, 'entire sets of her muscles have become habituated to moving in mechanistic, conjoint patterns, like the parts of machines; other muscles, perhaps partly atrophied, were not used at all.'

'We have subjected her to an intense exercise program,' said the man, 'but we have had little success. She does not yet feel as a female, so she does not yet move as a female. I think she does not yet know what it is to be a female.'

'That,' I said, 'she will learn from a man.'

'Are all the women of Earth like that?' asked the man.

'Many,' I said, 'not all.'

'It must be a dreary place,' said the man.

'On Earth,' I said, 'women try to be identical with men.'

'Why should that be?' asked the man.

'Perhaps because there are few men,' I said.

'The male population is small?' he asked.

'There are many males,' I said, 'but few men.'

'I find this hard to understand,' said the slave master.

I smiled. 'The distinction,' I said, 'makes little sense to a Gorean.'

He shrugged.

'I do not blame the males,' I said, 'nor the females. Both are fellow victims. In virtue of historical factors, social, institutional and technological, having to do with the development of a given world, the male, from the cradle, is programmed with antimasculine values, taught to distrust his instincts, to hate and fear them, and, ideally, to revel in his de-masculinization. He lives miserably, of course, unfulfilled, frustrated, subject to hideous diseases, and has little to console himself with other than the ignorant servility with which he has worn his chains, taking smug, righteous pride in his allegiance to them.'

'On such a world, then, women have won?' asked the man.

'No,' I said, 'the machine has won. Women, too, have lost.'

'Surely, someday on Earth,' said the man, 'the males will dare to be men?'

'I do not think so,' I said, 'save for rare individuals. The process of teaching, unconscious, subtle, pervasive, is too effective. It is not unusual for a woman to fear her womanhood; what is less generally recognized is that many men fear their own manhood; they conceal their blood; they pretend it does not exist; it is even dangerous, in such a society, to suggest that men consider honesty in such matters, to suggest that they dare to be men, to suggest that they might, if they wished, tear away their own chains. The weakest, the most trapped among them, are often the first, with hysteria, knowing they themselves are not strong enough to take their rightful freedoms, and envying others they fear might have the strength, to denounce such modest suggestions.'

'The weak,' said the man, 'are always those who fear the strong.'

'They fear, not strangely, a world in which not everyone is like themselves.'

'Let all be weak, for I am weak,' smiled the man.

'Yes,' I said.

'And what of the women?' asked the man.

'They attempt to imitate the masculinity they do not find in men,' I said.

'Grotesque,' said the man.

'It is depressing,' I said. 'Let us see the slave.'

The slave master clapped his hands, then called through the silver curtain. '92,683,' he said.

'She has a bit more fluidity, more sensuality, in her body movement now,' he said. 'She moves somewhat better than she did. Here are her exercises.' He thrust a sheet of paper to me. I looked at it. They were familiar exercises, slave-female exercises, designed to keep a girl supple, loose, vital, fit, for her master. 'You are familiar with matters of diet?' he asked.

'Yes,' I said. The diet of the slave girl was regulated with the same attention and care as that which a man of Earth would bestow on his prize hunting dogs, or otherwise esteemed domestic animals. Caloric intake was supervised with particular care. A common problem with slave girls was petty thievery, as they attempted to steal pastries or sweets. Many slave girls have a craving for sweets. These are commonly kept from them. A girl might have to perform superbly for hours before her master before he, in his generosity, would consent to throw her a candy.

'Her body, of course,' said the man, 'is now much more alive to the world about her.'

The stimulation chamber would have accomplished this. Now her skin would be much more aware of such tiny things as a change in air movement in a room, temperature, humidity, and such; also she would now be more keenly sensitive to differences in textures with which her body might come in contact, such as the granulation of the stones on which her feet walked, whether there was slight moisture on tiles, the fall of silk, in different varieties, on her shoulder, the precise feeling of the pile of a rug beneath her thigh, the exact feeling of a strap cinched on her body, the exact feeling of slave bracelets, cool and inflexible, on her small wrists. Her entire body would, now be alive, an organ of touch, a sheet of sentience and vitality. I was satisfied. It was a step toward sensuality.

'The slave, 92,683,' said a woman's voice.

Through the strings of the silver curtain emerged the girl. 'Kneel here, little Alyena,' said the slave master, in Gorean.

I observed as the girl knelt. I thought the slave master too modest. Subtly, but unmistakably, she was a different girl. She still had far to go, but there was no doubt as to the fact that improvement had been wrought in her. Interestingly, I sensed that the girl did not really understand certain changes which had been brought about in her. Doubtless she still thought herself the identical girl who had been placed in the pens. Certain of these changes, mostly in movements, and ways of holding the body, are, sometimes, unconscious concomitants of the training of the girl; they accompany, as pleasant consequences, a latent value, other forms of training which have rather different manifest objectives. An obvious example is the stimulation chamber training which is overtly concerned with honing a physical and psychological responsiveness to surface sensation; this responsiveness, however, is reflected in the entire attitude, and expressions, of the girl. One does not, so to speak, train the girl to 'look vital'; rather one makes her vital; she then, perhaps without even understanding it, or thinking about it, looks vital.

The girl knelt before the desk of the slave master. I sat to one side, in a curule chair. She knelt obediently, beautifully, as a pleasure slave. She was in the presence of free men. I saw her eyes briefly close, relishing the feel of the stone floor, as she knelt back on her heels, on her knees and the tops of her toes; I saw her body straighten itself, exposing itself, drinking in the atmosphere of the room. Her eyes were very much alive, very blue. She looked irritated.

'What about such things,' I asked the slave master, 'as giving pleasure to men.'

'We have shown her some simple things,' he said, 'about all she is now capable of.'

'Have you taught her to dance?' I asked.

'She is not yet ready to dance,' said the slave master.

I looked at the girl, to detect how much of the conversation, in Gorean, she understood. Her grasp was imperfect.

'Stand, Girl,' I said to her in Gorean.

Gracefully she stood. I observed her.

'Bracelets!' I said in Gorean, harshly.

The girl snapped to position, hands behind the small of her back, head lifted, chin up, turned to the left. In such a posture she may be conveniently put in bracelets, and leashed.

'Kneel,' I told her. Again she knelt, in the position of the pleasure slave.

To one side, her arms folded, the quirt in her hand, in leather strips and halter, with collar and ring, with high-laced sandals, stood the large female slave, who had originally conducted the girl from the room, and had brought her back today. She smiled.

I pointed to the stones at my feet. 'Crawl,' I said, in Gorean.

The girl slipped to her belly, and, as a slave girl, crawled to my feet. She put her lips to my foot; I felt her hair over it. 'Return,' I told her. On her belly, head down, she returned to where she had knelt.

'Kneel,' I said.

Again she knelt in the position of the pleasure slave. Her eyes were angry.

Excellent, I thought to myself.

'She has been diligent?' I asked the slave master.

'Yes,' he said.

I smiled. The girl had fallen into the rebellion of compliance. To avoid the deprivation of food, the whip, she obeyed perfectly, but outwardly. She was trying to retain an island in which she would be her own mistress. She thought she was deceiving us. I did not see that it was mine to do, but doubtless, in time, her master, when he wished, would shatter her, taking this island from her, making her completely a slave. For now, I thought I would let her think she was fooling us. Later, when a master wished, he would, when it pleased him, to her horror, break her totally to his will.

I had little doubt that the lovely Alyena would one day, in the arms of a strong man, for whom I was saving her, become a true slave, adoringly and vulnerably the property of her master.

I glanced to the large female slave, with the quirt, standing near the silver curtain.

'Why are you not in slave silk?' I asked her.

Her eyes flashed. Her hand clenched on the quirt.

'She is useful in the pens,' said the slave master. 'She terrorizes feminine girls.'

I turned to Alyena. 'What do you think,' I asked in English, 'of the female slave?'

'I fear her,' whispered small, lovely Alyena.

'Why,' I asked.

'She is so strong, so hard,' said Alyena.

82

'What you fear in her,' I said, 'is masculinity, but it is not a true masculinity; it is fraudulent.' I looked down at her. 'The masculinity you must learn to fear,' I told her, 'is the masculinity of men.'

'She is a match for any man,' said Alyena. Her eyes shone with pride.

I turned to the slave master. 'Fetch a male slave,' I said.

One was brought. He was not a large fellow. He was, however, an inch or so taller than the female slave.

'You certify me,' said I to the slave master, 'that this man is neither clumsy nor stupid, nor drunk, nor an instructor in combat intent upon increasing the confidence of his pupils.'

'It is so certified,' he smiled. 'He is used in cleaning the pens. He is a drover who falsified the quality-markings on spice crates.'

I placed a copper tarn disk on the desk of the slave master.

'Fight,' I said to the slaves.

'Fight,' said the slave master.

The man looked puzzled. With a cry of rage, shrill and vicious, the female slave leapt toward him, slashing him across the face with the quirt. She struck him twice before he, angry, took the quirt from her and threw it aside.

'Do not anger me,' he told her.

He turned and caught her kick on his left thigh. She leapt at him, fingers like claws, to tear out his eyes. He seized her wrists. He turned her about. She could not move. Then, with considerable force, as she cried out with misery, he flung her, the length of her body, belly front, against the stone wall. He then stepped back, jerked her ankles from under her and flung her to the stones, and knelt across her back. She wept and struck the stones with her fists. Then her halter was removed and her hands pulled behind her and bound with it. He discarded her belt and the strips of leather. He removed her sandals. With one of the long, straplike laces, he crossed and bound her ankles. Then, angrily, he turned her collar, hurting her, with its ring, to the back. With the other straplike lace run through the ring and tied to the binding on her ankles, he jerked her ankles up, high, fastening them there. Then he crouched over her and she lay bound at his feet. He turned her head, looking over her right shoulder, so that it faced him; he crouched so that she could not move; his right ankle was against her left cheek. He poised his thumbs, held downward, over her eyes.

'I am a woman at your mercy,' she wept. 'Please, Master, do not hurt me!'

He looked to the slave master. The slave master came to where the woman lay. He looked down at her. He called two slaves from behind the silver curtain. They looked down at the woman. Then the slave master said, 'Put her in slave silk, and give her to male slaves.'

She was freed of the cord binding her ankles to her collar ring.

She was jerked to her feet, and held there; she could not stand by herself for her feet were still crossed and bound. 'Who are the masters?' asked the slave master of her.

The woman, hair before her face, held upright by men, looked at Alyena. The woman trembled. 'Men,' she whispered. 'Men are the masters.'

Alyena's face turned white.

The woman was carried from the room, to the pens. For a silver tarsk I purchased the male slave, and freed him.

'Stand,' I said to Alyena, who was trembling.

I put the walking chains on her, which I had purchased a few days ago in the bazaar.

I looked down into her eyes. 'Who are the masters?' I asked.

She looked up at me, angrily. Then she said, 'Men – men are the masters.'

I then left the office of the slave master of Tor, followed by the slave girl.

On the back of the kaïila, on the road to the Oasis of Nine Wells, drowsily, I listened to the kaïila bells.

It was in the late afternoon. We would stop in an Ahn or two for camp.

Fires would be lit. The kaïila would be put in circles, ten animals to the circle, and fodder, by kaïila boys, would be thrown into the center of the circle.

The tents would be pitched. The opening of the Tahari tent usually faces the east, that the morning sun may warm it. Gor, like the Earth, rotates to the east. The nights require often, a heavy djellaba or an extra blanket. Many nomads build a small kaïila-dung fire in the tent, to smolder during the night, to warm their feet. I needed not to do this, of course, for at my feet slept the former Miss Priscilla Blake-Allen, the girl, Alyena.

At night the kaiila are hobbled. The slave girls, too, are hobbled. With the kaiila a simple figure-eight twist of a kaiila-hair rope, above the spreading paws, below the knees, is sufficient. A girl, of course, is chained. When finished with her, I would cross Alyena's ankles and, with the walking chain, suitably shortened, chain them together. That way she could not stand. I would then throw her her brief djellaba against the desert cold, and order her to a position of sleep. On the mat, toward morning, she would pull the hood over her face, fold her arms and pull up her legs, knees bent; the djellaba came far up her thighs; I would watch her sleeping, sometime, for she was quite beautiful. Once she opened her eyes. 'Master,' she said. 'Sleep, Slave,' I told her. 'Yes, Master,' she said. In the morning I would unchain her early that she might, like the other slave girls in camp, be about her duties. Once she stole a date. I did not whip her. I chained her, arms over her head, back against the trunk, to a flahdah tree. I permitted nomad children to discomfit her. They are fiendish little beggars. They tickled her with the lanceolate leaves of the tree. They put honey about her, to attract the tiny black sand flies, which infest such water holes in the spring. When we would break camp, I would lift her to the kurdah, placing her within.

I became aware of the pounding of kaiila pads on the dry surface. Suddenly I was alert, awake.

I spun the kaiila, and stood in the stirrups.

A man was riding by, the length of the caravan, one of the points. 'Riders!' he cried. 'Riders!'

I could see them now, more than a hundred of them, sweeping toward us over the crest of one of the hills, to my left, the west. Their burnooses whipped behind them as they mounted the crest of the hill and, the animals half sliding, descended the other side, approaching us. Guards from our caravan were hastening outward to meet them. I stood in the stirrups. I saw no one approaching from other directions. There might be, of course, such delayed charges. Reassured I was to see points riding out about the caravan, outriders, to guard against such surprise. I saw Farouk, merchant and caravan master, ride by, burnoose swirling behind him, lance in hand. With him were six men. I saw drovers, holding the reins of their beasts, shading their eyes, looking over the dust to the west. One of the kinsmen of Farouk went to the kurdahs of slave girls, hobble chains at his saddle pommel; he would rein in before a kurdah, throw the girl the hobble and order her, 'Shackle yourself'; he would wait the moment it took for the girl to snap the small ring about her right wrist and, behind her body, the larger one about her left ankle; the rings are separated by about six inches of chain; they are not sleeping hobbles, which confine only the ankles; then he would rush to the next kurdah, fling a hobble to the next girl, and repeat his command. I rode down the caravan until I came to Alyena's kurdah. She thrust her head out, veiled, her fists holding apart the rep-cloth curtain.

'What is going on?' she cried.

'Be silent,' I told her.

She looked frightened.

'Stay within the kurdah, Slave,' I warned her. 'And do not peer out.'

'Yes, Master,' she said.

I turned the kaiila, loosened the scimitar in the sheath.

'They are Aretai!' cried a man.

I thrust the scimitar back, deep in the sheath.

I saw, some hundred yards from the caravan, the riders reined up. With them I saw Farouk, conversing with their captain. The caravan guards, on nervous, prancing kaiila, were behind him. Lances were high, butts in the stirrup sheath, like needles against the hills.

I rode my kaiila out a few steps, toward the men, then returned it to the caravan.

'They are Aretai,' said one of the drovers. The caravan, I knew, was bound for the Oasis of Nine Wells. It was held by Suleiman, master of a thousand lances. He was high pasha of the Aretai.

Several of the newcomers fanned out to flank the caravan, at large intervals. A cluster of them rode toward its head, another cluster toward its rear. Some twenty of them, with Farouk, and certain guards, began to work their way down the caravan, beast by beast, checking the drovers and kaiila tenders.

'What are they doing?' I asked a nearby drover.

'They are looking for Kavars,' he said.

'What will they do with them if they find them?' I asked.

'Kill them,' said the man.

I watched the men, on their kaiila, accompanied by Farouk, the caravan master, moving, man by man, toward us.

'They are the men of Suleiman,' said the drover, standing

nearby, the rein of his kaiila in his hand. 'They have come to give us an escort to the Oasis of Nine Wells.'

Closer came the men, stopping, starting, moving from one man to the next, down the long line. They were led by a captain, with a red-bordered burnoose. Several of them held their scimitars, unsheathed, across the leather of their saddles.

'You are not a Kavar, are you?' asked the drover.

'No,' I said.

The riders were before us.

The drover threw back the hood of his burnoose, and pulled down the veil about his face. Beneath the burnoose he wore a skullcap. The rep-cloth veil was red; it had been soaked in a primitive dye, mixed from water and the mashed roots of the telekint; when he perspired, it had run; his face was stained. He thrust back the sleeve of his trail shirt.

The captain looked at me. 'Sleeve,' he said. I thrust back the sleeve of my shirt, revealing my left forearm. It did not bear the blue scimitar, tattooed on the forearm of a Kavar boy at puberty.

'He is not Kavar,' said Farouk. He made as though to urge his mount further down the line.

The captain did not turn his mount. He continued to look at me. 'Who are you?' he asked.

'I am not a Kavar,' I told him.

'He calls himself Hakim, of Tor,' said Farouk.

'Near the north gate of Tor,' said the captain, 'there is a well. What is its name?'

'There is no well near the north gate of Tor,' I told him.

'What is the name of the well near the stalls of the saddlemakers?' asked the captain.

'The well of the fourth passage hand,' I told him. Water, more than a century ago, had been struck there, during the fourth passage hand, in the third year of the Administrator Shiraz, then Bey of Tor.

I was pleased that I had spent some days in Tor, before engaging in the lessons of the scimitar, learning the city. It is not wise to assume an identity which one cannot cognitively substantiate.

'Your accent,' said the captain, 'is not of Tor.'

'I was not always of Tor,' I told him. 'Originally I was from the north.'

'He is a Kavar spy,' said one of the lieutenants, at the side of the captain.

'I have gems to sell Suleiman, your master,' said I, 'for bricks of pressed dates.'

'Let us kill him,' urged the lieutenant.

'Is this your kurdah?' asked the captain, gesturing to the kurdah on the nearby kaiila.

'Yes,' I said.

In making their examination of the caravan they had, with their scimitars, opened the curtains of the kurdahs, for there might have been Kavars concealed therein. They had found, however, only girls, slaves, their right wrists and left ankles locked in five-link slave hobbles.

'What is in it?' he asked.

'Only a slave girl,' I told him.

He pressed his kaiila to the kurdah, and, with the tip of his scimitar, prepared to lift back the curtain to his right.

My scimitar, blade to blade, blocked his.

The men tensed. Fists clenched on the hilts of scimitars. Lances were lowered.

'Perhaps you conceal within a Kavar?' asked the captain.

With my own scimitar tip I brushed back the curtain. In the kurdah, kneeling, frightened, naked save for collar and veil, the girl shrank back.

'Thigh,' said the captain.

The girl turned her left thigh to him, showing her brand. 'It is only a slave girl,' said the lieutenant, disappointed.

The captain smiled. He regarded the sweet, small, luscious, exposed slave curves of the girl. 'But a pretty little one,' he said.

'Face-strip yourself,' I ordered her.

The girl, fingers behind the back of her head, at the golden string, lowered her veil. Her body had lifted beautifully when her hands had sought the string behind her head. I noted how she had done it. I grinned to myself. She was a slave girl and did not know it.

'Yes,' said the captain, 'a pretty slave.' His eyes lingered on her unveiled mouth, then he drank in the rest of her, then the whole of her. He looked at me. 'I congratulate you on your slave,' he said.

I acknowledged his compliment, inclining and lifting my head.

'Perhaps, tonight,' he suggested, 'she may dance for us.'

'She does not know how to dance,' I said. Then, to the girl, in English, I said, 'You are not yet ready to dance for the pleasure of men.' She shrank back. 'Of course not,' she said, in English. But I could see that, in spite of her anger, her denial, her eyes had been excited, curious. Doubtless she had, from time to time, wondered what it would be like, a collared slave girl, to dance naked in the sand, in the light of the campfire, laboring vulnerably under whip-threat to please Gorean warriors. It would be a long time, I thought, before the cool, white-skinned Alyena would beg, 'Dance me! Dance me for the pleasure of men!'

'She is barbarian,' said I to the captain. 'She speaks little Gorean. I told her she was not yet ready to dance for the pleasure of men.'

'A pity,' said he. In Gorean female dances the girl is expected, often, to satisfy, fully, whatever passions she succeeds in arousing in her audience. She is not permitted merely to excite, and flee away; when, at the conclusion of the swirling music, she flings herself to the floor at the mercy of free men, her dance is but half finished; she has yet to pay the price of her beauty.

'You must have her taught to dance,' said the captain.

'It is my intention,' I said.

'The whip,' said the captain, 'can teach a girl many things.'

'Truly have you spoken,' I agreed.

'A pretty slave,' he said, and then turned his kaiila away, his men following, to continue his examination of the men of the caravan. As he turned his kaiila, the lieutenant, who had accompanied him, he who had asserted that I was a Kavar spy, he who had urged them to slay me, cast me a dark look. Then he, too, was with the rest, and Farouk, down the caravan line.

'It will not be necessary, Master,' said Alyena, loftily, in Gorean, 'to use the whip on me, to make me dance.'

'I know,' I laughed, '– Slave!'

Her fists clenched.

'Veil yourself,' I said.

She did so.

'Remain within,' I said, 'and do not peer out.'

'Yes, Master,' she said.

I saw her eyes, blue, angry, over the yellow veil, and then I, laughing, with my scimitar, brushed down the right-hand cur-

89

tain of the kurdah, it dropping, concealing her within, a slave girl.

Gradually, as a girl begins to realize she is a slave, truly, in a society in which there are slaves, and in which one can truly be just that, and without an escape, a fantastic transformation takes place in her. I could already see the beginnings of this transformation in Alyena. She was already becoming excited about her collar, and her ownership by men. She was becoming curious about them. She was becoming brazen, and shameless, as befits an article of property. She was now permitting herself thoughts and dreams that might have scandalized a free woman, but were for her, only a slave, quite appropriate. She was becoming petty, and pretty, and provocative. She was becoming sensual. She was becoming sly, clever, owned. Recently she had stooped to stealing a date. Though I had, of course, punished her for this, I was, secretly, quite pleased. It meant she was becoming a slave girl. Now I had seen her lift her body, beautifully, in removing her veil before men. I had seen her curiosity about what it would be to dance before them. She had informed me that it would not be necessary for me to use the leather on her, before she would apply herself to the lessons of the dances of slave girls. She thought herself, in herself, quite free, a slave only in name and collar, but in this she was deceiving herself. Let her keep that bit of pride, I thought, until some master takes it from her, and she, shattered, prone on the tiles, or submission mat, knows then, truly, she is only slave.

The lovely Alyena, though she did not know it, and would have refused to believe it, was coming along quite well.

She was becoming a slave girl.

FIVE

WHAT OCCURRED IN THE PALACE
OF SULEIMAN PASHA

'What do you want for her?' asked Suleiman. He sat on cushions, on rugs of Tor.

He wore the kaffiyeh and agal, the cording that of the Aretai.

Before us, on the smooth, scarlet, inlaid floor, stood the girl. Her body was relaxed, but, nonetheless, held beautifully. She was looking away. She seemed bored, a bit insolent.

Low on her hips she wore, on a belt of rolled cloth, yellow dancing silk, in Turian drape, the thighs bare, the front right corner of the skirt thrust behind her to the left, the back left lower corner of the skirt thrust into the rolled belt at her right hip. She was barefoot; there were golden bangles, many of them, on her ankles, more on her left ankle. She wore a yellow-silk halter, hooked high, to accentuate the line of her beauty. She wore a gold, locked collar, and, looped about her neck, many light chains and pendants; on her wrists were many bracelets; on her upper arms, both left and right, were armlets, tight, there being again more on the left arm. She shook her head, her hair was loose.

'Prepare to please a free man,' I told the girl.

She was blonde, blue-eyed, light-skinned.

She bent her knees, weight on her heels, lifted her hands, high over her head, wrists close together, back to back, on her thumbs and fingers, poised, tiny cymbals.

I nodded to the musicians. The music began. There was a bright flash of the tiny finger cymbals and Alyena danced for us.

'Do you like the slave?' I asked.

Suleiman watched her, through heavily lidded, narrow eyes.

His face betrayed no emotion. 'She is not without interest,' he said.

I removed from within my robes the belt in which I had concealed gems. I cut the stitching, which held the two sewn pieces together and, one by one, placed the gems on the low, inlaid, lacquered table behind which, cross-legged, sat Suleiman. He looked at the gems, taking them, one after the other, between the first finger and thumb of his right hand. Sometimes he held them to the light. I had made certain I knew, within marketing ranges, the values of the stones, and what, within reason, they would bring in weights of pressed dates.

To the right of Suleiman, languid, sat another man. He, too, wore kaffiyeh and agal, a kaftan of silk. He was a salt merchant, from Kasra.

'I regret,' said Ibn Saran, 'that we could not travel together to Kasra, and then Tor.'

'I was called away swiftly,' said I, 'on matters of business.'

'It was my loss,' smiled Ibn Saran, lifting to his lips a tiny, steaming cup of black wine.

Suleiman, with his finger, pushed back certain of the stones toward me.

I replaced these in my wallet. His greatest interest, apparently, lay in the sereem diamonds and opals.

Both sorts of stones were rare in the Tahari gem trade.

He lifted his eyes to Alyena. Her body seemed barely to move, yet it danced, as though against her will. It seemed she tried to hold herself immobile, as though fighting her own body, but yet that it forced her to dance, betraying her as a slave girl to the gaze of masters. Her eyes were shut, her teeth clenched on her lip, her face agonized; her arms were above her head, her fists clenched, and yet, seemingly in isolation, seemingly against her resolve, her body moved, forcing her to be beautiful before men. A fantastic intensity is achieved by this dancers' artifice. It was not lost on Suleiman, or Ibn Saran.

I had waited a month at the Oasis of Nine Wells before being granted an audience with Suleiman.

Ibn Saran, not taking his eyes from Alyena, lifted his finger. From one side a slave girl, barefoot, bangled, in sashed, diaphanous, trousered chalwar, gathered at the ankles, in tight, red-silk vest, with bare midriff, fled to him, with the tall, graceful, silvered pot containing the black wine. She was veiled. She knelt, replenishing the drink. Beneath her veil I saw the metal of her collar.

I had not thought to have such fortune. She did not look at me. She returned to her place with the pot of black wine.

Ibn Saran lifted another finger. From the side there hastened to him another girl, a fair-skinned, red-haired girl. She, too, wore veil, vest, chalwar, bangles, collar. She carried a tray, on which were various spoons and sugars. She knelt, placing her tray on the table. With a tiny spoon, its tip no more than a tenth of a hort in diameter, she placed four measures of white sugar, and six of yellow, in the cup; with two stirring spoons, one for the white sugar, another for the yellow, she stirred the beverage after each measure. She then held the cup to the side of her cheek, testing its temperature; Ibn Saran glanced at her; she, looking at him, timidly kissed the side of the cup and placed it before him. Then, her head down, she withdrew.

I did not turn to look back at the first girl, she who held the silvered pot.

I wondered if she belonged to Suleiman or Ibn Saran. I supposed to Suleiman, for it was within his palace that we sat, concerned with our business.

Suleiman, reluctantly, pushed two more stones back toward me. Not speaking, I put them in my wallet.

In her dance, Alyena turned. I smiled. Beneath the small of her back, on the left side, I could see, through the yellow silk, that the bruise had not yet healed. She had received it on the caravan march; four days earlier, before the bruise had been inflicted on her, we had been joined by the officers and escort sent forth from Nine Wells. She had received it at a watering place. She had been carrying a large bag of churned verr milk on her head. It had been given to her by an agile, broad-shouldered, handsome young nomad. I had seen it and, in my opinion, she had asked for it. She, with her burden, had walked past him, near him, and as a slave girl. He had leaped to his feet and, swift, with fingers like pliers, had administered a sharp, jocular bit of instruction to the bold wench. Her yelp resounded for a radius of a quarter of a pasang about the watering hole, startling even the verr and kaiila. She dropped the churned verr milk, the bag's seams fortunately for her not splitting, and spun to face him, but he was towering over her, not four inches from her. 'You walk well, Slave Girl,' he told her. She staggered backward, frightened, stumbling, until she was backed against the backward-leaning trunk of a flahdah tree. She looked up at him. 'You're a pretty little slave girl,' he said. 'I would not mind owning you.' She turned her head away. 'Oh!' she cried. His hand was on her body, and she, writhing, weeping, with her heels, pushing herself, back scraping on the bark, climbed almost a foot up the slanting trunk, before he, through her veil, kissed her, leaving a stain of blood on the silk, and, with his hands, knotted her hair about the trunk of the tree, then leaving her. She was weeping, on her knees at the tree, trying to undo the knots in her hair which bound her to it, which knots, being on the other side of the trunk, she could not see. It was more than ten Ehn before she had managed, to the amusement of the camp, to free herself. She was further discomfited by the fact that she was discovered by Aya, Farouk's slave woman who was training her. Aya was not pleased to find the girl hair-tied by the tree, the bag of churned verr milk lying to one side in the dust. Aya made clear her displeasure by striking the girl several times, before she could free herself, with her customary instrument of instruction, the knotted kaiila strap. 'Lazy girl!' she chided. 'There is a time for play and a time for work!' When Alyena had managed to free herself again, hastily, weeping, lifted and placed upon her head the bag of churned verr milk, steadying it, and proceeded to deliver it to the tent of Farouk. 'This is a time for work!' cried Aya. 'Yes, Mistress!' wept Alyena.

When Alyena had been released from her duties by Aya, the girl fled to me, recounting in tears what had occurred.

'Was he not a terrible beast?' asked Alyena.

'Yes, a terrible beast,' I agreed.

'Should you not have interfered?' she pouted.

I shrugged. 'I thought he handled you quite well,' I said.

'Oh,' she said. Then, after a time, she asked, 'Should you not have defended your property?'

'Perhaps if I thought it had any value,' I said.

'Oh,' she said. She looked down.

'Remove my slippers,' I told her.

She bent to my slippers.

That night, late, when she was in her djellaba, and hobbled, lying at my feet, she spoke. 'Master,' she said.

'Yes,' I said.

'He was a terrible beast, was he not?' she asked.

'Yes,' I said.

There was a long pause. Then I heard, 'Do you think I shall

94

ever see him again?'

'Nomads are poor,' I said. 'I thought you wanted to be owned by a rich man.'

'I do not want to be owned by him!' she cried. 'I hate him!'

'Oh,' I said.

After a time I heard, 'Master –'

'Yes,' I said.

'Do you think, Master,' she asked, 'that I shall ever see him again?'

'I do not know,' I said.

I heard the looped chain, wrapped several times about her crossed ankles, and locked, move. Then I was conscious of her in the darkness, kneeling in her hobble beside me. Her head, dark, was to the tent mat. 'Master,' she whispered.

'Yes?' I said.

'May I be taught to dance?' she asked.

'Who is "I"?' I questioned.

'Alyena, your slave girl, Master,' she whispered, 'begs to be taught to dance.'

'Perhaps she will be taught,' I said.

We were silent for a time.

'Alyena,' I said.

'Yes, Master,' she said.

'In your heart,' I asked, 'do you think of yourself as slave?'

'May a girl answer truthfully?' she asked.

'Yes,' I said.

'I can never be a true slave,' she said. 'I am a woman of Earth.'

'Oh,' I said. I smiled.

I listened to the night, the wind, the snorting of kaiila, the calls of the guards.

'Why does Alyena wish to learn to dance?' I asked her.

The girl thought for a bit. Then she sniffed. 'Alyena,' she said, 'thinks that it might give her pleasure, that it would give her something interesting to do, to occupy her time. She thinks it would be good for her health. It will help to keep her figure trim.'

'Alyena,' I said, 'wishes to learn to dance – to dance the true dances of a female – because in her heart, and she tells no one, there is a secret.'

'What is Alyena's secret?' asked the girl.

'That in her heart,' I said, 'she wants to be a slave girl.'

'Nonsense,' said the girl.

'But there is another secret,' I said. 'One which Alyena does not know.'

'And what is that?' she asked, angrily.

'That she who in her heart wants to be a slave girl is already a slave girl.'

'No, no!' cried the girl. 'No!'

'On such a girl,' I said, 'brand and collar are no more than emblems, mere tokens, proclaiming on her body the truth of her, the deepest truth of her, which no longer may she conceal.'

'No!' cried the girl.

'On such a girl,' I said, 'brazenly, making it evident to all, they tell the secret, which she is no longer permitted to hide, that she is slave, only slave.'

'No!' she cried.

'Your brand and collar, Alyena,' I said, 'fit you well.'

'No!' she wept. I heard her fingers pull at her collar.

'Rejoice,' said I, 'that they are on your body. Many slave girls never know them.'

She lay in the dark, twisting, weeping, hobbled, pulling at her collar.

Ibn Saran, watching the yellow-silked, collared slave dance, sipped his hot, black wine.

I saw that he was interested in the beauty.

She bent down, her leg extended and, moving it, flexing it, slowly, to the music, from her knee to the thigh, caressed it.

Alyena was good, because, in her belly, though she still did not know it, burned slave fire.

Sometimes she would look at us, her audience. Her eyes said to us, I dance as a slave girl, but I am not truly a slave girl. I am not tamed. I can never be tamed. No man can tame me.

In time she could learn she was truly slave. There was little hurry in such matters. In the Tahari men are patient.

Before Suleiman, now, there lay five stones, three sereem diamonds, red, sparkling, white flecked, and two opals, one a common sort, milky in color, and the other an unusual flame opal, reddish and blue. Opals are not particularly valuable stones on Earth, but they are much rarer on Gor; these were excellent speciments, cut and polished into luminescent ovoids;

96

still, of course, they did not have the value of the diamonds.

'What would you like for these five stones?' he asked.

'A hundred weights of date bricks,' I said.

'That is too high,' he said.

Of course it was too high. The trick, of course, was to make the asking price high enough to arrive at some reasonable exchange value later on, and, at the same time, not insult a man of Suleiman's position and intelligence. To make the first price too high, as though I were dealing with a fool, might result in unfortunate consequences for myself, the least among which might have been immediate decapitation, supposing that Suleiman had had an excellent breakfast and a pleasant preceding night with his girls.

'Twenty weights of date bricks,' he said.

'That is too low,' I said.

Suleiman studied the stones. He knew his suggested price was too low. He was merely concerned to consider what they might, competitively, be worth.

Suleiman was a man of discrimination, and taste; he was also one of high intelligence.

It had been he who had organized the trap.

It had been night, when I had first suspected the nature of the trap, the sixth night after the joining of the caravan of Farouk by the escort of Aretai soldiers.

The lieutenant to the captain, high officer of the escort, came to my tent. It had been he who had suspected me of being a Kavar spy, who had urged the killing of me. We bore one another little good will. His name was Hamid. The name of the captain was Shakar.

He looked about himself, furtively, then sat himself in the tent, unbidden, on my mats. I did not wish to kill him.

'You carry stones, which you wish to sell to Suleiman, high Pasha of the Aretai,' had said the lieutenant.

'Yes,' I had said.

He had seemed anxious. 'Give them to me,' he said. 'I will carry them to Suleiman. He will not see you. I will give you, from him, what they bring in pressed date bricks.'

'I think not,' I said.

His eyes narrowed. His swarthy face darkened.

'Go,' he said to Alyena. I had not yet hobbled her.

She looked at me. 'Go,' I said.

97

'I do not wish to speak before the slave,' he said.

'I understand,' I said. Only too well did I understand. Did he find it essential to slay me he would do well not to perform this deed before a witness, be it only a slave.

He smiled. 'There are Kavars about,' he said, 'many of them.'

To be sure, I had seen, from time to time, over the past few days, riders, in small groups, scouting us.

When the guards or the men of our escort rode toward them, they faded away into the hills.

'In the vicinity,' said Hamid, 'though do not speak this about, there is a party of Kavars, in number between three and four hundred.'

'Raiders?' I asked.

'Kavars,' he said. 'Tribesmen. And men of their vassal tribe, the Ta'Kara.' He looked at me closely. 'There may soon be war,' he said. 'Caravans will be few. Merchants will not care to risk their goods. It is their intention that Suleiman not receive these goods. It is their intention to divert them, or most of them, to the Oasis of the Stones of Silver.' This was an oasis of the Char, also a vassal tribe of the Kavars. Its name had been given to it centuries before, when thirsty men, who had moved at night on the desert, had come upon it, discovering it. Dew had formed on the large flat stones thereabout and, in the light of the dawn, had made them, from a distance, seem to glint like silver. Dew, incidentally, is quite common in the Tahari, condensing on the stones during the chilly nights. It burns off, of course, almost immediately in the morning. Nomads sometime dig stones before dawn, clean them, set them out, and, later, lick the moisture from them. One cannot pay the water debt, of course, with the spoonful or so of moisture obtainable in this way. It does, however, wet the lips and tongue.

'If there are so many Kavars about,' I said, 'and Ta'Kara, you do not have enough men to defend this caravan.' Indeed, in such a situation, militarily, so small an escort as a hundred men would seem rather to invite attack.

Hamid, lieutenant to Shakar, captain of the Aretai, did not respond to my remark. Rather he said, 'Give me the stones. I will keep them safe for you. If you do not give them to me, you may lose them to Kavars. I will see Suleiman for you. He will not see you. I will bargain for you. I will get you a good price in date bricks for them.'

'I will see Suleiman myself,' I said. 'I will bargain for my-self.'

'Kavar spy!' he hissed.

I did not speak.

'Give me the stones,' he said.

'No,' I said.

'It is your intention,' he said, 'to gain access to the presence of Suleiman, and then assassinate him!'

'That seems an ill-devised stratagem to obtain a good price in date bricks,' I said. 'You have drawn your dagger,' I observed.

He lunged for me but I was no longer there. I moved to my feet, and, kicking loose the pole which held the tent, slipped outside, drawing my scimitar. 'Ho!' I cried. 'Burglar. A burglar!'

Men came running. Among them came Shakar, captain of the Aretai, blade drawn, and several of his men. Drovers, slaves, crowded about. Inside the fallen tent, struggling, was a figure. Then the tent, as men held torches, at a sign from Shakar, was thrown back.

'Why,' cried I in amazement, 'it is the noble Hamid. Forgive me, Noble Sir. I mistook you for a burglar!'

Grumbling, brushing sand from his robes, Hamid climbed to his feet.

'It was clumsy to let a tent fall on you,' said Shakar. He sheathed his scimitar.

'I tripped,' said Hamid. He did not look pleased as, following his captain, looking back, he disappeared in the darkness.

'Set the tent right,' I told Alyena, who was looking up at me, frightened.

'Yes, Master,' she said.

I then went to find Farouk. There was little point in his losing men.

We did not have to wait long for the attack of the Kavars. It occurred shortly after the tenth hour, the Gorean noon, the following day.

Not much to my surprise the men of the escort of Aretai rushed forth to do battle, but, seeing the numbers of their enemy, which indeed seemed considerable, sweeping down from the hills, wheeled their kaiila and, abandoning the caravan,

99

rode rapidly away.

'Do not offer resistance!' cried Farouk to his guards, riding the length of the caravan. 'Do not fight! Do not resist!'

In a few moments the Kavars, howling, lances high, burnooses swirling, were among us.

The guards of Farouk, following his example, dropped their bucklers to the dust, thrust their lances, butt down, in the earth, took out their scimitars and, flinging them blade downward from the saddle, hurled them into the ground, disarming themselves.

Slave girls screamed.

With lances the Kavars gestured that the men dismount. They did so. They were herded together. Kavars rode down the caravan line, ordering drovers to hurry their animals into line.

With their scimitars, they slashed certain of the bags and crates on the kaiila, determining their contents.

One Kavar warrior, with the point of his lance, drew a line in the graveled dust.

'Strip your women,' he called. 'Put them on this line.' Women were hurried to the line. Some of them were stripped by the scimitar. I saw Alyena pulled by the arm from her kurdah and thrown to the gravel. As she knelt on her hands and knees in the gravel, looking up, terrified, a warrior, behind her, on kaiila, thrust the tip of his lance beneath her veil, between the side of her head and the tiny golden string, and, lifting the lance, ripped the veil from her, face-stripping her. She turned to face him, terrified, crouching in the gravel. 'A beauty!' he cried. 'Oh!' she cried. The steel, razor-sharp point of the lance was at her bosom. 'Run to the line, Slave Girl,' she was ordered. 'Yes, Master,' she cried.

'Why have you not disarmed yourself?' asked a Kavar, riding up to me.

'I am not one of Farouk's guards,' I said.

'You are a member of the caravan, are you not?' he asked.

'I am journeying with it,' I said.

'Disarm yourself,' he said. 'Dismount.'

'No,' I said.

'We have no wish to kill you,' he said.

'I am pleased to hear it,' I said. 'I, too, have no wish to kill you.'

'Find Aretai,' said a man, riding by. 'Kill them.'

'Are you Aretai?' asked the man.

'No,' I said.

I saw certain of the kaiila being led past. Others were left with their drovers.

There was dust about, raised by the paws of the animals. I saw the girls, standing on the line. There was dust on their ankles and calves and, light, on their bodies. Their eyes were squinting, half shut, in the dust and sun. Two of them coughed. Some of them shifted about, for the dust and gravel was hot on the soles of their small, bare feet. They were all stripped. None left the line. An officer rode rapidly back and forth the length of the line, examining them. He called orders. The first one to be prodded with the side of a lance from the line was Alyena.

This pleased me, that she had been found suitable to be a slave of Kavars.

'Stand there, Girl,' ordered a man.

It did not surprise me, however. She was becoming more beautiful each day, as she, not knowing it herself, and repudiating the very thought, was coming to love her collar. She was a slave. On Gor, sooner or later, she would be forced to face this fact; she would be forced to look deeply within herself; to confront herself, perhaps for the first time with candor, and uncompromising honesty; I wondered if, at that time, seeing herself, truly, she would go mad, or if, boldly, with joy, she would dare to be what she found that she was; a human of Earth she had been carefully conditioned to imitate stereotyped images, produced by others, alien to her own nature; what Earth most feared was the peril of men, and women, becoming themselves; on Earth it was regarded as horrifying that millions of beautiful, feminine women, in spite of conditioning, wanted to be the slaves of strong, powerful men; on Gor it was not regarded as horrifying but appropriate; indeed, what other sort of woman is worth putting in a collar; one of the most common emotions felt eventually by an enslaved girl, in a slave culture, where their sort, if not respected, is accepted, is, perhaps surprisingly, gratitude. I am not clear what they have to be grateful about. They are totally under the power of strong masters, and must do what they are told.

Eight other girls now stood behind Alyena, ready for chains. Some six girls had been rejected by the Kavars. 'Run to your masters,' cried a Kavar to the rejected girls. In tears they fled from the line. I could see that Alyena was pleased to lead the

101

line. I saw she was pleased that Aya, who had caused her much trouble, had been rejected. Alyena stood, naked, very proud, very straight, waiting for her chains. They would not be put on her, of course.

'It is my recommendation to you,' said the Kavar, 'to disarm yourself and dismount.'

'It is my recommendation to you,' I said, 'that you, and your fellows, ride for your lives.'

'I do not understand,' he said.

'If you were Aretai,' I asked, 'would you have surrendered the caravan without a fight?'

'Of course not,' he said.

His face turned white.

'Fortunately,' I said, 'I see only dust rising in the east. I would not, however, strike due west. That would be the natural path of departure of surprised, startled men. Others may await you there. Considering the extent of the terrain, and the likely numbers that the Aretai can muster, it will be difficult for them to encircle you unless you permit them to close with the caravan. My own recommendation, though it may be imperfect, given that I have not scouted the terrain, would be to depart, with haste, south.'

'South,' he said, 'is Aretai territory!'

'It seems unlikely they would expect you to move in that direction,' I said. 'You may always deviate from that course later.'

He stood in his stirrups. He cried out. An officer rode up. Together they looked to the east. Dust, like the blade of a dark scimitar, for pasangs, swept toward us.

'Let us fight!' cried a man.

'Without knowing the nature and number of the enemy?' I inquired.

The officer looked at me.

'What are their numbers?' he demanded.

'I'm sure I do not know,' I said, 'but I expect they are ample to accomplish what they have determined to do.'

'Who are you?' demanded the officer.

'One who is bound for the Oasis of Nine Wells,' I told him.

The officer stood in his stirrups. He lifted his lance. Men wheeled into position.

Kicking the kaiila in the flanks, angrily, the officer urged his mount from the camp. The swirling burnooses of the Kavars and Ta'Kara left the camp.

They rode south. I regarded their leader as a good officer.

I rode over to Alyena. She looked up at me. 'It seems you will not be chained,' I said.

'How pleased I am,' she cried.

'Do not be disappointed,' I told her. 'As a slave girl you will become quite familiar with chains. You will wear them often, and helplessly.'

'Oh?' she said, pertly.

'Certainly,' I assured her.

She looked up at me. 'I would have been the first chained,' she laughed. 'I was the first girl taken from the line. I would have led the slave chain!'

'There would have been no chain,' I said. 'One cannot march naked girls across the desert. You would have been chained and, individually, or in pairs, put across saddles.'

'Had there been a chain,' she said, 'I would have led it.'

'Yes,' I said. I lifted her to the saddle.

'And I am not the tallest,' she said. 'I am not the tallest!'

'Do you grow insolent?' I asked.

'Of course not, Master,' she said. 'But does it not mean I am the most beautiful?'

'Among tarsk,' I said, 'even a she-sleen looks well.'

'Oh, Master!' she protested. I placed her in the kurdah. She knelt there. With my lance tip I retrieved her veil from the dust, and put it to the side of her left knee. 'Repair it,' I said, 'and don it. With it conceal your mouth, which is rather loud of late.'

'Yes, Master,' she said.

I turned to look at the dust from the east. I could see riders now. There were four hundred of them.

'Master,' said the girl.

'Yes,' I said.

'I know that I am beautiful,' she said.

'How do you know that?' I asked.

She knelt there, naked, in the kurdah, the veil by her knee. She straightened herself. She put her hands on her collar. She lifted her head, her chin, proudly. Her neck was delicate, aristocratic, a bit long, as she held it, white. I saw the close-fitting, obdurate metal, inflexible, with its lock behind the back of the neck, encircling it. Her eyes were strikingly blue, and bright, lively; her hair, long, blonde, streamed behind her.

'How do you know that you are beautiful?' I asked.

She shook her head a little, arranging her hair, and then looked at me, saucily, directly, her fingers on the metal at her throat. 'Because I am collared,' she laughed.

With the tip of my scimitar I made ready to conceal her again within the kurdah.

The Aretai were nearing the caravan, a pasang or so away, sweeping down upon it. Now, from the west, too, I could see some two hundred men riding in. Neither group, of course, would find Kavars in the caravan. The plan had been a good one, only the Kavars, apparently, had escaped.

'Is it not true, Master?' she said.

'It is true,' said I, 'Slave Girl. Had men not found you beautiful they would have been quite content to leave you free. Only the most beautiful are thought worthy of the brand; only the most beautiful are found worthy of the collar.'

'But how miserable,' she moaned, 'that I fell slave!'

'The more excruciatingly beautiful a woman is,' I said, 'the more likely it is that she will be put in brand and collar.'

She looked at me.

'Any true man,' I said, 'who sees such a woman wishes to own her.'

'On this world,' whispered Alyena, 'they can!'

'On this world,' I said, 'they do.'

'Poor women!' said Alyena.

I shrugged.

'Master,' she said.

'Yes,' I said.

'May Alyena, your obedient girl, your dutiful girl, be taught to dance?'

'You have not forgotten your young nomad, have you?' I asked.

She looked down, sullenly.

'To be sure,' I said, 'it would be difficult to compete for him unless you could dance.'

'I do not even like him!' she cried. 'He is a beast! He is a terrible person! Did you not see how he abused me?'

'In his arms,' I laughed, 'he would treat you only as a slave.'

'Terrible,' she wept.

To her indignation I felt her body. It was hot and wet. 'Yes, pretty Alyena,' I said to her, 'I will have you taught to dance, for in your belly is slave fire.'

104

'No!' she wept.

'Slave fire,' I said.

I then brushed down the curtain of the kurdah, as she cried out with rage, closing her within.

The Aretai, from the east, and west, lances down, scimitars high, with much dust, crying out, shouting, swept into the caravan. They did not find the Kavars, or the Ta'Kara.

Suleiman was a man of discrimination, and taste; he was also one of high intelligence.

He studied the stones.

It had been he who had organized the trap.

'Twenty-five weights of date bricks,' he said.

'Ninety,' I said.

'Your price is too high,' he said.

'Your price, in my opinion,' I said, 'great pasha, is perhaps a bit low.'

'Where are the Kavars!' had cried Shakar, captain of the Aretai, when he had swept into the caravan, his kaiila rearing, his lieutenant, Hamid, behind him.

'They are gone,' I had told him.

Had the Kavars been caught in the trap there would have been a massacre.

Suleiman was a man to hold in respect.

The true worth of the stones, which I had had appraised carefully in Tor, against their best information as to the date yields, was between sixty and eighty weights in pressed date bricks. I was not interested, of course, in driving bargains, but in meeting Suleiman. I had been more than a month at the oasis. Only now had he consented to see me. Recently, too, had Ibn Saran, with a caravan, arrived at the oasis. Some twenty thousand people lived at the oasis, mostly small farmers, and craftsmen, and their families. It was one of the larger oases in the Tahari. It seemed important for me to see Suleiman. As a portion of my assumed identity, I wished to sell him stones. Moreover, with the dates purchased by these, I hoped to have a suitable disguise, as a merchant in date bricks, in moving eastward. I suspected that my being summoned to the presence of Suleiman was not unconnected with the arrival of Ibn Saran at the oasis. He had, I suspected, interceded in my behalf. For this I was surely grateful. He remembered me, of course, from the hall of Samos. Had I not seen Suleiman shortly I would have had to strike eastward myself. Without a guide this would have been incredibly dangerous. The men of the Tahari kill those who make maps of it. They know their own country, or their districts within it; they are not eager that others know it as well. Without a guide, who knew the locations of water, to enter the Tahari would be suicidal. I had offered good prices for guides. But none had volunteered. They protested fear of the imminent war, the dangers of being on the desert at such a time. I suspcted, however, that they had been told not to offer me their services. One fellow had agreed, but, the next morning, without explanation, he had informed me that his mind was changed. It would be too dangerous, in such times, to venture into the desert. Sometimes I had seen Hamid, the lieutenant of Shakar, captain of the Aretai, following me about. He still suspected, I supposed, that I was a Kavar spy. But when Ibn Saran had arrived at the oasis, Suleiman had invited me to his presence. I wondered if he had been waiting for Ibn Saran. Ibn Saran, it seemed to me, exercised more influence at the Oasis of the Nine Wells than one might have expected of a mere merchant of salt. I had seen men withdrawing from the path of his kaiila, standing aside, lifting their hands to him.

Alyena, in dancing, sensed the power of Ibn Saran. It is not diffiicult for a female dancer, lightly clad, displaying her beauty, to detect where among those who watch her lies power. I am not sure precisely how this is done. Doubtless, to some extent, it has to do with richness of raiment. But even more, I suspect, it has to do with the way in which they hold their bodies, their assurance, their eyes, as they, as though owning her, observe her. A woman finds herself looked upon very differently by a man who has power and one who does not. Instinctively, of course, to be looked upon by a man with power thrills a woman. They desire, desperately, to please him. This is particularly true of a slave girl, whose femaleness is most shamelessly and brazenly bared. Ibn Saran, languid, observed the dancer. His face betrayed no emotion. He sipped his hot black wine.

Alyena threw herself to the floor before him, moving to the music. I supposed she saw in him her 'rich man,' who would guarantee her a life in which she might be protected from the labors of the free woman of the Tahari, the pounding of grain with the heavy pestle, the weaving of cloth, the churning of milk in skin bags, the carrying of water, the herding of animals with sticks in the blistering heat. I saw her turn, and twist and writhe, and move, and, on her belly, hold out her hand to him.

Her lessons, which had been intensive, once we had arrived at the Oasis of Nine Wells, had cost little, and had, in my opinion, much increased her value, doubling or tripling it. The modest cost of the lessons had been, in my opinion, an excellent investment. My property had now increased, considerably, in value. But most credit, surely, had to go to the girl herself. With fantastic diligence had she applied herself to her lessons, and practices. Even so small a thing as the motion of the wrist she had practiced for hours.

Her teacher was a café slave girl, Seleenya, rented from her master; her musicians were a flutist, hired early, and, later, a kaska player, to accompany him.

Once I saw her, naked, covered with sweat and bangles, in the sand.

'Have you had to beat her often?' I asked Seleenya.

'No,' said the slave girl. 'I have never seen a girl so eager,' she said.

'Play,' said I to the musicians.

They played, until I, by lifting a finger, silenced them. At the same time, too, Alyena froze in the sand, her right hand high, left hand low, at her hip, her head bent to the left, eyes intent on the fingers of her left hand, as though curious to see if they would dare to touch her thigh; then she broke the pose, and threw back her head, breathing deeply. There was sand on her ankles and feet; perspiration ran down her body.

'Does your girl please you?' she asked.

'Yes,' I said. 'And doubtless, too,' I said, 'a young nomad would be pleased.'

She tossed her head, and sniffed. 'I have no longer an interest in such as he,' said she. She looked down, and bit her lip. 'I know, Master,' she said, 'you will do with me exactly what you please, but I would bring a higher price, surely, if I were sold to a rich man.' She knelt in the sand before me, in her sweat and bangles; she looked up, blue-eyed. 'Please, Master,' she said, 'sell me to a rich man.'

I motioned her to her feet. I signaled the musicians. She danced.

I observed her. I thought it not unlikely this slave might stir the interest of a man of means.

'Perhaps,' I said. I was thinking I might sell her to Suleiman. I watched her move.

'I have never seen a girl take so readily, so swiftly, so naturally to the dances of a slave,' said Seleenya.

'She is a natural slave,' I told Seleenya.

'In your arms,' said Seleenya, looking up at me, 'might not any woman find herself a natural slave?'

'Go to the alcove,' I told her. I was renting her.

'Yes, Master,' she whispered, gathering her silk about her and hurrying to the alcove.

'Continue your practices,' I told Alyena.

'The fact that I can dance as a slave,' said Alyena, moving before me, 'does not mean that I am a slave.'

I smiled, and turned away from her, going to the alcove. 'I am not tamed,' cried Alyena. 'No man tame me!'

I turned. 'Kneel,' said I. 'Say "I am tamed." '

Immediately she knelt. 'I am tamed,' she said. She smiled. It was the rebellion of compliance.

'Resume your practices,' I told her.

The musicians began again, and again the girl danced. It was superb. And it was incredible. She did not yet know she was a true slave. What a little fool she was.

I watched her move.

She smiled at me, disdainfully. I considered her blonde hair, now wild about her head as, suddenly, she entered into a series of spins. Her gaze focused to the last moment on a spot across the room from her, and then, suddenly, on each spin, her head snapped about, and she again found the focus. Then she finished the spins, and froze, hands over her head, body held high, stomach in, right leg flexed and extended, toes only touching the floor. Then she was again in basic position. Her white skin, in itself, in the Tahari, would bring a good price. Blonde hair and blue eyes, too, in this region, made her a rare specimen. But beyond these trivialities, though of considerable commercial import, was the fact that she was beautiful, both in face and figure. Her figure, though not full, was completely female, beautifully proportioned, and sweetly slung. She was, in Earth measurements, I would guess, some five feet four inches in height. Her face was incredibly delicate, and her lips. Her face was extremely sensitive, and feminine. It was a face on which emotion could be easily read. Her lip was swift to tremble, her eyes swift to moisten, filling with bright tears. Her feelings were easily hurt, a valuable property in a slave girl. Too, she could not control her feelings, another excellent property in a slave girl. Her feelings, vulnerable, deep, exploitable, in her expressions and on her face, betrayed her, exposing her to men, and their amusement, as helplessly as her stripped beauty. They made her more easily controlled, more a slave. I had once seen her handwriting. It, too, was extremely feminine. I watched her dance. Too, in her belly, perhaps most important of all, burned slave fire. She would do quite well. She would bring a high price. Only a rich man, I speculated, would be able to afford her.

It had been a stroke of brilliance, or of fortune, I surmised, to have brought the wench south. I had little doubt she would prove valuable.

'Master!' called Seleenya, the café slave girl, the rented girl, softly, from the alcove. She stood behind the beaded curtain. She had slipped off her silk. 'Please, Master!' she wept. I saw through the strings of hanging beads the collar on her throat.

I went to her.

Behind me, as I thrust apart the beads, I heard the pounding of the drums, the kaska, the silence, then the sound, as the flutist, his hands on her body, to the sound of the drum, instructed the girl in the line-length and intensity of one of the varieties of pre-abandonment pelvic thrusts.

'Less,' he said. 'Less. There must be more control, more precision. You are being forced to do this, but you are holding back. You are angry. This must show on your face.'

'Please do not touch me so, Master,' she said.

'Be silent,' he said to her. 'You are slave.'

'Yes, Master,' she said.

'Try again,' he said.

'Yes, Master,' she said.

I again heard the drum.

Seleenya lifted her arms to me, and parted her lips. I touched her.

'Is it the intention of Master to use me slowly?' she said.

'Yes,' I said.

'Seleenya loves Master,' she said.

At a languid gesture from Ibn Saran, Alyena lifted herself from the scarlet tiles, gracefully turning from her side to her knees, and then, head back, hair to the floor, slowly, inch by melodic protesting inch, arms before her body, lifted herself to a kneeling position, erect, the last bit of her to rise being her head, with a swirl of her blonde, loose hair. Then, looking to Ibn Saran, suddenly she bent forward, as though impulsively, as though she could not help herself, and, hands on the tiles, head down, kissed the tiles at his feet, before his slippers. She looked up at him. I gathered she wanted to be bought by him. He was her 'rich man.' He lifted his finger for her to rise. Her right leg thrust forth, brazenly, and then, from her kneeling position, slowly, hands above her head, moving, high, she rose swaying to her feet.

'May I strip your slave?' inquired Ibn Saran.

'Of course,' I said.

He nodded to the girl. To the music she unhooked her slave halter of yellow silk and, as though contemptuously, discarded it, I saw she was excited to see his interest in her. Only too obviously was she interested in him making a purchase of her. The churning of milk and the pounding of grain were not for lovely Alyena. That was for ugly girls and free women. She was too desirable, too beautiful, to be set to such labors.

I decided I might care to taste the steaming, black wine. I lifted my finger. The girl in whose charge was the silver vessel, filled with black wine, knelt beside a tiny brazier, on which it sat, retaining its warmth. Seeing my signal, she stiffened; she hesitated. She was white, dark-haired. She wore a high, tight vest of red silk, with four hooks; her midriff was bare; she wore the chalwar, a sashed, diaphanous trousered garment, full but gathered in, closely, at the ankles; she was barefoot; her wrists and ankles were bangled; she was veiled; she was collared. She rose swiftly to her feet. She knelt, head down, before me. She poured, carefully, the hot, black beverage into the tiny red cup. I dismissed her. Beneath her veil I had not been able to read the lettering on her collar, which would tell who owned her. I supposed it was Suleiman, since she was serving in the palace. The other girl, the white-skinned, red-haired girl, also in vest, chalwar and veil, and bangles and collar, lifted her tray of spoons and sugars. But I turned away. She was not summoned. The girls, white-skinned, were a matched set of slaves, one for the black wine, one for its sugars.

Alyena, now, slowly, disengaged the dancing silk from her hips, yet held it, moving it on and about her body, by her hands, taunting the reclining, languid, heavy-lidded Ibn Saran, to whom she knew, at his slightest gesture, she must bare herself.

He regarded her veil work; she was skillful; he was a connoisseur of slave girls.

I, too, in my way, though doubtless less skillful than the noble Ibn Saran, was a connoisseur of slave girls. For example, the dark-haired slave, she who was one of the matched set, she who was charged with the careful pouring of black wine, was a piece of delicious woman meat, a luscious, if inadequately disciplined piece of female flesh. To see her was to want her.

I had once had a chance to buy her, but, like a fool, I had not done so, carrying her in chains to my ship, to be taken to my house.

I had later sent Tab, one of my captains, a trusted man, to Lydius to buy her, but already had she been sold.

Her whereabouts had been unknown.

She had once disobeyed me, a male. For this she must be punished. I had not bought her in Lydius. Then I had been seeking Talena, to free her in the northern forests, and return her safe to Port Kar, where we might, as I had then thought, renew the companionship. Surely would it have seemed inappropriate to have returned in triumph with Talena, with that dark-haired wench, such a fantastic beauty, nude, wearing my chains, in the hold of my ship. Would Talena not have cut her throat, under the metal collar? And had I freed her would she not, soon, have fallen again to a man's collar? Her flight from the Sardar had not won her freedom. She, a girl of Earth, had been swiftly caught by Panther Girls, and displayed, tied, roped, to a pole, on the banks of the Laurius, hands over head, ankles, throat and belly bound to it, a beautiful, taken slave. Sarpedon, a tavern keeper from Lydius, had bought her from Panther Girls. It was in his chains that I had found her, a lowly paga slave in his establishment. She had, in fleeing the Sardar, taken my tarn. Yet, when I found her in Lydius, I had not slain her for this act. I had only used her, and left her slave. The tarn had later returned; in fury I had driven it away. She had cost me the tarn; it was worth ten times the cost of her body on a public block. None but its master should it have permitted its saddle! Of what value is a tarn of war who permits a stranger, even a girl, a mere wench, to ascend to its saddle? I had driven it away. When I thought of the tarn I sometimes wanted to lash her beauty to the bone. Yet I recalled that once had she labored, as I, before her flight, her disobedience, for Priest-Kings. I, in my courtly simplicities, my romantic delusions of those times, had wished to return her safe to Earth.

111

She had declined, fleeing the Sardar. It had been a brave act. But it had been not without its consequences. She had gambled. She had lost. I left her slave.

At a signal from Ibn Saran, Alyena drew the veil about her body, and around it, and, with one small hand, threw it aside. She stood boldly before him, arms lifted, head to the side, right leg flexed. The veil, floating, wafted away, a dozen feet from her, and gently, ever so gently, settled to the tiles. Then, to the new melodic line, she danced.

Did the girl, in Lydius, truly think I would have freed her, yielding to her pleadings, I, in whose veins flowed Gorean blood, whose tarn she had cost him? I had not slain her. What a pretty little fool she was! I recalled her pleading that I buy her. Only a slave would so plead. I had not realized until then that she was truly a slave. I recalled, to my chagrin, that once, long ago, we had thought we had cared for one another. I recalled that once, in delirium, in weakness, when poison had burned in my body, I had cried out for her to love me. But when, long later, after I had learned the lessons of Torvaldsland, I ridded myself of the poison in the cleansing delirium of the antidote, I had not cried out, in weakness, for her love, begging it, but rather, in strength, laughing, had collared her, putting her to my feet and making her my slave. Proud women, their pride stripped from them, belong at the feet of prouder men. She had begged to be freed. She was a slave. And I, once, had been fool enough to care for her. Once, it was true, she had served Priest-Kings, but then, so, too, had I. And that was long ago. And then we did not know, and she did not know, that she was a true slave, as was revealed in a tavern in Lydius. We had thought her a free woman, pretending to be slave. Then, in a tavern in Lydius, we learned she was slave. It was now out of the question that she, a slave, might serve Priest-Kings. The collar, by Gorean law, cancelled the past. When Sarpedon had locked his collar on her throat her past as a free woman had vanished, her current history as a slave had begun. 'She fled the Sardar,' had said Samos to me. 'She disobeyed. She is untrustworthy. And she knows too much.' He had wished to send men to Lydius to purchase her, and return her to Por Kar that she might be, under his direction, thrown to urts in the canals. 'She cannot be depended on,' said Samos. 'And she knows too much.'

'There are better things to do with a beautiful slave,' I told him, 'than throw her into the canals, to feed the urts.'

Samos had grinned at me. 'Perhaps,' he had said. 'Perhaps.'

What a fool I had been to be willing to return such a luscious piece of female to Earth. Had I had my wits about me I would have put a collar on her then and fastened her to the slave ring at the foot of my couch. I could not deny that I was now pleased she was not, in innocuous triviality, ensconced on Earth. I was pleased rather that her beauty was on Gor, where I, and other males, might have access to it. She might have been safe on Earth; she had chosen to be unsafe, as any beautiful woman without a Home Stone must be, on Gor. She would now pay the penalties, and well, exacted of her beauty by the powerful men of a primitive culture. She had gambled. She had lost. I was pleased she had lost. My only regret was that I had not bought her in Lydius, and returned her to Port Kar, to keep her as one of my own slaves. I had thought, at that time, however, that I would find Talena. Talena, unless she, too, were collared, and had no choice, would not be likely to accept such a beauty beneath the same roof with her. If she did not kill her, she would have soon sold her, probably to a woman, or, for a pittance, to the most despicable master she could find. I had not known until Lydius that Vella, the former Miss Elizabeth Cardwell, of Earth, was a true slave.

I glanced casually back to look upon her, kneeling beside the slender, silvered, long-spouted vessel of black wine, resting over its tiny brazier, she only one of a pair, a matched set, of slaves. Her eyes were angry, over her veil. Her bare midriff, long, between the high, hooked vest of red silk and the low-slung, sashed chalwar, about her hips, some inches below her navel, was quite attractive. To see her was to want her; and to want her was to wish to own her.

Alyena now to a swirl of music spun before us, swept help-less with it, bangles clashing, to its climax.

Then she stopped, marvelously, motionlessly, as the music was silent, her head back, her arms high, her body covered with sweat, and then, to the last swirl of the barbaric melody, fell to the floor at the feet of Ibn Saran. I noted the light hair on her forearms. She gasped for breath.

Ibn Saran, magnanimously, gestured that she might rise, and she did so, standing before him, head high, breathing deeply.

Ibn Saran looked at me. He smiled thinly. 'An interesting slave,' he said.

'Would you care to bid upon her?' I asked.

Ibn Saran gestured to Suleiman. He acknowledged the courtesy. 'I would not bid against a guest in my house,' he said.

'And I,' said Ibn Saran, 'would not feel it gracious to bid against the host in whose house I find such welcome.'

'In my Pleasure Gardens,' smiled Suleiman, 'I have twenty such women.'

'Ah,' said Ibn Saran, bowing.

'Seventy weights of dates for the stones,' said Suleiman to me. The price was fair, and good. In his way, he was being magnanimous with me. He had bargained earlier, and had, in this, satisfied himself as a trader of the desert. It was now as Suleiman, Ubar and Pasha of Nine Wells, that he set his price. I had little doubt it was firm. He cut through much haggling. Had he been truly interested in bargaining and dates I suspected I would not have been permitted to deal with him at all, but one of his commissary officers.

'You have shown me hospitality,' I said, 'and I would be honored if Suleiman Pasha would accept these unworthy stones for sixty weights.'

Had it not been for Ibn Saran, I suspected I would not have been admitted even to the presence of the Pasha of Nine Wells.

He bowed. He called a scribe to him. 'Give this merchant in gems,' said he, 'my note, stamped for eighty weights of dates.'

I bowed. 'Suleiman Pasha is most generous,' I said.

I heard a noise from afar, some shouting. I did not think either Ibn Saran or Suleiman heard it.

Alyena stood on the scarlet tiles, head back, sweating, breathing heavily, nude save for her ornaments and collar, the bangles about her ankles and wrists, the armlets, the several chains and pendants looped about her neck. She brushed back her hair with her right hand.

I now heard some more shouting. I heard, too, incongruous in the palace of the Pasha of Nine Wells, from afar, the squealing of a kaiila.

'What is going on?' asked Suleiman. He stood, robes swirling.

Alyena looked about.

At that instant, buffeting guards aside, sending them sprawling, to our amazement, in the carved, turret-shaped portal of the great room, claws scratching on the tiles, appeared a war kaiila, in full trappings, mounted by a veiled warrior in swirling burnoose. Guards rushed forward. His scimitar leapt from its sheath and they fell back, bleeding, reeling to the tiles.

He thrust his scimitar back in his sheath. He threw back his head and laughed, and then tore down the veil, that we might look on his face. He grinned at us.

'It is the bandit, Hassan!' cried a guard.

I drew my scimitar and stood between him and Suleiman.

The kaiila pranced. The man uncoiled a long desert whip from his saddle.

'I come for a slave,' he said.

The long blade of the whip lashed forth. Alyena, her head back, cried out with pain. Four coils of the whip, biting into her, lashing, snapped tight about her waist. He yanked her, stumbling, the prisoner of his whip, to the side of his kaiila. By the hair he yanked her across his saddle.

He lifted his hand to us. 'Farewell!' he cried. 'And my thanks!' He then spun the kaiila and, as guards swarmed after him, to our astonishment, leapt the kaiila, catlike, between pillars, through one of the great arched windows of the palace room. He struck a roof below, and then another roof, and then was to the ground, racing away, men turning to look after him.

I, and others, turned back from the window. On the cushions lay Suleiman, Pasha of Nine Wells. I ran to him. I saw Hamid, who was the lieutenant of Shakar, captain of the Aretai, slip swiftly behind hangings, a dagger, bloodied, held within his cloak.

I turned Suleiman. His eyes were open. 'Who struck me?' he said. There was blood deep in the silk of the cushions.

Ibn Saran drew forth his scimitar. He did not seem languid now. His eyes blazed. He seemed a silken panther, lithe, tensed for the spring. He pointed the scimitar at me. 'He!' he cried. 'I saw it! He did it!'

I leaped to my feet.

'Kavar spy!' cried Ibn Saran. 'Assassin!'

I spun about, facing steel on all sides.

'Cut him down!' cried Ibn Saran, raising his scimitar.

SIX

A SLAVE GIRL TESTIFIES

The bodies of the two girls, stripped, lay on the narrow rectangles, networks of knotted ropes, on the racks. The ropes, slung, were pressed down with their weight. Their hands were at their sides, but ropes were attached to them, and fixed on the axle of the windlass, above their heads. Both wore collars. Their ankles were roped to the foot of the device.

I knelt on the circle of accusation. My wrists were manacled behind my back. On my neck, hammered, was a heavy ring of iron, with two welded rings, one on each side, to which chains were attached, these chains in the hands of guards. I was stripped. My ankles were chained.

'Cut him down!' had cried Ibn Saran, raising his scimitar.

'No!' had said Shakar, captain of the Aretai, staying his arm. 'That would be too easy.'

Smiling, Ibn Saran had sheathed his weapon.

Ropes had been put upon me.

I struggled in the chains. I was helpless.

'Let the testimony of slaves be taken,' said the judge.

Two brawny male slaves, stripped to the waist, spun the two handles on the racks.

The red-haired girl, she who had been one of the matched set of slaves, who had had in her charge the tray of spoons and sugars, wept. Her wrists, and those of the other girl, as the long wooden handles turned, were pulled up and over her head. The red-haired girl writhed on the cords. 'Master!' she wept.

Ibn Saran, in silken kaftan, and kaffiyeh and agal, strode to the rack.

'Do not be frightened, pretty Zaya,' he said. 'Remember to tell the truth, and only the truth.'

'I will, Master!' she wept. 'I will.'

116

At a sign from the judge the handle moved once, dropping the wooden pawl into the ratchet notch. Her body was now tight on the rack; her toes were pointed; her hands were high over her head, the rough rope slipped up her wrists, prohibited from moving further by its knots and the wide part of her hands.

'Listen carefully, little Zaya,' said Ibn Saran. 'And think carefully.'

The girl nodded.

'Did you see who it was who struck noble Suleiman Pasha?'

'Yes,' she cried. 'It was he! He! It was he, as you, my Master, have informed the court.' The girl turned her head to the side, to regard me. 'He!' she cried.

Ibn Saran smiled.

'Hamid it was!' I cried, struggling to my feet. 'It was Hamid, lieutenant to Shakar!'

Hamid, standing to one side, did not deign to look upon me. There were angry murmurs from the men assembled in the court.

'Hamid,' said Shakar, not pleased, standing near, 'is a trusted man.' And he added, 'And he is Aretai.'

'Should you persist in accusing Hamid,' said the judge, 'your penalties will be the more severe.'

'He it was,' said I, 'who struck Suleiman.'

'Kneel,' said the judge.

I knelt.

The judge signaled again to the slave who controlled the handle of the red-haired girl's rack. 'No, please!' she screamed.

Once more the handle moved and the pawl slipped into a new notch on the ratchet. Her body, now, was lifted from the network of knotted ropes and hung, suspended, between the two axles of the rack.

'Masters!' she cried. 'Masters! I have told the truth! The truth!'

The pawl was moved yet another notch. The girl, now hurt, screamed.

'Have you told the truth, pretty Zaya?' inquired Ibn Saran.

'Yes, yes, yes, yes, yes!' she wept.

At a signal from the judge the handle was released. The axle of the windlass at the girl's head spun back and her body fell into the network of knotted ropes. One of the slaves removed the ropes from her wrists and ankles. She could not

117

move, so terrified she was. He then threw her to the side of a wall, where another slave, pushing against the side of her neck, fastened a snap catch on her collar, securing her by a chain to a ring in the floor. She lay there, trembling.

'Let the testimony of the second slave be taken,' said the judge.

Her wrists were already over her head. She was stripped. She looked at me. She wore a collar.

'Think now, my pretty,' said Ibn Saran. 'Think carefully, my pretty.'

She was the other girl of a matched set, the other white-skinned wench, who had had in her charge the silvered, long-spouted vessel of black wine.

'Think carefully now, pretty Vella,' said Ibn Saran.

'I will, Master,' she said.

'If you tell the truth,' he said, 'you will not be hurt.'

'I will tell the truth, Master,' she said.

Ibn Saran nodded to the judge.

The judge lifted his hand and the handle on the girl's rack moved once. She closed her eyes. Her body was now tight on the rack; her toes were pointed; her hands were high over her head, the rope tight, taut, on her wrists.

'What is the truth, pretty Vella?' asked Ibn Saran.

She opened her eyes. She did not look at him. 'The truth,' she said, 'is as Ibn Saran says.'

'Who struck noble Suleiman Pasha?' asked Ibn Saran, quietly.

The girl turned her head to look at me. 'He,' she said. 'He it was who struck Suleiman Pasha.'

My face betrayed no emotion.

At a signal from the judge the slave at the handle of the girl's rack, pushing it with his two hands, moved the handle. When the pawl slipped into its notch her body was held, tight, suspended, between the two axles of the rack.

'In the confusion,' said Ibn Saran, 'it was he, the accused, who struck Suleiman Pasha, and then went, with others, to the window.'

'Yes,' said the girl.

'I saw it,' said Ibn Saran. 'But not I alone saw it.'

'No, Master,' she said.

'Who else saw?' he asked.

'Vella and Zaya, slaves,' she said.

'Pretty Zaya,' said he, 'has given witness that it was the accused who struck Suleiman Pasha.'

'It is true,' said the girl.

'Why do you, slaves, tell the truth?' he asked.

'We are slaves,' she said. 'We fear to lie.'

'Excellent,' he said. She hung in the ropes, taut. She did not speak.

'Look now again, carefully, upon the accused.'

She looked at me. 'Yes, Master,' she said.

'Was it he who struck Suleiman Pasha?' asked Ibn Saran.

'Yes, Master,' she said. 'It was he.'

The judge gave a signal and the long handle of the rack, fitting through a rectangular hole in the axle, moved again.

The girl winced, but she did not cry out.

'Look again carefully upon the accused,' said Ibn Saran. I saw her eyes upon me. 'Was it he who struck Suleiman Pasha?'

'It was he,' she said.

'Are you absolutely certain?' he asked.

'Yes,' she said.

'It is enough,' said the judge. He gave a signal. The handle spun back. The girl's body fell into the network of knotted ropes. She turned her face to me. She smiled, slightly.

The ropes were removed from her wrists and ankles. One of the male slaves lifted her from the rack and threw her to the foot of the wall, beside the other girl. The slave there took her by the hair, holding her head down, and, between the back of her neck and the collar, thrust a snap catch, closing it. He then, roughly, burning the side of her neck, slid the catch about her collar, to the front; there he jerked it against her collar; the chain then, which fastened her, like the other girl, to a ring in the floor, ran to her collar, under her chin. She kept her head down, a slave.

SEVEN

I AM INFORMED OF
THE PITS OF KLIMA;
AN ESCAPE IS ARRANGED

I lifted my head.

I smelled it, somewhere near. But I saw nothing. I tensed. I sat against the stone wall, formed of heavy blocks. I pulled my head out from the wall, but it would not move far. To the heavy collar of iron, to each of its two, heavy welded rings, one on each side, there was fastened a short chain, fixed to a ring and plate, bolted through the drilled stone. My hands, each, were manacled to the wall, too, on short chains, to my left and right. I was naked. My ankles, in close chains, were fastened to another ring, in the floor, before me, it, too, on a plate, bolted through the floor block.

I sat forward, as far as I could, listening. I sat on the stone, on straw, soiled, which was scattered on the floor to absorb wastes. I looked to the door, some twenty feet across the stone floor; it was of beams, sheathed with iron. There was a small window, high in the door, about six inches in height, eighteen inches in width. It bore five bars. There was a musty smell, but the room was not particularly damp. Light reached it from a small window, barred, some twelve feet above the floor, in the wall to my right. It was just under the ceiling. In the placid, diagonal beam of light, seeming to lean against the wall, ascending to the window, I saw dust.

I distended my nostrils, screening the scents of the room. I rejected the smell of moldy straw, of wastes. From outside I could smell date palms, pomegranates. I heard a kaiila pass, its paws thudding in the sand. I heard kaiila bells, from afar, a man shouting. Nothing seemed amiss. I detected the odor of kort rinds, matted, drying, on the stones, where they had been

120

scattered from my supper the evening before. Vints, insects, tiny, sand-colored, covered them. On the same rinds, taking and eating vints, were two small cell spiders. Outside the door I could smell cheese. The smell, too, of Bazi tea was clear. I heard the guard move, drowsy, on his chair outside the door. I could smell his sweat, and the veminium water he had rubbed about his neck.

Then I sat back against the stones. It seemed I had been mistaken.

I closed my eyes. 'Surrender Gor,' had come the message, presumed from the steel worlds. 'Surrender Gor.' And, earlier, months ago, a caravan boy, Achmed, the son of the merchant, Farouk of Kasra, had found the inscription on a rock, 'Beware the steel tower.' There had been, too, the message girl, Veema, whose very body had borne the warning, 'Beware Abdul.' I thought little of that now, however, for Abdul had been the water carrier in Tor, surely a minor agent of Others, the Kurii, little to be feared, no more than a gnat in the desert. I had not chosen to press the juices from the body of that insect. I had let him flee in terror. I still did not know, however, who had sent the warning, 'Beware Abdul.' I smiled. There seemed little reason to beware of such a nonentity.

On the trip to Nine Wells, in the company of Achmed; his father, Farouk; Shakar, captain of the Aretai; Hamid, his lieutenant, and a guard of fifteen riders, I had seen the stone, led to it by Achmed.

'The body is gone!' cried Achmed. 'It lay here!'

The stone, however, remained, and the message scratched upon it. It was scratched in Taharic, the lettering of the Tahari peoples. Their language is Gorean, but they, like certain other groups, usually isolated groups, did not use the common Gorean script. I had studied the Taharic alphabet. Since the alphabet is correlated with Gorean phonemes, it is speedily mastered, little more than an incomplete cipher, by one who knows Gorean. One oddity about it, from the point of view of one who reads Gorean, is that it possesses signs for only four of the nine vowels in Gorean. There was, however, even for me, no difficulty in reading the inscription. No vowel sound had to be interpolated, or determined from context, in this message. Each sign was clear. The message as a whole was explicit, unmistakable. The vowel sounds which are explicitly represented, incidentally, are represented by tiny marks near the other

121

letters, rather like accent marks. They are not, in themselves, full-fledged letters. Vowel sounds which are not explicitly represented, of course, must be inserted by the reader. At one time in Taharic, apparently, no vowel sounds were represented. Some Taharic scholars, purists, refuse to countenance vowel signs, regarding their necessity as a convenience for illiterates.

'There is no body here now,' had said Shakar, captain of the Aretai.

'Where could it have gone?' asked Hamid, his lieutenant.

His question was not an ill-advised one. There was no sign about of picked bones, or of the work of scavengers. Had there been sand storms the rock, too, presumably, would have been covered. Sand storms in the Tahari, incidentally, though upon occasion lengthy and terrible storms, may rearrange dunes, but they seldom bury anything. The whipping sand is blasted away almost as swiftly as it is deposited. Further, of course, a body in the Tahari decomposes with great slowness. The flesh of a desert tabuk which dies in the desert, perhaps separated from its herd, and unable to find water, if undisturbed by the salivary juices of predators, remains edible for several days. The external appearance of the animal, beyond this, can remain much the same for centuries.

'It is gone,' said Shakar, turning his kaiila, and returning to the caravan.

The others followed him.

I lingered a bit longer, looking on the inscription. 'Beware the steel tower.' Then I, too, turned my kaiila, and returned to the caravan.

'Surrender Gor,' I thought.

I leaned back against the stone. I moved my head a bit, turning my neck inside the heavy collar. I pulled a bit at the wrist manacles, on my left and right. I heard the chain subside to the stones. I felt a trickle of sweat move down my left forearm, and slip under the iron on my left wrist. I pulled wildly against the wrist manacles; the collar cut into my neck; I twisted my ankles in the ankle irons, and pulled the chain against the ring. Then, furious, I sat back against the stones. I was a prisoner. I was absolutely helpless.

I closed my eyes again. Suleiman had not died. The blow of the assassin, in the confusion, had failed to find its mark.

The judge, on the testimony of Ibn Saran, and that of two white-skinned, female slaves, one named Zaya, a red-haired girl, the other a dark-haired girl, whose name was Vella, had sentenced me as a criminal, a would-be assassin, to the secret brine pits of Klima, deep in the dune country, there to dig until the salt, the sun, the slave masters, had finished with me. From the secret pits of Klima, it was said, no slave had ever returned. Kaiila are not permitted at Klima, even to the guards. Supplies are brought in, and salt carried away, by caravan, on which the pits must depend. Other than the well at Klima, there is no other water within a thousand pasangs. The desert is the wall at Klima. The locations of the pits, such as those at Klima, are little known, and, to protect the resource, are kept secret by mine agents and merchants. Women are not permitted at Klima, lest men kill one another for them.

Then again, unmistakably, this time, the odor came to my nostrils. The hair rose on the back of my neck.

I strained against the iron, the chains. I was nude. I was completely helpless. I could not even put my hands before my body.

I must wait.

I smelled Kur.

'Is there someone there?' called the guard. I heard his chair scrape. I heard him get to his feet.

He received no answer. There was only silence.

I sat still. I moved not even the chain.

He walked toward the threshold of the large room, or hall, which gives access to the cells. He walked carefully. There is no door on the threshold. It is a narrow threshold, lying at the foot of a set of narrow, twisting, concave stairs.

'Who is there?' he called. He waited. There was no answer.

He turned about, and went back to his chair. I heard him sit down again. But in a moment, suddenly, the chair scraped back again, and he was on his feet. 'Who is there!' he challenged. I heard his scimitar leave its sheath.

'Who is there!' I heard him cry once more, then heard him turning, wildly, facing about, here and there, in the hall.

Then I heard a startled inarticulate cry of horror, quick cut short. There was a snap, as of gristle.

There was little sound then, only that of a large tongue, moving in blood, tasting, curious. The man had had smeared about the base of his neck veminium water.

I heard then the body dropped. I did not hear the sound of feeding. I heard a pawing about the body, and its clothing.

123

Then I sensed, outside, a large body lift itself to its feet, and turn, slowly, toward the door of my cell.

I sensed then that it stood before the door of my cell. I could not take my eyes from the small window in the door. I saw nothing outside. Yet I sensed that it stood there, and that it was looking through the bars.

I heard the key move in the lock.

The door swung open. I saw nothing in the threshold. Beyond, crumpled on the floor, I saw the remains of the guard, the head, awry, lying on its side, strung by torn vessels to the body, the back of the neck bitten through. I saw straw move within the cell. The smell of Kur was strong. I sensed it stood before me.

The chain at my left wrist was lifted. Twice, it was pulled against the wall ring. Then it was dropped to the stones.

I sensed that the beast stood.

In a moment I heard voices, those of several men. They were nearing.

Among them, imperious, I heard the voice of Ibn Saran. I heard men descending the steps. There was a cry of horror. I could see through the door of my cell, now swung open. Ibn Saran, himself, in black cloak, and white kaffiyeh with black cording, emerged through the threshold.

Instantly was his scimitar unsheathed, the reflex of a desert warrior. He did not look upon the gruesome sight which lay upon the stones at his feet. Rather did he, with one lightning glance, examine the room.

'Unsheath your weapons,' cried he to his daunted men. Some of them were unable to take their eyes from what lay on the stones. With the flat of his blade he struck more than one of them. 'Back to back,' he said. 'Stand ready!' Then he said, 'Block the door!'

He looked within the cell. I saw him, outside. I was chained in a sitting position. I could not pull far against the ring of my ankle irons for my back was against the wall; I could not pull forward, nor to the side, from the wall because of the chains on my collar; my hands were chained down and toward the wall, on each side, back from my body; I could, by the intention of my captors, exert little leverage; I was perfectly chained. Ibn Saran smiled. 'Tal,' said he. I was his prisoner. 'Tal,' said I. I could see his scimitar.

'What could have done this horrible thing?' asked one of his men.

'I was warned of this,' said Ibn Saran.

'A Djinn?' asked one of the men.

'Smell it?' said Ibn Saran. 'Smell it! It is still here!'

I heard the Kur breathing, near me.

'Block the door!' said Ibn Saran.

The two men by the door, who had been standing there, looked about themselves, brandishing their scimitars, frightened.

'Do not fear, my fellows,' said Ibn Saran. 'This is not a Djinn. It is a creature of flesh and blood. But be wary! Be wary!' He then formed his men into a line, against the far wall of the outer room, that into which the threshold gave access. 'I had warning of this possibility,' he said. 'It has now occurred. Do not fear. It can be met.'

The men looked to one another, wild-eyed.

'Upon my signal,' said Ibn Saran, speaking in swift Gorean, 'attacking in a line, slash every inch of this room. He who first makes contact, let him cry out, and the others, then, must converge on that spot, cutting, as it were, the very air into pieces.'

One of the men looked at him. 'There is nothing here,' he whispered.

Ibn Saran, scimitar poised, smiled. 'It is here,' he said. 'It is here.' Then suddenly he cried, 'Ho!' and leapt forward, the blade, in rapid, diagonal figure-eight strokes, backhand upswept, shallowly curved, blade turning, forehand descending, shallowly curved, tracing its razor pattern. His right, booted foot stamped forward, his body turned to the left, minimizing target, his head to the right, maximizing vision, his rear foot at right angles to the attack line, maximizing leverage, assuring balance. His men, some of them timidly thrusting out, poking, touching, followed him. 'There is nothing here, noble master,' said one of them.

Ibn Saran stood in the threshold of the cell. 'It is in the cell,' he said.

I observed the scimitar. It was a wickedly curved blade. On such a blade, I knew, silk dropped, should the blade be moved, would fall parted to the floor. Even a light stroke of such a blade, falling across an arm, would drop through the flesh, leaving its incised record, a quarter of an inch deep, in the bone beneath.

125

'It will be most dangerous,' said Ibn Saran, 'to enter the cell. You will follow me swiftly, forming yourselves in a line, backs against the near wall.'

'Let us close the door, and lock it,' said a man, 'trapping it within.'

'It would tear the bars from the window and escape,' said Ibn Saran.

'How could it do this?' asked the man.

I gathered that the man did not know the strength of Kurii. I found it of interest that Ibn Saran did.

'Such a beast,' said he, 'must not be found within the cell. Its body must be disposed of.'

I could understand the reasoning of this. Few on Gor knew of the secret war of Priest-Kings and Others, the Kurii. The carcass of a Kur, lying about, would surely prompt many questions, much curiosity, perhaps shrewd speculations. It might also, of course, attract the vengeance of Kurii on the community or district involved.

'I will first enter the cell,' said Ibn Saran. 'You will then follow me.' There seemed nothing soft or languid about Ibn Saran now. When there is need the men of the desert can move with swift, menacing efficiency. The contrast with their more normal, acculturated, paced form of motion, unhurried, even graceful, is startling. I further decided that Ibn Saran was a brave man.

With a cry, thrusting through the threshold of the cell, then slashing about, he leaped into the cell. His men, frightened, sped into the cell behind him, and, white-faced, backed themselves against the wall in a line behind him. No longer was the outer threshold, that opening onto the twisting, ascending stairs, guarded. The door to the cell, however, by Ibn Saran, was.

'There is nothing here, Master!' cried one of the men. 'This is madness!'

'It is gone,' I told Ibn Saran.

Ibn Saran smiled. 'No,' he said. 'It is here. It is here somewhere.' Then he said to his men. 'Be silent! Listen!'

I could not even hear men breathing. The light fell from the barred window onto the gray stones of the straw-strewn floor. I looked at the men, the walls, the matted, dried kort rinds on the floor, near the metal dish. On the rinds the spiders continued to hunt vints.

We did hear a man calling outside, selling melons. We

126

heard two kaiila plod by, their bells jangling.

'The cell is empty,' said one of the men, whispering.

Suddenly one of the men of Ibn Saran screamed horribly. I looked up, in the collar, chains pulling at my throat. I jerked at my wrist chains, held. Men shrank back, 'Save me!' cried the man. 'Help!'

Abruptly, horribly, had he seemed, from his feet, sideways, to hurtle upward. Ten feet in the air, against the stones of the ceiling, twisting, crying out, screaming, he writhed.

'Help me!' he cried.

'Do not break your position,' said Ibn Saran. 'Hold position!'

'Please!' wept the man.

'Hold position!' said Ibn Saran.

Then the man, the sleeves of his garments, above his elbows, tight to his body, was slowly lowered.

'Please!' he said.

Then he cried out, a short cry, brief; there was a sound, exploding, velvet-soft, like a bubble of air being forced upward through water; the side of his neck had been bitten away; arterial blood, driven by the blind pump of the heart, pulsed.

'Hold position!' cried Ibn Saran.

I admired his generalship. Had his men charged, initially, the captured man would have been hurled against them. In the breaking of their formation the Kur would have slipped away. Had they now rushed to their comrade, again the formation would be broken, and the Kur, by now, had assuredly changed his position.

Ibn Saran himself, a brave man, blocked the open door to the cell.

'Scimitars ready!' he cried. 'Ho!'

Across the floor, now wet with blood, and blood-soaked straw, the men, in their line, Ibn Saran remaining at the door, charged. The blood, between the stones, formed tiny rivers.

'Aiii!' cried a man, wheeling back, horrified. There was blood on his scimitar. He was terrified. 'A Djinn!' he cried.

In that moment, Ibn Saran, at the door, thrust out, wickedly, deeply.

There was a roar of pain, a howl of rage, and I saw that his scimitar, to six inches, was splashed with bright blood of the Kur, clearly visible.

'We have it!' cried Ibn Saran. 'Strike! Strike!' The men looked about. 'There!' cried Ibn Saran. 'The blood! The blood!' I saw a stain of blood on the floor, and then a bloody print, of a heavy, clawed foot. Then drops of blood, as if from nowhere, dropping, one after the other, to the stones. 'Attack at the blood!' cried Ibn Saran. The men converged at the blood, striking. I heard two more howls of rage, for twice more they had struck the beast. Then a man reeled back, turning. His face was gone.

The men now circled where the blood fell, which marked the path of the beast.

Suddenly there was a scrambling sound and I saw the bars in the small window shake and scrape, one wrenching loose, with a shower of stone and dust from the wall.

'To the window!' cried Ibn Saran. 'It will escape!' He leaped to the barred window, striking madly about, against the stone. His men followed, striking, crying out.

I smiled, seeing, in the confusion, the blood, drop by drop, slip to the door of the cell, move across the stones, out into the hall, and through the threshold, then up the twisting, narrow, concave stairs.

It had been an excellent diversion on the part of the Kur. It would have known it would not have had the time to wrench loose the bars and slip through the narrow window before being hacked to pieces. But the ruse had drawn Ibn Saran from the door.

Ibn Saran spun from the wall, his blade battered, nicked and dull, from pounding on the stone. He saw the blood. He cried out with rage and, turning, fled from the cell.

On the kort rinds the spiders continued to hunt vints.

'We have killed it,' said Ibn Saran. 'It is dead.'

I surmised that they had had little difficulty in following the trail of blood. The animal, at least four times, had been struck, and with razor-sharp scimitars of the Tahari. Once, by Ibn Saran, it had been wounded to a depth of some six inches. I had adjudged this by the blood rain on the scimitar, in its rivulets. So struck, four times, I found it not difficult to believe that the animal, even if unfound, would have sought a dark place, and there, in silence, bled to death.

'We have disposed of the body,' said Ibn Saran.

I shrugged.

'It threatened your life,' he said. 'We have saved your life.'

'My gratitude,' I said.

It was midnight, in the cell. Outside, the three moons were full.

The cell had been cleaned, straw and wastes removed, rinsed down; most of the blood had been scrubbed from the stones; behind remained, here and there, only some stubborn, darkish stains; new straw had been spread; the kort rinds had been taken. Little remained to give evidence of the conflict which had earlier transpired in the chamber. Even the barred window had been repaired. The scrubbing, and cleaning, to my interest, had been done by jailers. I would have expected such work to be done by nude female slaves, in work collar, chain and ankle ring, to keep them on their knees with their brushes, but it had not been; one of the administrative penalties of he who is sent to the brine pits of Klima is commonly to be deprived of the sight of female bodies; there are no women at Klima; there is little but the salt, the heat, the slave masters and the sun; sometimes men go mad, trudging into the desert, trying to escape; but there is no water within a thousand pasangs of Klima; I would have liked to have seen a female slave, before being chained for the march to Klima; but I was not permitted this.

Often I had to force from my mind the look on the face of the second slave, she called Vella, of triumph, as she, small and lovely, luscious, freed of the rack ropes, had sat up on the knotted ropes, after her testimony had confirmed that of others, of Zaya, the other girl, and Ibn Saran, sending me to the brine pits of Klima. She had been pleased. I would go to Klima. The slave girl had had her vengeance. She, with her lie, confirming those of others, had determined the matter well. Then, her testimony done, she, with the other wench, had been chained as a slave. I recalled her smile, and that I, though innocent, was to go to Klima.

I was not pleased with the female slave.

I looked up. With Ibn Saran were four men. One of them held up a tharlarion-oil lamp.

'Do you understand what it is,' asked Ibn Saran, 'to be sent to Klima – to be a salt slave?'

'I think so,' I told him.

'There is the march to Klima,' said he, 'through the dune country, on foot, chained, on which many die.'

I said nothing.

'And should you be so unfortunate,' said he, 'to reach the

129

vicinity of Klima, your feet must be bound with leather to your knees, for you will sink through the salt crusts to your knees, and, unprotected, your flesh, by the millions of tiny, heated crystals, would be grated and burned from your bones.'

I looked away, in the chains.

'In the pits,' he said, 'you pump water through underground deposits, to wash salt, with the water, to the surface, and re-pump again the same water. Men die at the pumps, in the heat. Others, the carriers, in the brine, must fill their yoke buckets with the erupted sludge, and carry it from the pits to the drying tables; others must gather the salt and mold it into cylinders.' He smiled. 'Sometimes men kill one another for the lighter assignments.'

I did not look at him.

'But you,' said he, 'who attempted to assassinate our noble Suleiman Pasha, will not be given light assignments.'

I pulled at the chains.

'It is the steel of Ar,' he said. 'It is excellent, brought in by caravan.'

I fought the manacles.

'It will hold you quite well,' said he, '– Tarl Cabot.'

I looked at him.

'It will amuse me,' he said, 'to think of Tarl Cabot, laboring in the brine pits. As I rest in my palace, in the cool of the rooms, on cushions, relishing custards and berries, sipping beverages, delighted by my slave girls, among them your pretty Vella, I shall think of you, often, Tarl Cabot.'

I tore at the chains.

'The famed agent of Priest-Kings, Tarl Cabot,' he said, 'in the brine pits! Excellent! Superb!' He laughed. 'You cannot free yourself,' he said. 'You cannot win.'

I subsided in the chains, helpless.

'The day at Klima,' he said, 'begins at dawn, and only ends at darkness. Food may be fried on the stones at Klima. The crusts are white. The glare from them can blind men. There are no kaiila at Klima. The desert, waterless, surrounds Klima, for more than a thousand pasangs on all sides. Never has a slave escaped from Klima. Among the less pleasant aspects of Klima is that you will not see females. You will note that, following your sentencing, the sight of such flesh has been denied you. But then you can always think of your pretty Vella.'

130

In the manacles, my fists clenched.

'When I make her serve me,' he said, 'I will think of you.'

'Where did you find her?' I asked.

'She has a very lively body, hasn't she?' asked Ibn Saran.

'She is a female,' I said. 'Where did you find her?'

'In a tavern in Lydius,' he said. 'It is interesting. We bought her, originally, simply as a slave. We keep our eyes open for good female flesh. It is useful to our purposes, in infiltrating houses, in obtaining secrets, in seducing officers and important men, and, of course, to reward our followers and, naturally, as a simple item for exchange, a form of currency; the slave girl is usually in demand, particularly if beautiful and trained; at our wish, such women are conveniently marketable; there is little trouble in selling them; furthermore, they attract little undue commercial attention, for they are a familiar type of merchandise; thus, the slave girl, for us, if beautiful, and particularly if trained, constitutes a reliable, safe, readily negotiable form of wealth.'

'For anyone,' I said.

'Yes,' he said.

'And Vella?' I asked.

'The former Miss Elizabeth Cardwell, of New York City, of the planet Earth?' he asked.

'You seem to have learned much,' I said.

'The Earth slave girl has taught us much,' he said. 'She was a lucky catch. We were fortunate to get our chain on her collar.'

'What has she told you?' I asked.

'Whatever we wished to know,' he said.

'Oh,' I said, 'I see.'

'Torture was not required,' said Ibn Saran. 'Its threat was sufficient. She is only a woman. We chained her nude in a dungeon, with urts. In an hour, weeping, hysterical, she begged to speak. She was interrogated for the night. We learned all she knew. We learned much.'

'Surely you then freed her?' I asked, smiling. 'For such aid?'

'It seems we promised to do so,' said he, 'but, later, as I recall, it slipped our mind. We keep her slave.'

'Full slave?' I asked.

'Full slave,' he said.

'Fitting,' I said.

'She is a slave,' he said.

'I know,' I said.

131

'What, in particular,' I asked, 'did you learn from the Earth slave girl, the former Miss Cardwell?'

'Many things,' said he, 'but, doubtless of most importance, the weakness of the Nest.'

'You will now attack?' I asked.

'It will not be necessary,' he said.

'An alternate plan?' I asked.

'Perhaps,' he said.

'What she told you, of course,' said I, 'may not be true.'

'It tallies with the reports of other humans, who, once, long ago, fled the Sardar.'

These would have been the Nest's humans who, following the Nest War, had elected to return to the surface of Gor.

'But are these reports true,' I asked, 'or only, sincerely, believed to be true?'

'They could, of course, be implanted memories,' admitted Ibn Saran. 'It could be a trick to lure an attack into a trap.'

I was silent.

'We are not unaware of such possibilities,' he said. 'We have typically proceeded with caution.'

'But now it may matter less?' I asked.

'Now,' said he, 'it may matter not at all. No longer need we listen with such care to the blabbering of slave girls.'

'You have a new strategy?' I asked.

'Perhaps,' he said, smiling.

'Perhaps you would share it with one bound for the brine pits of Klima?' I asked.

He laughed. 'And you might speak it to guards, or others!'

'My tongue could be cut out,' I said.

'And your hands cut off?' he laughed. 'And then what good would you be in the pits?'

'How did you learn that the slave, purchased only for her beauty in Lydius, was the former Elizabeth Cardwell?' I asked.

'Fingerprints,' he said. 'Her accent, certain mannerisms, suggested Earth origin. We took her prints, curious. On our records they matched those of Miss Elizabeth Cardwell, of New York City, Earth, who had been brought to Gor to wear the message collar to the Tuchuks.'

I recalled the collar. When first I had seen her, her stockings in shreds, her brief, yellow, Oxford-cloth shift dusty and stained, her neck bound to a capture lance, her wrists bound behind her, on the plains of the Wagon Peoples, a captive of

Tuchuks, she had worn it. She had understood so little then, been so innocent of the affairs of worlds.

Now the girl was less innocent.

'The message collar,' said Ibn Saran, 'failed to bring about your death, the termination of your quest for the last egg of Priest-Kings,' He smiled. 'Indeed, the girl even became your slave.'

'I freed her,' I said.

'Courtly fool,' he said. 'Investigating her further, understanding she accompanied you to the Sardar, with the last egg of Priest-Kings, we looked for further connections. Soon it became clear that she had been your confederate, spying for you, in contriving the downfall of the house of Cernus, one of our ablest operatives.'

'How could you know this?' I asked.

'One who knew the house of Cernus, freed from slavery, was brought to my palace. To her terror, he immediately identified her. We then stripped her and put her in shackles in the dungeon, with the urts. In an Ahn she begged to tell us all, and did.'

'She betrayed Priest-Kings?' I asked.

'Completely,' said Ibn Saran.

'She serves Kurii now?' I asked.

'She serves us well,' he said. 'And her body is exquisite, and delicious.'

'You are fortunate,' said I, 'to possess such a slave.'

Ibn Saran nodded.

'I was interested to note, as well,' said I, 'that she testified that I had struck Suleiman Pasha.'

'So, too, did Zaya,' said Ibn Saran.

'That is true,' I said.

'Neither needed urging,' said Ibn Saran. 'Both are slaves.'

'Vella,' said I, 'is a highly intelligent, complex woman.'

'Such make the best slaves,' said Ibn Saran.

'True,' I said. Indeed, who would want to collar any other sort of woman? To take the most brilliant, the most imaginative, the most beautiful women, and put them at your feet, impassioned, helpless slaves, is victory.

'She hates you,' said Ibn Saran.

'I see,' I said.

'It has to do with Lydius, it seems,' said he.

I smiled.

'It was with much pleasure that the vicious little slave falsely testified that it had been your blade which had struck Suleiman Pasha. It is with much pleasure that she sends you to the brine pits.'

'I see,' I said.

'A woman's vengeance is not a light thing,' said Ibn Saran.

'Doubtless,' said I.

'But one thing troubled her,' said Ibn Saran, 'a matter in which, fearing for herself, she was apprehensive.'

'What was that?' I asked.

'The security of Klima,' he said. 'She feared you might escape.'

'Oh?' I said.

'But I assured her that there was no escape from the pits of Klima, and, thus encouraged, it was with enthusiasm that she rehearsed her testimony.'

'Pretty Vella,' I said.

He smiled.

'It is no accident,' I said, 'that she was, her identity discovered, brought to the Tahari.'

'Of course not,' said Ibn Saran. 'She was brought here, collared, to serve me.'

'She has served you well,' I said.

'She has much aided, as we had anticipated, in your reception. She, permitted once, secretly, to look upon you in the streets of Nine Wells, through the tiny veil of a haik, she nude beneath, in the keeping of one of my men, later confirmed, stripped on her knees before me, her lips to my feet, your identity – as Tarl Cabot, agent of Priest-Kings. And what she did not accomplish with the message collar in the land of the Wagon Peoples, she has well accomplished here on the rack in the chamber of justice.'

'She has served you well,' I said.

'She is an excellent little slave,' said Ibn Saran, 'and most pleasing on the cushions.'

'Pretty Vella,' I said.

'Think of her, Salt Slave,' said Ibn Saran, 'in the pits of Klima.'

He turned, cloak swirling, and left the chamber, followed by his men, the last bearing the tharlarion-oil lamp.

Outside the three moons were full.

*

134

I did not think, truly, I would be sent to the brine pits of Klima.

I was thus not surprised when, an Ahn later, that same moonlight night, before I was to be taken to Klima in the morning, two men, hooded, cloaked, furtive, appeared in the hall outside the cell door.

There would be danger in conducting or transporting a slave to Klima in these times of unrest between the Kavars and the Aretai and their vassal tribes.

It was not impossible that the penal caravan, with me, and presumably, others, would be intercepted.

If I had been Ibn Saran I would not have taken this risk.

The door to the cell opened.

'Tal, noble Ibn Saran,' said I, 'and gracious Hamid, lieutenant to Shakar, captain of the Aretai.'

In Ibn Saran's hand was his scimitar, unsheathed. I moved in the chains. They carried no light, but the moonlight, streaming through the barred window into the cell, permitted us to regard one another.

'It seems,' I said, 'I am not to reach the brine pits of Klima.'

I observed the scimitar. I did not think they would slay me in the cell. This would seem, to the magistrates of Nine Wells, inexplicable, an accident demanding the most rigorous and exacting inquiry.

'You mistake us,' said Ibn Saran.

'Of course,' I said. 'Actually you are agents of Priest-Kings, secretly seeming to work for Kurii. Before your men you were forced to conduct your charade of complicity in their schemes, lest your true loyalties be discovered. Doubtless you have fooled them all, and well, but not me.'

'You are perceptive,' said Ibn Saran.

'Obviously it was the intention of Kurii to kill me, for they sent one of their kind to do so. You, however, saved me from its merciless fangs.'

Ibn Saran inclined his head. He sheathed his scimitar.

'We have little time,' he said. 'Outside your kaiila awaits, saddled, with a weapon, the scimitar, and water.'

'But is there no guard?' I asked.

'He was outside,' said Ibn Saran. 'We have slain him for you.'

'Ah,' I said.

'We will drag the body into the cell when you have made good your swift escape.'

135

The manacles on my wrists and ankles were locked shackles. Hamid thrust the key in, unsnapping them. 'And Hamid,' I said, 'by intent, did not strike Suleiman to the death, but feigning clumsiness, wounded him only.'

'Precisely,' said Ibn Saran.

'Had I wished to kill,' hissed Hamid, 'the blow would have told.'

'Doubtless,' I said.

'It was essential for us, to protect appearances with Kurii, to appear to attempt to delay you, to forestall you in the completion of your inquiry for Priest-Kings.'

'Of course,' I said. 'But now, appearances kept, you free me to continue my work.'

'Precisely,' said Ibn Saran.

From within his cloak Hamid produced a chisel and a hammer.

'Open the collar,' I told him, 'rather than merely break the links. It will take more time, but it will be more comfortable.'

'Someone will hear!' said Ibn Saran.

'I am confident,' I told him, 'none will hear.' I smiled. 'It is late.'

I had a special reason for wishing to delay my escape some quarter of an Ahn.

'Open the collar,' said Ibn Saran, angrily.

'It is a lovely moonlight night,' I observed. 'It will thus, in my escape, make it easier for me to see my way.'

Ibn Saran's eyes flashed. 'Yes,' he said.

'I am pleased,' I said, 'to learn that you labor in the service of Priest-Kings.'

Ibn Saran inclined his head.

'Will my escape not require an explanation?' I asked.

'The guard was bribed,' said Ibn Saran. 'Then you, in treachery, in your escape, slew him.'

'We will leave the body here, with the tools,' said Hamid.

'You are thorough,' I admitted.

I eased my neck from the collar, it scraping the sides of my neck. It hung against the stones, on the two chains. It caused me great pain to stand. I moved my arms and legs. I wondered how far I was supposed to get. If it were true that a saddled kaiila, my own, awaited, I gathered the strike would be made in the desert, probably just outside the oasis.

It must be well planned. It must be, in their opinion, fool-proof, far surer than the likelihood, which would be high, of my reaching Klima in penal caravan.

I left the cell. On a table outside was clothing. I donned it. It was my own. I checked the wallet. It contained even the gems which I had placed there, after removing them from my interior belt, when I had been negotiating with Suleiman.

'Weapons?' I asked.

'The scimitar, at the saddle,' said Ibn Saran.

'I see,' I said. 'And water?'

'At the saddle,' he said.

'It seems,' I said, 'that it is twice I owe you my life. You have saved me this afternoon from the beast's attack, and to-night you free me, rescuing me from the brine pits of Klima. I am indebted to you, it seems.'

'You would do as much for me,' he said.

'Yes,' I said.

His eyes clouded.

'Hurry,' said Hamid. 'The guard will be soon changed.'

I climbed the stairs. I strode through the outer room, and out the portal onto the sand.

'Be less bold. Be more careful,' said Ibn Saran.

'No one is watching,' I assured him. I smiled. 'It is late,' I said.

I saw the kaiila. It was my own. It was saddled; water bags were at its flanks; a scimitar sheath, with weapon, on straps, hung at a saddle ring on the right. I checked the girth straps, the kaiila rein. They were in order. I hoped that the beast had not been drugged. I lifted my hand near its eye; it blinked, even to the third lid, the transparent lid; very lightly I touched its flank; the skin shook, twitching, beneath the finger.

'What are you doing?' asked Ibn Saran.

'I am greeting my kaiila,' I said.

The reflexes of the beast seemed fit. I doubted then that it had been drugged. If it had been drugged with a quick-acting agent, the quarter of an Ahn I had purchased, delaying my escape, in demanding that the collar be removed, rather than the links broken, would have given the drug time to be evident in the behavior of the beast. I doubted that a slow drug would have been used, because time would be significant in these matters. Ibn Saran would not have cared to risk giving me an

137

Ahn's start on a fast kaiila. I was pleased that the animal had not, apparently, been drugged.

It suddenly occurred to me that perhaps Ibn Saran, as he proclaimed, was indeed an agent for Priest-Kings. Perhaps Hamid, too, was such an agent.

If so, my dalliance, increasing their risks, had jeopardized their lives.

I mounted.

'May your water bags be never empty,' said Ibn Saran. 'May you always have water.' He put his hand on the bulging water bag, which hung behind the saddle, on the left side of the beast, balanced by another on the right. One drinks alternatively from the bags, to maintain the weight distribution. Such weight, of course, slows down the kaiila, but, in the desert, one must have much water.

'May your water bags be never empty,' I said. 'May you always have water.'

'Ride north,' said Ibn Saran.

'My thanks,' I said, and kicking the beast in the flanks, sand scattered back from its claws, I pressed the beast to the north.

As soon as I was out of earshot of Ibn Saran and Hamid, and among the walls of the oasis buildings, I reined in.

I looked back and noted, high, lofting in the moonlight night, an arrow, with a silver pennon attached to it. It climbed more and more slowly to the height of its arc, seemed to pause, and then, gracefully, turned and looped down, faster and faster, the moonlight sparkling on the fluttering, silvered pennon.

I examined the paws of the kaiila, I found that for which I searched inserted in the right forepaw of the animal. I removed from its paw the tiny, rounded ball of wax, held in place by threads; within the wax, which would soon, in the riding and pounding, and by the heat of the animal's body, disintegrate, concealed, I found a needle; I smelled it; it was smeared with kanda, a deadly toxin, prepared from the ground roots of the kanda bush; I wiped the needle, with a ripping from my shirt sleeve, cleaning it, and discarded needle and cloth in a refuse pile.

I sampled the water in the two water bags. It was, as I had expected, heavily salted. It was not drinkable.

I removed the scimitar from its sheath. It was not mine. I examined the blade and found the flaw, neatly filed, under the hilt, concealed by the guard. I tapped the blade into the sand; it fell from the hilt, which I retained in my hand. I concealed both blade and hilt in the refuse pile.

I drew the kaiila back into the shadows. Two men rode by, Ibn Saran and Hamid.

I poured the salt water into the sand. It was late. I decided I would seek an inn for the night.

EIGHT

I BECOME GUEST OF
HASSAN THE BANDIT

I did not sleep as well as I might have that night, for from time to time, clouds of riders, with bows, and lances, swept through the streets of Nine Wells, returning from one sortie into the desert or another. For better than fifty pasangs about the terrain was apparently combed, again and again, but yielding not even a trail.

I did, however, get several hours of uninterrupted sleep toward morning, when, worn, exhausted, thirsty, slack in their saddles, the bulk of the search parties returned to Nine Wells.

I patronized an unimportant, rather poor sort of establishment, whose proprietor, I suspected, would have had better things to do than attend trials at the chamber of justice. Fortunately this was true. He was, however, informed on the public news. 'The assassin fled last night, into the desert,' he told me, 'escaping!'

'Incredible,' I said. My response was appropriate, for I, for one, did not believe it.

I had arisen about the ninth hour, which, on Gor, is the hour before noon.

The kaiila I fed in the stable, where he occupied a rear stall, I watered it, too, deeply.

While at breakfast I sent a stableboy on small errands. When I finished breakfast the lad, a sprightly young fellow, had returned.

In my burnoose and sash, a rather ostentatious yellow and purple, befitting, however, a local merchant, or peddler, who wishes to call attention to himself, I myself went about the shops, making purchases. I obtained a new scimitar. I did not need a sheath and belt. I obtained, too, a set of kaiila bells, and two sacks of pressed-date bricks. These are long, rectangular bricks, weighing about a stone apiece, or, in Earth weight, about forty pounds.

In a short while, at the public well near the chamber of justice, I had filled my water bags and collected the latest gossip. 'Out of my way,' said a soldier, reaching down to splash water in his face. I deferred to him, which seemed to me was advisable for a local date merchant. Besides he had had a difficult night of it in the desert. 'Have you found the assassin yet?' I asked. 'No,' he growled. 'Sometimes I fear I am not safe,' I said. 'Do not fear, Citizen,' said he. 'Very well,' I said.

The search parties would recuperate during the afternoon and night, I had learned. There was little chance of picking up a subtle trail by moonlight. It was impractical to begin again, the men and animals exhausted, until morning. That would give me a start, I speculated, of some fifteen Gorean hours.

It would be more than sufficient.

In the neighborhood of noon, moving slowly, in the yellow and purple burnoose, with sash, water bags at the flanks of my kaiila, sacks of pressed-date bricks tied across the withers, kaiila bells ringing, calling attention to myself and my wares, I left the oasis. Once, the lofty palms small behind me, I had to turn aside, to avoid being buffeted by the return of the last of the search parties.

On a hill, more than two hundred pasangs north and east of Nine Wells, two days after I had left the oasis, I reined in, the kaiila turning on the graveled crest.

Below, in the valley, between the barren, rocky hills, I observed the small caravan being taken.

Two kurdahs were seized in the hand of a rider, by their frames, and jerked to the side on the kaiila, spilling their occupants, free girls, in a flurry of skirts, to the gravel.

Drovers and merchants were being herded, at lance point, to a side. A guard, holding his right shoulder, hurried by a lance tip, was thrust with them.

The packs of kaiila were being slashed, to determine the value of the merchandise carried, and whether it would be of value to raiders.

Some of the kaiila were pulled together, their reins in the hands of a rider.

One of the burdens tied among others on the back of one of

the pack kaiila was transferred to another beast, one whose rein was held by the rider.

The hands of the free girls were bound before their bodies. Their free hands were bound at the end of long straps. The lengthy, free end of these tethers, then, was, by their captor, looped and secured about his pommel.

One man tried to break and run. A rider, wheeling after him, struck him in the back of the neck with the butt of his lance. He fell sprawling in the dust and rocks.

I saw a water bag being slashed, the water dark on the side of a kaiila, it shifting and rearing, the water falling, soaking into the dust.

I saw other bags thrown to the ground, before the cornered man.

Packs were cut from kaiila, their contents spilling on the ground. These were goods not desired. The kaiila, then, freed of reins and harness, with the flat of scimitars, and cries, were driven into the desert.

The two girls now stood naked in the dust, stripped by the blade of their captor. One of the girls had her hands, wrists bound, in her hair, pulling at it, crying out with misery. The other girl seemed angry. She looked at her bound wrists, her tether, as though she could not believe herself secured to the pommel. Her head was high. She had long, dark hair.

Their captor, who seemed to be chief of the raiders, mounted. He stood in his stirrups. He shouted directions to his men. The raiders, then, as one man, turned their kaiila, and, unhurried, rode slowly from the trail. Two of the men held the reins of two pack kaiila; another man, by the rein, pulled another beast, shambling after him. The leader, his scimitar across his saddle, rode first, his burnoose gentle, swelling in the hot wind, behind him. Tied to his pommel, stumbling, followed his two fair captives.

Behind, the men shouted. Some dared to raise their fists. Others went to their water bags.

On foot, on the trail, they would have only enough water to reach the tiny oasis of Lame Kaiila, where there would be for them doubtless sympathy, but little aid in the form of armed men. Indeed, it lay in a direction away from Nine Wells, which was the largest, nearest oasis where soldiers might be found. By the time word of the raid reached Nine Wells the raiders might be thousands of pasangs away.

I turned my kaiila and dropped below the crest of the hill. I had scouted the camp of the raiders last night.

I would meet them there. I had business with their leader.

'You work well,' I told the slave girl. The camp was abandoned save for her.

She cried out. The heavy, round-ended pestle, some five feet in height, more than five inches wide at the base, dropped. It weighed some thirty pounds. When it dropped, the heavy wooden bowl, more than a foot deep and eighteen inches in diameter, tipped. Sa-Tarna grain spilled to the ground. I held her by the arms, from behind.

Like the camps of many nomads the camp was on high ground, which commanded the terrain, but was itself concealed among scrub brush and boulders. There was a corral of thorn brush, uprooted and woven together, which served for kaiila. Within it, now, were four pack kaiila. There were five tents, each of tawny, inconspicuous kaiila-hair cloth, each pegged down on three sides, each with the front, facing east, for warmth of the morning sun, left open. These tents, typical nomad tents, were small, some ten feet in depth, some ten to fifteen feet wide; they were supported on wooden frames; the ground, within them, leveled off, was covered by mats. At the back the tents were low, stretching to the ground. It is at the backs that goods are stored. In a normal family situation the household articles and the possessions of women are kept on the left side of the area, and the goods of the men, blankets, weapons, and such, are kept on the right. These goods, both men and women, are kept in leather bags of various sizes. These, made by the women, are often fringed, and of various colors, and beautifully decorated.

I looked about; there was little difference between this camp and a typical nomad camp. One crucial difference, of course, was the absence of free women and small children. In this camp there was only a slave girl, left behind to pound grain and watch kaiila.

I smiled. This was a camp of raiders.

I released the girl.

She turned about. 'You!' she cried. Alyena was fully dressed. She wore a long bordered skirt, with scarlet thread at its hem, which swirled as she turned; she wore a jacket, tan, of soft kaiila-cloth, taken from the animal's second coat, which had a hood, which she had thrown back; beneath the jacket she wore

143

a cheap, printed blouse of rep-cloth, blue and yellow, which well clung to her.

At her throat was a metal collar, no longer mine.

I observed the drape of the skirt on her hips, the sweet, delicate, betraying candor of her blouse.

Her master had not given her undergarments. What need has a slave for such?

She wore slippers.

She looked at me frightened, her eyes very blue, the hair loose and lovely.

'I see, pretty Alyena,' I said, 'you now wear earrings.'

They were golden loops, large, barbaric. They fell beside her neck.

'He did it to me,' she said. 'He pierced my ears with a saddle needle.'

I did not doubt it, in this out-of-the-way place. The operation, usually of course, is performed by one of the leather workers.

'He put them on me,' she said. She lifted her head, and brushed one. I could see she was proud. 'They are from his plunder,' she said.

Alyena, as an Earth girl, acculturated to earrings, did not object to them, not in themselves. If she had had objections doubtless they would have pertained to other matters, such as the fact that, against her will, her ears had been pierced; that she had not chosen the rings, but he; and that he, as a master, giving her no choice, not considering her feelings, because it had pleased him, had simply put them on her, making her, his slave, wear them. But she did not seem displeased. She had a healthy flush to her features. Alyena, though she seemed apprehensive, did not seem unhappy.

'Earrings,' I said to her, 'by Gorean girls, are regarded as the ultimate degradation of a female, appropriate only in sensual slave girls, brazen, shameless wenches, pleased that men have forced them to wear them, and be beautiful.'

'Do free women on Gor not wear earrings?' asked Alyena.

'Never,' I said.

'Only slave girls?'

'Only the most degraded of slave girls,' I said. 'Are you not shamed?'

She laughed, merrily. 'Slaves are not permitted pride,' she said proudly.

She turned her head from side to side, the loops swinging.

144

'Many slave girls,' I said, 'once they become used to earrings, come to love them, and even beg them of their masters.'

'I love mine,' she said.

'Only a collar makes a woman more beautiful,' I said.

'I wear both!' said Alyena. She lifted her head, smiling.

'But surely you object?' I inquired.

'Oh, certainly!' she said, quickly. She looked at me. 'A slave girl is supposed to object, is she not?'

'I suppose so,' I said.

'Then,' she said, smiling, 'I suppose that I object.'

'But your master does with you what he pleases?' I asked.

She squared her shoulders. She stood very straight. Her eyes flashed. 'My master,' she said, 'does with me precisely what he pleases. He is not weak!'

'I did not mean to imply that he was,' I said.

'My will must bend to his, perfectly, completely, in all things,' she said. 'I am nothing. He is all. He is the master.'

'I see,' I said.

'I am owned,' she said. 'He commands perfect obedience in me. I have no choice but to give it. I am his slave.'

'And how do you feel about this?' I asked.

She looked at me. Then she said, 'I love it.'

'Make the tea,' I said.

Lifting her skirt the girl went to the tent, to make tea. Far off I could see a subtle, almost invisible lifting of dust. The raiders were returning.

I went to the tent, and, on one of the mats, near its entrance, sat down, cross-legged.

I brushed back the hood of the burnoose. It was hot. There is an almost constant hot wind in the Tahari.

'I feared, when first I saw you,' said the girl, measuring the tea, from a tiny box, 'that you had come to carry me off. But, I suppose, had that been your intention, you would have already done so.' She had, in the tent, removed the tan jacket of kaiila hair, with hood. As she bent down, her breasts hung lovely against the cheap rep-cloth of the blue-and-yellow-printed blouse.

'Perhaps not,' I said.

Her hand shook, slightly, on the metal box of tea. Her eyes clouded.

'You are worked hard here?' I asked.

'Oh, yes!' she laughed. 'From morning to dark I am worked.

I must gather brush and kaiila dung and make fires; I must cook the stews and porridges, and clean the pans and the bowls; I must shake out the mats and sweep the sand in the tents; I must rub the garments and polish the boots and leather; I must do the mending and sewing; I weave; I make ropes; I bead leather; I pound grain; I tend the kaiila; twice daily I milk the she-kaiila; I do many things; I am much worked.' Her eyes sparkled. 'I do the work here of ten women,' she said. 'I am the only female in the camp. All unpleasant, light, trivial work devolves upon me. Men will not do it. It is an insult to their strength.' She looked up. 'You, yourself,' she said, 'have made me make your tea.'

'Is it ready?' I asked. I looked at the tiny copper kettle on the small stand. A tiny kaiila-dung fire burned under it. A small, heavy, curved glass was nearby, on a flat box, which would hold some two ounces of the tea. Bazi tea is drunk in tiny glasses, usually three at a time, carefully measured. She did not make herself tea of course.

Casually I glanced at the horizon. The dust was nearer now. On a pole, beside the entrance of the tent, hung a water bag.

'And at night,' I asked the girl, 'you are permitted to rest from your labors?'

She was still stained from sweat, from pounding the grain outside the tent.

'My diurnial labors,' she laughed, 'may be those of a free woman, but do not forget what I am.'

I regarded her.

'I am a slave girl!' she laughed.

'In the night,' I said, 'you remove your slippers, and put on silk and bells.'

'If permitted,' she smiled. 'Often I serve nude.' She laughed. 'It is at night that I truly labor! Oh, the things he has made me do, things I would never have dreamed of!'

'Are you happy?' I asked.

'Yes,' she said.

'Do the other riders share you?' I asked.

'Of course,' she said. 'I am normally the only girl in camp.'

'From time to time there are others?' I asked.

'Sometimes,' she said. 'Free women, slave girls, taken from caravans.'

'What happens to them?'

'They are taken to oases, to be sold,' she said. 'My labors as

146

a slave,' she confided, 'are not limited to the nights. He uses me often. Sometimes, when his need is on him, he calls me in, sweaty, from work, and makes me serve him. Sometimes he merely throws my skirt over my head and hurls me to the mats, taking me swiftly, then ordering me to resume my work outside.'

'Are you often whipped?' I asked.

She turned about pulled up her blouse, showing me her back. 'No,' she said. There were few marks on her back, though I saw the traces of a beating or two. There was no scarring. The soft, pliant, broad-bladed five-strap lash had been used. It is the common instrument, if not the switch, used on girls. It is a valuable tool. It punishes with a terrible efficiency, and does not leave the girl permanently marked.

'I was punished twice,' she said, 'once, early in the tents, when I dared to be insolent, a second time when I was clumsy.' She smiled. 'I have not been insolent, nor clumsy since,' she said. She lifted the kettle from the fire and, carefully, poured me a tiny glass of tea.

I took the glass. 'Is your master brutal?' I asked.

'No,' she said, 'he is not brutal, but he is severe.'

'Harsh?' I asked.

'Yes,' she said, 'I would say he is harsh.'

'But not brutal?'

'No,' she said.

'Your relation to him?'

'Slave.'

'His relation to you?'

'Master.'

'Discipline?' I asked.

She smiled. 'I am kept under the strictest of discipline,' she said.

'But you are seldom whipped?'

'Almost never,' she said. 'But I know that he is fully capable, as he has demonstrated, of whipping me. Should I not be pleasing, I know that I, as a slave girl, will be lashed.'

'You live under the threat of the whip?'

'Yes,' she said. 'And the threat is not empty.' She looked at me. 'He is strong enough to get what he wants out of me. He knows it. And I have learned it. He is strong enough, if I do not please him, to lash me.'

'How do you find this?' I asked.

147

'Meaningful,' she said, '– and thrilling!'

'You seem to enjoy being dominated by a male,' I said.

'I am a woman,' she said. She looked down. 'I have discovered feelings I never knew I had,' she said. She looked up. 'I have discovered, in the arms of a strong, uncompromising man, how fantastic, how deep and glorious is my female sexuality.'

'You do not speak as a woman of Earth,' I observed.

'I am a Gorean slave girl,' she said, kneeling straight, touching her earrings.

'It seems to me,' said I, 'you care for your master.'

'If not restrained by his command,' she said boldly. 'I would lick the dust from his boots!'

Suddenly she looked about. She, too, now, saw the dust. She recognized the raiders were returning. Her eyes, suddenly, were frightened.

'You must flee!' she said. 'They may kill you if they find you here!'

'I have not finished my tea,' I said.

'Is it – is it,' she said, standing, uncertainly, 'your intention to do harm to my master?'

'I have business with him,' I said, simply.

She backed away. I set the tea down on the sand, between two mats, beside me. I did not think it would spill. She took another step backward. I reached to the side, to pick up a length of chain which lay there, one of several, doubtless ready for securing slaves, anticipated perhaps as prizes from the afternoon's caravan raid. Alyena turned, and, with a cry, fled from the tent, toward the dust. The length of chain hurled from my hand, bola-like, caught her about the ankles, whipping about, and she, in a flurry of skirt and blonde hair, sprawled, hands outstretched, to the dust. In an instant I was on her, kneeling across her back, my left hand across her mouth, pulling her head up, painfully, and back. I then put my right hand swiftly over her mouth, before she could cry out, and, my left hand in her hair, pulled her to her feet and dragged her back into the tent. I looked about, and found some materials at hand, which I kicked together into a pile on the mats. I then put her on her back on the mats, and, kneeling across her body, transferring my left hand from her mouth, I thrust a scarf, wadded, deep into her mouth, then fastened it there with several turns of sash, using the extra length of the sash,

148

tying it, to blindfold her. I then threw her on her stomach. With a length of strap I tied her hands behind her back, and, with another scarf, crossed and bound her ankles. I then threw her to the back of the tent, on the right side, which is that side of the nomad's tent reserved for the possessions of men.

I then went and stood near the entrance of the tent. My kaiila was tethered in the rear.

First over the rise, on his kaiila, with the two girls tethered, stumbling, exhausted, feet bleeding, to the pommel, was the leader. Instantly he saw me and was alert. He cried out to his men. They deployed, circling.

I saw the scimitar, lifted, in the hand of the leader.

Unlooping, swiftly, with his left hand, the tethers of the prisoners from his pommel, he threw the straps to one of his men. Behind them I could see the captured pack kaiila. There were nine men, not including the leader. The leader's kaiila reared. I saw it was his intention, not dismounting, to ride the kaiila against and through the tent, it striking against the beast's forequarters. It would be ripped from its pegs, the frame shattered, but he, leaning down from the saddle, would have his stroke.

I lifted the water bag from the pole, where it hung, outside the entrance of the tent.

One of the men cried out with rage.

I lifted the bag, drinking deeply. I replaced the plug and put back the bag, wiping my mouth on my sleeve.

The leader resheathed his scimitar and, lightly, dismounted from the kaiila.

I returned to the mats, sat again cross-legged upon them, and picked up my small glass of tea, which I had not yet finished.

He entered the tent, bending down.

'Tea is ready,' I said to him.

He went to the back of the tent and, with a knife, freed Alyena of her restraints. She looked up at him, terrified. But he was not irritated with her. It is nothing for a man to over-power a female.

'Serve us tea,' he said.

Trembling she measured him a tiny glass of tea. His men stood outside, wary.

'The tea is excellent,' I said.

In sharing their water I had made myself, by custom of the Tahari, their guest.

NINE

ZINA, A BEAUTIFUL TRAITRESS, IS DEALT WITH IN THE FASHION OF THE TAHARI

'Chain the two prisoners,' said the leader of the raiders, to one of his men.

He then looked at me.

One of the men came into the tent and picked up the chains which had lain, coiled, on the mats, in readiness. One length of chain he retrieved from the dust, where I had hurled it, snaring the fleeing Alyena by her ankles.

'Kneel,' said one of the men.

'No, Hassan!' cried one of the girls. The other girl, she who had torn at her hair, when captured, knelt. The girl who had, when captured, looked disbelievingly at the bonds on her wrists, stood, angry, defiant.

She came and stood before him, naked in the tent, on the mats. Her body was covered with sweat. The legs, from the thighs down, were covered with dust, dark in her sweat, and scratched by the myriad thrusts of brush through which, tethered, she had been dragged at her captor's stirrup.

'It was I, Zina,' she said, 'who, for a tarn disk of gold, betrayed the caravan into your hands, giving you its inventory, its schedule, its route!'

Such matters, I knew, were usually carefully guarded in the Tahari, even in times of relative peace.

The other girl cried out in anger at her, but did not dare rise. 'Chain her,' said Hassan, indicating the kneeling girl. One of the men, from behind, put ankle rings on her, joined by about a foot of chain. I heard the two, heavy snaps of the locks. He then unbound her wrists and coiled the tether. Before her body he locked her wrists in three-link slave bracelets.

150

'In the sun,' said Hassan to two others of his men. They departed and, shortly, returned with a heavy, pointed stake. It was some four feet in height, some four inches in diameter. One man held the stake and the other, with a heavy hammer, drove it deeply, firmly, into the earth, until only some two inches of it were visible. At this end, fastened to a bolted band, fitted into a groove at the termination of the stake was a metal ring. The man who had held the stake then took a snap collar, with chain and snap lock, about a yard in length, and secured the girl, on her knees, by the neck, to the stake.

'Free me!' demanded the girl, Zina.

'Free her,' said Hassan.

One of his men took the binding fiber from her wrists.

'Pay me!' she demanded.

At a gesture from Hassan, one of the men, from a small coffer to one side, drew forth a golden tarn disk, and gave it to the girl. She clenched it in her hand.

'Give me clothing,' she said.

'No,' said Hassan.

She looked at him, frightened.

'You have been paid,' he said. 'Go.'

She looked about herself, fearfully. She looked at the tarn disk.

'Give me water,' she said.

'No,' he said.

'I will buy it,' she said, frightened.

'I do not sell water,' he said. 'Go.'

'No!' she wept.

'Go,' he said.

'I will die in the desert,' she cried. The golden tarn disk glinted in her hand.

'I betrayed the caravan to you!' she cried.

'You have been paid,' he said.

She looked from man to man, into the eyes of each. Her lip trembled. 'No,' she whispered. 'No!'

She looked at Alyena, who knelt beside the tea, looking down at the mats, not daring to raise her eyes. Alyena's shoulders shook. Her breasts, pendant, were sweet, loose, inside the rep-cloth blouse. The naked girl knelt beside her, frantic, timid, and reached out to touch her shoulder.

'Plead for me,' begged Zina.

'I am only a slave,' wept Alyena.

151

'Plead for me!' begged Zina.

Alyena, anguished, tears in her eyes, looked at Hassan, her master. 'I plead for her, Master!' she cried.

'Leave the tent or be lashed, Slave,' said Hassan.

Alyena leapt to her feet, weeping, and fled from the tent.

The girl then, again, now half crouching, looked about at the men, from face to face. She looked into the eyes of each. Their eyes were merciless.

She leapt to her feet. 'No, Hassan! No!' she cried, the golden tarn disk clutched in her small palm.

'Leave the camp,' he said.

'I will die in the desert,' she whispered.

'Leave the camp,' he said.

'Keep me as a slave girl!' she cried.

'Are you not a free woman?' he asked.

'Please, Hassan,' she wept, 'keep me as a slave girl!'

'But you are free,' he said.

'No!' she cried. 'In my heart I have always been a true slave girl. I only pretended to be free. Whip me for it! Though I was fortunate enough never to be collared or branded, or mastered, I am a natural slave! Though I have lived as a free woman since birth, I concealed the fact that I was a true slave!'

'And when did you learn this fact?' asked Hassan.

'When my body changed,' she said, looking down. The men laughed.

I looked upon her. Her contours were lovely. It was not unlikely she would please a master.

She stood before Hassan, relaxed, soft, though frightened, her right foot at a right angle with her left, turning her hip out, opening her beauty to him, as a slave girl. 'I confess to you, Hassan,' she said, 'what I have never confessed to any other man – that I am a slave girl.'

'Legally,' said he, 'clearly you are free.'

'More real than the law is the heart,' said the girl, quoting a proverb of the Tahari.

'It is true,' said Hassan.

'Keep me,' she said.

'I do not want you,' he said.

'No!' she cried.

'I do not want you,' he said. Then he said, 'Conduct this free woman from the camp.'

One of the men seized her by the arm.

'Let me sell myself!' she wept.

As a free woman she could do this, but, of course, she could not revoke the transaction for, after its completion, she would be only a slave.

'I will sell myself into slavery,' she said.

Hassan indicated to his man that he should release the girl. He did so.

'Do you understand what you are saying?' asked Hassan.

'Yes,' she said.

'Kneel,' he said.

She knelt before him.

'What have you to offer?' he asked.

She held out the golden tarn disk.

He looked at it, held in her small palm, proffered to him, piteously.

'Please, Hassan,' she said.

'I see that you are a true slave, Zina,' he said.

'Yes, Hassan,' she said. 'I am a true slave.'

'It is far more than you are worth,' he said.

'Take it,' she begged.

He looked at her.

'Please take it!' she begged.

He smiled.

She took a deep breath; she closed her eyes. Then she opened her eyes. 'I sell myself into slavery,' she said.

His hand, open, was poised over the coin. Her eyes looked into his. His hand closed upon the coin; the transaction was completed.

'Chain this slave,' he said.

Roughly the girl, whose name had been Zina, but who was now as nameless as a newborn she-kaiila, was taken from the tent and thrown on her belly in the gravel by the slave stake. The collar, from behind, was put about her throat and locked; her head was jerked sideways as, by the collar chain, in the fist of one of Hassan's men, she was secured by the snap lock at the chain's free end, to the stake ring. Her ankles were chained, snapped into the ankle rings; her right wrist was then locked in a slave bracelet; Hassan's man, reaching under her right leg, by the dangling bracelet, rudely jerked her right hand and wrist under her right leg; he then locked her left wrist in the bracelet, confining her hands behind and below her right leg. She lay on her side in the gravel, miserable. When free

153

women and slave girls are chained together, it is common to respect the distinction between them by chaining them somewhat differently; in this case the free girl's hands were braceleted before her body, the slave's were fastened below her right leg; it is common for the slave to be placed under greater restraint, and more discomfort, than her free sister; this acknowledges the greater nobility of the free woman, and is a courtesy often extended to her, until she, too, is only a slave; 'Give the free girl a switch,' said Hassan; it was done; the free girl wielded the switch with two hands; the slave, as she was chained, could not defend herself.

Hassan slipped the golden tarn disk into his wallet. 'Alyena!' he called.

The girl came running to him, and knelt before him. 'Yes, Master,' she said.

'Give us more tea,' said Hassan.

'Yes, Master,' she said.

'Are you not afraid the free girl will kill her?' I asked Hassan. I referred to the switching in progress of the recently imbonded wench at the slave stake.

She who had been Zina was now shrieking for mercy. She was not receiving it.

'No,' said Hassan.

'Slave! Slave! Slave!' screamed the free girl, lashing down at the imbonded traitress.

But, after a time, he signaled to one of his men, and he, standing behind the free girl, who was on her knees, caught the switch on the backswing and, to her fury, took it from her. 'It is enough,' he said to the free wench. She sat angrily in the gravel, her head down, her neck chained to the stake.

'Please, Mistress. Please, Mistress,' wept the slave, moaning.

'Alyena,' said Hassan.

'Yes, Master,' she said.

'Gather brush and dung,' he said. 'Make a fire. Heat well an iron.'

'Yes, Master,' she said.

'Tonight,' he said, 'we brand a slave.'

'Yes, Master,' she said.

I had little doubt that it would be the Tahari brand which, white hot, would be pressed into the thigh of the new slave, marking her thenceforth as merchandise. The contact surface of the iron would be formed into the Taharic character 'Kef',

154

which, in Taharic, is the initial letter of the expression 'Kajira', the most common expression in Gorean for a female slave.

Taharic is a very graceful script. It makes no distinctions between capital and small letters, and little distinction between printed and cursive script. Anyone who can read printed Taharic will have no difficulty in following cursive Taharic. The men of the Tahari are content to form their letters carefully and beautifully, being fond of them. To scribble Taharic is generally regarded not as proving oneself a swift, efficient fellow, but something of a boor, insensible to beauty. The initial printed letter of 'Kajira', rather than the cursive letter, as generally, is used as the common brand for women in the Tahari. Both the cursive letter in common Gorean and the printed letter in Taharic are rather lovely, both being somewhat floral in appearance.

'Give the free girl water,' said Hassan. It was done. 'The slave will wait until she is branded before she drinks,' said Hassan.

'Yes, Hassan,' said one of the men.

'Water her after the kaiila,' said Hassan to Alyena.

'Yes, Master,' she said.

'You have lost some money on these women, haven't you,' I asked, 'if you brand her before bringing her to the market.'

Hassan shrugged.

Many men like to think they are buying a fresh girl, one who was free. Many men enjoy breaking a girl to slavery. Furthermore, slavers tend to pay more highly for free women than slave girls. Slave girls, less guarded, less protected, are more easily acquired. Slave girls, too, are less likely to be the objects of determined rescue attempts. No one cares too much what happens to a slave girl. So they wear the collar of one man or another, in one city or another. What does it matter? They are only slave. Sometimes it seemed to me that, at least in the north, a tacit agreement existed among the isolated cities. Beautiful slave girls, barefoot, bangled, in scandalously brief slave livery, well displaying their considerable charms, collared, hair free, flowing in the wind, vital, walking exhilaratedly, were common on the high bridges of the city, extending between the numerous cylinder towers, whereas free women, sedate, dignified, restricted, in their confining robes of concealment, were discouraged from the use of such bridges. Each city's young tarnsmen, then, in testing their mettle, were offered

155

convenient, well-displayed, delicious, female acquisition-targets. Who would care to risk his life for a free woman, who, stripped, might prove disappointing, when, for less risk, he could get his capture loop on a known quantity, a girl who has quite probably been trained like an animal to deliciously satisfy the passions of a man? A girl who, responsive, helpless under his touch, his hands and mouth igniting her slave reflexes, will beg and strive to be a loving and obedient joy to him. These arrangements, I suspected, had to do with the attempt of cities to protect their free women who, in numbers, seldom fall to the enemy, unless the city itself should fall, and then, of course, they would find themselves, like slaves, under the victory torches, their clothing removed completely, strapped on the pleasure racks of the conquerors, thereafter, in the morning following the victory feast, to be chained and branded. Men respected free women; they desired, fought for, sought and relished their female slaves.

'As a free woman,' smiled Hassan, 'she would have brought me nothing.' He referred to the one who had been Zina. 'As a free woman,' said he, 'I would have put her out into the desert. As a slave girl I will make a little on her.' He grinned. 'And, of course,' he said, 'her brand will be fresh.'

'That is true,' I acknowledged.

'Besides,' he said, 'it will give me great pleasure to brand her.'

I smiled.

'In her slavery,' said he, laughing, 'let her remember who it was who put the brand on her.'

'Hassan, the bandit,' I said.

'He,' acknowledged the desert raider. 'Now let us have more tea.'

TEN

HASSAN DEPARTS FROM
THE OASIS OF TWO SCIMITARS

The oasis of Two Scimitars is an out-of-the-way oasis, under the hegemony of the Bakahs, which, for more than two hundred years, following their defeat in the Silk War of 8,110 C.A., has been a vassal tribe of the Kavars. The Silk War was a war for the control of certain caravan routes, for the rights to levy raider tribute on journeying merchants. It was called the Silk War because, at that time, Turian silk first began to be imported in bulk to the Tahari communities, and northward to Tor and Kasra, thence to Ar, and points north and west. Raider tribute, it might be noted, is no longer commonly levied in the Tahari. Rather, with the control of watering points at the oasis, it is unnecessary. To these points must come caravans. At the oases, it is common for the local pashas to exact a protection tax from caravans, if they are of a certain length, normally of more than fifty kaiila. The protection tax helps to defray the cost of maintaining soldiers, who, nominally at any rate, police the desert. It is not unusual for the genealogy of most of the pashas sovereign in the various oases to contain a heritage of raiders. Most of those in the Tahari who sit upon the rugs of office are those who are the descendants of men who ruled, in ruder days, scimitar in hand, from the high, red leather of the kaiila saddle. The forms change but, in the Tahari, as elsewhere, order, justice and law rest ultimately upon the determination of men, and steel.

It was late at night, in single file, over the sands, silvered in the light of the three moons, that we came to Two Scimitars.

Men rushed forth from the darkness, with weapons, encircling us.

'It is Hassan,' said a voice.

'One cannot be too careful these days,' said another voice.

'Tal,' said Hassan to the merchant who stood at his stirrup.

'We have water,' said the merchant, greeting the bandit.

Hassan stood in his stirrups, looking about at the palms, the red-clay walls, the buildings of mud, some domed, of the oasis, the gardens.

'You have goods for me?' asked the merchant.

'Yes,' said Hassan. He sat back in the saddle. The girl, back arched, head down, belly up, bound over the withers of the kaiila, before the saddle, twisted, whimpering. She was Zina. Only she now wore the name which she had borne as a free woman as a slave name, to shame her, given to her by her master, Hassan, the Bandit. Her companion prize, whose name was Tafa, was bound similarly before the saddle of one of Hassan's men. The soft interiors of the thighs of both girls were bloodied, stained reddish brown, to the side of the knee, but only one of them wore in her flesh, on the outside of her left thigh, recently imprinted, the Tahari slave mark. She only, Zina, was, of now, a slave girl. Others of the men of Hassan led pack kaiila, containing in their burdens goods taken from the caravan plundered four days ago.

The mud buildings at an oasis such as that of Two Scimitars last for many years. In such an area one often goes years without rain.

When rain does fall, however, sometimes it is fierce, turning the terrain into a quagmire. Following such rains great clouds of sand flies appear, wakened from dormancy. These feast on kaiila and men. Normally, flying insects are found only in the vicinity of the oases. Crawling insects of various sorts, and predator insects, however, are found in many areas, even far from water. The zadit is a small, tawny-feathered, sharp-billed bird. It feeds on insects. When sand flies and other insects, emergent after rains, infest kaiila, they frequently alight on the animals, and remain on them for some hours, hunting insects. This relieves the kaiila of the insects but leaves it with numerous small wounds, which are unpleasant and irritating, where the bird has dug insects out of its hide. These tiny wounds, if they become infected, turn into sores; these sores are treated by the drovers with poultices of kaiila dung.

'Six days ago,' said the merchant, 'soldiers, Aretai, from Nine Wells raided the Oasis of the Sand Sleen.'

It puzzled me that the merchant should say this.

I looked about me. In the moonlight I could see that kaiila had trodden the gardens. I saw two walls broken, the high walls of red clay used to shade courtyards and as a protection against raiders. I counted eleven palm trees, date palms, cut down, their trunks fallen at an angle into the dust, the palm leaves dried and lifeless, the fruit unripened. It takes years for such a tree to grow to the point at which it will bear fruit.

'They struck here last night,' said the merchant. 'But we drove them off.'

'Aretai are sleen,' said Hassan.

I wondered that he should feel so deeply about such matters, he, a bandit.

'They broke a well,' said the merchant.

No one spoke for some time. Hassan, nor his men, did not even cry out in outrage.

Then Hassan said, thinly, 'Do not jest.'

'I do not jest,' said the merchant.

'Aretai are sleen,' said Hassan, 'but yet are they of the Tahari.'

'The well is broken,' said the merchant. 'Do you wish to see?'

'No,' said Hassan.

'We are attempting to dig out the rock, the sand,' said the merchant.

Hassan's face was white.

It is difficult for one who is not of the Tahari to conjecture the gravity of the offense of destroying a source of water. It is regarded as an almost inconceivable crime, surely the most heinous which might be perpetrated upon the desert. Such an act, regarded as a monstrosity, goes beyond a simple act of war. Surely, in but a few days, word that Aretai tribesmen had destroyed, or attempted to destroy, a well at Two Scimitars would spread like fire across the desert, inflaming and outraging men from Tor to the Turian outpost merchant fort, and trading station, of Turmas. This act, perpetrated against the Bakahs at Two Scimitars, a vassal tribe of the Kavars, would doubtless bring full-scale war to the Tahari.

'Even now the war messengers ride,' said the merchant.

The tribes, at the various oases, and in the desert, in their nomad territories, and at their kasbahs, would be summoned. It would be full war.

A well had been broken.

159

'Business must go on,' said the merchant. He was looking up at Hassan. His hand was on Zina's body.

'Are you sure the raiders were Aretai?' I asked the merchant.

'Yes,' he said. 'They did not deign to conceal the fact.'

'On what do you base your conjecture?' I asked.

'What is your tribe?' he asked.

'He is Hakim of Tor,' said Hassan. 'I vouch for him.'

'The agal cording was Aretai,' said the merchant. 'The saddle markings, too. And they cried out, in their attack, "For Nine Wells and Suleiman!"'

'I see,' I said.

'If the Aretai want war – to the destruction of water – they shall have it,' said the merchant.

'I wish to leave before dawn,' said Hassan.

'Of course,' said the merchant. 'What have we here?' he asked. 'One free woman, one slave.' He turned to two of his men. 'Bring the pack kaiila into my courtyard,' he said, 'and display the goods.'

They hastened to obey him.

'Interesting, Hassan,' smiled the merchant, 'that it should be the slave you choose to carry before your saddle.'

Hassan shrugged.

'Her brand is fresh,' smiled the merchant.

'True,' said Hassan.

'Doubtless you put the iron to her body yourself,' said the merchant.

'Yes,' said Hassan.

'It is an excellent job,' said the merchant. 'You have a steady hand, and firmness.'

The girl whimpered.

'I have branded many women,' said Hassan.

'And superbly,' said the merchant.

His hands, sure, exact, made a preliminary assessment of the curves of the slave captive.

'Is she alive?' asked the merchant.

'Touch her, and see,' said Hassan.

The girl writhed before the saddle, twisting in her bonds, helpless. She cried out, her eyes shut, her teeth clenched, her head flung, wild, from side to side.

'She is alive,' commented the merchant.

Girls are usually brought hot to the oasis. It is not difficult

160

to ensure their responsiveness, bound as they are. One begins approximately an Ahn before the time of arrival.

The merchant then went to Tafa, the free woman. She, too, cried out, helpless, twisting in the ropes that confined her fair limbs.

'Are you free?' asked the merchant.

'Yes, yes!' she wept.

'You leap in the ropes like a slave girl,' he told her. She moaned in protest. Then, mercifully, he let her subside.

'Bring them in,' said he to Hassan, and his man. 'We will put them on the circle of assessment, and I will give you a price on them.'

The merchant then turned and entered his courtyard. Hassan, his man, I, and others of his men, slowly, on kaiila, filed into the courtyard, following the merchant.

Tafa was drawn weeping from the circle of assessment. Her left wrist was locked in a slave bracelet and she was put, kneeling, against a wall; her left side faced the wall; the opened bracelet, that not closed about her left wrist, was snapped shut about a slave ring bolted in the wall, the ring was approximately at her left shoulder; her head was down, hair forward; she knelt there, weeping, her left wrist fastened at her shoulder level to the wall.

'No!' cried Zina.

She was thrown unceremoniously, nude, to the circle of assessment. She crouched there, under the torches, on the seven-foot scarlet circle, angry, frightened.

She was quite beautiful, the slave girl. I wondered how another slave girl, Vella, once Miss Elizabeth Cardwell of New York City, of Earth, who had betrayed Priest-Kings, would look thrown nude upon such a circle.

When the whip snapped, a heavy whip in the hand of one of the merchant's brawny aides, the girl cried out, and her body reacted, in terror, as though struck. But the leather, of course, had not touched her body. Its snap was only admonitory. It would not touch her body unless the men were not pleased with her.

'Stand!' said the merchant. 'Head back! Hands behind head! Bend backwards! Farther! Farther!' He turned to us. 'Acceptable,' he said. Then to the girl he issued orders, rapidly, harshly. I watched, with interest, as the girl, tears in her eyes, responded to his swiftly issued, abrupt commands. For more than four Ehn he put her through a swift, staccato regimen of movement, a set of slave paces, assessment paces, deigned to exhibit, vulnerably, decisively and publicly, her beauty, in all of its major attitudes and positions. 'Hands on hips! Be insolent! Hands behind back! Hands crossed before you, as though bound! Hands at throat, as though chained to collar, fingers before mouth! Fall to the floor! Kneel! Head down! Head up! Bend backwards! Farther! Roll to the floor, on your side, on your back, right leg high, now flexed, left leg high, now flexed, to your side, right leg extended, palms on floor, left leg extended, palms on floor! Appear angry! Appear frightened! Appear aroused! Smile!' He did this with the same swift, expert objectivity, and clinical detachment, that a physician might bring to a routine medical examination; this examination, of course, was a beauty examination, assessing the desirability of a female slave. The whip cracked again. She cried out in misery, shuddering.

She looked up at him, in terror.

'Hassan?' asked the merchant.

'Very well,' said Hassan. He stepped to the edge of the circle.

'Crawl to his feet,' ordered the merchant.

The girl began to do so.

'On your belly,' said the merchant.

'She did so. At his feet, unbidden, she pressed her lips to his slippers. 'Keep me, Hassan,' she begged.

'To my lips,' he said.

She crept to her feet and lifted her lips to his. He tasted her well.

'Keep me, Hassan!' she wept.

He threw her back to the center of the marble circle. 'What is she worth?' asked Hassan of the merchant.

'I will give you a silver tarsk for her,' said he, 'for she is only slave.'

'Hassan!' cried the girl.

'Done,' said Hassan, selling his slave.

'No, Hassan!' she cried.

'And two tarn disks of gold, of the mintage of Ar, for the free wench,' said the merchant.

'Agreed,' said Hassan.

'Hassan!' cried the slave girl.

'Take this slave away,' said the merchant.

A slave bracelet was locked about the left wrist of Zina and she was dragged to the wall, where she, on her knees, was put, facing the wall. The bracelet not locked about her left wrist was then put through the slave ring and, this done, her right wrist was locked in it, confirming both her wrists at the ring, her belly facing the wall. She looked over her right shoulder at Hassan. 'Hassan!' she cried.

Hassan took the moneys from the merchant. 'In the next room,' said the merchant, 'we will deal for the other goods.'

'Yes,' said Hassan.

'Hassan!' cried the girl.

He left the room. He did not speak to the traitress. He was of the Tahari.

'More, Masters?' asked the girl, kneeling beside the low, tem-wood-inlaid table. She wore a high, red-silk vest, swelling, fastened with a single hook; diaphanous red-silk chalwar, low on her hips, gathered at the ankles; two golden bangles on her left ankle; collar.

'No, Yiza, retire,' said the merchant.

'Yes, Master,' she said.

She lowered her eyes and, taking the tray with black wine and sugars, rose gracefully to her feet, backed away, turned, and left the room.

She moved sweetly. She had been aroused from sleep, not permitted to veil herself, and instructed to prepare and serve black wine. This she had done. At the interior corners of her eyes had been the signs of sleep; she had yawned like a cat when kneeling to one side; her face, and her mouth, had revealed the heavy, sweet lassitude of the beautiful woman who is weary; when she had left, though she held herself erect, as an imbonded girl must, there had been a slow, felicitous swing to her gait, graceful, languid, somnolent, subtly betraying the weariness of her beauty, awakened and forced so early to serve. Her haunches flowed beneath the silk, and then she had disappeared. I did not think it would take her long to remove her clothing, draw her rep-cloth sheet about her and, drawing her knees up, fall asleep on the straw of her cell, which, under pain of death, she would shut behind her, locking it.

When she had left the room she had used the runner at the side of the room. Rooms in private dwellings, in the Tahari, if rich, usually are floored with costly rugs. The rooms are seldom crossed directly, in order to prevent undue wear on the rugs; long strips of ruglike material line the edges of the room; these are commonly used in moving from room to room; children, servants, slaves, women, commonly negotiate the rooms by keeping on the runners, near the walls. Men commonly do also, if guests are not present.

'The breaking of a well,' said the merchant, 'is an almost inconceivable criminal act.'

Neither of us, Hassan, nor myself, responded to him. What he said was true. Earlier, though it had not been our original intention, following our commercial interaction, in which Hassan had exchanged his plunder, flesh and otherwise, for gold, we had been conducted by the merchant to the well, shattered, perhaps ruined. Under torches men had labored, removing stone and sand in leather buckets on long ropes. Hassan's fists had clenched. We had then retired to the merchant's house for black wine. It was two Ahn before dawn.

The various prices and coins had totalled eleven tarn disks of Ar, and four of Turia. To his nine men, apiece, he had thrown a tarn disk of Ar. The rest he kept for himself. A gold tarn disk of Ar is more than many common laborers earn in a year. Many low-caste Goreans have never held one in their hand. His men, outside, waited, the reins of their kaiila in hand.

'And strangest of all,' said the merchant, leaning forward, looking at us intently, 'is the fact that the Aretai raiders were led by a woman!'

'A woman?' asked Hassan.

'Yes,' said the merchant.

'And the war messengers have already been sent?' asked Hassan.

'To all the oases of the Kavars and their vassal tribes,' said the merchant.

'Has there been talk of truce, of discussion?' asked Hassan.

'With those who have cost water?' asked the merchant. 'Of course not!'

'And what word,' asked Hassan, 'has been heard from Haroun, high pasha of the Kavars?'

'Who knows where Haroun is?' asked the merchant, spreading his hands.

'And of his vizier, Baram, Sheik of Bezhad?'

164

'The war messengers have been sent,' said the merchant.

'I see,' said Hassan.

'The tribes gather,' said the merchant. 'The desert will flame.'

'I am weary,' said Hassan. 'And I do not think it wise to be too publicly in Two Scimitars by daylight.'

'Hasaad Pasha knows that raiders come to Two Scimitars,' smiled the merchant. 'It is useful to our economy. We are not on main trade routes.'

'He does not know officially,' said Hassan, 'and I do not wish him to have to dispatch a hundred soldiers to ride about in the desert searching for us, to satisfy outraged citizens. I do not feel like a hard ride now, and doubtless, too, neither do the soldiers. Besides, if we actually encountered one another, it would be quite embarrassing to both parties. What would we do?'

'Ride past one another shouting wildly?' suggested the merchant.

'Perhaps,' smiled Hassan.

'You would probably have to kill one another,' said the merchant.

'I suppose so,' said Hassan.

'At night,' said the merchant, 'you, and others, are always welcome in Two Scimitars.'

'Welcomed by night, sought by day,' said Hassan. 'I think that I shall never understand honest men.'

'We are complicated,' admitted the merchant.

'I wish that the men of other oases were so complicated,' said Hassan. 'In many of them they would pay high to have my head on a lance.'

'We of Two Scimitars,' said the merchant, 'cannot be held accountable for the lack of sophistication in such simple rogues.'

'But to whom do you sell the goods I bring you?' asked Hassan.

'To such simple rogues,' smiled the merchant.

'They know?' asked Hassan.

'Of course,' said the merchant.

'I see,' said Hassan. 'Well, it will soon be light, and I must be going.'

He rose to his feet, somewhat stiffly, for he had been sitting cross-legged for some time, and I joined him.

'May your water bags be never empty. May you always have

water,' said the merchant.

'May your water bags be never empty,' we rejoined. 'May you always have water.'

Outside, shortly before dawn, when drops of moisture beaded on the rocks, Hassan and I, and his men, put our left feet into the stirrups of our saddles and mounted our swift beasts.

'Hassan,' said I.

'Yes,' said he.

'The merchant told us that six days ago Aretai from Nine Wells raided the oasis of the Sand Sleen.'

'Yes,' said Hassan.

'Six days ago,' said I, 'the soldiers at Nine Wells were in the vicinity of the oasis, hunting for a fugitive, escaped from their prison, who had been sentenced to the pits of Klima for an alleged attempt on the life of Suleiman Pasha.'

'Did he escape?' asked Hassan, smiling.

'It seems so,' I said.

'That, too, is my intelligence,' said Hassan.

'If the soldiers of Nine Wells were at their oasis six days ago,' said I, 'they were not, too, at the oasis of the Sand Sleen.'

'No,' said Hassan.

'And it does not seem likely,' said I, 'that, last night, Aretai from Nine Wells would be here.'

'It would be hard riding,' said Hassan. 'And this seems an obscure oasis, far from trading routes.'

'Where would they have disposed of loot from the oasis of the Sand Sleen?' I asked.

'It might have been hidden in the desert,' suggested Hassan.

'Why Two Scimitars?' I asked. 'It is a small oasis, not even Kavar.'

'I do not know,' said Hassan.

'Suleiman, Pasha at Nine Wells,' said I, 'lies in his palace in critical condition. It seems an unusual time for his Aretai to rush raiding about the countryside.'

'It does, indeed,' smiled Hassan.

'Yet the raiders wore the garments of Aretai, the saddle markings, shouted 'For Nine Wells and Suleiman!'

'You and I, too,' smiled Hassan, 'might arrange such matters, and shout boldly.'

I said nothing.

'Odd,' said Hassan, 'that they should shout "For Nine Wells and Suleiman!"'

'Why?' I asked.

'The names of leaders,' said Hassan, 'do not figure in the war cries of Aretai, nor of most tribes. It is the tribe which is significant, not the man, the whole, not the part. The war cry of the Aretai, as I am familiar with it, is "Aretai victorious!"'

'Interesting,' I said. 'Do the Kavars have a similar cry?'

'Yes,' said Hassan. 'It is "Kavars supreme!"'

'It seems reasonably clear, then,' said I, 'that Aretai did not raid Two Scimitars.'

'No,' said Hassan, 'Aretai did not raid Two Scimitars.'

'How can you be sure?' I asked.

'A well was broken,' said Hassan. 'The Aretai are sleen, but they must be respected as foes. They are good fighters, good men of the desert. They would not destroy a well. They are of the Tahari.'

'Who, then,' I asked, 'raided the oasis of the Sand Sleen, the oasis of Two Scimitars?'

'I do not know,' said Hassan. 'I would like to know. I am curious.'

'I, too, am curious,' I said.

'If war erupts, fully, in the desert,' said Hassan, 'the desert, for all practical purposes, will be closed. Trade will be disrupted, armed men will roam, strangers will be more suspect than normally. Few chances will be taken. They will, presumably, be put to death.'

His remark did not much cheer me.

'Strange,' said Hassan, 'that these matters should occur now.'

'Why strange now?' I asked.

'Doubtless it is only a coincidence,' said Hassan.

'I do not understand you,' I said.

'I was intending an expedition into the unexplored dune country,' said he.

'I, too, am a traveler,' I said.

'I thought so,' said he.

'What do you expect to find there?' I asked.

'What are you?' he asked.

'A lowly gem merchant,' I said.

'I saw you in Tor,' said he, 'with the scimitar.'

'Oh,' I said.

'I saw you again, noting your progress, at a watering place on the route to Nine Wells.'

'It was there,' said I, 'that you, in nomad's guise, so abused

167

my blond-haired, blue-eyed slave.'

'She was insolent,' he said. 'It was there that I determined I would have her for my own slave.'

'After your touch, and abuse,' said I, 'she begged to be taught the dances of a slave girl.'

He smiled.

'You took her boldly in the palace of Suleiman,' I said.

He shrugged.

'I have never seen a better whip-capture of a girl,' I said.

He inclined his head, accepting my compliment.

'It is thought, I understand,' he said, 'that it was you, Hakim of Tor, who struck Suleiman.'

'I did not do so,' I said.

'Why would they think you would have done so?' he said.

'It is thought,' I said, 'I am a Kavar spy.'

'Oh?' he smiled.

'Yes,' I said.

'Is it known to you, Hakim of Tor,' asked he, 'who it was who actually struck Suleiman?'

'Yes,' I said, 'it is known to me. It was Hamid, lieutenant to Shakar, captain of the Aretai.'

'I find it of interest, that it should have been Hamid,' he said. Then he said, 'I have wanted to meet you.'

'Oh?' I asked.

'I thought,' said he, 'that when I stole your pretty little slave you would pursue me into the desert. I did not know, of course, that Hamid would strike Suleiman, and that you would be detained.'

'You wish to speak to me?' I asked.

'I am keeping the girl, of course,' he said. He looked at me. 'Do you wish to do contest for her?' he asked.

'I do not need to decide that at the moment, do I?' I asked.

'Of course not,' said Hassan. 'You are my guest.' He grinned. 'You may use her at any time you wish, of course,' he said.

'Hassan is generous,' I laughed.

'From the first instant I put my hands on her,' he said, 'I decided that I would have her for my own.'

'Are you accustomed to taking what women you wish?' I asked.

'Yes,' he said.

'If I had lost your trail,' I said, 'how then would you have made contact with me?'

168

'You would not have lost the trail,' he said.

'But if so?' I asked.

'Then you would have been informed where to find your – my – pretty Alyena in chains. We would then have met.'

'But what if I attempt to slay you now?' I asked.

'You will not, for you are my guest,' said Hassan. 'Besides, why should you bring such a slave into the desert with you, a blonde-haired, white-skinned, blue-eyed wench?'

'Why?' I asked.

'Not as a simple slave,' he said. 'You could buy and rent girls at any oasis. You brought her for a purpose. You wished to sell her, or give her, to someone, in exchange for something, for aid, for information, for something.'

'You are astute,' I said.

'I hope,' he said, 'that the female slave will not complicate relations between us.'

'How could a mere female slave, who is nothing, do that?' I asked.

'True,' said Hassan.

'She seems happy in your chains,' I said.

'She is a slave,' he said.

'It is unfortunate,' said I, 'that she is white-skinned, blonde-haired, blue-eyed.'

'Why is that?' he asked.

'Such women,' said I, 'are cold.'

'Not when collared,' he said.

'Is she hot?' I asked.

I knew that the metal collar of a female slave, that obdurate circlet of steel, locked, which she could not remove, so contrasting with her softness, so proclaiming its vulnerability and rightlessness, often transformed even an inhibited, hostile, cold wench, hating men, into an abandoned, yielding, man-vulnerable, passionate slave girl, loving to lie helpless at the mercy of their touch, that of masters.

Hassan threw back his head and laughed. 'She is the hottest thing I have ever held in my arms,' he said.

I smiled. I wondered how scandalized, how embarrassed and shamed the former Miss Priscilla Blake-Allen would be to hear her needs and her performance so boldly and publicly spoken of. The poor thing, however, could not help herself in the arms of a master.

'She loves you,' I told Hassan.

'I have given her no choice,' he said.

I supposed it true.

I supposed, further, that the rare event had here taken place of a girl meeting her true master, and a man his true slave girl. The girl, one among thousands less fortunate, had encountered a male, surely, too, one among thousands, who could be, and was, to her and for her, her absolute and natural master, the ideal and perfect male for her, dominant and uncompromising, who could, and would, demand and get her full, yielding sexuality, which a woman can give only to a man who owns her totally, before whom, and to whom, she can be only an adoring slave. This happens almost never on Earth, where the normal male/female relationship is the result of a weak, pleasant male's releasing of the female's maternal instinct, rather than her usually frustrated instinct to submit herself fully to a truly dominant male as a held and owned, penetrated, submissive female; it does occur, however, with some frequency on Gor, where girls, slaves, are more frequently traded and exchanged. One tries different girls until one finds she, or those, who are the most exquisite, the most pleasing; one tends then, to keep them; this tends, too, to work out to the advantage of the women, the female slaves, but few, except themselves, are concerned with them, or their feelings; men, it is clear, have a need to dominate; few deny this; none deny it who are informed; in the Gorean culture, as it is not on Earth, institutions exist for the satisfaction of this need, rather than its systematic suppression and frustration; the major Gorean institution satisfying this need is the widespread enslavement of human females; the master/slave relationship is the deepest, clearest recognition of, and concession to, this masculine need, felt by all truly vital, sexual males; but, in the Gorean theory, this masculine need to dominate, which, thwarted, leads to misery, sickness, and petty, vicious, meaningless aggressions, is not an aberration, nor an uncomplemented biological singularity in males, but has its full complementary, correspondent need in the human female, which is the need, seldom satisfied, to be overwhelmed and mastered. In primitive mate competitions, in which intelligence and cunning, and physical and psychological power, were of biological importance, rather than wealth and status, the best women, statistically, would fall to the strongest, most intelligent men; it is possible, and likely, that women, or the

170

best women, were once fought for, literally, as well as symbolically, as possessions; if this were the case then it is likely that something in the female, genetically, would respond to dominance and strength; most women do not, truly, want weak men; they wish their children to be born not to an equal but a superior; how could they respect a man who in stature and power was no more than themselves, the equal of a woman, a prize? Given the choice to bear the child of an equal, or a master, most women would choose to bear the child of a master; women long to bear the children of men superior to themselves; it is a defeated woman whose body grows fat with the child only of an equal; just as evolution, at one time, selected strong, intelligent men, capable of combat, because they were successful in mate competitions, so, too, correspondingly, in the transmission of genetic structures, it would be selecting women who responded to, and yielded to, such men, women who were the biologically specified and rightful property of such men, our ancestors. The dominant male is thus selected in mate competition; the undominant male tends, statistically, to lose out to his stronger, more intelligent foe; correspondingly, evolution selected the female who responds to the dominant male; she who fled such men either mated with weaker men, her children then being less well adapted for survival, or, perhaps, fled away, and her genes were lost, for better or for worse, to the struggling human groups. The female who was excited by such men, and longed to belong to them, to masters, and keep by them and serve them, had the best chance of survival; she was the best protected; her children would be the best protected; further, her children would be more intelligent and stronger, being the offspring of more intelligent and stronger men; her lusts, and her love being owned by such men, and her pride in their possession of her, would contribute substantially to not only her survival but that of her children; too, the woman would, over generations, become more beautiful and desirable, and sexually exciting, as vital males exercising their masculine prerogatives selected among the daughters of the daughters of such women; men chose for mating women who pleased them, and women who pleased them were not the ugly, the gross, the belligerent and stupid, but the intelligent, loving, desirable and beautiful. The twin dynamics of evolu-

171

tion, natural and sexual selection, thus formed over thousands of years the biological nature of the human female; originally there might have been only random tendencies to respond to masculine domination, but those who had them had the best chance of survival; such tendencies were then transmitted, becoming pervasive genetic characteristics of women; owned women lived; the most beautiful and best of these were selected by the strongest, most intelligent and powerful men. It is from such intricate workings of nature that has come the intelligent, beautiful, sensitive woman, the feminine woman with full complement of normal feminine hormones, who longs in her heart to lie lovingly, obediently, excitedly in the arms of a strong man, his woman; beyond this, one might note that dominance and submission are genetically pervasive in the animal kingdom; among mammals in general, and primates universally, it is the male who dominates and the female who submits; this is not an aberration; the abberation is its conditioned frustration, possible, interestingly enough, only in an animal complicated enough to be subject to extensive conditioning regimes, where words may be used to induce counterinstinctual responses, to the detriment and misery of the individual organism, though perhaps subservient to a given conception of economic and social relationships. We are bred hunters; we are made farmers.

'It is near dawn,' said Hassan. 'Let us leave the oasis.'

I rode beside him.

'Why should you wish to speak to me?' I asked him.

'I think,' he said, 'we have a common interest.'

'In what?' I asked.

'In travel,' he said.

'Travelers often seek out curiosities,' I said.

'I intend a venture into the desert,' he said.

'It will be dangerous in these times,' I said.

'Are you familiar with a stone,' asked he, 'near the route between Tor and Nine Wells, which bears an inscription?'

'Yes,' I said.

'And there was a man,' said he, 'who lay near the stone, he who had scratched the inscription.'

'Yes,' I said. 'But when I saw the stone he was gone.'

'I took the body,' said Hassan. 'In a great pyre of brush I saw it burned. Its ashes I had committed to the sands.'

'You knew him?' I asked.
'He was my brother,' said Hassan.
'What do you seek in the desert?' I asked.
'A steel tower,' he said.

ELEVEN

RED ROCK, WHERE SALT IS SHARED;
HASSAN AND I ENCOUNTER TARNA

'You do not wear bells on your kaiila harness!' said the man, threatening us with his lance.

'We come in peace,' said Hassan. 'Have you seen, or heard aught, of a tower of steel?'

'You are mad!' cried the man.

Hassan turned aside his kaiila, with its single rein, and continued our journey, his nine men, myself, and the slave girl, Alyena, following, on our kaiila.

Standing afoot, in the dust, with his lance, the nomad watched us turn away. Behind him was a herd of eleven verr, browsing on brownish snatches of verr grass. He would have defended the small animals with his life. Their milk and wool were his livelihood, and that of his family.

'Perhaps there is no steel tower,' I suggested to Hassan.

'Let us continue our search,' he said.

I had now seen the Tahari in many moods. For twenty days we had been upon the desert.

Once, when a rising edge of blackness, whipping with dust, had risen in the south, we had dismounted, hobbled our kaiila and turned their backs to the wind. We had made a wall with our packs and crouched behind it, drawing our burnooses about us. Hassan, in his own burnoose, sheltered the girl, Alyena, commonly keeping her wrists braceleted behind her, that she not forget she was slave. For two days the sand had hurtled about us, and we had waited, in the manner of the Tahari, patiently in the blasting half darkness of the sand. We had scarcely moved, save to pass about a verrskin of water and a leather pouch of Sa-Tarna meal. Then, as swiftly as it had come, the sand fled, and the sun, bright and immediate,

raw with its ferocity and beauty, held again, untroubled, for-
getful, the scepter, the constant, merciless mace, of its light
and heat over the wide land.

Hassan was the first to stand. He shook the sand from his
burnoose. He unbraceleted Alyena. She stretched like a she-
sleen. Sand was banked against the wall of packs.

'A terrible storm,' I said.

He smiled. 'You are not of the Tahari,' he said. 'Be pleased
that now, in the spring, the wind did not blow from the east.'
Then he said to Alyena, 'Make tea.' 'Yes, Master,' she said,
happily.

Two days later there had been rain.

The flies had now gone.

I had, at first, welcomed the clouds, and thrown back my
burnoose to feel the swift, fierce rain pelt my face. The temperature fell by more than fifty degrees in a matter of Ehn.
Alyena, too, was much pleased. The men of the Tahari, however, sought quickly the highest ground in the vicinity. There
is little rain erosion in the Tahari, with the result that there
are few natural and ready paths to convey water. When it falls,
it often falls heavily, and on flat land, in the loose dust. Within
minutes of the rain beginning to fall we had to dismount, to
drag and pull our struggling, frightened kaiila to higher ground.
They sank to their knees in the mud, snorting, eyes rolling,
and we, mud to our hips, pushing and pulling, sometimes
actually seizing one of their mired limbs, freeing it and moving
it, brought them to the place Hassan had designated, the lee
side of a rocky formation.

Hassan put Alyena, whom he had carried, beside him.

'This is only the fourth time,' he said, 'I have seen rain.'

'It is beautiful!' cried Alyena.

'Can one drown in such mud?' I asked.

'It is unlikely,' said Hassan. 'It is not as deep as a man.
Small animals, in effect, swim in it. The danger is primarily
that the kaiila may, struggling, and falling, break their limbs.'
I noted that Hassan's men had thrown blankets over the heads
of the kaiila, to prevent them from seeing the storm, and keep
rain from striking their faces, which phenomenon, frightening
them, tends to make them unmanageable. 'One must not, of
course,' said Hassan, 'camp in a dried watercourse. A storm,
of which one is unaware, perhaps pasangs away, can fill such a
bed with a sudden flow of water, washing away one's camp and

endangering life.'

'Are men often drowned in such accidents?' I asked.

'No,' said Hassan. 'Men of the Tahari do not camp in such places. Further, those who are foolish enough to do so, can usually, struggling and washed along, save themselves.'

Many men of the Tahari, incidentally, and interestingly, can swim. Nomad boys learn this in the spring, when the waterholes are filled. Those who live at the larger, more populous oases can learn in the baths. The 'bath' in the Tahari is not a matter of crawling into a small tub but is more in the nature, as on Gor generally, of a combination of cleaning and swimming, and reveling in the water, usually connected with various oils and towelings. One of the pleasures at the larger oases is the opportunity to bathe. At Nine Wells, for example, there are two public baths.

Within an Ahn after the cessation of the rain, the sun again paramount, merciless, in the now-cloudless sky, the footing was sufficiently firm, the water lost under the dust and sand, to support the footing of kaiila. The animals were unhooded, we mounted, and again our quest continued.

It was only a day later that the flies appeared. I had thought, first, it was another storm. It was not. The sun itself, for more than four Ehn was darkened, as the great clouds moved over us. Suddenly, like darting, black, dry rain, the insects swarmed about us. I spit them from my mouth. I heard Alyena scream. The main swarms had passed but, clinging about us, like crawling spots on our garments, and in and among the hairs of the kaiila, in their thousands, crept the residue of the infestation. I struck at them, and crushed them, until I realized the foolishness of doing so. In less than four Ahn, twittering, fluttering, small, tawny, sharp-billed, following the black clouds, came flights of zadits. We dismounted and led the kaiila, and let the birds hunt them for flies. The zadits remained with us for more than two days. Then they departed.

The sun was again merciless. I did not find myself, however, longing for a swift return of rain.

'Where, friend,' asked Hassan, of another nomad, 'is the steel tower?'

'I have never heard of such,' said he, warily. 'Surely in the Tahari there are no towers of steel.'

And we continued our quest.

The Tahari is perhaps most beautiful at night. During the day one can scarcely look upon it, for the heats and reflections. During the day it seems menacing, whitish, shimmering with heat, blinding, burning; men must shade their eyes; some go blind; women and children remain within the tents; but, with the coming of the evening, with the departure of the sun, there is a softening, a gentling, of this vast, rocky, harsh terrain. It is at this time that Hassan, the bandit, would make his camps. As the sun sank, the hills, the dust and sky, would become red in a hundred shades, and, as the light fades, these reds would become gradually transformed into a thousand glowing tones of gold, which, with the final fading of the light in the west, yield to a world of luminous, then dusky, blues and purples. Then, it seems suddenly, the sky is black, and wide and high and is rich with the reflected sands of stars, like clear bright diamonds burning in the soft, sable silence of the desert's innocent quietude. At these times, Hassan, cross-legged, would sometimes sit silently before his tent. We did not then disturb him. Oddly enough he permitted no one near him at such times but the collared slave girl, Alyena. She alone, only female and slave, would be beside him, lying beside him, her head at his left knee. Sometimes he would, in these times, stroke her hair, or touch the side of her face, almost gently, almost as though her throat were not encircled by a collar. Then, after the stars would be high for an Ahn or so, he would, suddenly, laughing, seize the girl by the arms and throw her on her back on the mats, thrust up her dress and rape her as the mere slave she was. Then he would knot her skirt over her head, confining her arms within it, and throw her, she laughing, to his men, and to me, for our sport.

'No,' said a man, 'I have seen no tower of steel, nor have I heard of such. How can there be such a thing?'

'My thanks, Herder,' said Hassan, and again led us on our quest.

The camps of nomads were becoming less frequent. Oases were becoming rare.

We were moving east in the Tahari.

Some of the nomads veil their women, and some do not. Some of the girls decorate their faces with designs, drawn in charcoal. Some of the nomad girls are very lovely. The children of nomads, both male and female, until they are five or six years of age wear no clothing. During the day they do not venture from the shade of the tents. At night, as the sun goes down, they emerge happily from the tents and romp and play. They are taught written Taharic by their mothers, who draw the characters in the sand, during the day, in the shade of the tents. Most of the nomads in this area were Tashid, which is a tribe vassal to the Aretai. It might be of interest to note that children of the nomads are suckled for some eighteen months, which is nearly twice the normal length of time for Earth infants, and half again the normal time for Gorean infants. These children, if it is significant, are almost uniformly secure in their families, sturdy, outspoken and self-reliant. Among the nomads, interestingly, an adult will always listen to a child. He is of the tribe. Another habit of nomads, or of nomad mothers, is to frequently bathe small children, even if it is only with a cloth and cup of water. There is a very low infant mortality rate among nomads, in spite of their limited diet and harsh environment. Adults, on the other hand, may go months without washing. After a time one grows used to the layers of dirt and sweat which accumulate, and the smell, offensive at first, is no longer noticed.

'Young warrior,' asked Hassan, of a youth, no more than eight, 'have you heard aught of a tower of steel?'

His sister, standing behind him, laughed. Verr moved about them brushing against their legs.

The boy went to the kaiila of Alyena. 'Dismount, Slave,' he said to her.

She did so, and knelt before him, a free male. The boy's sister crowded behind him. Verr bleated.

'Put back your hood and strip yourself to the waist,' said the boy.

Alyena shook loose her hair; she then dropped her cloak back, and removed her blouse.

'See how white she is!' said the nomad girl.

'Pull down your skirt,' said the boy.

Alyena, furious, did so, it lying over her calves.

'How white!' said the nomad girl.

The boy walked about her, and took her hair in his hands. 'Look,' said he to his sister, 'silky, fine and yellow, and long.' She, too, felt the hair. The boy then walked before Alyena. 'Look up,' said he. Alyena lifted her eyes, regarding him. 'See,' said he to his sister, bending down. 'She has blue eyes!'

'She is white, and ugly,' said the girl, standing up, backing off.

178

'No,' said the boy, 'she is pretty.'

'If you like white girls,' said his sister.

'Is she expensive?' asked the boy of Hassan.

'Yes,' said Hassan, 'young warrior. Do you wish to bid for her?'

'My father will not let me own a girl,' said the youngster.

'Ah,' said Hassan, understanding.

'But when I grow up,' said he, 'I shall become a raider, like you, and have ten such girls. When I see one I want I will carry her away, and make her my slave.' He looked at Hassan. 'They will serve me well, and make me happy.'

'She is ugly,' said the boy's sister. 'Her body is white.'

'Is she a good slave?' asked the boy of Hassan.

'She is a stupid, miserable girl,' said Hassan, 'who must be often beaten.'

'Too bad,' said the boy.

'Tend the verr,' said his sister, unpleasantly.

'If you were mine,' said the boy to Alyena, 'I would tolerate no nonsense from you. I would make you a perfect slave.'

'Yes, Master,' said Alyena, stripped before him, her teeth gritted.

'You may clothe yourself,' said the boy.

'Thank you, Master,' said Alyena. She pulled up her skirt and drew on her blouse, adjusted her cloak and hood. Whereas she could dismount from the kaiila blanket, which served her as saddle, she could not, unaided, reach its back. I, with my left hand under her foot, lifted her to her place. 'The little beast!' whispered Alyena to me, in English. I smiled.

'Have you seen, or heard, aught, young warrior,' asked Hassan, 'of a tower of steel?'

The boy looked at him and laughed. 'Your slave, Raider,' said he, indicating the irritated Alyena, now again mounted, well vexed, on her kaiila, 'apparently makes your tea too strong.'

Hassan nodded his head, graciously. 'My thanks, young warrior,' said he.

We then left the boy, and his sister, and their verr. She was scolding him about the verr. 'Be quiet,' he told her, 'or I will sell you to raiders from Red Rock. In a year or two you will be pretty enough for a collar.' He then skipped away as she, shouting abuse, flung a rock after him. When we looked back again they were prodding their verr, leading them, doubtless, away from their camp. On our kaiila harness, we knew, we wore no bells.

'The oasis of the Battle of Red Rock,' said Hassan to me, 'is one of the few outpost oases maintained by the Aretai. To its west and south is mostly Kavar country.'

At noon of the next day, I cried out, 'There is the oasis.'

'No,' said Hassan.

I could see the buildings, whitish, with domes, the palms, the gardens, the high, circling walls of red clay.

I blinked. This seemed to be no illusion. 'Can you not see it?' I asked Hassan, the others.

'I see it!' said Alyena.

'We, too, see it,' said Hassan, 'but it is not there.'

'You speak in riddles,' I said.

'It is a mirage,' said he.

I looked again. It seemed to me unlikely that this was a mirage. I was familiar with two sorts of mirages on the desert, of the sort which might be, and often were, seen by normal individuals under normal circumstances, not the mirages of the dehydrated body, the sun-crazed brain, not private hallucinatory images. The most common sort of mirage is simply the interpretation of heat waves, shimmering on the desert, as the ripples in water, as in a lake or pond. When the sky is reflected in the rising, heated air, the mirage is even more striking, because then the surface of the 'lake,' reflecting the sky, seems blue, and, thus even more waterlike. A second common sort of mirage, more private than the first, but quite normal, is the interpretation of a mixed terrain, usually rocks and scrub brush, mixed with rising heat waves, as an oasis with water, palms and buildings. Perception is a quite complicated business, involving the playing of energies on the sensors, and the transduction of this energy into an interpreted visual world. All we are in physical contact with, of course, is the energy applied to the sensors. These physical energies are quite different from the 'human world' of our experience, replete with color, sound and light. There is, of course, a topological congruence between the world of physics and the world of experience. Evolution has selected such a congruence. Our experimental world, though quite unlike the world of physics, is well coordinated with it. If it were not we could not move our physical bodies conveniently among physical objects, manage to put our hands on things we wished to touch, and so on. Different sensory systems, as in

180

various types of organisms, mean different experiential worlds. Each of these, however, the world of the man, the cuttlefish, the butterfly, the ant, the sleen, the Priest-King is congruent, though perhaps in unusual ways, with the presumably singular, unique physical world. Beyond this, perception is largely a matter of interpreting a flood of cues, or coded bits, out of which we construct a unified, coherent, harmonious world. Though the eye is a necessary condition for seeing, one does not, so to speak, 'see' with the eye, but, oddly enough, with the brain. If the optic nerve, or, indeed, certain areas of the brain, could be appropriately stimulated one could have visual experiences without the use of eyes. Similarly, if the eyes were in perfect condition, but the visual centers of the brain were defective, one could not 'see.' Perhaps it is more correct to speak of a system of components necessary for visual experience, but, even if so, it is well to understand that what impinges upon the eyes are not visual realities but electromagnetic radiations. Further, what one sees is a function not simply of what exists in the external world, but of a number of other factors as well, for example, what one has familiarly seen before, what one expects to see, what others claim is there to be seen, what one wants to see, the physical condition of the organism, its conditioning and socialization, the conceptual and linguistic categories available to organism, and so on. It is thus not unusual that, in a desert situation, a calm, normal person may, misinterpreting physical cues, make an oasis, complete with buildings and trees, out of energies reflected over a heated surface from rock and brush. There is nothing unusual in this sort of thing.

But this did not seem to me a mirage sort of experience. I rubbed my eyes. I changed the position of my head. I closed and opened my eyes.

'No,' I said. 'I see an oasis clearly.'

'It is not there,' said Hassan.

'Does the oasis of the Battle of Red Rock have, at its north-east rim, a kasbah, with four towers?'

'Yes,' said Hassan.

'Then I see it,' I said.

'No,' said Hassan.

'There are palm groves, five of them,' I said.

'Yes,' he said.

'Pomegranate orchards lie at the east of the oasis,' I said. 'Gardens lie inward. There is even a pond, between two of the groves of date palms.'

'True,' said Hassan.

'There is Red Rock,' I said.

'No,' said Hassan.

'I could not imagine these things,' I said. 'I have never been to Red Rock. Look. There is a single gate in the kasbah, facing us. On the towers two flags fly.'

'Pennons,' said Hassan, 'of the Tashid and Aretai.'

'I shall race you to the oasis,' I said.

'It is not there,' he said. 'We shall not arrive there until to-morrow, past noon.'

'I see it!' I protested.

'I shall speak clearly,' said Hassan. 'You see it and you do not see it.'

'I am glad,' I said, 'that you have chosen to speak clearly. Had you spoken obscurely I might not have understood.'

'Ride ahead,' suggested Hassan.

I shrugged, and kicked the kaiila in the flanks, urging it downward, from the sloping hill, toward the oasis. I had ridden for no more than five Ehn when the oasis vanished. I reined in the kaiila. Before me was nothing but the desert.

I was sweating. I was hot. Before me was nothing but the desert.

'It is an interesting phenomenon, is it not?' asked Hassan, when he, and the others, had joined me. 'The oasis, which is some seventy pasangs distant, is reflected in the mirror of air above it, and then again reflected downward and away, at an angle.'

'It is like mirrors?' I asked.

'Precisely,' said Hassan, 'with layers of air the glass. A tri-angle of reflected light is formed. Red Rock, more than seventy pasangs away, is seen, in its image, here.'

'It is only then an optical illusion?' I asked.

'Yes,' said Hassan.

'But did it not seem real to you?' I asked.

'Of course,' he said.

'How did you know it was not Red Rock?' I asked.

'I am of the Tahari,' he said.

'Did it look different to you?' I asked.

'No,' he said.

'Then how could you tell?' I asked.

He shrugged. 'I am of the Tahari,' he said.

182

'But how could you tell?' I asked.

'By the distances and times,' he said. 'We had not come far enough, nor at our pace, fast enough, for it to be Red Rock.'

'Seeing it,' I said, 'one who was unwise, and not of the Tahari, might ration water unwisely, and die.'

'In the Tahari,' said Hassan, 'it is well to be of the Tahari, if one would live.'

'I will try to be of the Tahari,' I said.

'I will help you,' said Hassan.

It was the next day, at the eleventh Ahn, one Ahn past the Gorean noon, that we arrived at the Oasis of Red Rock.

It was dominated by the kasbah of its pasha, Turem a'Din, commander of the local Tashid clans, on its rim to the northeast. There were five palm groves. At the east of the oasis lay pomegranate orchards. Toward its lower parts, in its center, were the gardens. Between two of the groves of date palms there was a large pool. The kasbah contained a single gate. On the summits of its four towers flew pennons, those of the Tashid and Aretai.

'Do you fear to enter the oasis of the vassal tribe of the Aretai?' asked Hassan.

'We are from Nine Wells,' I said.

'I think, too, there is little danger,' said Hassan.

We entered the oasis slowly, single file, in caravan style. There is almost always a constant, hot wind on the Tahari. Our burnooses lifted behind us, slowly, swelling, over the flanks of our animals. The girl, Alyena, rode next to the last in our line, in the position of least status; she was followed by one of Hassan's men, the guard; such a guard is commonly posted; he, from time to time, watches the trail behind the caravan and, of course, prevents the escape of slave girls.

The oasis which we were entering is named for the battle of Red Rock, which is a large shelf of reddish sandstone behind the oasis, north by northeast from its lowest point, and center. It was used as the vantage point for the Aretai commander at that time, Hammaran, who also launched at a crucial point in the struggle, his picked cavalry, and bodyguard, from that height, turning the battle's tide. The Tashid commander of the time, Ba'Arub, died on the shelf of red stone, with ten men, trying to reach Hammaran. It was said that he came within ten yards of him. Ba'Arub was, it was said, a brave man. It was also

183

believed that if he had stood siege in his kasbah, in time Hammaran would have been forced to retire. It is difficult to maintain a lengthy siege in the Tahari. Food supplies at the oasis are short, except for the stores in the kasbah, and supply lines are long, and difficult to defend. Had Ba'Arub destroyed or fouled the public wells at Red Rock, those outside the walls of the kasbah, Hamaran would have been forced to retire in twenty-four hours, and perhaps lose most of his men on the return march to his country. But being of the Tahari, Ba'Arub, as it is told in the stories related about the campfires, would not do this. It is said he came within ten yards of Hammaran.

Men regarded us with some curiosity, as is common when newcomers arrive at an oasis, but I detected neither apprehension nor hostility. The wars and raids, I gathered, had not touched Red Rock.

A child ran beside the stirrup of Hassan, playing. 'You have no bells on your kaiila,' said the child.

'They were stolen by raiders,' said Hassan. The boy laughed and ran beside him.

'We shall seek an inn,' said Hassan.

The battle of Red Rock, for which the oasis is named, took place more than seventy years ago, in 10,051 C.A., or in the sixth year of the reign of Ba'Arub Pasha. Since that time the Tashid have been a vassal tribe of the Aretai. Though there are some token tributes involved, exemptions for Aretai merchants from caravan taxes, and such, the vassal tribe is, in its own areas, almost completely autonomous, with its own leaders, magistrates, judges and soldiers. The significance of the relationship, is crucially, interestingly, military alliance. The vassal tribe is bound, by its Tahari oaths, sworn over water and salt, to support the conquering tribe in its military endeavors, with supplies, kaiila and men. The vassal tribe is, in effect, a military unit subordinate to the conquering tribe which it, then, may count among its forces. Enemies conquered become allies enlisted. One's foe of yesterday becomes one's pledged friend of today. The man of the Tahari, conquered, stands ready, his scimitar returned to him, to defend his conqueror to the death. The conqueror, by his might and cunning, and victory, has won, by the right of the Tahari, a soldier to his cause. I am not clear on the historical roots of this unusual social institution but it does tend, in its practice, to pacify great sections of the Tahari. War, for example, between conquering tribes and rebellious

184

vassal tribes is, although not unknown, quite rare. Another result, perhaps unfortunate, however, is that the various tribes tend to build into larger and larger confederations of military related communities. Thus, if war should erupt between the high tribes, the conquering tribes, the entire desert might become engulfed in hostilities. This was what was in danger of happening now, for the Aretai and the Kavars were the two high tribes of the Tahari. Not all tribes, of course, are vassal or conquering tribes. Some are independent. War, incidentally, between vassal tribes is not unknown. The high tribes need not, though often they do, support vassal tribes in their squabbles; the vassal tribes, however, are expected to support the high, or noble, tribes, in their altercations. Sometimes, it is made quite clear, by messenger and proclamation, whether a war is local or not, say, between only the Ta'Kara and the Luraz, who have some point of dispute between them. All in all, the relation of vassal tribe to conquering tribe probably contributes more to the peace of the Tahari than to its hostilities. It is fortunate that some such arrangement exists, for the men of the Tahari, like Goreans generally, are extremely proud, high-strung, easily offended men, with a sense of honor that is highly touchy. Furthermore, enjoying war, they need very little to send them to their saddles with their scimitars loose in their sheaths. A rumor of an insult or outrage, not inquired closely into, perhaps by intent, will suffice. A good fight, I have heard men of the Tahari say, licking their lips, justifies any cause. It may be appropriate here to mention that the reason that Hammaran came to Red Rock seventy years ago is not even known, by either Aretai or Tashid. The cause of the war was forgotten, but its deeds are still recounted about the fires. There were seventy men in the bodyguard of Hammaran. When the battle was lost to him, Ba'Arub tried to reach him. It said he came within ten yards.

'We shall stop here,' said Hassan, reining in before an inn. We dismounted. We took the packs from our kaiila, the saddles and accoutrements. Boys came out to meet us, to take our kaiila to the stables. Two of Hassan's men went with them, to see that the animals were well cared for. One of Hassan's men helped Alyena to dismount. She took short steps and went to kneel beside Hassan, her head down, at his left thigh.

'Stand, Slave,' he said to her.

'Yes, Master,' she said.

He took one of the water bags, which was still full, which held some twenty gallons of water.

'Carry this burden, Slave,' he said.

'Yes Master,' she said.

He threw it over her shoulders. She gasped. She bent forward, her hands steadying the bag. It was heavy for the slight beauty. She almost lost her balance. If she dropped it, she would be much beaten.

The men then gathered their saddles, their weapons, the other water and goods, and their belongings. Alyena waited for us, bent, face strained, bearing across her small shoulders the weight of the water.

Each man carried his own saddle. Saddles are prized on the Tahari and each man cares for his own, and sees to its safety. Among nomads they are brought into the tent each night, and placed on the right side of the tent, at the back.

The water which we had brought with us would not now be wasted but, by Tahari custom, emptied into the cistern of the inn. In this fashion the water is still used, and, to some extent, it saves the inn boys from carrying as much water as they might otherwise do, from the wells of the oasis, to the inn's cistern. In leaving an oasis, of course, similarly, as a courtesy to the inn and its hospitality, the bags are commonly filled not at the cistern, but at the public well.

Hassan then, carrying his saddle and other belongings, went into the inn. His men, and I, followed him. Last to enter the inn, head down, was Alyena.

'Here, Slave,' said one of the inn boys to her, indicating the way to the inn's cistern. Alyena, slowly, half stumbling, followed him. He did not, of course, help her. She emptied the water into the cistern. Those of Hassan's men who carried water, too, emptied the water into the cistern. Before Alyena returned to us, the boy brushed back her hood, revealing her hair and face. His hand was in her hair. 'You are a pretty slave,' he said. 'Thank you, Master,' whispered Alyena. He turned her head from side to side. Then he released her, snapping his fingers and pointing to his feet. She knelt before him, and kissed his feet, her hair falling over them. He then turned away. She rose to her feet and went to kneel beside Hassan, who was sitting at a bench before a table. She knelt perpendicular to his thigh, and put her head gently, sideways, on his left leg. He handled her head and hair with a rough gentleness,

186

sometimes running his fingers, caressing her, between her throat and the collar.

'Have you heard aught of a tower of steel?' Hassan was asking the master of the inn.

None, it seemed, at Red Rock had either seen, or heard, of so strange an architectural oddity as a tower of steel in the desert.

This was irritating to Hassan, and did not much please me either, for the oasis of the Battle of Red Rock was the last of the major oases of the Tahari for more than two thousand pasangs eastward; it lay, in effect, on the borders of the dreaded dune country; there are oases in the dune country but they are small and infrequent, and often lie more than two hundred pasangs apart; in the sands they are not always easy to find; among the dunes one can, unknowingly, pass within ten pasangs of an oasis, missing it entirely. Little but salt caravans ply the dune country. Caravans with goods tend to travel the western, or distant eastern edge of the Tahari; caravans do, it might be mentioned, occasionally travel from Tor or Kasra to Turmas, a Turian outpost and kasbah, in the southeastern edge of the Tahari, but even these commonly avoid the dune country, either moving south, then east, or east, then south, skirting the sands. Few men, without good reason, enter the dune country.

I had little doubt, nor did Hassan, that it was within the dune country that lay the steel tower, if there was indeed such an unusual edifice.

It seemed reasonably clear that if such were not the case someone, nomad or merchant, or innkeeper or drover, or guide or soldier, would have heard of it.

But such a tower might exist in the dune country for ten thousand years, remote and undiscovered.

The Others, the Kurii, had stopped slave runs from Earth to Gor. 'Surrender Gor,' had been the ultimatum delivered to the Sardar. A Kur, alone, had been apprehended, apparently on his way to the dune country. A message had been inscribed on a rock: Beware the steel tower. And a message girl had been brought to Samos, of Port Kar. Her message, revealed in the shaving of her head, had been 'Beware Abdul.' Only that portion of the mystery seemed well solved. Abdul had been the lowly water carrier in Tor, a minor agent, presumably of Others, the Kurii, who had wished to keep me from the Tahari. That part of the mystery only had I now well solved. Still, however, I did not know who had sent the message. I wondered on the Kur which had entered, invisible, my cell at Nine Wells. He had been much wounded. He had not killed me. Ibn Saran had told me the beast had been slain. There was much, yet, which I did not understand.

'We shall leave in the morning,' said Hassan to me, stretching. 'None here seem to know of a steel tower.'

Indeed, to my surprise, word of the attack, putatively by Aretai, on the Bakah oasis of Two Scimitars, of some days ago, had not yet seemed to reach Red Rock. None here spoke of it. Had they known of the raid it would, surely, have been the topic of pervasive converse in the oasis. It seemed to me clear that none here, at least of the common population, knew of it. Had it truly been by Aretai I had no doubt but what the oasis would be preparing itself, even now, for Kavar reprisals. It was not odd, of course, for Red Rock not to have yet heard of the attack. It was explained so simply as by no man yet having brought them the news. No one had yet journeyed to them, who knew of the attack, or knew of it and would tell them. Since Red Rock was an oasis under the governance of the Tashid, a vassal tribe of Aretai, of course, no Bakah, or other member of the Kavar confederation, would be likely, particularly in such times, to drop in and, in friendly fashion, convey this intelligence to them. Indeed, they would tend to avoid Aretai and Aretai-dominant oases, at least until they could come in force, paying the respects of the Tahari with steel.

'I am weary,' said Hassan. 'I shall retire.' Already he had sent Alyena up to his room. His men, too, were lodged on the second floor.

Hassan looked about himself. 'What is the hour?' asked Hassan.

One of the inn boys, sitting in an apron, on a bench near the large, cylindrical sand clock, glanced at it. 'Past the nineteenth hour,' he said. He yawned. He would stay up until the twentieth hour, the Gorean midnight, at which time he would turn the clock, and retire.

'Are masters well content in my house?' asked the innkeeper.

188

'Yes,' said Hassan. Then Hassan said, 'Soldiers are returning.'

I listened carefully. I had not noticed the sound. Hassan's fingers, on the table, had caught the subtle vibration.

I could now hear the drumming of galloping kaiila.

'No soldiers are out,' said the innkeeper.

Hassan leaped to his feet, throwing over the table. In a bound he had fled upstairs.

'Do not go to the window!' I cried.

But already the innkeeper had thrown back the shutters. I heard Hassan shouting upstairs. I heard the sound of feet. The innkeeper turned to face me, his face white; he fell rolling to the floor, snapping off the shaft of the arrow. 'Kavars supreme!' I heard. I rushed to the window, my scimitar thrust through and the figure, in burnoose, screamed, clutched at the dark side of the window, and fell back, bloodied, into the darkness. I reached to close the shutters. Two arrows struck the wood, splintering needles of wood into my cheek; then the shutters were pulled closed, fastened; another arrow burst half through one, hanging on our side. The inn boy stood by the sand clock, looking wildly about. We heard the paws of kaiila, their squeals and snorts, and hisses. I heard a man cry out. Somewhere I heard a door splintering, though not, I thought, of the inn. 'Kavars supreme!' I heard.

'Upstairs!' cried Hassan. 'To the roof!'

I took the stairs four at a time, climbing to the second floor. The inn boy, terrified, fled through a door to the kitchen.

Alyena, white faced, stood, her arm in the grip of one of Hassan's men.

'Follow me,' said Hassan. Other guests at the inn fled downstairs. A woman screamed.

We climbed a narrow ladder, pushing up a trap door to the roof. We stood under the three moons of Gor. The desert looked white. Beneath us, in the streets, people were running, some carrying belongings. 'To the kasbah!' cried a man. 'Seek safety in the kasbah!' Among the running people rode warriors, slashing about themselves, slaying and freeing for themselves a path for their mounts. 'Kavars supreme!' they cried.

'Kavars!' I cried.

Hassan looked at me, wildly, angrily. 'To the stable yard,' he said. We ran across the roof to the walled stable yard. He cried orders, swiftly. Saddles were fetched, two men leaped

189

down from the roof to the ground below, then leaped up, running to the stables. I saw a fire arrow loop in the sky over palms. I heard the sounds of axes. There was, on the other side of the wall, much screaming. We heard the door of the inn splintering. Below us, in the stable yard, holding the reins of kaiila, came Hassan's men. 'Guard the trap door,' said Hassan to one of his men. Almost at that moment the trap door thrust up and a man's face appeared; Hassan's man thrust his scimitar through the jaw and wrenched it free, loose with blood and teeth and kicked shut the door.

'To the kasbah!' cried a man below in the street, terrified.

'Into the desert!' cried a woman. 'The kasbah is bolted against raiders! People die at the gate, cut down, pounding to enter!'

'Fire!' I cried. An arrow had fallen within the stable yard, striking through the straw in the storage stall at the right. We saw a man climbing over the gate to the stable yard. He fell back, thrust from the gate by a lance in the hands of one of Hassan's men. The interior of the stable yard was now well lit, by the blazing straw. The kaiila squealed in fright. Hassan's men threw their burnooses over the heads of the animals. Two were saddled.

'Look there!' I cried. Two raiders had climbed to the roof, leaping from their kaiila. Hassan and I met them, fiercely, forcing them back over the edge, into the crowded, dark, screaming throng below. I saw a palm tree falling. Four buildings were afire.

A woman screamed below.

More riders, slashing, pressed by, below us. 'Their garments, their saddles,' said Hassan, 'are Kavar!'

From the roof we could see men and women, and children, running through the palm groves and gardens.

Another building, this time to our left, caught fire. I smelled smoke. 'The inn is afire,' I said.

'Tarna!' we heard. 'Tarna!'

Hassan went to the edge of the wall looking down into the now-blazing stable yard. 'Follow them!' cried Hassan, indicating his two men below, to the rest of his men, even to he who guarded the trap door. They vaulted the edge of the roof, striking below in the stable yard. Hastily they saddled their kaiila. I could now see fire, in a bright, geometrical, right-angled line, glowing from below, about the trap door's edge.

Hassan tore off his own burnoose and, putting it under Alyena's arms, lowered her from the roof to the arms of one of his men, mounted on his kaiila. Alyena looked upward at Hassan, wildly. 'Master!' she cried. But he had gone.

We ran again to the other edge of the roof. We could see more raiders coming. There were flights of them, paced out, perhaps hundreds altogether.

'On my signal,' said Hassan, 'have them throw open the gate to the stable yard, and ride!'

I went to the edge of the roof overlooking the burning yard. I saw the man to whom Alyena had been lowered. She was now on her own kaiila. It was wedged in, among the others.

'I relay the signal of Hassan,' said I. 'Upon this signal, take flight!'

'Two kaiila are saddled for you,' said he, indicating two mounts.

'Upon the signal,' said I, 'take flight.'

'What of you,' he cried, 'and Hassan!'

'Upon the signal,' I said, 'take flight.'

'Prepare to open the gate,' said the man to two of his fellows, who, mounted, waited near it. Each would draw back one of the bars.

'Hassan!' screamed Alyena. 'Hassan!'

One must watch, to see when the escape might best emerge from the yard, another must convey the signal.

'Hassan!' screamed Alyena, from below.

I smiled to myself. She had dared to soil the name of her master by putting it on her lips which, though beautiful, were only those of a slave. Girls are not, commonly, permitted to speak the name of their master. He is addressed as, or responded to, as 'Master' or 'my Master.' If Hassan survived, he would, I suspected, well beat her for this lapse. Some masters, it might be noted, however, permit the girl to speak their name, if it is accompanied by an acknowledgement of title, as in, say, 'Hassan, Master,' or 'Hassan, my Master.' Hassan, however, was not so lenient; he had, as yet, not permitted his pretty Alyena this liberty. I had little doubt, should he survive, the lovely, little wench would be well whipped for her oversight, her agonized outburst, bordering on insolence.

His hand was lifted. His head was low, looking over the ledge. I heard a flight of riders thunder by. His hand fell.

'Go!' I said.

The bars were withdrawn; the gates swung wide; the burnooses were thrown from the heads of the animals, and the kaiila bolted from the blazing stable yard into the suddenly illuminated street.

We heard men shouting.

In moments the kaiila and their riders had vanished down the street.

'There are two kaiila remaining, saddled,' I called to Hassan. 'Hurry!'

'Take one!' he cried. 'Be off! There is time! Be off!'

Instead I joined him at the edge of the roof.

Now another flight of the kaiila riders sped by beneath the roof. We kept our heads low.

'Are you not coming?' I asked.

'Be off!' he whispered. 'Wait!' he said.

Then, below, through the streets, in swirling purple and yellow burnooses, came eleven riders.

'Tarna!' we heard. 'Tarna!'

They reined in, almost below the edge of the roof. Several other riders, raiders, were with them, behind.

'Tarna!' we heard.

The leader of the riders, in blue and purple burnoose, stood in the stirrups, surveying the carnage.

Reports were made by lieutenants to this leader. Orders were issued to these men and they, on their kaiila, sped away. The leader, graceful, slight, vital, stood in the stirrups, scimitar in hand.

'The wells?' asked a man.

'Destroy them,' she said.

He sped away, followed by a cloud of riders. The leader sat back in the saddle, burnoose swelling in the wind, light, wickedly curved scimitar across the pommel.

'Destroy the palms, burn the buildings,' she said.

'Yes, Tarna,' said the lieutenants, and they wheeled their mounts, going to their men.

The girl looked about and then, rapidly, with a scattering of dust, she moved her kaiila in the direction of the kasbah. She was followed, swiftly, by the ten riders who had accompanied her, and several others of the raiders.

'Get your kaiila, escape!' said Hassan. The roof was hot; the inn, below, was burning; to our right, through the roof, flames licked upwards.

'Are you not coming?' I asked.

'Presently,' he said. 'I am curious to see one of these Kavars.'

'I am coming with you,' I said.

'Save yourself,' said he.

'I am coming with you,' I said.

'We have not even shared salt,' he said.

'I shall accompany you,' I said.

He looked at me, for a long time. Then he thrust back the sleeve of his right hand. I pressed my lips to the back of his right wrist, tasting there, in the sweat, the salt. I extended to him the back of my right wrist, and he put his lips and tongue to it.

'Do you understand this?' he asked.

'I think so,' I said.

'Follow me,' said he. 'We have work to do, my brother.'

Hassan and I leaped from the roof, which was now partly aflame, to the stable yard. There, tethered, shifting, their nostrils stung with smoke, their heads covered with saddle blankets, were our two kaiila. By the reins we led them from the yard, once outside removing the saddle blankets. I saw the body of one of the inn boys to one side, against the wall of the opposite building. It must have been past the twentieth Gorean hour. The sand clock had not been turned. We heard the roof of the inn fall. Far off there was screaming. We led the beasts through the streets of the oasis. Twice we skirted pockets of fighting men. Once, four Tashid soldiers sped by.

Once, looking through an alley, to the street at its end, we saw mounted men fighting. There were some ten Tashid soldiers, on kaiila, attacking the command group of the raiders. Then they were forced back, with lances, by dozens of raiders. They wheeled away, pursued by the raiders, the command group, in its purple and yellow burnooses following. I saw Tarna, the leader of the raiders, standing in her stirrups, scimitar high, urging her men forward, then joining in the pursuit.

'Who are you?' cried a voice.

We spun about.

'Aretai sleen!' cried the man. He, mounted on his kaiila, urged the beast forward. We blocked the charge with our kaiila. The animals squealed and grunted. None of us, because of the animals, could get a good stroke at the other. The man, with a cry of rage, pulled his animal back, and sped into the darkness. It was not unwise on his part. In the alley, with two

193

of us, it might not have gone well for him.

'We have lost him,' I said.

'There are others,' said Hassan.

In a few moments we came to a high, thick wall of red clay. Before this wall were some six of the raiders, four with scimitars drawn. Against the wall, kneeling, stripped, bellies pressed tight against it, points of the scimitars against their backs, between their shoulder blades, chins high, against the wall, hands high over their heads, palms pressed tight against the wall, were four beautiful girls. One of the men with sheathed scimitar was preparing to bracelet the first girl; the other man with sheathed scimitar was unlooping a light slave chain with snaplocks to put the lovely prisoners in throat coffle.

'Tal,' said Hassan, greeting them.

They spun to face him. Each wore the garments, the agal cording of the Kavars. The saddles on their nearby kaiila were Kavar.

They rushed toward us, the two with sheathed scimitars last, freeing their weapons. By the time they reached us, the other four were down. They backed away, then turned and ran. We did not pursue them.

The girls, remained as they had been placed. They did not even dare to turn their heads.

Hassan kissed one on the back of the neck. 'Oh!' she cried.

'Are you female slaves?' he asked.

'No, Masters!' cried one.

'Run then to the desert,' said Hassan.

They turned about, crouching, by the wall, trying to cover themselves.

'But we are stripped,' cried one.

'Run!' said Hassan, smacking her smartly with the flat of his blade.

'Oh!' she cried and fled, the others following, into the darkness.

We laughed.

'They are pretty,' said Hassan. 'Perhaps we should have kept them.'

'Perhaps,' I admitted. One, a wide-hipped little brunette, I thought, would have looked well at my feet.

'Yet,' said Hassan, 'this seems scarcely a time propitious for the braceleting of wenches.'

'You are right,' I observed.

'Besides,' said Hassan, 'they were young. In two years or so they would be more ripe for the picking.'

'Others may have them then,' I said.

He shrugged. 'There are always young, beautiful wenches to make slaves,' he said.

'True,' I said.

He looked at our fallen foes. We saw in the light of the moons, and in the light of a torch in a ring on a wall opposite the wall.

'Here,' said Hassan, kneeling beside one of the fallen men. I joined him. Hassan thrust up the left sleeve.

'He is Kavar,' I said. I saw on the man's left forearm the blue scimitar.

'No,' said Hassan. 'Look. The point of the scimitar curves inward, toward the body.'

'So?' I asked.

'The Kavar scimitar,' he said, 'points away from the body, to the outside, toward the foe.'

I looked at him.

Hassan smiled. He thrust up his left sleeve. Startled, I saw the mark on his left forearm.

'This,' said Hassan, smiling, 'is the Kavar scimitar.'

I saw the point, as he had said, was curved away from the body, to the outside, as he had said, toward foes.

'You are Kavar,' I said.

'Of course,' said Hassan.

We spun about. We heard the tiny noise. We looked up. We stood within a ring of mounted warriors, with purple and yellow burnooses, others behind them in more common desert garb. Lances threatened us, pinning us at the wall. Arrows, fitted to bows, were trained upon our hearts.

'There they are,' said the man whom we had skirmished with earlier in the alley.

'Shall we kill them?' asked one of the men in the purple and yellow burnoose.

'Discard your weapons,' said Tarna.

We did so.

'Stand,' she said.

We did so.

'Shall we kill them?' asked the man.

'Lift your heads,' said the girl.

We did as she had commanded.

195

'Tarna?' he asked.

'No,' she said. 'They are handsome and strong. They are not without interest to me. Take them as slaves.'

'Yes, Tarna,' said the man.

'This one,' said the girl, looking down at me, calmly, 'strip him, and chain him to my stirrup.'

TWELVE

WHAT OCCURRED
IN TARNA'S KASBAH;
HASSAN AND I DECIDE TO TAKE
OUR LEAVE FROM THAT PLACE

I rolled about, on my back, splashing in the water.

It was quite pleasant. The temperature of the water, perhaps, was a bit warm. Also, it was perfumed. Yet I did not mind. It had been weeks since I had had a bath. I was appreciative of this hospitality in the male seraglio of the kasbah of Tarna, bandit chieftain of the Tahari.

'Hurry, Slave,' said the tall, dark-haired girl, bare-armed, in an ankle-length, flowing white garment. 'The mistress will be ready for you soon.' She held four large, heavy snowy towels, each of a different absorbency. To one side another girl, clad similarly, was replacing in a rack bath oils, with which I had been rubbed prior to entering the second sunken bath. I had now rinsed them from my body, but I was not eager to leave the water. I reveled in it.

Hassan, in a brief, white-silk garment, sat cross-legged nearby. 'You do not appear too dismal,' said he to me.

'Is your mistress, Tarna, pretty?' I asked the tall dark-haired girl.

'Emerge and towel yourself,' said the girl.

'I can well use the bath,' I said to her, grinning.

'That is true,' she conceded. 'Hurry!'

Four days ago, at dawn, Tarna, at the head of her men, left the Oasis of the Battle of Red Rock in flames. Only its citadel, its kasbah, had been impregnable. Its palm groves had been cut down, its gardens destroyed, four of its five public wells caved in and filled. The other well, by too many men, had been defended with too much vigor. There had been some four or five hundred raiders. When they left Red Rock their kaiila had been heavy with loot. Some forty female slaves, coffled, braceleted, had been taken. Two males, too, had been taken, myself and Hassan. As Tarna had left Red Rock, not looking back, straight in the saddle, burnoose swelling in the morning wind over the sand, I had marched beside her, stripped, wrists manacled behind my back, chained by the neck to her stirrup. Hassan, similarly secured, trudged at the stirrup of one of her lieutenants. Before the sun was high and the sands burning we reached her loot wagons, kept in the desert. There Hassan and I, locked in slave hoods, and chained, were thrown into one of the wagons, with other loot. Even the female slaves, when fastened in their wagons were hooded. The location of the kasbah of Tarna, bandit chieftain of the Tahari, her lair, was secret. We had reached its vicinity this morning, shortly after dawn. We, and the other prisoners, had been unhooded. Then, again, Hassan and I had been chained at stirrups. I at Tarna's own, by her boot. 'Where are we?' I had asked Hassan. The kaiila crop of a guard had struck me across the mouth. 'I do not know,' had said Hassan. He, too, was struck. The female prisoners were ranged, in coffle, between two riders, one at the head and one at the foot of the chain. A chain from the neck of the first, some ten feet in length, ascended to the pommel of the lead guard; a chain from the neck of the last, some ten feet in length ascended to the pommel of the guard bringing up the rear. They were marched this way that residents and the garrison of the kasbah, in the great yard, behind the gate, regardless of the side on which they stood, might, with unimpeded vision, see the flesh loot well displayed. The canvas covers of the wagons, too, were thrown back, that the goods taken at Red Rock could be seen in their abundance and richness.

As the raiders returned, from their column, by mirror, a signal was flashed to the kasbah. On receipt of this signal a pennon, a victory pennon, was raised on the gate tower. We saw the gate swinging open.

Suddenly Tarna kicked her kaiila in the flanks and bolted from the column. The chain tore at the back of my neck and I was thrown from my feet and dragged through the brush and dust, twisting. She rode for a hundred yards and reined in the kaiila. 'Have you stamina? Can you run?' she asked. I looked at her, coughing, covered with dust, cut by brush. 'On your feet!' she said, her eyes bright over the purple veil. 'I will teach you to crawl,' she said. I struggled to my feet. She walked the kaiila, then, widely circling, increased its pace, gradually, smoothly. 'Excellent!' she cried. I was of the warriors. She increased the pace. 'Excellent,' she cried, 'excellent!' Even among warriors I had been agile, swift. My heart pounded; I fought for breath. More than a pasang she ran me into the desert. 'Incredible!' she laughed. Then, laughing, she kicked the kaiila and I was again hurled from my feet, and wrists manacled behind me, was dragged, rolling, twisting, behind her. After a quarter of a pasang she let me regain my feet, then, cantering, I bloody and stumbling, body shaking, neck burning, vision black at the edges, returned to the head of her column; I sank to my knees in the dust below her stirrup; 'Look up,' said she, 'Slave'; I looked up; 'I will make you crawl,' she said; then she said, 'On your feet.' I got up. She seemed startled. She did not think that I could yet stand. 'You are strong,' she said. I felt the tip of her scimitar beneath my chin, forcing it up. 'I enjoy running men at my stirrup,' she said. 'You are strong. I shall enjoy taming you.' Then she turned in the saddle and, with her scimitar, indicated her distant kasbah. 'Onward!' she cried, and the column, with loot and slaves, made its way toward the high, arched gate of her desert fortress. To my interest I noted that this was but one of two kasbahs. Another, even larger, lay to its east some two pasangs. I did not know to whom this larger kasbah belonged.

Soon Tarna, with her men, and loot and slaves, entered the great gate of her fortress. She lifted her arms and scimitar, acknowledging the cheering.

'Hurry, Slave,' said the tall, dark-haired girl, bare-armed, in her ankle-length, flowing white garment. 'The mistress will be ready for you soon.'

'Is your mistress pretty?' I asked her. I had not, because of the purple sand veil worn by Tarna, which she had looped loosely about her face, well looked upon her. What I had seen of her seemed to me not only pretty, but beautiful. I had little doubt that she was a proud, striking female. I had not been able, of course, to well judge, in her mannish garb, and burnoose, the lineaments of her body. The beauty of a woman can only be judged well when she is naked, as female slaves are sold.

'She is as ugly as a sand sleen,' snapped the dark-haired

199

girl. 'Hurry!'

'We have never seen our mistress,' said the other girl, in long garment, who was in charge of the bath oils.

'Hurry, Slave,' said the first girl, 'or we will call the guards, to have you beaten!' She looked anxiously about. I had little doubt that it might be she who would be held responsible if I were not ready on time for the pleasure of the mistress. I saw the other girl laying out a light tunic of red silk, and a necklace of yellow, rounded beads, which I supposed was for me. 'Get out now,' she said, 'and towel yourself!'

I rolled back in the water. I had been well fed. I had slept much since morning. I felt refreshed, and rested. I had a long kaiila ride before me tonight.

'What,' I asked the girl, 'is the fate of the female slaves taken from Red Rock?'

'Even now,' she said, 'under guard, in wagons, they are bound for the markets of Tor, where they will be sold.'

'Are there, then, few girls kept in the fortress?' I asked.

'Girls are kept, of course, some girls,' she said, '– for the men.'

'Where?' I asked.

'On the lower levels of the kasbah,' she said.

'But you are not kept for the men?' I asked.

'Of course not!' she said, angrily.

There were several of Tarna's males sitting about, in silken tunics, some with jewelry, curious about Hassan and myself. Some of them were rather sullen. The mistress had not, this night, chosen one of them for her evening's pleasure. One of them, earlier, a fellow in a ruby necklace, had said, 'I am more handsome, surely, than he,' referring to me. I supposed it were true. On the other hand, Hassan and myself had a certain advantage, I supposed, in freshness and novelty. I was pleased that I had been selected for the night. I found the kasbah's seraglio pleasant, but I did not wish to remain here longer than necessary.

'I do not understand how it is that I, Hassan,' Hassan had said, 'was not first picked for the pleasure of the mistress.'

'Doubtless I am the most fascinating,' I said to him.

'There is no accounting for the taste of women,' he had said.

'That is true,' I said. 'I have noted that Alyena much prefers you to me.'

'That is true,' he said.

200

'She is, of course,' I pointed out, 'only slave.'

'It is true that she is only a slave,' he said, 'but she, though slave, is an extremely intelligent young woman.'

'That is true,' I admitted. The slave raiders of the Kurii, the Others, selected, among other things, high intelligence in their victims. Their two major criteria, as nearly as I could determine, were femininity and intelligence. These two traits, hormonal and intellectual, almost always produce a vulnerable, fragile, alert, sensitive beauty, one almost ready for the collar. Extremely intelligent, feminine girls, as most Goreans know, make excellent slaves. Goreans show little interest either in stupid women, though some are sexually attractive, or in mules. Stupid women are too stupid to be good slaves; mules are not even women. But the true female, the awakened, helpless prisoner of her instincts and blood, with a fine mind, a deep, lovely, sensitive mind, imaginative and inventive, is the one the Goreans want, head down, at their feet. What man would want his collar on anything less precious? 'Yet, Tarna,' I suggested, 'does not seem to be obtuse.'

'No,' he admitted. 'That is true.'

'And it is I who have been first chosen,' I pointed out.

'There is no accounting for the taste of women,' he said. 'Alyena,' he said, 'who is better, prefers me.'

'I have not seen Tarna stripped and tied at the slave ring,' I said. 'I do not know if Alyena is better or not.'

'Let us assume she is,' proposed Hassan.

'Very well,' I said.

'She prefers me,' he said.

'There is no accounting for the taste of women,' I said.

At this point I had been summoned by the two bare-armed, white-garbed girls, for my bath.

'Do you object, Ali?' asked one of the silken fellows.

'No, I do not,' snapped the girl in the white garment, with towels.

I had not understood, for a moment, to whom he might be speaking. The girl, however, had answered him. I recalled I had asked her if she were kept for the men, and that she had responded, angrily, 'Of course not!' He had then asked, 'Do you object, Ali?'

I swam to the side of the bath and looked up at her. 'What is your name?' I asked.

She stepped back. 'Ali,' said she.

201

'That is a man's name,' I said. 'Or a boy's.'

'My mistress,' said the girl, 'gives me what name she pleases.' She was angry.

The fellow who had spoken before laughed.

'Be silent, Fina!' she snapped, sharply.

His face turned white. He put his head down. 'Yes, Mistress,' he said.

'Fina,' I said to her, 'is a woman's name, or a girl's.'

'It pleases the mistress,' said she, 'to give us what names she pleases.' She glanced at the males about, in their silk. 'Each,' said she, 'all of them have such names, the names of girls.' She glared at Hassan, and myself. 'You two, too, will be so designated!' Then she cried, 'Go! Go to your alcoves, Slaves! Go!'

The men, some of them frightened, with the exception of Hassan who sat, puzzled, by the side of the bath, scurried to their tiny alcoves.

The two girls, in white garments, as I had come to understand, were dominant in the seraglio, rather in the nature of eunuchs, imposing order upon it and keeping its slaves in harmonious discipline. Their word, imperiously delivered, with the confidence of unquestioned command, doubtless backed by the whips and scimitars of male guards outside, served as law to the inmates of Tarna's seraglio; when they spoke, men obeyed; when they spoke sharply, men feared; in the seraglio, backed by the power of Tarna's guards, these two beautiful women were dominant over the men; they, particularly the taller, dark-haired one, obviously despised the silken males in her charge; openly she held them, to their misery, in contempt.

We heard the outer gate of the seraglio, at the far end of the corridor, being pounded on.

'Hurry!' cried the girl. 'They are coming for you! Get out! Towel yourself!'

I reached out and, from the bath, seized her right ankle. The other girl, she who laid out the red-silk tunic, the yellow beads, gasped. I looked up at the tall girl. 'You do not wear a collar,' I said.

'No,' she said. Then she said, 'Release my ankle, bold sleen!'

'This does not seem the ankle of a male,' I said. I held her ankle in my grip.

'Release me!' she said.

About the ankle there was, welded, an iron ring. 'What is this?' I asked her.

202

'It is thus that Tarna marks her female seraglio slaves!' said the girl. 'Release me!'

The pounding was louder. 'Release me!' she cried. 'I will have you whipped!'

'But then I may not be ready in time for the mistress,' I said.

'I will have you beaten to the bone tomorrow!' she hissed.

'Then, tonight,' I said, 'I will have to explain to the mistress why I cannot much please her.'

The girl turned white. 'You seduced me,' I explained.

'No! No!' she cried.

'What were you called as a woman?' I asked.

'Lana!' she cried out in agony. She tried to pull away. 'Release me!'

We heard the outer gate, by guards, being opened. 'They will be here in a moment!' she cried. 'Please!'

I released her ankle, and lifted myself, dripping, from the bath.

She thrust the towels at me, almost in a frenzy. We heard the arriving guards outside the inner door conversing with those who guarded it.

'Towel yourself!' she said.

I lifted my arms. 'Towel me, Lana,' said I.

'Sleen!' she cried.

I looked about at the seraglio. It was lovely. There were high separated, decorated columns, many arches, much carving, rich hangings, much tile, floors marbled and mosaiced, too. It was lofty, spacious, beautiful. I regretted I did not have more time to spend here.

'Sleen!' wept the girl, beginning to rub me with the first of the towels. 'Help me!' she cried to the other girl, who was frightened.

'No,' I said. 'Only you, Lana.'

Weeping, furious, Lana applied the towel to my body. 'Oh!' she cried. For I then had her in my arms. I reached behind her body. She put her head back. 'No!' she cried. 'Are you mad? I am your seraglio mistress! No!' The garment, hooks broken, fell to her ankles.

'You do not have the body, either, of a male,' I observed.

'Please,' she wept.

I kissed her on each breast, for they were beautiful.

'I am your seraglio mistress!' she wept.

203

I kissed her fully on the mouth, holding her helplessly. 'No,' I said, 'you are only a beautiful slave girl.'

I released her and she, clumsily, in haste, applied the towels to my body. When she had finished she was at my feet, drying them. I lifted her to her feet and put her back against one of the cool, narrow marble columns supporting the arched roof of the seraglio. I stood close to her, our lips but an inch parted. With my finger tips, on either side, I caressed the sides of her throat. 'This throat,' I said, 'is aristocratic and beautiful. It would look well in a collar.' Her eyes met mine. 'I wish it wore yours,' she said. '– Master.' I kissed her.

I heard the bolt sliding back on the inner door. The other girl threw me the red-silk tunic and I slipped it on, dropping the yellow necklace inside the tunic.

The door opened. Two guards stood there, in purple and yellow burnoose.

'Is the slave ready?' asked one of the guards, looking about. 'What is going on here?' asked the other, surveying the exposed beauty of Lana, the seraglio mistress. She, frightened, hands before her mouth, pressed back against the column.

'She is preparing to bathe,' I told them. I went to her and took her by the left arm, over the elbow, and the right ankle, and upended the beauty, headfirst, into the pool.

I glanced to Hassan, and to the other girl. 'I shall return shortly,' I told him.

'Very well,' he said, edging toward the other girl.

'The mistress,' said one of the guards, 'does not finish with her males shortly.'

Lana's head, sputtering, blinking, emerged from the bath.

'She will tonight,' I told him. Then I turned to Hassan, 'Be ready,' I told him. 'We have a long kaiila ride this night.'

'Very well,' he said. The guards looked at me as though I might be mad. He was now standing almost directly behind the other girl, she who had handled the bath oils.

'Let us hurry,' I said to the guards. 'We must not keep the mistress waiting.'

'He is eager,' laughed one of the guards.

'He is a fool,' said the other.

Lana, dripping, head down, crawled from the bath. I saw Hassan measuring the distance between the two girls.

I led the way, swiftly, through the inner door of the seraglio. 'Is your mistress pretty?' I asked one of the guards, who was

204

hurrying to follow.

'She is as ugly as a sand sleen,' he growled.

He bolted the door behind him, shutting and locking the seraglio from the outside. There were two guards, I noted, at the door. Down the corridor, some fifty yards of tile and hangings, there was the outer door. This was knocked upon, and, from the outside, opened. There were two guards there, too.

'Come now,' I said, 'truly, is your mistress pretty?'

'She is as ugly as a sand sleen,' said the guard.

'I am Tarna,' said the woman. She reclined on the wide couch, resting on one elbow, regarding me.

I looked about the room. I went to the window, and looked down, into the courtyard.

'The drop,' she said, 'is some seventy feet.'

I examined the walls, the door.

'The door,' said she, 'by the guards outside, opens only to my signal.'

'Come,' said she, 'stand at the foot of my couch.'

'We are alone?' I asked.

'Guards stand outside the door,' she said, puzzled.

'That is acceptable,' I said.

I regarded her. 'You are a strange slave,' she said. She reclined, resting, on one elbow. She wore a soft gown, flowing, yellow, long, of Turian silk; it was sheer and, with its deep neckline, and about the hips, well betrayed her. Her hair was black, and long, and rich, and well displayed against the yellow cushion behind her.

I was pleased to see that she was not as ugly as a sand sleen. I was pleased to see, contrariwise, that she was stunningly beautiful. Her eyes were very dark.

'I own you,' she said.

'I have a long kaiila ride ahead of me tonight,' I told her.

'You are a strange slave,' she said.

'There is another kasbah nearby,' I said, 'one which lies within two pasangs. Whose kasbah is it?'

'It does not matter,' she said. 'Do you like being a slave?' she asked.

There were red silken sheets on the great couch, on which she reclined. At its foot there was a slave ring.

'It is my understanding, following merchant law, and Tahari custom,' I said, 'that I am not a slave, for though I am a prisoner, I have been neither branded nor collared, nor have I performed a gesture of submission.'

'My bold slave,' she said.

I shrugged.

'Do you find me pleasing,' she asked, 'out of mannish desert garb?'

I regarded her. 'Yes,' I said.

In her hands I saw she held a kaiila crop. 'I am mistress,' she said.

'You are quite beautiful,' I said. 'You should be a slave girl.'

She put back her head and laughed. 'Bold, bold slave,' said she. 'I like you! You seem different from the others. Perhaps I will not, even, give you a girl's name.'

'Perhaps not,' I admitted.

'I have wondered, sometimes,' said she, 'what it would be like to be a woman.'

'Surely you are a woman,' I said.

'Am I attractive?' she asked.

'Yes,' I said.

'Do you know that, with a scimitar,' she asked, 'I am quite skilled, more skilled than any man?'

'No,' I said, 'I did not know that.'

'But I have wondered sometimes,' she said, '– what it would be like to be a woman.'

I smiled.

'A true woman,' she said, '– at the mercy of a man.'

'Oh?' I asked. I looked about the room. There were, here and there, in coffers, scarves, and, from which the hangings depended, suitable cords.

The guards would have to be dealt with.

Then her manner changed. She became arrogant, angry. 'Serve me wine, Slave,' she said.

I went to the wine table and, from the curved vessel, poured a small cup of wine. I gave this to her. She sat, on the edge of the couch, and sipped it. Then her eyes became irritated. 'Orders I gave,' said she, 'that you were to be presented to me this night in yellow slave beads. I see that I must have the seraglio mistress beaten in the morning.'

'No,' I said. 'I have them here, inside my tunic.'

'Put them on,' she said.

'No,' I said.

She put down the wine. 'No?' she asked.

'No,' I said.

She laughed. 'But I may have you whipped,' she said, 'tortured, destroyed.'

'I doubt it,' I said.

'Kneel to the whip,' she said. She lifted the crop.

'No,' I said.

She stood back. She did not attempt to strike me. 'I do not understand,' she said. 'Surely you must understand that, in this room, in this kasbah, in the Tahari, you are mine, to do with as I please. I have complete power over you! You are my slave, absolutely!'

'No,' I said.

'What a fantastic slave you are,' she said. 'I do not know if I should have you killed or not.' She looked at me. 'Are you not afraid?'

'No,' I said.

'You are different,' she said, 'different from all the others. I must handle you carefully. I do not even know if it would be wise to break you, to make you cringe and grovel.' She seemed lost in thought.

I poured myself a small cup of the wine, and drank it, replacing the cup on the table.

'You are beautiful,' I said, looking at her. 'Your lips,' I said, 'are interesting.' They were a bit full, protruding, pouting. They would crush well beneath a man's teeth.

'How is that?' she asked.

'It would be easy,' I said, 'to bring blood from them in a master's kiss.'

Her eyes flashed. 'Go to the slave ring!' she hissed.

'No,' I said.

She stood back, as though stunned. 'I will call the guards,' she said.

'Do so,' I suggested.

But it was clear she did not wish to do this.

'You do not obey me,' she said.

'You are the woman,' I said. 'It is you who must obey.'

'Insolent sleen!' she cried, turning away, gown swirling. 'Insolent sleen!' Then she faced me. 'I shall call the guards, now,' she said, 'to enter and destroy you!'

'But you will not then learn,' I said, 'what it is to be a woman, a true woman – at the mercy of men.'

She went to the window angrily, furiously, and looked out, over the walls of the kasbah to the sands silvered by the light of the three moons. Overhead the stars were bright.

She turned to face me, fists clenched, her right fist on the kaiila crop.

'Surely you have been curious to learn, sometime, what it would be like to be a true woman – at the mercy of men.'

'Never!' she cried. 'Never! I am Tarna. I do not have such thoughts! I am Tarna! I am Tarna!'

She turned away, to the window.

'Call the guards,' I said.

She turned to face me. 'Teach me to be a woman,' she said.

'Come here,' I said. She came and stood before me, angry. I put out my hand. She looked at it. Then slowly she put the long, supple, leather kaiila crop into my hand.

'Would you dare to strike me?' she asked.

'Certainly,' I said.

'Is it your intention to strike me?' she asked.

'If you do not obey,' I said.

'You would,' she said. 'You would!'

'Yes,' I said.

'I will obey,' she said.

I threw the kaiila crop to one side, to the floor. It slid along the tiles. She watched it.

'Fetch me the crop,' I said.

She did so, and again placed it in my hand. 'Turn about,' I told her. 'Go to the couch, lie upon it.'

Her shoulders shook with defiance. But then she turned about, and went to the couch, lying upon it.

I let her lie there for a moment. I watched her eyes. I had little doubt, from her eyes, and her breathing, that if I were to touch her body, intimately, my hand would be hot and soaked with the helplessness of her arousal. Seldom had I seen a woman so ready.

Tarna, I gathered, had waited long to be a woman.

I threw aside the kaiila crop.

'Do you not want the crop,' she asked, 'to discipline me?'

'Fetch it,' I said.

She rose from the bed, scarcely able to stand, bent over, so much was her need upon her.

'No,' I said.

She looked at me.

208

'On your knees,' I said, 'in your teeth.'

She crawled to the crop and, putting her head down, sideways, took it in her teeth. She, on her hands and knees, brought it to me. I took it roughly from her mouth. 'Get on the couch,' I told her.

'Yes, Warrior,' she whispered, again crawling upon the scarlet sheets. I put the crop beside the couch, at hand. I doubted that it would be necessary to use it.

I went to one of the coffers and picked out two scarves.

'What are they for?' she asked.

'You will see,' I told her.

I dropped them to the pillow beside her. 'You made me fetch a kaiila crop,' she said, 'on my hands and knees, and in my mouth, as though I might be a she-sleen.'

'You are a she-sleen,' I said. 'You will be treated as one.'

'I am not in the habit,' she said, 'of fetching kaiila crops in my teeth for men.'

'If you knew more men,' I said, 'true men, the experience would be less unfamiliar.'

'I see,' she said.

'The she-sleen,' I said, 'is a sinuous and beautiful animal, and very dangerous. One cannot show weakness with such an animal. They will turn and rend the master. One must keep them under perfect discipline.'

'And if one keeps the she-sleen under perfect discipline?' asked Tarna.

'Then,' said I, 'it is a superb, and beautiful, and most pleasing pet.'

'And I am the she-sleen?' she asked.

'Yes,' I said.

'And,' she asked, 'am I, your she-sleen, to be kept under perfect discipline?'

'Of course,' I said.

'You are a beast,' she said.

'Yes,' I said.

'If I were a she-sleen,' she said, snuggling back into the pillow, 'I think I would like a master such as you.'

'You are a she-sleen,' I said.

'And you?' she asked.

'I am your master,' I said.

'Keep me under perfect discipline, Master,' she said.

'I will,' I said.

She looked up at me, her lips parted, her eyes bright.

'I give you my permission,' she said, 'to do with me what you want.'

'I do not need your permission,' I said.

Her hands were beside her head, on the pillow. 'What are you going to do with me?' she asked.

'You will see,' I told her. I stood beside the couch, looming over her, looking down upon her.

I saw she wished to say something. I waited. She rose up, on her elbows.

'I have never felt this way before,' she said.

I shrugged. I had no interest in her feelings.

'You are different from the others,' she whispered, 'the docile, weak ones.'

'It is you, a female,' I said, 'who is weak, and it will be you who will be docile.'

'A she-sleen?' she smiled.

'You are not truly a she-sleen,' I said.

'Oh?' she asked. 'What am I, truly?'

'What do you feel like?' I asked.

'I have strange feelings,' she said. 'I have never felt them before.' She looked at me. 'I feel, before you,' she said, 'weak, vulnerable. I want to be overwhelmed by you, and held. I imagine a slave girl must have some such feelings, before a strong master.'

I smiled.

'You are so different,' she said, 'so different from the others, the weak, docile ones.'

'It is you,' I told her, 'who is weak.' I held her hands down, pinned, under mine, beside her head. She could not free herself.

'Yes,' she said, 'I am weak.' She smiled up at me.

'And it is you,' I told her, 'who will be docile.'

'Yes,' she said, 'I will be docile.'

I freed her hands, and looked down at her.

'Yes,' she said, 'I am helpless. I will be docile.'

'You would make a pretty slave,' I said.

'Would I?' she asked.

'Yes,' I said.

'What are you going to do with me?' she asked.

'You will see,' I said.

'I beg your favor,' said she. 'Warrior.'

'What do you want?' I asked.

'Tonight – please, Warrior,' she said, 'tonight let me be truly as a female slave. Treat me not as your mistress, who owns you, but as only a slave girl, whom you own, at your mercy. Treat me as a slave girl! Please, Warrior, treat me as a slave girl!'

'Oh?' I asked.

'Teach me,' she begged, 'to be a woman!'

'I do not have time,' I said.

She looked at me, wildly.

'I have a long kaiila ride ahead of me this night,' I said. One of the scarves, which I had been surreptitiously wadding at the side, I thrust swiftly, deeply, into her mouth. She could not speak, but twisted, only tiny, fumbling sounds coming from her mouth. Kneeling across her, pinning her arms to her sides, I then, with the other scarf, tied the wadding securely in her mouth. Holding both her hands in my left hand I then dragged her from the couch to the side of the room where, with my right hand, I tore down some of the soft cords used to arrange the voluminous, decorative drapes and hangings which adorned the chamber. I then threw her to the slave ring and, with the cords, tied her wrists behind her back, and then, passing the cord through the ring, crossed and tied her ankles together, pulling them rather close to her bound wrists. I then put her on her knees, bound hand and foot, at the slave ring. She struggled to face me, squirming, her eyes wild with rage.

I looked to the door, considering the distance.

Swiftly I pulled the binding of the wadding free. I then, moving swiftly, so as to be in place, went to the door. Head-down, furious, Tarna fought to expel the wadding. It took her a moment longer to do so than I had anticipated, but it did not disarrange my plans. She spat out the wet, heavy scarf. She threw back her head. 'Guards!' she cried. 'Guards!'

In a moment the door flew open and the two guards, scimitars drawn, entered the room.

They saw Tarna at the slave ring. They stopped, startled. I was behind them. I took the neck of each and, in the instant before they could react, struck together their heads, felling both.

I closed the door.

Tarna was looking at me, wildly. 'You tricked me,' she

cried, squirming at the ring.

I thrust the wadding back, deeply, in her mouth, securing it with the other scarf.

'Yes,' I said.

I dragged the two unconscious guards to the side. I took the garments of one, and tied both, gagging them, to one side. One of the luxurious hangings I flung over them.

I moved swiftly to the door, and, opening it a crack, reconnoitered.

I looked back to Tarna. She was enraged. She struggled. She had, of course, been bound by a warrior. She was helpless. Near the red silk I had cast aside, when donning the desert garments of the guard, on the tiles, I saw the vulgar, wooden, rounded, yellow slave beads, the necklace, which I had not chosen to permit being placed upon me.

Tarna shrank back. She shook her head. I scooped up the beads, which were in five strands, and, kneeling behind her, pulling down her gown a bit, from the shoulders, to better display them, fastened them tightly about her throat. I then set a large mirror across the room from her, that she might see how beautiful she was. 'Do not struggle, overmuch,' I warned her, 'or, when your men come, they will find you stripped to the thighs.'

I could not make out what she said, but it is perhaps just as well.

'Perhaps I shall return someday,' I said, 'to make you a slave.'

She squirmed in the cords, writhing, enraged, then stopped suddenly, furious; in another move she would have stripped herself.

I blew her a kiss, in the Gorean fashion, brushing the kiss with my finger tips toward her.

Her eyes were wild over the gag, furious, enraged.

Perhaps I would return someday and make her a slave. I thought that she would make a pleasing slave girl.

I shut the door upon her.

I made my way, swiftly, through the palace, recalling the way from my being conducted earlier to the boudoir of this kasbah's chieftainess, the much-feared Tarna.

It was late and I encountered few guards. The sand veil was high about my face, as though I were a messenger incognito. The garments were sufficient to permit me passage.

212

At the outer door of the seraglio I demanded entrance, to fetch the slave, Hassan, to the quarters of Tarna.

I was admitted. At the inner door, I was challenged.

'I have this letter of passage,' I said, reaching into my cloak. The letter of passage was the back of my hand, flying up and to the right, while, at the same time, with my left fist, I drove into the diaphragm of the man on my left. He could make no sound, doubled up. Before the man on my right could recover, or unsheath his weapon, I had struck him unconscious; I then, at my leisure, did the same with the other fellow. I gagged and tied both of them.

I then swung open the inner door to the seraglio.

'Greetings,' said Hassan.

'Greetings,' I said.

'Did all go well?' he asked.

'Yes,' I said. 'Is all in order here?' I asked.

'It seems so,' he said.

I heard the muffled sounds of the two seraglio mistresses, Lana and she in whose charge had been the oils of the bath.

They had been bound and gagged with strips of their white garments. They stood, naked, each backed against one of the slender, lofty, cool marble pillars which supported the roof of the seraglio; their wrists were fastened behind them, about the pillars. Each uttered tiny sounds of protest; their eyes were wild over their gags.

There was a reddish stain down the interior of the left thigh of the one girl, she who had handled the oils of the bath.

'She was virginal,' I remarked.

'Yes,' said Hassan.

'What of this one?' I asked Hassan, indicating Lana.

'I tested her,' said Hassan. 'She, too, is virginal. I left her for you.'

Lana shrank back against the pillar.

'What have we here?' I asked. I noted one silken fellow, he with the ruby necklace, trying furtively to slip about the side of the room to the door.

He broke into a run, but I managed to trip him, and Hassan leaped upon him and carried him, squirming to the bath. 'We will be beaten,' whimpered the fellow. 'Give the alarm!' he shouted to his fellow mates. Two or three stood about, but they did not cry out. Hassan took the fellow and threw him on his belly by the bath and held his head under water, for

213

about an Ehn. When he pulled the fellow's head up, he said to him, 'You might be drowned in the bath. Such accidents can happen.' Then he thrust his head again under the water. When he pulled it up the second time the fellow cried out for mercy. Hassan threw him to two of the other males. 'If he attempts to give the alarm,' said Hassan, 'drown him.' 'Very well,' said one of the other fellows. I gathered there was little lost affection for the fellow in the ruby necklace in the seraglio of Tarna. He was, I had learned, a weak fellow, an informer, one constantly alert to opportunities to ingratiate himself with the mistress who despised him, one of her most obsequious pets, held in contempt by all. 'You may blame his drowning on us, of course,' said Hassan. 'Naturally,' said one of the silken fellows. The fellow in the ruby necklace shuddered. 'I will be silent,' he said. 'You will be silent, or be silenced,' said one of the fellows. 'Remember,' said another, 'whatever happens, eventually, you will be put back with us.' 'I will remember,' said the fellow. 'I will do as you wish.'

'Take him to an alcove,' I said. 'Bind and gag him. Then, too, retire to your alcoves.'

'Very well,' they said, retiring, taking with them the stumbling, miserable fellow in the ruby necklace.

The seraglio, then, seemed empty, silent. We heard the torches crackle.

I looked again to Lana. She shrank back. She, the seraglio mistress, unprotected, bound, gagged, helpless, was alone with us.

'I left her for you,' said Hassan.

Swiftly I untied her hands and then retied them, so that they were above her head and behind it, fastened at the sides of the pillar. I then, lifting her, lowered her gently to the tiles. She squirmed, helplessly. By the ankles I pulled her as far from the pillar as the bonds on her wrists, fashioned by Hassan from the strips from her white, removed clothing, would permit. She lifted one knee. I thrust her knees apart. She lifted her head, trying to put her gagged mouth against me. I saw pain in her eyes. I pulled down the gag, for a moment, and let her free herself of the wadding. 'I love you, Master,' she whispered. 'I love you!' I kissed her, thrust back the wadding, and regagged her.

I rose to my feet.

'You have ruined her, I judge,' said Hassan, 'as an effective

214

mistress of the seraglio.'

The girl was trying to put her leg against me, reaching for me. I took her ankle, and crouching, kissed it, on the top, and then pressed my lips to the bottom of her foot, near the instep, then beneath and behind the shin, then again, twice, near the bottom of the foot, at the instep.

I judged her responses, the movements of her eyes. 'Yes,' I said, 'I expect so.'

Lana lifted her body to me, helplessly, 'I will guarantee, my dear,' I said to her, 'that, hereafter, you will be given to men.' I then, with her virgin blood, on her belly, traced the Tahari slave mark. Seeing this, the mark of a free man's satisfaction with her, I had little doubt that Tarna would dismiss her from the seraglio, sending her in chains to the lower levels, where, with low-order slave girls, she might be used to serve the lusts of her raiders. Lana's eyes shone with pleasure. I had found her acceptable. I had, furthermore, indicated this upon her flesh. She would now be done with the seraglio. She would now have to do with free men, with true men, she the slave. She lay bound and gagged, proudly. She stretched her body, as she could, luxuriantly, reveling in the sensation in her body and the feel of the coolness of the tiles upon her flesh.

I noted that Hassan, following my example, had also indicated his pleasure on the flesh of the other girl.

'We must leave soon,' he said.

'There are two guards outside the outer door,' I said. 'They will expect me, soon, to bring you through.'

'Surely,' said he, 'I should be better dressed for riding in the night.'

'One of the guards outside the outer door,' I said, 'may perhaps be persuaded to loan you garments, weapons and accoutrements.'

'He would be a good fellow, indeed,' said Hassan.

'They seemed to me good fellows,' I said.

THIRTEEN

AN ACQUAINTANCE IS RENEWED

My left foot broke through the crust of salt. 'Kill us! Kill us!' I heard a man cry. I heard the stroke of the lash behind me, and another cry, long, miserable. My left leg, to the thigh, slipped into the brittle layers of crust. I fell, unable to break my fall because of the manacles confining my wrists at my waist, fastened to the loop of chain, burning in the sun, about my waist. I could not see, for the slave hood. My back, and body, burned. Our feet, to the knees, were wrapped in leather, but, in many places, in making our way across the crusts, the weight of our bodies forced us deeper than this into the crusts. The salt, working its way into the leather wrappings, found its way to the feet. I could feel blood inside the wrappings. Some men, though I did not know how many, had gone lame. They were no longer with the chain. They had been left behind, their throats cut, lying in the crusts. The chain on the collar at my throat jerked. I lay still for a precious moment in the burning crusts. The lash struck me. The chain jerked again and I struggled to my feet. Again the lash fell. I stumbled on. The path is broken by a kaiila, whose long, haired legs, with broad pads, break through, and lift themselves free, of the crusts.

'I did not think a woman could hold you,' had said the man.

Scarcely had Hassan and I, clad in the garments of guards, astride kaiila taken from the stables of Tarna's kasbah, emerged from the fortress's gate than, on the path to Red Rock, clouds of riders had swept before us. Wheeling our kaiila we had sought escape, only to discover we were surrounded. In the bright moonlight of Gor's three moons we turned. On every side were riders, many with crossbows.

'We have been waiting for you,' said one of the riders. 'Will it be necessary to kill the kaiila?' The riders were veiled in red.

'No,' had said Hassan. He had disarmed himself, and dismounted. I followed his example.

Ropes were put on our throat; our hands were tied behind our backs.

On foot, among our captors, tethered by the neck to saddle rings, bound, we trudged to the larger of the pair of kasbahs, that other than Tarna's. The journey was not long, only some two pasangs.

At the foot of the great gate we stopped. The walls were more than seventy feet high. The battlements, square and looming, of which there were seventeen, assuming general symmetry and counting the two flanking the central gate, soared to ninety feet. The front wall was some four hundred feet in length; the side walls were some four hundred and fifty feet in length. The walls in such a kasbah are several feet thick, formed of stones and mud brick; the walls in this kasbah, as in most, too, were covered with a sheen of plaster, whitish pink, which, in the years of exposure to the heat and sun, as is common, had flaked abundantly.

'You are Tarl Cabot,' said the leader of the men who had captured us, indicating me.

I shrugged. Hassan looked at me.

'And you,' said the man, indicating Hassan, 'are Hassan, the bandit.'

'It is possible,' admitted Hassan.

'It is as naked prisoners that you will enter this kasbah,' said the man.

We were stripped by the scimitar.

Naked, bound, standing in the sand, tethered, surrounded by kaiila and riders, we looked up at the lofty walls of flaking plaster, the battlements flanking the great gate. The moonlight reflected from the walls of pinkish, flaking plaster.

Two of the kaiila snorted, pawing the sand.

The great gate, on its heavy hinges, opening in the middle, slowly swung back.

We faced the opening.

'You two have been troublesome,' said the rider. 'You will be troublesome no more.'

We could see the whitish courtyard, its sand, beyond the gate, lamps set in walls.

'Whose kasbah is this?' I asked.

'It can be only,' said Hassan, 'the kasbah of the Guard of the Dunes.'

'That of the Salt Ubar?' I asked.

'That,' agreed Hassan. I had heard of the Salt Ubar, or the Guard of the Dunes. The location of his kasbah is secret. Probably, other than his own men, only some few hundred know of it, primarily merchants high in the salt trade, and few of them would know its exact location. Whereas salt may be obtained from sea water and by burning seaweed, as is sometimes done in Torvaldsland, and there are various districts on Gor where salt, solid or in solution, may be obtained, by far the most extensive and richest of known Gor's salt deposits are to be found concentrated in the Tahari. Tahari salt accounts, in its varieties, I would suspect, for some twenty percent of the salt and salt-related products, such as medicines and antiseptics, preservatives, cleansers, bleaches, bottle glass, which contains soda ash, taken from salt, and tanning chemicals, used on known Gor. Salt is a trading commodity *par excellence*. There are areas on Gor where salt serves as a currency, being weighed and exchanged much as precious metals. The major protection and control of the Tahari salt, of course, lies in its remoteness, the salt districts, of which there are several, being scattered and isolated in the midst of the dune country, in the long caravan journeys required, and the difficulty or impossibility of obtaining it without knowing the trails, the ways of the desert. A lesser protection and control of the salt, though a not unformidable one, lies in the policing of the desert by the Salt Ubar, or the Guard of the Dunes. The support of the kasbah of the Salt Ubar comes from fees supplied by high salt merchants, the measure of which fees, of course, they include in their wholesale pricings to lesser distributors. The function of the kasbah of the Salt Ubar, thus, officially, is to administer and control the salt districts, on behalf of the Tahari salt merchants, primarily by regulating access to the districts, checking the papers and credentials of merchants, inspecting caravans, keeping records of the commerce, etc. For example, caravans between Red Rock, and certain other oases, and the salt districts, will travel under an escort of the Guard of the Dunes. Many salt caravans, incidentally, travel only between the districts and local oases, while others travel between the local oases and the distant points, often culminating with Kasra or Tor. Some caravans, of course, journey through from the distant points to the salt districts, accepting the danger and inconvenience of trekking the dune country, but thereby avoiding the higher charges of picking up salt from the storehouses in the local oases. Even these caravans, of course, once in the dune country are accompanied by the men of the Guard of the Dunes. The Guard of the Dunes, however, does not obtain the title of the Salt Ubar in virtue of his complacent magistracy of the salt districts, subservient to the Tahari merchants. There are those who say, and I do not doubt it true, that it is he, and not the merchants, who controls the salt of the Tahari. Nominally a sheriff of the Tahari merchants, he, ensconced in his kasbah, first among fierce warriors, elusive and unscrupulous, possesses a strangle hold on the salt of the Tahari, the vital commerce being ruled and regulated as he wills. He holds within his territories the right of law and execution. In the dunes he is Ubar and the merchants bow their heads to him. The Guard of the Dunes is one of the most dreaded and powerful men in the Tahari.

'Kneel, Slaves,' said the rider, the leader of the men who had captured us.

Hassan and I knelt.

'Kiss the sand before the gate of your master,' said the man.

Hassan and I pressed our lips to the sand before the great, open portal.

'On your feet, Slaves,' said the man. Hassan and I rose to our feet.

'You have been troublesome, Slaves,' said the man. 'You will be troublesome no more.'

The gate stood open before us. We could see the courtyard, whitish beyond, the moonlight on its sand, the small lamps set in the far walls.

'Herd the slaves before their master,' said the rider, he the leader of our captors.

I felt the point of a scimitar in my back.

'What is the name of the Salt Ubar?' I asked Hassan.

'I thought everyone knew his name,' said Hassan.

'No,' I said. 'What is his name?'

'Abdul,' said Hassan.

The scimitar pressed in my back. I, and Hassan, entered the

kasbah of the Guard of the Dunes, the Salt Ubar, he whose name was Abdul.

Opulent were the halls and lofty chambers of the kasbah of Abdul, the guard of the dunes, he known as the Salt Ubar of the Tahari.

Rich and smooth were the variegated, glossy tiles, sumptuous the hangings, slender the pillars and columns, ornate the screens and carvings, brilliant and intricate the stylized floral inlays, the geometrical mosaics. High vessels of gold, some as tall as a girl, gleaming dully in the light of the lamps, were passed on our journey through the halls, into the upper rooms, too, great vases of red and yellow porcelain, many of which were as large as a man, imported from the potteries of Tyros. Beaded curtains did we pass, and many portals, looming and carved.

We did not soil the polished floors, nor bring sand within. At the foot of the great stairs, marble and spiraling, leading to the upper rooms, we, and our guards, those accompanying us, some dozen men, paused. Their desert boots were removed by kneeling slave girls, who then, with lavers and veminium water, and oils, pouring and cleansing, washed their feet. The girls were not of the Tahari, and so dried the men's feet with their hair. To make a Tahari girl, even though slave, do this, is regarded as a great degradation. As discipline, of course, what is routine for a girl not of the Tahari, in miserable Tahari enslavement, may be forced on a slave girl whose origin is itself the Tahari. When the men's feet were cleansed, they were fitted by the girls with soft, heelless slippers, of the sort commonly worn indoors in permanent residences in the Tahari, with extended, curling toes. The feet of myself, and those of Hassan, too, were washed, and dried. The girl who cared for me had long hair, almost black. She bent to her work. Once she looked up at me. She might once have been of high family in Ar. She was now only a Tahari slave girl. She looked down, finishing her labors.

'In there,' said the man who had led our captors. We had now stopped before a great portal, narrower at its bottom, then swelling, curving, gracefully expanding, outward and upward, then narrowing again, gracefully concluding in a point. It might have been in the design of a stylized lance, or flame or leaf. This portal lay at the end of our trek, through several

220

halls, and up more than one flight of stairs.

There were men within, seated about a central figure, on rugs, on a dais. The men were veiled, in the manner of the Char. Girls, docile, belled and collared, served them.

A girl emerged from the room. Our eyes met. Her eyes fell. She did not know us. She found herself examined. Her body blushed red, from hair to ankles. Though Hassan and I were stripped, she was more naked than we, for she wore Gorean slave silk.

'In there,' said the man. Again I felt the incitement of the point of the scimitar in my back.

On ropes, hands bound behind our back, Hassan and I entered the lofty chamber.

Those within the chamber looked up.

We were thrust before the dais. 'Kneel, and kiss the tiles before the feet of your master,' said the man. Hassan and I knelt. Scimitars stood at the ready. We kissed the tiles. We straightened ourselves. Failure to comply in such a situation means immediate decapitation.

The man on the dais, sitting cross-legged, regarded us.

We said nothing.

He lifted his finger. 'You may again show respect,' said the man behind us.

We again kissed the tiles. We again straightened ourselves. Again we said nothing.

'I did not think a woman could hold you,' smiled the man on the dais.

We did not respond.

'I expect to have better fortune,' said the man. He was veiled, in the manner of the Char, as were the others with him. He picked a grape from a bowl of fruit on a small table near him, and, holding the veil from his face, as do the men of the Char, put the bit of fruit into his mouth, and bit into it. It was pitted. He chewed on the fruit.

I looked about the room.

It was a marvelous and lofty room, high-ceilinged, columned and tiled, ornately carved, open and spacious in aspect, rich in its decoration. A vizier, a pasha, a caliph, might have held audience in such a chamber.

'She is an excellent tool,' said the man on the dias, finishing the fruit, rinsing the fingers of his right hand in a small bowl of veminium water, and drying them on a cloth to his right, 'but only, when all is said and done, a woman. I did not think she could hold you. You were little more than twenty Ahn in her keeping.'

'We fell into your trap,' said Hassan.

The man shrugged, a Tahari shrug, tiny, subtle, like a swift smile, acknowledging the compliment of Hassan.

'It is not clear to me,' said Hassan, 'why a simple date merchant, like my friend, Hakim of Tor, and I, a lowly bandit, would be of interest to one so august as yourself.'

The man regarded Hassan. 'Once,' said he, 'you took something from me, something in which I was interested.'

'I am a bandit,' said Hassan, in cheerful explanation. 'It is my business. Perhaps I could return it to you, if you were serious about its recovery.'

'I have recovered it myself,' said he.

'Then I have little with which to bargain,' admitted Hassan. 'What was it I took, in which you were interested?'

'A trifle,' said the man.

'Perhaps it was another bandit,' suggested Hassan. 'Many of us, veiled, resemble one another.'

'I witnessed the theft,' said he. 'You did not deign to conceal your features.'

'Perhaps that was unwise on my part,' volunteered Hassan. He was clearly curious. 'Yet I do not recollect purloining anything upon an occasion on which you were present. Indeed, this is my first visit to your kasbah.'

'You did not recognize me,' said the man.

'I did not mean to be uncivil,' said Hassan.

'You were in reasonable haste,' said the man.

'My business must often be conducted with dispatch,' admitted Hassan. 'What was it I took?' he asked.

'A bauble,' said the man.

'I hope that you will forgive me,' said Hassan. 'Further, in the light of the fact that you have recovered that in which you were interested, whatever it is, I trust that you will be willing to let bygones be bygones, and permit myself and my friend to depart, returning to us our kaiila, garments and accoutrements, and perhaps bestowing upon us some water and supplies. We will then be on our way, commending your generosity and hospitalities at the campfires, and will bother you no longer.'

'I am afraid that will not be possible,' said the man.

'I was not optimistic,' admitted Hassan.

'You are a bandit,' pointed out the figure on the dais.

'Doubtless each of us has our own business,' said Hassan. 'Being a bandit is my business. Surely you would not hold one's business against him.'

'No,' said the man, 'but I, too, have my business, and part of my business is to apprehend and punish bandits. You would surely not hold my business against me.'

'Of course not,' said Hassan. 'That would be not only irrational, but discourteous.' He indicated me with his head. 'I have been traveling with this fellow,' he said, 'a clumsy, but well-meaning oaf, a boorish date merchant, Hakim of Tor, not overly bright, but good-hearted. We fell together by accident. Should you free him, your generosity and hospitality would be commended at the campfires.'

I did not care greatly for Hassan's description. I am not boorish.

'They must find other things of which to speak at the campfires,' said the man.

He looked about himself. On the dais, with him, were several men, low tables of food, fruit, stews, tidbits of roast verr, assorted breads. He, and the males were veiled. About the dais, kneeling, waiting to serve, were slave girls, some in high collars, clad in strands of slave silk. They were not veiled. Among the upper classes in the Tahari, it is scandalously erotic, generally, that a female's mouth should not be concealed. To see a girl's lips and teeth is a charged experience. To touch a girl's teeth with your teeth is prelude to the seizure of her body, an act that one would engage in only with a bold, brazen mate, or with one's shameless slave girl, with whom one can do, to her joy, precisely as one pleases.

'I have waited long to have you at my feet,' said the man. Then he lifted his finger. Four of the girls, with a jangle of slave bells, fled to Hassan and myself. They regarded the figure on the dais, veiled, sitting cross-legged. 'Please them,' he said. We struggled. With lips, and tongues, and small fingers, the girls addressed themselves to our pleasures. The binding fiber cut into our wrists. The ropes on our neck held us in place. We could not free ourselves. Again the veiled man lifted his finger. Other girls, with bits of food, gave us to feed, with their tiny fingers placing tidbits, delicacies, into our mouths. One girl held back our head, and others, from goblets, gave

223

us of wines, Turian wine, sweet and thick, Ta wine, from the famed Ta grapes, from the terraces of Cos, wines even, Ka-la-nas, sweets and drys, from distant Ar. Our heads swirled. We heard music. Musicians had entered the room. 'Feast,' said the man on the dais. He clapped his hands. We shook our heads, trying to clear the wines from them. We struggled. I pulled with my head away from the eager lips and hands of the slave girl who sought to hold me and kiss me. 'Tafa loves you,' she whispered, kissing me. A guard's hand held my hair, keeping my head in place. I felt the ropes burn on my neck. I closed my eyes. I felt her lips beneath my left ear, biting and kissing. 'Tafa loves you, Master,' she whispered. 'Let Tafa please you.' I was startled. Suddenly I realized that this was the same girl who had been one of the pair captured by Hassan in the desert, shortly before I had first made his acquaintance. She had been the proud free woman, sold at Two Scimitars, with Zina, the traitress. It was difficult now to see in this las-civious, delicious slave, who seemed born to the collar, the proud free woman whom Hassan had earlier captured, and who had been later sold at the Bakah oasis of Two Scimitars. Some Goreans maintain that all women are born to the collar, and require only to find that man strong enough to put it on them.

I tried to pull away, but was held. 'Tafa loves you,' she whispered. 'Let Tafa give you pleasure.' I felt the lips of another girl at my leg and waist.

The men, veiled, observed complacently.

Again the man on the dias clapped his hands. Before us now on the tiles, in the basic position of the slave dance, too, her hands lifted over her head, wrists back to back, stood a chained girl.

Hassan's eyes were hard.

It was Alyena.

'Do you remember this one?' asked the veiled man, of Hassan.

'Yes,' said Hassan.

'This is that of which,' said the man, 'I spoke earlier. This is that in which I was once interested. This is that which you once took from me. This is the trifle, the bauble. I have now recovered it.'

Alyena trembled under the eyes of Hassan. She wore graceful, golden chains.

'It was recovered,' he said, 'in the vicinity of Red Rock.'

There were tears in Alyena's eyes. She stood in the position of the slave dance, a girl waiting to be commanded to please men.

'She was with several men,' said the man on the dais. 'They fought well, with skill and savagery, and broke through to the desert beyond Red Rock.'

How was it then, I wondered, that lovely Alyena stood here, on these tiles, slave?

'Then, most peculiarly,' said the man, 'when apparently safe, escaped with her escort, she, suddenly, turned her kaiila about, returning, fleeing back to Red Rock.'

The oasis, or much of it, I knew, would have been in flames at that time.

'She was, of course, almost immediately captured,' said the man. 'She was crying the name "Hassan".'

I could see that this did not please Hassan at all. His will had been disobeyed. Further, I recalled that the girl had, in Red Rock, under stress, cried his name, speaking it, though she was only a girl in bondage.

'I love you, Master,' cried the girl. 'I wanted to be with you! At your side!'

'You are a runaway slave girl,' he said.

She wept, but did not break the position of the slave dance. 'Too,' said he, 'at the oasis you cried my name.' These were serious offenses.

'Forgive me, Master,' she cried. 'I love you!' She had risked her life to return to Hassan. She loved him. Yet a slave girl owes her master absolute obedience. She had violated his will in two particulars. I did not think it would go easily with her. Love on Gor does not purchase a girl lenience; it does not mitigate her bondage, nor compromise her servitude, but rather renders it the more complete, the more helpless and abject.

'Master,' wept the girl.

What a beautiful piece of slave flesh Alyena was, so vulnerable, so feminine, but how could she have been otherwise when owned by Gorean men? The man on the dais languidly lifted his finger. The musicians readied themselves. Alyena looked upon Hassan, agonized. 'What shall I do, Master?' she begged. She wore a golden metal dancing collar about her throat, golden chains looped from her wrists, gracefully to the collar ring, then fell to her ankles; there are varieties of Tahari dancing chains; she wore the oval and collar; briefly, in readying a girl, after she has been belled and silked, and bangled, and has been made up, and touched with slave perfume, she kneels, head down in a large oval of light gleaming chain, extending her wrists before her; fastened at the sides of the top of the oval are two wrist rings, at the sides of the lower loop of the oval two ankle rings; the oval is then pulled inward and the wrist and ankle rings fastened on the slave; her throat is then locked in the dancing collar, which has, under the chin, an open snap ring; with the left hand the oval is then gathered together, so the two strands of chain lie in the palm of the left hand, whence, lifted, they are placed inside the snap ring, which is then snapped shut, and locked; the two strands of chain flow freely in the snap ring; accordingly, though the girl's wrists and ankles are fastened at generous, though inflexible limits from one another, usually about a yard for the wrists and about eighteen inches for the ankles, much of the chain may be played through, and back through, the collar ring; this permits a skillful girl a great deal of beautiful chain work; the oval and collar is traditional in the Tahari; it enhances a girl's beauty; it interferes little with her dance, though it imposes subtle, sensuous limits upon it; a good dancer uses these limits, exploiting them deliciously; for example, she may extend a wrist, subtly holding the chain at her waist with her other hand; the chain slides through the ring, yet short of the expected movement; the chain stops her wrist, her wrist rebels, but is helpless; it must yield; her head falls; she is a chained slave girl.

'Master, what shall I do?' begged Alyena. How beautiful she was.

All eyes were upon her. Aside from her jewelries, her bells, the oval and collar, the cosmetics, the heady slave perfume, she wore six ribbons of silk, yellow, three before and three behind, some four feet in length, depending from her collar. I had always admired her brand. It was deep and delicate, and beautifully done.

'Master!' cried Alyena.

The finger of the man on the dais, he veiled in red, prepared to fall.

'Dance, Slave,' said Hassan.

The man's finger fell languidly, the musicians began to play.

226

Alyena, before us, in the chains of the Tahari, danced. She was a most beautiful trifle, a most lovely bauble.

We feasted late, and were much pleased by the beauties of the Salt Ubar.

Finally, he said, 'It is late. And you must retire, for you must rise before dawn.'

Hours before, Alyena had been dismissed from the audience chamber of the Guard of the Dunes, the Salt Ubar.

'Take her to the guard room,' he said. 'There let her give pleasure to the men.' Alyena, still in her chains, was pulled by the hair from the room.

'You veil yourself in the manner of the Char,' I said, 'but I do not think you of the Char.'

'No,' said the man on the dais.

'I had not known you were the Salt Ubar,' said I.

'Many do not know that,' said the man.

'Why are you and your men veiled?' I asked.

'It is customary for the men of the Guard of the Dunes to veil themselves,' said he. 'Their allegiance is to no tribe, but to the protection of the salt. In anonymity is a disguise for them. Freely may they move about when unveiled, none knowing they are in my fee. Veiled, their actions cannot be well traced to an individual, but only to an institution, my Ubarate.'

'You speak highly of your office,' I said.

'Few know the men of the Salt Ubar,' said he. 'And, veiled, anonymous, all fear them.'

'I do not fear them,' said Hassan. 'Free me, and give me a scimitar, and we shall make test of the matter.'

'Are there others here, too, I know?' I asked.

'Perhaps,' said the man. Then he turned to the others. 'Unveil yourselves,' he said.

The men removed the scarlet veils. 'Hamid,' said I, 'lieutenant to Shakar, captain of the Aretai.' I nodded.

The man looked at me with hatred. His hand was at a dagger in his sash. 'Let me slay him now,' he said.

'Perhaps you would have better fortune than when you in stealth struck Suleiman Pasha,' I said.

The man cried out in rage.

The leader, the Salt Ubar, lifted his finger and the man subsided, his eyes blazing.

'There is another here I know,' I said, nodding toward a

227

small fellow, sitting beside the Salt Ubar, 'though he is now more richly robed than when last I saw him.'

'He is my eyes and ears in Tor,' said the Salt Ubar.

'Abdul the water carrier,' said I. 'I once mistook you for someone else,' I said.

'Oh?' he said.

'It does not matter now,' I said. I smiled to myself. I had thought him to be the 'Abdul' of the message, that which had been placed in the scalp of the message girl, Veema, who had been sent mysteriously to the house of Samos in Port Kar. I still did not know who had sent the message. As now seemed clear to me, the message must have referred to Abdul, the Salt Ubar. He who had sent the message had doubtless been of the Tahari. It had doubtless not occurred to him that the message might have been misconstrued. In the historic sense, the planetary sense, there would have been only one likely 'Abdul' in the Tahari at this time, the potent, powerful, dreaded Guard of the Dunes, the Salt Ubar. He would be a most formidable minion of Kurii. Neither Samos nor myself, however, though we had heard of the Salt Ubar, had known his name. Further, his name is not often casually mentioned in the Tahari. It is difficult to know who are and who are not his spies. His men belong to various tribes. I might have behaved differently in the Tahari had I earlier known the name of the Salt Ubar. I wondered who had sent the message, 'Beware Abdul.' How complacent I had been, how sure that I had earlier penetrated that mystery.

'May I cut his throat?' asked the water carrier.

'We have other plans for our friend,' said the Salt Ubar. He had not unveiled himself, though his men, at his command, had done so.

'Have you long been known as Abdul?' I asked the Salt Ubar.

'For some five years,' said he, 'since I infiltrated the kasbah and deposed my predecessor.'

'You serve Kurii,' I said.

The man shrugged. 'You serve Priest-Kings,' said he. 'We two have much in common, for we both are mercenaries. Only you are less wise than I, for you do not serve upon that side which will taste the salt of victory.'

'Priest-Kings are formidable enemies,' said I.

'Not so formidable as Kurii,' said he. 'The Kur,' said he,

'is persistent. It is tenacious. It is fierce. It will have its way. The Priest-Kings will fall. They will fail.'

I thought that what he said might be true. The Kur is determined, aggressive, merciless. It is highly intelligent, it lusts for blood, it will kill for territory and meat. The Priest-King is a relatively gentle organism, delicate and stately. It has little interest in conflict; its military posture is almost invariably defensive; it asks little more than to be left alone. I did not know if Priest-Kings, with all their brilliance, and all their great stores of knowledge on their scent-tapes, had a glandular and neurological system with which the motivations and nature of Kurii could be understood. The true nature of the Kurii might elude them, almost physiologically, like a menacing color they could not see, a terrible sound to which their sensors were almost inert. A man, I felt, could know a Kur, but Priest-Kings, I suspected, could only know about a Kur. They could know about them, but they could not know them. To know a Kur one must, perhaps, in the moonlight, face it with an ax, smell the musk of its murderous rage, see the eyes, the intelligence, the sinuous, hunched might of it, the blood black at its jaws, hear the blood cry, stand against its charge. A creature who had not known hatred, lust and terror, I suspected, would be ill-fitted to understand the Kur, or men.

'What you say is quite possibly true,' I said.

'I shall not ask you to serve Kurii,' said the man.

'You honor me,' I said.

'You are of the Warriors,' he said.

'It is true,' I said. Never had I been divested of the scarlet. Let who would, with steel, dispute my caste with me.

'Well,' said the man on the dais, 'it is late, and we must all retire. You must be up before dawn.'

'Where is Vella?' I asked.

'I have confined her to quarters,' he said.

'Must I address you,' I asked, 'as Abdul?'

The man lowered his veil. 'No,' he said, 'not if you do not wish to do so.'

'I know you better under another name,' I said.

'That is true,' said the man.

Hassan began to struggle. He could not part the fiber on his wrists. The ropes burned on his throat. He was held by the guards on his knees.

The blade of a scimitar stood at his throat. He was quiet.

'Are we to be slain at dawn?' I asked.

'No,' he said.

I looked at him puzzled. Hassan, too, seemed shocked.

'You will begin a journey, with others, at dawn,' said the man. 'It will be a long journey, afoot. It is my hope that you will both arrive safely.'

'What are you doing with us?' demanded Hassan.

'I herewith,' said Ibn Saran, 'sentence you to the brine pits of Klima.'

We struggled to our feet, but each of us, by two guards, was held.

'Tafa, Riza,' said Ibn Saran, to two of the girls. 'strip.' They did so, to collar and brand. 'You will be taken below, to the dungeons,' said Ibn Saran to us. 'There you will be chained by the neck in separate cells. In the cell of each, we will place a naked slave girl, she, too, chained by the neck, her chain within your reach, that you may, if you wish, pull her to you.'

'Ibn Saran is generous,' I said.

'I give Hassan a woman,' said he, 'for his audacity. I give you, too, a woman, for your manhood, and for we are two of a kind, mercenaries in higher wars.' He turned to one of the girls. 'Straighten your body, Tafa,' he said. She did so, and stood beautifully, a marvelous female slave. 'Chain Riza,' said he to one of the guards, selecting the woman who would serve us, by his will, 'beside Hassan, this bandit, and Tafa by the side of this man, he of the Warriors, whose name is Tarl Cabot.'

Metal leashes were snapped on the girls' throats.

'Regard Tafa, Tarl Cabot,' said Ibn Saran. I did so. 'Let Tafa's body give you much pleasure,' he said. 'For there are no women at Klima.'

We were turned about and taken from the audience hall of the Guard of the Dunes, Abdul, the Salt Ubar, he who was Ibn Saran.

FOURTEEN

THE MARCH TO KLIMA

I took another step, and my right leg, to the knee, broke
through the brittle crusts. The lash struck again across my
back. I straightened in the slave hood, my head thrown back
by the stroke. The chain on my neck jerked forward and I
stumbled in the salt crusts. My hands clenched in the manacles, fastened at my body by the loop of chain. My left leg
broke through a dozen layers of crust, breaking it to the side
with a hundred, dry, soft shattering sounds, the rupture of in-
numerable fine crystalline structures. I could feel blood on
my left leg, over the leather wrappings, where the edge of a
crust, ragged, hot, had sawed it open. I lost my balance and
fell. I tried to rise. But the chain before me dragged forward
and I fell again. Twice more the lash struck. I recovered my
balance. Again I waded through the crusts toward Klima.

For twenty days had we marched. Some thought it a hundred. Many had lost count.

More than two hundred and fifty men had been originally
in the salt chain.

I did not know how many now trekked with the march.
The chain was now much heavier than it had been, for it,
even with several sections removed, was carried by far fewer
men. To be a salt slave, it is said, one must be strong. Only
the strong, it is said, reach Klima.

In the chain, we wore slave hoods. These had been fastened
on us at the foot of the wall of the kasbah of the Salt Ubar.
Before mine had been locked under my chin I had seen the
silver desert in its dawn. The sky in the east, for Gor, like the
Earth rotates to the east, had seemed cool and gray. It was
difficult to believe then, in the cool of that morning, as early
as late spring, that the surface temperatures of the terrain we

would traverse would be within hours better than one hundred and fifty degrees Farenheit. Our feet, earlier, had been wrapped in leather sheathing, it reaching, in anticipation of the crusts later to be encountered, to the knees. The moons, at that time, had been still above the horizon. Rocks on the desert, and the sheer walls of the Salt Ubar's kasbah, looming above us, shone with dew, common in the Tahari in the early morning, to be burned off in the first hour of the sun. Children, and nomads, sometimes rise early, to lick the dew from the rocks. From where we were chained, I had been able to see, some two pasangs to the east, Tarna's kasbah. A useful tool had the Salt Ubar characterized her. She had not been able to hold Hassan and me. The Salt Ubar had speculated that he would enjoy better fortune in this respect. The collar was locked about my throat.

An Ahn before dawn I had been aroused. Tafa, sweet and warm, on the cool stones, on the straw, lay against me, in my arms. On her throat was a heavy cell collar, with ring; attached to the ring was some fifteen feet of chain, it attached to a plate near our heads. I was similarly secured. The plates were no more than five inches apart. When we had been placed in the cell a tiny lamp had been put on a shelf by the door. The stones were broad, heavy blocks, cool, wet in places, over which lay a scattering of damp straw. We were perhaps a hundred feet below the kasbah. The cell had not been much cleaned. There was a smell, as of humans, and urts. Tafa screamed but she, unleashed, was thrown to the wall, and her fair throat placed in the waiting cell collar, it then snapped shut. I was then, too, secured. 'Do not keep me in this place!' screamed Tafa. 'Please! Please!' But they did not unlock the collar. An urt scampered across the stones, disappearing between two blocks of stone in the wall. Tafa screamed and threw herself to the feet of one of the jailers, holding his legs, kissing at him. With his left and right hand he checked the collar at her throat, holding it with his left hand and, with his right, jerking the chain twice against the ring, then threw her from him, to the straw. The other man similarly checked my collar. Then, with a knife, he cut the two ropes from my throat, and freed me of the binding fiber. He took the shreds of rope and binding fiber with him when he left the cell. The heavy door, beams of wood, sheathed with plates of iron, together some eight inches thick, closed. The hasps were flung over the staples, two, heavy, and two locks were shut on the door. At the top of the door, some six inches by ten inches, barred, was an observation window. The guards looked in. Tafa sprang to her feet and ran to the length of her chain, her hands and fingers outstretched, clawing toward the bars. Her fingers came within ten inches of the bars. 'Do not leave me here,' she cried. 'Please, oh, please, oh Masters!' They turned away. She moaned, and turned from the door, dragging at the chain with her small hands. She fell to her hands and knees and vomited twice, from fear and the stench. An urt skittered past her, having emerged from a crack in the floor between two stones and moved swiftly across the floor, along one wall, and vanished through the crack which had served as exit for its fellow a few moments earlier. Tafa began to weep and pull hysterically at the chain and collar on her throat. But it was obdurately fastened upon her. I checked my own collar and chain, and the linkage at the ring and plate. I was secured. I looked at the tiny lamp on the shelf near the door. It smoked, and burned oil, probably from tiny rock tharlarions, abundant south of Tor in the spring. I looked at Tafa. She shook her head. 'No,' she said. 'You are sentenced to Klima.'

I leaned back against the wall. 'You will be only a salt slave,' she said.

I watched her. With the back of her right wrist she wiped her mouth. I continued to watch her. She half knelt, half sat, her head down, the palms of her hands on the floor of the cell.

I picked up, where it lay on the stones, fastened to the plate and ring near mine, the chain which ran, looped, lying on the floor, to her collar, several feet away.

'No!' she cried angrily. I held the chain. I did not pull it to me. 'Salt slave!' she cried. She jerked the chain taut with her two hands, on her knees, backing away. My hand rested on the chain, lightly. It was tight on its ring, taut. I removed my hand from the chain.

Watching me, catlike, Tafa lay on her side in the straw. I looked away. Tafa, no longer under the eye of her master, the feared Ibn Saran, had a slave girl's pride. She was, after all, a lock-collar girl, who had been once free, who was beautiful, who had, at Two Scimitars, brought a high price, a price doubtless improved upon, if only slightly, by the agents of Ibn Saran, when they had bought her for their master. Slave

233

girls, commonly obsequious and docile with free males, who may in an instant put them under discipline, are often insolent and arrogant with males who are slave, whom they despise. Salt slaves, in the Tahari, are among the lowest of the male slaves. The same girl who, joyously, would lasciviously writhe at the feet of the free male, begging him for his slightest touch, would often, confronted with male slaves, treat them with the contempt and coldness commonly accorded the men of Earth by their frustrated, haughty females; I have sometimes wondered if this is because the women of Earth, cheated of their domination by the aggressor sex, see such weaklings, perhaps uneasily or subconsciously, as slaves, men unfit to master, males determined to be only the equals of girls, stupid fools who wear their own chains, slaves who have enslaved themselves, fearing to be free. Goreans, interestingly from the point of view of an Earthling, who has been subjected to differing historical conditioning processes, do not regard biology as evil; those who deny the truths of biology are not acclaimed on Gor, as on Earth, but are rather regarded as being curious and pathetic. Doubtless it is difficult to adjudicate matters of values. Perhaps it is intrinsically more desirable in some obscure sense to deny biology and suffer from mental and physical disease, than accept biology and be strong and joyful, I do not know. I leave the question to those wiser than myself. For what it is worth, though doubtless it is little pertinent, the men and women of Gor are, generally, whole and happy; the men and women of Earth, generally, if I do not misread the situation, are not. The cure for poison perhaps is not more poison, but something different. But this matter I leave again to those more wise than myself.

My hand again picked up Tafa's chain, where it was fastened to the plate near mine. Instantly, her eyes, which she had closed, her arm under the left side of her head, opened. I took up a fist of the chain. 'Salt slave!' she said. She rose to her knees. She jerked with her weight against the chain. This time I did not release it. Her hands slipped on the chain. She tried to jerk it again, holding it more firmly. I did not release the chain. It was as though it had been fastened anew, but a fist shorter than it had been. 'No!' she cried. I took up another fist of chain. She sprang to her feet. 'No! No!' she cried. I put my two hands on the chain. I drew it another few inches toward me. She stumbled forward some inches, then stood,

234

bracing herself, her hands on the chain. 'No!' she cried. I took up another fist of chain, her neck and head were pulled forward. She was in an awkward position. She could not brace herself. She gave some inches and again braced herself, throwing her weight back against the chain. It did not yield. She wept. 'No! No!' she said. It interested me that she would attempt to pit her strength against mine. The strength of a full-grown woman is equivalent to that of a twelve-year-old boy. Goreans read in this an indication as to who is master. Foot by foot, slowly, across the floor of the cell, she slipping, screaming, struggling. I drew her toward me. I saw the small oil lamp was growing dim, the oil almost depleted, the wick smoking. Then my fist was in the girl's collar and I threw her to her back at my side. With my left hand I lifted the heavy collar chain from her body and threw it over her head and behind her. I saw her wild eyes, frightened. With some straw I wiped her mouth, cleaning it, for earlier, in her revulsion and terror, her horror at the place and manner in which she found herself incarcerated, she had from her own mouth soiled both herself and the cell. 'Please,' she said. 'Be silent,' I told her. The lamp sputtered out.

An Ahn before dawn I had been aroused, Tafa, sweet and warm, on the cool stones, on the straw, lay against me, in my arms.

Five men, two with lamps, entered my cell. A loop of chain was placed about my belly. My wrists were manacled before me, the manacles fixed with a ring in the chain. Two of the men, one on each side, then thrust a bar behind my back and before my elbows, by means of which, together, they could control me. The fifth man unsnapped the collar from my throat, and dropped it, with its chain, to the stones. I was pulled to my feet.

Tafa, frightened, awake, knelt at my feet. She bent to my feet. I felt her hair on my feet. I felt her lips kiss my feet. She knelt as a slave girl. In the night I had conquered her.

By means of the bar, not looking back, I was thrust from the cell.

We had stood, the salt slaves being readied for the march to Klima, at the foot of the wall of the kasbah of the Salt Ubar. The moons were not yet below the horizon. It was cool, even chilly at that hour in the late spring. Dawn, like a shadowy scimitar, curved gray in the east. I could see Tarna's kasbah, some two pasangs away. Hassan stood, some four men from me, similarly manacled. Our feet had already been wrapped in leather. I saw the collar of the chain lifted, snapped on his throat. Dew shone on the plastered walls of the kasbah looming over me, on rocks scattered on the desert. A rider, on kaiila, was moving toward us, on the sand about the edge of the wall. The scarlet sand veil of the men of the Guard of the Dunes concealed his countenance, and a length of it fluttered behind him as he rode, and the wide burnoose lifted and swelled behind him. The cording of the agal, over the scarlet kaffiyeh, was gold. Men beside me lifted the chain and collar. The rider pulled the kaiila up beside me, drawing back on the single rein. The collar was snapped about my throat. I felt the weight of the chain.

'Greetings, Tarl Cabot,' said the rider.

'You rise early, noble Ibn Saran,' said I.

'I would not miss your departure,' he averred.

'Doubtless in this there is triumph for you,' said I.

'Yes,' said he, 'but, too, regret, Comrade. One gains a victory, one loses an enemy.'

The men of the Guard of the Dunes were fastening slave hoods on the prisoners of the chain. There were several men behind me. This slave hood does not come fitted with a gag device. It is not a particularly cruel hood, like many, but utilitarian, and merciful. It serves four major functions. It facilitates the control of the prisoner. A hooded prisoner, even if not bound, is almost totally helpless. He cannot see to escape; he cannot see to attack; he cannot be sure, usually, even of the number and position of his captors, whether they face him, or are attentive, or such; sometimes a hooded prisoner, even unbound, is told simply to kneel, and that if he moves, he will be slain; some captors, to their amusement, leave such prisoners, returning Ahn later, to find them in the same place; the prisoner, of course, does not know if they have merely moved a hundred feet away or so, to rest or make camp; all he knows is that if he does move a foot from his place he may feel a scimitar pass suddenly through his body. In the hood, too, of course, the prisoner does not know who might strike or abuse him. He is alone in the hood, with his confusion, his ignorance, his unfocused misery, his anguish, helpless. The

236

second major function of the hood is to conceal from the prisoner his location, where he is and where he is being taken. It produces disorientation, a sense of dependence on the captor. In the case of the march to Klima, of course, the hood serves to conceal the route from the prisoners of the chain. Thus, even if they thought they might live for a time in the desert, in trying to flee, they would have little idea of even the direction to take in their flight. The chance of their finding their way back to the kasbah of the Salt Ubar, and thence, say, to Red Rock, would be small, even if they were not hooded; hooded, on the Klima march, of course, the chance, unhooded, of finding their way back at a later time would be negligible. This disorientation tends to keep men at Klima; fewer of them, thus, die in the desert. The second two functions of the slave hood, relative to the march to Klima, were specific to the march. Mercifully, the hood tended to protect the head from the sun; one does not go bareheaded in the desert; secondly, the darkness of the hood, when the salt crusts were reached, prevented blindness, from the reflection of the Tahari sun off the layered, bleak, white surfaces. These hoods, used on the march to Klima, have a tiny flap, closed and tied with a leather string, at the mouth, through which, several times during the day, opened, the spike of a water bag, carried by kaiila, is thrust. The men are fed twice, once in the morning, once at night, when the hood is opened, and thrust up some inches to permit eating. Food is thrust in their mouths. It was generally dried fruit, crackers and a bit of salt, to compensate for the salt loss during the day's march, consequent on perspiration. Proteins, meat, kaiila milk, vulo eggs, verr cheese, require much water for their digestion. When water is in short supply, the nomads do not eat at all. It takes weeks to starve, but only, in the Tahari, two days to die of thirst. In such circumstances, one does not wish the processes of digestion to drain much needed water from the body tissues. The bargain would be an ill one to strike.

Ibn Saran had turned his kaiila toward Hassan. He looked at him for a time. Then he said, 'I am sorry.' Hassan did not speak. It had puzzled me that Ibn Saran had spoken thusly to Hassan, a bandit. Then Ibn Saran turned his kaiila again, and prepared to depart the chain.

'Ibn Saran,' I said.

He paused, and guided the kaiila to my side. The men were

closer now, fastening on the prisoners the slave hoods.

'Slave runs to Earth by agents of Kurii,' I said, 'have been discontinued.'

'I know,' he said.

'Does that not seem curious?' I asked.

He shrugged.

'Priest-Kings,' I said, 'received an ultimatum, "Surrender Gor." '

'That is known to me,' said he.

'Might you clarify that ultimatum?' I asked.

'I assume,' he said, 'it betokens an intention to invite capitulation, before some aggressive strategem is initiated.'

'A strategem of what nature?' I asked.

'I am not privy,' said he, 'to the war conferences of the Kurii.'

'What is your charge in the desert, on behalf of Kurii?' I inquired.

'Their work,' said he.

'And of late?' I asked.

'To precipitate war,' said he, 'between the Kavars and the Aretai, and their vassal tribes, to close the desert to strangers, intruders.'

'Such as agents of Priest-Kings?' I asked.

'They, and any others unwelcome now in the dune country,' said he.

'Can your men not police the dune country?' I asked.

'We are too few,' said he. 'The risk of some strangers slipping through would be too great.' In Gorean, the same expression is used for stranger and enemy.

'So you enlist the desert on your behalf?' I said.

'Inadvertently,' he said, 'thousands of warriors, preparing, hasten even now to do my bidding, to fly at one another's throats.'

'Many men will die,' cried Hassan, 'both Kavars and Aretai, and of the vassal tribes! It must be stopped! They must be warned!'

'It is necessary,' said Ibn Saran to him. 'I am sorry.'

A slave hood was pulled over the head of Hassan. His fists were clenched. It was locked under his chin.

'One gains a victory,' said Ibn Saran, 'but one loses an enemy.' He looked at me. He unsheathed his scimitar.

'No,' I said. 'I will march to Klima.'

'I am prepared to be merciful,' said he, 'Comrade.'

'No,' I said.

'It is cool here,' he said. 'Your death would be swift.'

'No,' I said.

'You are of the Warriors,' said he. 'You have their stupidity, their grit, their courage.'

'I will march to Klima,' I said.

He lifted the scimitar before me, in salute. 'March them,' said he, 'to Klima.' He resheathed the blade, swiftly. He turned his kaiila. He rode down the line, the burnoose swelling behind him.

Hamid, who was lieutenant to Shakar, captain of the Aretai, now in the red sand veil of the men of the Guard of the Dunes, stood near. 'I ride with the chain,' he said.

'I shall enjoy your company,' I said.

'You will feel my whip,' he said.

I saw the kneeling kaiila of the guards, the guards now mounted, lifting themselves to their feet. I surveyed the number of kaiila which bore water. 'Klima is close,' I said.

'It is far,' he said.

'There is not enough water,' I said.

'There is more than enough,' said he. 'Many will not reach Klima.'

'Am I to reach Klima?' I asked.

'Yes,' said Hamid, 'should you be strong enough.'

'What if difficulties should arise, unanticipated, on the journey?' I asked.

'Then,' said Hamid, 'unfortunately, I shall be forced to slay you in the chain.'

'Is it important that I reach Klima?' I asked.

'Yes,' said Hamid.

'Why?' I asked.

'You have given Kurii, and their agents, much trouble,' said he. 'You have opposed yourself to their will. Tarl Cabot, thus, will serve at Klima.'

'Tarl Cabot, thus,' I repeated, 'will serve at Klima.'

'Look,' said Hamid. He pointed to a window, narrow, high in the wall.

I looked up.

At the window, veiled in yellow, behind her slave master, stood a female slave.

Gracefully the girl, doubtless with the permission of the slave

239

master, removed her veil. It was Vella.

'You remember, perhaps,' said Hamid, looking up, 'the delicious slave, Vella, whom the Kurii found of much use, who testified against you in the court at Nine Wells, who, by her false testimony, attempted to send you to the pits of Klima?'

'I recall the slave,' I said. 'She is the girl-property of Ibn Saran.'

I recalled her well.

'It is she,' said Hamid, indicating the girl in the narrow window, the slave master behind her.

'Yes,' I said. 'I see.'

The girl looked down upon me. She smiled, scornfully. She had begged in Lydius to be freed. I had not known until then that she was true slave. But I would have known it now, seeing the insolence, the petty, collared beauty of her. I stood below her in the chain of salt slaves. Female slaves, cringing and obsequious, fearing free men, often display contempt for male slaves. Sometimes they even flaunt their beauty before them, in their walk and movements, to torture them, knowing that the male slaves may be slain for so much as touching their silk. I could see that she was much pleased to see me, helpless and in the chain to Klima. I could see in her smile how she looked upon me, as a female slave upon a male slave, but I could see, too, in her smile, the pleasure of her triumph.

'A delicious day for the slave,' said Hamid.

'True,' I said.

Then the girl, reaching within her silk, withdrew from her bosom a light square of silk, some eighteen inches square, scarlet, clinging, diaphanous.

She turned to the slave master behind her. She requested of him something. He seemed adamant. Her attitude was one of begging. With a laugh, he acceded to her request. Triumphantly she turned again to the window and dropped the silk from the aperture. Gracefully, it wafted downward, settling on the sand at the foot of the wall near us.

'Bring it,' said Hamid to a man.

The man picked it up, smelled it and laughed, and brought it to Hamid.

Hamid held it. It was laden with slave perfume. It was slave silk.

'A token,' I said.

'The token of a slave girl,' said Hamid contemptuously.

Hamid thrust and twisted the square of silk in the metal of my collar, and yanked it tight. 'Remember her at Klima,' he said.

She had testified against me at Nine Wells. She had smiled when I had been sentenced there to the pits of Klima.

I looked up, the silk fastened in my collar.

She looked down upon me, as a female slave upon a male slave. And, too, more than this, she looked down upon me in triumph. Her face was flushed. It was red with pleasure, transfused with joy. How deliciously sweet did she find her petty feminine vengeance! How foolish I thought her. Did she not know I was Gorean? Did she not know I would come back for her?

But it was said none returned from Klima.

I looked at her.

I resolved that I would return from Klima.

'Remember her at Klima,' said Hamid.

'Yes,' I said.

I would remember her. I would remember her well.

In the window the girl stiffened. The man behind her had said something to her. She turned to him, agonized. She pleaded with him. This time his face remained impassive. Angrily she turned to the window again. She smiled. She blew a kiss toward me, in the Gorean fashion, brushing it toward me with her fingers. Then, swiftly, she turned and left the window.

'Is she not,' I asked, 'to be permitted to look out, to see us begin the march to Klima?'

'She is a slave girl,' said Hamid. 'It will not be permitted her.'

'I see,' I said.

One often denies slave girls small pleasures and gratifications. It teaches them, the more deeply, that they are slaves.

Some kaiila moved by, laden with various supplies. Some guards rode by.

I smelled the slave perfume. I recalled it from the palace of Suleiman Pasha, when the girl, with Zaya, the other slave, had served black wine. A rich master will often have individual perfumes specially blended and matched to the slave nature of his various girls. All are slaves, completely, but each girl, collared, imbonded, is deliciously different. Some slave perfumes are right for some slaves, and others not. Vella's perfume, had suited her superbly. It fitted her well, like a measured collar.

I smiled. Perhaps Vella, even now, had been returned to the quarters for female slaves, where she would wait until commanded by men, perhaps to her exercises or bath, or silks, or cosmetics, to her beautification, or to small, suitable servile tasks, or perhaps to the couch of her master, or to those to whom he saw fit to give her. But it was early. Doubtless her silk had merely been taken from her and she had been commanded to her stomach, head to the wall, in her alcove, and the small, square gate had been locked behind her. These two precautions are common in female seraglios in the Tahari. When the girl lies on her stomach, her head to the wall, she cannot prevent the door from locking behind her. Furthermore, the small opening, approximately eighteen inches square, and set some ten inches off the floor, in the bars, with its small, heavy gate, can be easily negotiated only on the hands and knees. A girl cannot dart from a typical Tahari female-slave alcove. That she must enter and leave it on her hands and knees is thought to have a desirable psychological effect on the girl, impressing on even a haughty girl that she is only slave. Too, of course, this posture, on the girl's part, makes it convenient to leash her upon leaving the alcove.

I looked up at the window, in which the girl had stood. It was now empty.

Doubtless Vella, even now, in the quarters for female slaves, lay in her cushioned, barred alcove. Perhaps her small fists were clenched as she lay nude on the silks, the cushions, on her stomach, head to the wall, behind the ornate bars of her tiny, luxurious kennel. The tiny, iron door, heavy, barred, would shut behind her, locking. She was not to be permitted to watch in triumph my departure for Klima. What she had failed to do at Nine Wells, her master, Ibn Saran, sliken, pantherlike and lithe, had well accomplished. The small, delicious, owned brunette would not be permitted to watch. She would be denied that gratification, that pleasure. She would be shut instead in her alcove-cell. She was slave, only slave.

I smiled. I inhaled the perfume. Hamid took from a man nearby a slave hood. I saw the sky, grayish, the descending moons, the desert, and then the hood was pulled over my head, jerked tight, and locked.

*

242

We trudged, climbing, chained, and hooded, half dragged, tortuously, up the long slope. Time seemed measured in steps, the blows of the whip, the slow turning of the sun, over the Ahn, from one shoulder through the heat to the other.

For twenty days had we marched. Some thought it a hundred. Many had lost count. More than one man raved, insane in the chain. We had begun with some two hundred and fifty men. The chain was heavier now. Lengths had been removed from it. But still it was heavier. We did not know how many now carried the chain, or the remaining lengths.

Normally one does not move on the desert in the day, but the march to Klima is made in the sun, that only the strong will survive. We were given little to eat, but much water. In the desert, without water, even the strong die swiftly.

'Kill us! Kill us!' one man kept screaming.

At the crest of the slope we heard a man call 'Hold!' The chain stopped.

I sank to my knees, the crusts about my thighs. The inside of the slave hood seemed bright and granular. Even within it I closed my eyes. I held my hands, my neck, as still as possible, for the least movement would shift the collar, the manacles, the chain at my waist, and stir burning iron in the raw, abraided flesh. I did not wish to lose consciousness. Too many I feared who had lost it had not regained it. The guards of the chain did not see fit to dally overlong with the inert.

The salt clung to my body.

The sun was the sun of the late spring in the Tahari. The surface temperature of the crusts would be in the neighborhood of 160 degrees Fahrenheit. The air temperature would range from 120 to 140 degrees Fahrenheit. The marches to Klima are not made in the Tahari summer, only in the winter, the spring, and fall, that some will survive them.

I lifted my head to the sun, and shut my eyes against the redness, the heat and refulgence that seemed to fill the hood. I put down my head. Even in the hood I sensed the reflected heat radiating from the crusts.

It pleases Kurii, I thought, that Tarl Cabot will serve at Klima. How amusing they would find that. There was a bit of silk, now doubtless bleached by the sun, thrust and wrapped in my collar. Doubtless another, too, would be pleased that I served at Klima.

A kaiila moved swiftly past me, its paws scattering salt. I

felt it in the marks on my back, and in the chain sores.

'Kill us! Kill us!' the man screamed again, from somewhere in the chain behind me, several collars away.

Another kaiila moved past me, moving toward the front of the chain. My fists clenched.

I wondered if I could endure another day. I knew that I could. I had much to live for. There was a bit of silk, wrapped, fastened in the collar I wore.

'Kill us! Kill us!' screamed the man.

'There are too many,' I heard one of the guards say.

'Alternate collars,' said a voice.

'No!' a voice screamed. 'No!'

The guards knew the water. We did not.

It seemed a long time we knelt in the crusts. After some Ehn I heard men afoot near me. They were moving down the chain. I tensed in the hood. Suddenly the chain before me, jerked. I heard no sound. Then the chain pulled down. I struggled to my feet, pulling against the chain with my neck, wild, not able to see. 'Kneel,' said a voice. I knelt. I tensed. I could not see in the hood. I knelt, a chained captive in the crusts. I could not lift my hands before my body. I was helpless, absolutely. 'No,' I heard a voice cry, 'No!' The chain at my throat, from behind, shook, and sprang taut. I heard feet, scraping in the crusts, slipping. There was a cry, and I felt, through the chain, a drag, and shudder. Then the men continued on their way.

'I misjudged the water,' I heard Hamid say.

'It does not matter,' said someone.

We knelt in the crusts. Somewhere, a few feet from me, I heard a man singing to himself.

Another man came down the chain. I heard him open the collars on either side of me.

I heard, a short time later, wings, the alighting of one or more large birds. Such birds, broad-winged, black and white, from afar, follow the marches to Klima; their beaks, yellowish, narrow, are long and slightly hooked at the end, useful for probing and tearing.

The birds scattered, squawking, as a Kaiila sped past. The birds are called zads.

'On your feet, Slaves!' I heard. The lash struck me twice. I did not object to it. I could feel it. The blood coursed through my body. The pain was sharp, rich, and deep, and

244

keen. I did not object to the pain, for I could feel it. Elation coursed through me, fierce, uncontrollable, for I was alive. The lash struck again. I laughed, struggling to my feet. I stood straight. 'March, Slaves!' I heard, and I began again the march, moving first with the left foot, then the right, that the march be uniform, that the chain be carried evenly. It was heavier than before, but I carried it lightly, for I was alive. No longer did I object to the salt in my flesh, the heat. It was enough that I lived. How foolish it seemed then, suddenly, that one should want more. How should one want more, save perhaps health and honor, and a woman, slave at one's feet? I marched onward again, brushing through feeding zads, once more toward Klima. I hummed to myself a simple tune, a tune I had never forgotten, a warrior tune from the northern city of Ko-ro-ba.

Four days later, on a crest, the voice again called 'Hold!' and the chain held.

'Do not kill us! Do not kill us!' screamed a voice. I recognized it. It was the voice of the man who, through much of the march, had cried for us to be killed. He had been silent since the noon halt of four days ago. I had not known whether he had survived or not.

Kaiila moved past us.

I heard collars being opened. For the hood I could not see. The silk which was tied in my collar was removed. It was tied, by order of Hamid, who rode near, about my left wrist, under the manacle. I felt the silk in the circular wrist sore. A heavy key was then thrust in the lock of my collar. The lock contained sand and salt. In the heat the metal was expanded. The lock resisted. Then the key, forced, with a heavy snap, turned, freeing the lock bolt. The collar was opened. The collar was jerked from my throat, and dropped, with the chain, in the crusts. The man then moved to the next prisoner.

No man fled from the chain.

'We may not take kaiila in,' said a man.

We stood for some minutes. I felt the blood and salt in the split shreds of the leather wrappings on my legs. I took care not to move the manacles and chain.

I felt a key inserted in the lock of the slave hood. To my surprise it was thrust up, and jerked from my head. I cried out in sudden pain, the unbelievable white light, hot, fierce,

245

universal, merciless, shuddering in the scalding air of the encircling, blazing crusts, from horizon to horizon, exploding,
stabbing, searing like irons at my face and eyes. 'I'm blind,'
cried a man. 'I'm blind!'

Kaiila moved along the line. It would be long minutes before we could see.

We heard chains being looped and gathered. More Kaiila
passed me.

My limbs felt weak, and ached. I was dizzy. I could scarcely
move. I could scarcely stand.

'Take salt,' said a voice. It was Hassan!

'You live!' I cried.

'Take salt,' he said.

He fell to his knees, and thrust his face into the salt. He
bit at the crusts. He licked crystals from them.

I followed his example. We had not had salt in four days.

'Look,' cried one of the guards. We lifted our heads. We
struggled to our feet. We gritted our eyelids, to shut out the
heat, the blinding light.

'Water!' cried a voice. 'Water!'

It was a man, come from the desert about. He had not
been in the chain. He wore no manacles.

'Water!' he cried. He staggered toward us. He wore a bit
of cloth. His body moved awkwardly. His fingernails were
gone. His mouth and face seemed split, like dried crust.

'It is an escaped slave from the desert,' said Hamid. He
unsheathed his scimitar, and loped toward the man. He bent
down easily from the saddle, the blade loose, but he did not
strike, but returned to the other guards. The man stood in the
crusts, looking after the rider, stupidly. 'Water,' he said. 'Please,
water.'

'Shall we have sport?' asked Hamid of two of his fellows.

'The trek has been long,' grinned one, 'and there has been
little diversion.'

'The head?' asked one. 'The left ear?'

'Agreed,' said the other. They loosened their lances.

'Water,' said the man. 'Water.'

The first man, kicking the kaiila forward, missed his thrust.
The gait of the kaiila in the crusts was not even. The mark,
too, was not an easy one. To strike it would require considerable skill.

The haggard man stood in the crusts, stupidly.

'The right ear,' said the next man, grasping the long, slim lance, eight feet Gorean in length, marked with red and yellow swirling stripes, terminating in an extremely narrow point, razored, steel, some eleven inches in length, and lanceolate, as the leaf of the flahdah tree. All the time he had not taken his eyes from the target.

'Water!' cried the man. Then he screamed as the lance struck him, turning him about.

The second rider had been skillful. The blade had penetrated below the helix and opened the ear, lifting and parting, in its upward movement, the helix.

The man staggered back in the crusts, he lifted his hand. The first rider cursed. He had charged again. This time, the man, stumbling, trying to turn away, had been struck on the left arm, high, just below the shoulder. I was startled that there was so little blood, for the wound was deep. It was as though the man had no blood to bleed. There was a ridge of reddish fluid at the cut. I watched through narrowed eyelids, grimacing against the light. To my horror I saw the man press his mouth to the wound, sucking at the bit of blood. He did not move, but stood in the crusts, sucking at the blood.

Hamid, easily, on the kaiila, his scimitar still light in his hand, rode behind the man. I did not watch, but turned away.

'The point is to Baram,' said Hamid. Clearly the second rider had been the finest.

'We may not take the kaiila in,' said one of the guards.

'We have water sufficient for the return trip,' said another, 'moving at an unimpeded pace.'

To my amazement I saw one of the guards unlocking the stomach-chain and manacles of one of the prisoners. Already the man's slave hood had been removed. And we had, already, been freed of the neck chain.

I looked about, through half-shut eyes. I stood unsteadily. I counted. There were twenty prisoners standing in the crusts. I shuddered.

Hamid rode to my side. He had wiped his blade in the mane of his kaiila. He resheathed the blade. I felt the heat. We stood on a crest, overlooking a broad, shallow valley.

Hamid leaned down. 'There,' he said, pointing into the broad valley. 'Can you see?'

'Yes,' I said.

In the distance, below, perhaps five pasangs away, in the

247

hot, concave, white salt bleakness, like a vast, white, shallow bowl, pasangs wide, there were compounds, low, white buildings of mud brick, plastered. There were many of them. They were hard to see in the distance, in the light, but I could make them out.

'Klima,' said Hamid.

'I have made the march to Klima,' said one of the prisoners. He cried out, elatedly, 'I have made the march to Klima!' It was the man who had, for many of the days, cried out for us to be slain. It was he who had, since the noon halt of four days ago, been silent.

I looked at the prisoners. We looked at one another. Our bodies were burned black by the sun. The flesh, in many places, had cracked. Lighter colored flesh could be seen beneath. There was salt on us, to our thighs. The leather wrappings about our legs were in tatters. Our necks and bodies were abraided, raw from collar and chain. In the last days we had been denied salt. Our bodies were cruel with cramps and weakness. But we stood, all of us, and straight, for we had come to Klima.

Twenty had come to Klima.

The first prisoner, whose bonds had been removed, was thrust in the direction of the compounds. He began to stagger down the slope towards the valley, slipping in the crusts, sometimes sinking in to his knees.

One by one the prisoners were freed. None attempted to flee into the desert. Each, as he was freed, began to trudge toward Klima. There was nowhere else to go.

The man who had cried out, 'I have made the march to Klima!' was freed. He staggered toward the compounds, running, half falling, down the long slope.

Hassan and I were freed. Together we trudged toward Klima, following the straggling line of men before us.

We came upon a figure, fallen in the salt. It was he who had run ahead, who had cried out, disbelievingly, joyously, 'I have made the march to Klima!'

We turned the body over in the salt. 'He is dead,' said Hassan.

Together, Hassan and I rose to our feet.

Nineteen had come to Klima.

I looked back once, to see Hamid, he who was in the fee of the Guard of the Dunes, the Salt Ubar, who was supposedly the faithful lieutenant to Shakar, captain of the Aretai. He turned his kaiila, and, with a scattering of salt, following the others, disappeared over the crest.

I looked up toward the merciless sun. Its relentless presence seemed to fill the sky.

I looked down.

About my left wrist, knotted, bleached in the sun, was a bit of slave silk. On it, still, lingered the perfume of a slave girl, one who, purchased, had been useful to Kurii, who had testified falsely against me at Nine Wells, who had, contemptuously, insolently, cast me a token of her consideration, a bit of silk and scent, to remember her by, when I served at Klima. I would not soon forget pretty Vella. I would remember her well.

I looked up at the sun again, and then, bitter, looked away. I put the wench from my head. She was only a slave girl, only collar meat.

The important work was that of Priest-Kings. Hassan and I had not found the steel tower. We had failed.

I was bitter.

Then I followed Hassan, who had trudged on ahead, wading in the salt, following him toward Klima.

FIFTEEN

T'ZSHAL

At Klima, and other such areas, salt is an industry. Thousands serve there, held captive by the desert. Klima has its own water, but it is dependent on caravans for its foods. These food stores are delivered to scouted areas some pasangs from the compounds, whence they are retrieved later by salt slaves. Similarly, the heavy cylinders of salt, mined and molded at Klima, are carried on the backs of salt slaves from storage areas at Klima to storage areas in the desert, whence they are tallied, sold and distributed to caravans. The cylinders are standardized at ten stone, or a Gorean 'Weight,' which is some forty pounds. A normal kaiila carries ten such cylinders, five to a side. A stronger animal carries sixteen, eight to a side. The load is balanced, always. It is difficult for an animal, or man, of course, to carry an unbalanced load. Most salt at Klima is white, but certain of the mines deliver red salt, red from ferrous oxide in its composition, which is called the Red Salt of Kasra, after its port of embarkation, at the juncture of the Upper and Lower Fayeen.

In Gor's geologic past it seems that the salt districts, like scattered puddles of crystalline residue, are what remains of what was once an inland salt sea or several such. It may be that, in remote times, an arm of Thassa extended here, or did extend here and then, later, in seismic dislocations or continental drift became isolated from the parent body of water, leaving behind one or more smaller salt seas. Or it may be that the seas were independent, being fed by rivers, washing down accumulated salt from rocks over millions of square pasangs. It is not known. In the salt districts salt is found either in solid form or in solution. Klima, among the salt districts, is most famous for its brine pits. Salt can be found in solid form either above or below ground. With the subsidence of the sea and the shifting of strata, certain cubic pasangs of salt, in certain areas, became pressed into granitelike formations, through which one many actually tunnel. Some of these deposits are far below the surface of the Tahari. Men live in some of them, for weeks at a time. In other areas, certain of these solid deposits are exposed and are worked rather in the manner of open mines or quarries. In places these salt mountains are more than six hundred feet high. At Klima, however, most of the salt is in solution. It is the subterranean residue of portions of the vanished seas themselves, which have slipped through fissures and, protected from the heat, and fed still by the ancient seeping rivers, now moving sluggishly beneath the surface, maintain themselves, the hidden remnants of oceans, once mighty, which long ago swelled upon the surface of Gor itself. The salt in solution is obtained in two ways, by drilling and flush mining and, in the deeper pits, by sending men below to fetch the brine. In the drilling and flush mining, two systems are used, the double-pipe system and the separate-pipe system. In the double-pipe system fresh water is forced into the cavity through an outer pipe and the heavier solution of salt and water rises bubbling through the second pipe, or inner pipe, inserted within the larger. In the separate-pipe system, two pipes, separated by several yards, are used, fresh water being forced through one, the salt water solution, the salt being dissolved in the fresh water, rising through the other. The separate-pipe system is, by most salt masters, regarded as the most efficient. An advantage of the double-pipe system is that only a single tap well need be drilled. Both systems require pumping, of course. But much of the salt at Klima comes from its famous brine pits. These pits are of two kinds, 'open' and 'closed.' Men, in the closed pits, actually descend and, wading, or on rafts, negotiate the sludge itself, filling their vessels and later, eventually, pouring their contents into the lift sacks, on hooks, worked by windlasses from the surface. The 'harvesting' vessel, not the retaining vessel, used is rather like a perforated cone with a handle, to which is attached a rope. It is dragged through the sludge and lifted, the free water running from the vessel, leaving within the sludge of salt, thence to be poured into the retaining vessels, huge, wooden tubs. The retaining vessels are then emptied later into the lift sacks, a ring which fits over

251

the rope hooks. In places, the 'open pits', the brine pits, are exposed on the surface, where they are fed by springs from the underground rivers, which prevents their dessication by evaporation, which would otherwise occur almost immediately in the Tahari temperatures. Men do not last long in the open pits. The same underground seepage which, in places, fills the brine pits, in other places, passing through salt-free strata, provides Klima with its fresh water. It has a salty taste like much of the water of the Tahari but it is completely drinkable, not having been filtered through the salt accumulations. It contains only the salt normal in Tahari drinking water. The salt in the normal Tahari fresh water, incidentally, is not without its value, for, when drunk, it helps to some extent, though it is not in itself sufficient, to prevent salt loss in animals and men through sweating. Salt, of course, like water, is essential to life. Sweating is dangerous in the Tahari. This has something to do with the normally graceful, almost languid movements of the nomads and animals of the area. The heavy garments of the Tahari, too, have as two of their main objectives the prevention of water loss, and the retention of moisture on the skin, slowing water loss by evaporation. One can permit profuse perspiration only where one has ample water and salt.

Besides the mines and pits of the salt districts, there are warehouses and offices, in which complicated records are kept, and from which shipments to the isolated, desert storage areas are arranged. There are also processing areas where the salt is freed of water and refined to various degrees of quality, through a complicated system of racks and pans, generally exposed to the sun. Slaves work at these, raking, stirring, and sifting. There are also the molding sheds where the salt is pressed into the large cylinders, such that they may be roped together and eventually be laden on pack kaiila. The salt is divided into nine qualities. Each cylinder is marked with its quality, the name of its district, and the sign of that district's salt master.

Needless to say, Klima contains as well, incidental to the salt industry centered there, the ancillary supports of these mining and manufacturing endeavors, such as its kitchens and commissaries, its kennels and eating sheds, its discipline pits, its assembly areas, its smithies and shops, its quarters for guards and scribes, an infirmary for them, and so on. In many respects

Klima resembles a community, save that it differs in at least two significant respects. It contains neither children, nor women.

When we had approached Klima Hassan had said to me, 'Leave the bit of silk about your wrist in the crusts, hiding it.'

'Why?' I had asked.

'It is slave silk,' he said, 'and it bears, still, the scent of a woman.'

'Why should I leave it?' I asked.

'Because, at Klima,' he said, 'men will kill you for it.'

I hid the bit of silk in the crusts, at the edge of one of the low, white plastered buildings.

The man who spoke was T'Zshal, Master of Kennel 804. 'You are free to leave Klima whenever you wish,' he said. 'None is here held against his will.'

He stood before us.

We sat on the floor of the shed, naked, together. We were tied together by the neck, by a light rope. It would have suficed, truly, to hold only girls. Yet none of us parted it; none tore it from him.

'I do not jest,' said the man.

We had been four days now at Klima. We had been well watered and adequately fed. We had been kept in the shade. The rope had been placed on us when we had straggled in from the desert, to keep us together. We were told not to remove it; we did not remove it. Four men, however, had been cut from it. They had died of exposure, from the march to Klima. Thus, in the end, all told, only fifteen had survived the march.

'No,' laughed T'Zshal. 'I jest not!'

He wore desert boots, canvas trousers, baggy, a red sash; in the sash was thrust a dagger, curved. He was bare-chested, and hairy; he wore kaffiyeh and agal, though of rep-cloth, the cording, too, of rep-cloth, twisted into narrow cord. He was bearded. He carried a whip, the 'snake,' coiled, symbol of his authority over us. Behind him, armed with scimitars, stood two guards, they, too, bare-chested, in flat rep-cloth turbans. Light entered the kennel from an aperture in the ceiling.

He approached us. Several shrank back. He drew the curved dagger and slashed the light rope from our throats.

'You are free to go,' he said.

He strode to the door of the kennel and thrust it open. Out-

253

side we could see the sun on the crusts, the desert beyond.

'Go,' he laughed, 'Go!'

Not one of the men moved.

'Ah,' said he, 'you choose to remain. That is your choice. Very well, I accept it. But if you remain you must do so on my terms.' He suddenly snapped the whip. The crack was loud, sharp. 'It is understood?' he asked.

'Yes!' said more than one man, swiftly.

'Kneel!' barked T'Zshal.

We knelt.

'But will you be permitted to remain?' he asked.

Several of the men cast apprehensive glances at one another.

'Perhaps, yes. Perhaps, no,' said T'Zshal. 'That decision, you see, is mine.' He coiled the whip. 'It is not easy to earn one's keep at Klima. At Klima the cost of lodging is high. You must earn your right to stay at Klima. You must work hard. You must please me – much.' He looked from face to face.

He did not ask if we understood. We did.

'We may, however,' asked Hassan, 'leave Klima when we wish?'

T'Zshal regarded him. Clearly he was wondering if Hassan were insane. I smiled. T'Zshal was puzzled. 'Yes,' he said.

'Very well,' said Hassan, noting the point.

'There is little leather at Klima,' said T'Zshal. 'There are few water bags. Those that exist are of one talu. They are guarded.'

Water at Klima is generally carried in narrow buckets, on wooden yokes, with dippers attached, for the slaves. A talu is approximately two gallons. A talu bag is a small bag. It is the sort carried by a nomad herding verr afoot in the vicinity of his camp. Bags that small are seldom carried in caravan, except at the saddles of scouts.

'Is it your intention,' inquired T'Zshal of Hassan, 'to purloin several bags, fill them, battling guards, and walk your way out of Klima?'

Even, of course, if one could obtain several such bags, and fill them with water, it did not seem likely that one could carry enough water to find one's way afoot out of the desert.

Hassan shrugged. 'It is a thought,' he said.

'You must think you are strong,' said T'Zshal.

'I have made the march to Klima,' said Hassan.

'We have all made the march to Klima,' said T'Zshal.

254

We were startled that he had said this.

'There is none at Klima,' said T'Zshal, 'who has not made that march.' He looked at us. 'All here,' said he, 'my pretties, are slaves of the salt, slaves of the desert. We dig salt for the free; we are fed.'

'Even the salt master?' asked Hassan.

'He, too, long ago, once came naked to Klima,' said T'Zshal. 'We order ourselves by the arrangements of skill and steel. We, slaves, have formed this nation, and administer it, as we see fit. The salt delivered, the outsiders do not disturb us. In our internal affairs we are autonomous.'

'And we?' said Hassan.

'You,' grinned T'Zshal, 'are the true slaves, for you are the slaves of slaves.' He laughed.

'Did you come hooded to Klima?' asked Hassan.

'Yes, as have all, even the salt master himself,' said T'Zshal.

This was disappointing information. Hassan had doubtless had in mind the forcing of a guard, or kennel master, perhaps T'Zshal himself, to guide him from Klima, could he obtain water. As it now turned out, and we had no reason to doubt the kennel master, none at Klima could serve in this capacity.

We knew, generally, Red Rock, the kasbah of the Salt Ubar and such, lay northwest of Klima, but, unless one knows the exact direction, the trails, this information is largely useless. Even in a march of a day one could pass, unknowingly, an oasis in the desert, wandering past it, missing it by as little as two or three pasangs.

Knowledge of the trails is vital.

None at Klima knew the trails. The free, their masters, had seen to this.

Moreover, to protect the secrecy of the salt districts, the trails to them were not openly or publicly marked. This was a precaution to maintain the salt monoplies of the Tahari, as though the desert itself would not have been sufficient in this respect.

T'Zshal smiled, seeming human for the moment, and not kennel master. 'None, my pretties,' said he, 'knows the way from Klima. There is thus, in the desert, no way from Klima.'

'There is a way,' said Hassan. 'It need only be found.'

'Good fortune,' said T'Zshal. With his whip he indicated the opened door of the kennel. 'Go,' he said.

'I choose to stay, for the time,' said Hassan.

255

'My kennel is honored,' said T'Zshal, inclining his head. Hassan, too, bowed his head, in Taharic courtesy acknowledging the compliment.

T'Zshal smiled. 'Know this, though,' he said, 'that should you leave us our feelings would be injured, that our hospitality be rejected. Few return to Klima. Of those that do, few survive the pits of discipline, and of those who do, it is to dig in the open pits.' He lifted the whip, noting its graceful curve. It was the snake, many fanged, tiny bits of metal braided within the leather. 'Klima,' said T'Zshal, slowly, 'may seem to you a fierce and terrible place. Perhaps it is. I do not know. I have forgotten any other place. Yet it is not too different, I think, from the world on the other side of the horizon. At Klima, you will find, as in all the world, there are those who hold the whip, and those who dig, and die.' He looked at us. 'Here,' he said, 'in this kennel, it is I who hold the whip.'

'How,' I asked, 'does one become kennel master?'

'Kill me,' said T'Zshal.

SIXTEEN

HASSAN AND I AGREE
TO ACCOMPANY T'ZSHAL

I held the line coiled, in my left hand, it tied to the handle on the metal, perforated cone, swinging in my right.

It was cool in the pit, on the large raft. At each corner of the raft, mounted on a pole, was a small, oil-fed lamp. It was dark in the pit, save for our lamps, and those of other rafts. I could see two other rafts, illuminated in the darkness, one some two hundred yards away, the other more than a pasang distant over the water. In places we could see the ceiling of the pit, only a few feet above our head, in others it was lost in the darkness, perhaps a hundred or more feet above us. I estimated our distance beneath the surface to be some four hundred feet. The raft in the dark, sluggish waters, stirred beneath our feet.

I flung the cone out from the raft into the darkness, allowing the line to uncoil from my left hand, following the vanishing, sinking cone.

I shared the raft with eight others, three, who handled cones as I, the 'harvesters,' four polemen and the steersman. Harvesters and polemen, periodically, exchange positions. The raft is guided by a sweep at its stern, in the keeping of the steersman. It is propelled by the polemen. The poles used are weighted at the bottom, and are some twenty feet in length. One of the poles, released in deep water, will stand upright in the water, about a yard of it above the surface. The weight makes it easier to keep the pole, which is long, submerged. It may be thus be used with less fatigue. The floor of the brine pit, in most places, is ten to fifteen feet below the surface of the water. There are areas in the pits, however, where the depth exceeds that of the poles. In such areas, paddles, of which each raft is equipped with four, near the retaining vessels, are

257

used. It is slow, laborious work, however, moving the heavy raft with these levers. The raft is some twelve feet in width and some twenty-four or twenty-five feet in length. Each raft contains a low frame, within which are placed the retaining vessels, large, wooden salt tubs, each approximately a yard in height and four feet in diameter. Each raft carries four of these, either arranged in a lateral frame, or arranged in a square frame, at the raft's center. Ours were arranged laterally. The lateral arrangement is more convenient in unloading; the square arrangement provides a more convenient distribution of deck space, supplying superior crew areas at stem and stern. From the point of view of 'harvesting,' the arrangements are equivalent, save that the harvesters, naturally, to facilitate their work, position themselves differently in the two arrangements. If one is right-handed, one works with the retaining vessel to the left, so that one can turn and, with the right hand, tip the harvesting vessel, steadying it with the left hand.

I allowed time for the cone to sink to the bottom.

The retaining vessels are, at the salt docks, lifted from the rafts by means of pulleys and counterweights. The crew of a given raft performs this work. When the retaining vessels are suspended, they are tipped, and the sludge scooped and shoveled from them into the wide-mouthed, ring-bearing lift sacks. These, drawn and pushed on carts, fitted onto wooden, iron-sheathed rails, are transported to the hooked lift ropes. These ropes run in systems to the surface and return. Men at windlasses on the surface lift the sacks, which, when emptied, return on the slack loop. The weighted loop cannot slip back because each hook, in turn, preceding the sack being emptied, engages one of several pintles in the machinery, which is so geared that it can turn in only one direction. There are twelve of these pintles, mounted in a large circle; when a given hook drops off one, freed by gravity, another hook is already engaged on another, held there by the weight of the ascending lift sacks. Empty sacks are placed on slack hooks, below the machinery, to be returned to the pit.

The steersman, when not attending to his sweep, carried a lance. We were not alone in the pits.

Hand over hand, I drew the cone through the sludge toward the raft.

I had been amazed to learn that the brine pits, in effect a network of small subterranean marine seas, were not devoid

258

of life. I had expected them to be sterile bodies of water, from the absence of sunlight, percluding basic photosynthesis and the beginning of a food chain, and the high salt content of fluid. A human body, for example, will not sink in the water. This is one of the reasons, too, it is particularly desirable, in this environment, to weight the raft poles, to help counter the unusual bouyancy of the saline fluid. In my original conjecture, however, as to the sterility of these small seas, I was mistaken.

'Look there,' called the harvester.

I saw it, too. The other men came to my side of the raft, and we noted it, moving in the water. The steersman dropped the point of the lance toward the water, watching, too.

I slowly drew up the metal, perforated cone. Water drained from it, in tiny irregular streams, spattering back into the sea, and onto the boards of the raft. Then I lifted the cone and deposited the sludge in the retaining vessel, the large wooden tub behind me and to my left. I did not again coil and cast the line. I, too, watched the water.

The light of our lamps flickered on the surface, yellowly, in broken, shifting refractions.

'There!' said one of the men.

Lelts are often attracted to the salt rafts, largely by the vibrations in the water, picked up by their abnormally developed lateral-line protrusions, and their fernlike craneal vibration receptors, from the cones and poles. Too, though they are blind, I think either the light, or the heat, perhaps, from our lamps, draws them. The tiny, eyeless heads will thrust from the water, and the fernlike filaments at the side of the head will open and lift, orienting themselves to one or the other of the lamps. The lelt is commonly five to seven inches in length. It is white, and long-finned. It swims slowly and smoothly, its fins moving the water very little, which apparently contributes to its own concealment in a blind environment and makes it easier to detect the vibrations of its prey, and of several varieties of tiny segmented creatures, predominantly isopods. The brain of the lelt is interesting, containing an unusually developed odor-perception center and two vibration-reception centers. Its organ of balance, or hidden 'ear,' is also unusually large, and is connected with an unusually large balance center in its brain. Its visual center, on the other hand, is stunted and undeveloped, a remnant, a vague genetic memory of an organ long discarded in its evolution. Among the lelts, too, were, here and there, tiny salamanders, they, too, white and blind. Like the lelts, they were, for their size, long-bodied, were capable of long periods of dormancy and possessed a slow metabolism, useful in an environment in which food is not plentiful. Unlike the lelts they had long, stemlike legs. At first I had taken them for lelts, skittering about the rafts, even to the fernlike filaments at the sides of their head, but these filaments, in the case of the salamanders, interestingly, are not vibration receptors but feather gills, an external gill system. This system, common in the developing animal generally, is retained even by the adult salamanders, who are, in this environment, permanently gilled. The gills of the lelt are located at the lower sides of its jaw, not on the sides of its head, as is common in open-water fish. The feather gills of the salamanders, it seems, allow them to hunt the same areas as the lelts for the same prey, the vibration effects of these organs being similar, without frightening them away, thus disturbing the water and alerting possible prey. They often hunt the same areas. Although this form of salamander possesses a lateral-line set of vibration receptors, like the lelt, it lacks the craneal receptors and its lateral-line receptors do not have the sensitivity of the lelt's. Following the lelt, not disturbing it, often helps the salamander find prey. On the other hand, the salamander, by means of its legs and feet, can dislodge prey inaccessible to the lelt. The length of the stemlike legs of the salamander, incidentally, help it in stalking the water. It takes little prey while swimming freely. The long legs cause little water vibration. Further, they enable the animal to move efficiently, covering large areas without considerable metabolic cost. In a blind environment, where food is scarce, energy conservation is essential. The long narrow legs also lift the salamander's head and body from the floor, enabling it, with its sensors, to scan a greater area for prey. The upright posture in men delivers a similar advantage, visually, in increasing scanning range, this being useful not only in the location of prey, but also, of course, in the recognition of dangers while remote, hopefully while yet avoidable.

But it was not the lelts nor the salamanders which explained our interest in the waters.

'There!' cried the man. 'There it is again!' But then it was gone. I had not seen it.

In the pits there is no light, save that which men bring there. Without light, there cannot be photosynthesis. Without photosynthesis there cannot be the reduction of carbon dioxide, the formation of sugar, the beginning of the food chain. Ultimately, then, food brought into the pits, generally in the form of organic debris, from hundreds of sources, many of them hundreds of miles distant; this debris is carried by the fresh-water feeds, through minute faults and fissures, and even porous rock, until it reaches the remains of the ancient seas, now sunken far beneath the surface. On and in this debris, breaking it down, are several varieties of bacteria. These bacteria are devoured by protozoons and rotifers. These, in turn, become the food for various flatworms and numerous tiny segmented creatures, such as isopods, which, in turn, serve as food for small, blind, white crayfish, lelts and salamanders.

These latter, however, do not stand at the top of the food chain. Sometimes one picks up the lelts and salamanders in the cones. It was not these that had excited the interest of the men.

'Is it the Old One?' asked one of the men.

'I cannot tell,' said another. The steersman stood ready with the lance.

'There!' cried one of the men, pointing.

I saw it then, moving in, slowly, then turning about. The lelts and salamanders vanished, disappearing beneath the water. The thing disappeared. The waters were calm.

'It's gone,' said one of the men.

'Was it the Old One?' asked one of the men.

'I do not know,' said the steersman, with the lance. The Old One had not been seen in the pit for more than a year.

'It is gone now,' said another of the men.

'Look!' I cried. This time it was close, surfacing not ten feet from the raft. We saw the broad, blunt head, eyeless, white. Then it submerged, with a twist of the long spine and tail.

The steersman was white. 'It is the Old One,' he said. On the whitish back, near the high dorsal fin, there was a long scar. Part of the dorsal fin itself was rent, and scarred. These were lance marks.

'He has come back,' said one of the men.

The waters were still.

At the top of the food chain in the pits, a descendant, dark-adapted, of the terrors of the ancient seas, stood the long-bodied, nine-gilled salt shark.

The waters were calm.

'Let us gather salt,' said a man.

261

'Wait,' said the steersman. 'Watch.'

For more than a quarter of an Ahn we did nothing.

'It is gone,' said a man.

'We must make our quotas,' said one of the harvesters.

'Gather salt,' said the steersman.

Again we took our ropes and cones, and bent to the labor of dredging for salt.

'The lelts have not returned,' said the steersman to me.

'What does this mean?' I asked.

'That the Old One is still with us,' he said, looking down at the dark waters. Then he said, 'Gather salt.' Again I flung out the rope and cone.

It was growing late.

The oil in the lamps, on the poles at the corners of the raft, grew low.

On the surface it would be dusk.

I wondered how one might escape from Klima. Even if one could secure water, it did not seem one could, afoot, carry water sufficient to walk one's way free of the salt districts. And, even if one could traverse the many pasangs of desert afoot, there would not be much likelihood, in the wilderness, of making one's way to Red Rock, or another oasis. Those at Klima, by intent of the free, their masters, knew not the trails whereby their liberty might be achieved. I remembered, too, the poor slave who had encountered the chain on its march to Klima. He had been the subject of sport, then slain. None, it was said, had come back from Klima.

I thought of Priest-Kings, and Others, the Kurii, and their wars. They seemed remote.

It came very suddenly, from beneath the water, not more than five feet from me, erupting upward. I saw the man screaming in the jaws. The head was more than a yard in width, white, pits where there might have been eyes. The raft tipped, struck by its back, as it turned and, twisting, glided away into the darkness.

'Poles!' screamed the steersman. 'Poles!' The poleman seized the poles, lowering them into the water.

One of the lamps sputtered out.

I heard screaming now, far off, then silence. Because of the saline content of the water the salt shark, when not hunting, often swims half emerged from the fluid. Its gills, like those of lelt, are below and at the sides of his jaws. This is a salt adaptation which conserves energy, which, otherwise, might be constantly expended in maintaining an attitude in which oxygenation can occur.

'I cannot touch the bottom,' cried one of the men, in misery. The raft had drifted.

'Paddles,' cried the steersman, leaning on the sweep. The polemen seized up the broad levers near the retaining vessels. Another of the lamps sputtered out.

Slowly the raft turned.

Only two lamps now burned.

'You others,' said the steersman, 'take poles!' We did so. It was our hope that the men with paddles could move the raft sufficiently to bring it to a place where we could use the poles.

'It is gone now,' said one of the men with paddles.

'It is the Old One,' said the steersman. 'It is dusk.' I then understood, from his words, the meaning of the scarcity of food in the pit. When the hunting is good, one hunts. One can return later to earlier kills, driving away scavenging lelts. Further, I wondered at the salt shark, blind, living in total darkness. Yet it hunted at dusk, and at dawn, driven apparently by ancient biological rhythms. The long-bodied, ghostly creature, hunting in the black waters, followed still the rhythms of its dark clock, set for its species a quarter of a billion years ago in a vanished, distant, sunlit world.

'Make haste!' cried the steersman. 'Make haste!'

The third lamp sputtered out. There was now but a single lamp burning, on the port side, aft. Then it, too, sputtered out.

We were in darkness. Somewhere near, below us, or about us, moved the Old One.

We were in absolute darkness. There was no moonlight, not even starlight. In the world in which we stood even a Kur would be blind. We stood waiting, alone, in the world of the Old One.

When it came, it came swiftly, hurling itself upwards from the water. We, in the darkness, felt the salt water drench us, heard the great body, more than twenty feet long, fall back in the water.

Then, for a time, it was quiet again.

We heard the raft bumped, felt the movement in the wood. We then felt the body of the Old One beneath the raft. The raft tipped, but fell back. We clung in the darkness to the re-

263

taining vessels, the salt tubs. Twice more the raft tipped, and fell back.

More than a quarter of an Ahn passed. We thought the Old One no longer with us. Then the raft, on the port side, seemed to dip into the water. A man cried out, in horror, striking with a paddle. The heavy head slipped back into the water. The Old One had placed his head on the raft, sensing in the darkness.

We drifted for more than an Ahn in silence, in the darkness. Then, suddenly, hurling itself from the water, the great body, thrashing, fell across the raft, twisting, the mighty tail flailing and snapping. I heard splintering wood, the retaining vessels, the salt tubs, struck and shattered, flung bounding and rolling from the frame. I heard men scream, sensed men struck yards from the raft, heard them strike the water.

I threw myself on my stomach into the remains of the splintered frame, clutching at torn wood.

There was screaming in the darkness. I heard more than one man taken. 'I cannot see!' cried one man.

Four more times the great body threw itself onto the raft, thrashing.

Once I felt it roll over my back, my body protected by the remains of the frame. Its skin was not rough, abrasive, like that of free-water sharks, but slick, coated with a bacterial slime. It slipped over me, not tearing me from the frame. Though it touched me I could see nothing.

'Where are you?' I heard from the water.

'Here!' I cried. 'Here is the raft!' I knelt on the raft. I did not know if I were alone on it or not. 'Here!' I cried. 'Here! Here!'

'Help!' I heard. 'Help!' I heard two men crawl onto the raft. One began screaming. Another man crawled onto the raft and then, insanely, began to wander about. 'Stay down!' I cried. 'Save yourselves!' he cried. He leaped into the water. 'Come back!' I cried. It is my supposition that it was his intention to swim to the dock, more than four pasangs away. He did not turn back, even when I warned him that his direction was false. 'Poor fool,' said a voice. 'Hassan!' I cried. 'It is I,' he said, near me.

'Help!' I heard. I felt for one of the raft poles, found it, and, extending it, thrust it toward the voice. I pulled the man aboard. I tried to save a second man, similarly, but he was

264

taken from the pole, screaming, by the Old One.

I saw lights across the water, another raft, approaching. On its bow, lance raised, I saw T'Zshal.

The two rafts gently struck one another. We boarded the other raft.

'There is another man in the water, somewhere,' I said to T'Zshal. 'He swam that way.'

'Fool,' said T'Zshal, 'fool.' He looked upon us. 'The Old One,' he said, not asking.

The steersman nodded. He had lived.

'Let us go back,' said one of the polemen on T'Zshal's raft.

T'Zshal regarded us. I and Hassan had survived, and the steersman, and the man I had saved. I did not know if the man who had entered the water had survived or not. I did not think his chances were good.

'Let us return now, swiftly to the docks,' said one of the men on T'Zshal's raft.

T'Zshal looked out over the dark waters. 'The Old One has returned,' he said. 'And he has not forgotten his tricks.'

'Let us return swiftly to the dock,' said a man, insistently.

'A man of mine,' said T'Zshal, 'remains in the water.' He indicated with his hand the direction the men were to pole.

They moaned, but did not disobey the kennel master.

T'Zshal himself stood at the bow of the raft, the lance in one hand, in his other a lantern, lifted.

An Ahn later he found the man. 'Greetings,' said the fellow. 'Greetings,' said T'Zshal, drawing him from the water. 'I have been swimming,' said the man. 'Yes,' said T'Zshal. T'Zshal put him on the planks of the raft. The man seemed to have no recollection of the Old One, nor of what he was doing in the water. He fell asleep.

'Return to the dock,' said T'Zshal.

The heavy raft turned, and began to move toward the docks.

Hassan and I looked at one another. We had decided that we would not kill T'Zshal.

'Tomorrow,' said T'Zshal, 'at dusk, I am returning to this area.'

'I shall accompany you,' I said. 'And I, too,' said Hassan.

SEVENTEEN

WHAT OCCURRED IN THE PIT

I think there was no man on the raft that evening who had
not lost at least one comrade, recently or long ago, to the Old
One.

'We hunt the Old One,' T'Zshal had said. He had visited
various pits, some open, some sheltered, the warehouses, the
refining vats. 'We hunt the Old One,' he had said. And they
had followed him. Even in the shadow of Klima's Keep itself,
the squarish, stout, fortresslike building which houses the
weaponry, domicile and office of the Salt Master himself did
we recruit our crew. On the height of the keep I saw, tight in
the bright, hot wind, under the merciless sun, defiant to the
pits and desert itself, the flag of Klima, the whip and scimitar. None had been ordered; not one upon the raft had, under
the uplifted whip coil, nor upon the advice of unsheathed steel,
been commanded. Many were older men, sober and mature,
many blackened by the sun. Each was slave, but each came
not as a slave, but came unbidden, as a man. 'We hunt the
Old One,' had said T'Zshal. He said this in the pits, the warehouses, among the refining vats. 'We hunt the Old One,' he
said. And men had followed him.

I think there was no man on the raft that evening who had
not lost at least one comrade, recently or long ago, to the Old
One.

'Awaken me,' had said T'Zshal, 'when the lelts have gone.'

Far into the pit, distant from the salt docks, we slowed the
raft, and steadied it with the long poles, holding it as nearly
as we could in place. He who had been the steersman with us
yesterday, during the atack of the Old One, held the sweep
that governed the movements of that open, sluggish platform

which constituted our vessel. Beside he, only Hassan, on the other side, and myself, of yesterday's crew, accompanied T'Zshal. At the corners of the raft burned four lamps, mounted on poles. Torches, however, stood ready, to be lit from these, and held over the water, should there be need.

'Awaken me when the lelts have gone,' had said T'Zshal. 'I will sleep now.'

He had then laid down, behind the frame within which the salt tubs are stored, aft, and had slept. Beside him lay the long lance, some nine feet in length.

'Will you not use poison on the blade?' had asked a man at the salt dock. No one of those who accompanied T'Zshal had asked the question.

'No,' had said T'Zshal.

I wondered if he had once been of the Warriors.

I observed T'Zshal as he slept, the bearded head on one arm. I wondered why it was that none killed him, to become kennel master in his place. How was it, he holding the precarious sovereignty of our kennel, that he dared to sleep among slaves, who might win his kaffiyeh and agal, though they were only rep-cloth, so simply as the dagger, slipped from his sash, might enter his throat? The kennel master, though slave, too, is Ubar, with power of life and death, in the squalor of his domain. How is it, I wondered, that such a man can survive a night, that such a man dare turn his back upon the fierce, envious sleen among whom, with whip, and laughter, he walks. His will, his word, in the kennel decrees law. He may, if he choose, stake out, or whip or slay a man who fails his quota of gathered salt, or strikes a fellow, administering fierce, dread discipline as the whim may seize him, and yet, should he himself be slain, his slayer is not punished, but accedes to his authority and, in his place, becomes master of the kennel. How is it, I wondered, that men survive at Klima, and that they do not die at one another's throats?

I looked at the heads of the lelts, and, scattered among them, the heads of the pale salamanders, thrust from the dark water, attracted by the movement, or the awareness of the light or heat, of the lamps.

They had been with the raft now for better than an Ahn, appearing some quarter of an Ahn after we had steadied the sluggish vessel in place.

It is difficult to bespeak the darkness of the pit.

T'Zshal slept.

Beside him lay the lance; in his reddish sash was thrust the dagger of his office.

'The lelts remain with us,' said one of the men near me, he, too, with a pole.

I looked upon the lelts, and, among them, here and there, the salamanders. Their blunt, whitish heads protruded from the water, curious, each head oriented toward one or the other of the four lamps on the raft. I knelt down on the raft, and, quickly, scooped, holding it, one of the lelts from the water. It was inclosed in my hand. It struggled briefly, then lay still. The lelt is a small fish, long-bodied for its size, long-finned. It commonly swims slowly, smoothly, conserving energy in the black, saline world encompassing its existence. There is little to eat in that world; it is a liquid desert, almost barren, black, blind and cool. It swims slowly, conserving its energy, not alerting its prey, commonly flatworms and tiny segmented creatures, predominantly isopods. I turned the lelt, looking at the small, sunken, covered pits in the sides of its head. I wondered if it was capable, somehow, of a dim awareness of the phenomenon of light. Could there be some capacity, some genetic predisposition for the recognition of light, like an ancient, almost lost genetic memory, buried in the tiny, simple, linear brain at the apex of its spinal column? It could not be possible I told myself. The tiny gills, oddly beneath and at the sides of its jaws, closed and opened. There was a minute sound. I lowered my hand and let the lelt slip again, a few feet from the raft. Again its head protruded from the water, again oriented to the same lamp at the corner of the raft.

'Why did you not eat it?' asked the man near me.

I shrugged. Some salt slaves eat the lelt, raw, taken from the water, or gleaned from their harvesting vessels. The first bite is taken behind the back of the neck.

I regarded the fish.

Perhaps they have some dim awareness of light. Perhaps it is only the heat that draws them. I suppose, in the salt pit, one of our small lamps might seem to those who had in their lives only known darkness like the glory of a thousand suns. We know little about the lelt. We do know it will come from the darkness and lift the blind pits of its eyes toward a source of light.

'You could have given it to me,' said the man near me.

'I did not think of it,' I told him.

We know little about men, too, I thought. We do know they will seek the truth. I do not know if they can see it. Perhaps if they touched it, they would die, burning in its flames. Perhaps we cannot see truth. Perhaps nature has denied us this gift. Perhaps we can sense only its presence. Perhaps we can sense only its heat. Perhaps to stand occasionally in its presence is sufficient.

'The lelts have gone,' said the man.

The waters were dark, seemingly empty. The lelts, the salamanders, had gone.

'Waken, T'Zshal,' said the man. The hair rose on the back of my neck.

Suddenly then I understood the institution of the kennel master, and the dark laws governing his tenure, how they regulated and ordered behavior at Klima.

'The lelts have gone,' whispered a man.

I glanced at T'Zshal, his heavy head, bearded, resting on his arm, the lance beside him.

I had wondered why men did not kill T'Zshal, and the other kennel masters, why the societal arrangement was as stable as it was. I now knew. It was because the killer then, in turn, would be the kennel master. The dread responsibility would then be his to bear. His then would be the fearful burdens of autonomy, of freedom. One must speak carefully whose words become law. It is not easy to be master at Klima. Too, he would be the next to die. It is a high price to pay for the whip. One must think carefully before slaying a kennel master, for the reasons for which one performs this action, if sufficient to justify his slaying must, too, be sufficient to justify the slaying of his successor. There are two major controls on the office of kennel master, one on the men, the other on the master. The control on the men is that the killer of the kennel master must asume the office of his victim, with its vulnerabilities and hazards. The control on the kennel master is the incipient rage and menace of his desperate charges. If he does not govern shrewdly and well, if he does not do rough justice, he invites the lesions of resentment, which among the grim, trapped men of Klima must, sooner or later, culminate in the moment of insurrection. He cannot be easy with the men, of course, for he himself is subject to the sanctions of his superiors, in par-

269

ticular in connection with the salt quotas imposed upon his kennel. Men do not wish to be kennel master. But yet one must be sovereign; one must accept the burden. It is steel alone, and will, which prevents catastrophe and slaughter. The whip must be held. Who will be courageous enough, strong enough, to lift it among the savage, condemned beasts of Klima? Who will be bold enough, generous enough, to accept the dreadful office of kennel master at Klima?

'Waken T'Zshal,' whispered a man near me.

I went to the recumbent figure of the kennel master. I put my hand on his shoulder. 'Awaken, T'Zshal,' said I. 'The lelts have gone.'

T'Zshal opened his eyes. He sat up. With his fingers, and some fresh water, from a skin, he rubbed his eyes. He took a drink. He stretched, and stood up on the raft. He studied the waters about the raft, black and quiet. He removed his shirt, and his boots.

The waters were quiet.

He was bare-chested. He wore the kaffiyeh and agal. He was barefoot. The dagger was thrust in his sash. He examined the long blade of the lance, running his finger along the edge of the blade. The blade was bound in the shaft by four rivets. From his sash he took a long, narrow lacing of rawhide, which he bound about the base of the lance blade, where it was riveted in the shaft, thus, for about six inches, reinforcing the shaft. He then took fresh water from the skin and soaked the lacing. He then laid the lance over the tops of two of the large retaining vessels, the salt tubs, on the raft.

There was no stirring, or movement, near the raft.

None of the men spoke.

T'Zshal was the first to see it. We saw it only after we sensed his movement, slight.

It was some forty feet away, aft on the starboard side. Then it disappeared.

T'Zshal took the lance, holding the point down. He gripped it in both hands.

'Stand back from the edge of the raft,' he said.

We moved back.

I felt exhilarated. Gone from my mind suddenly was the brooding on realities and truths that might not be disclosed to men. It is enough to know they exist. One need not stand forever, one's face pressed against a wall that may not be penetrated. One must turn one's back in time upon the impenetrable wall. One must laugh, and cry out, and be a man. Man can think; he must act. In the midst of impenetrable mysteries, not caring for him, beyond him, he behaves, he chooses, he acts. Wisdom decrees that the tree of thought must not be planted where it cannot bear fruit. A man may starve trying to feed on the illusion of nourishment. There are realities, truths, which lie open to man. These are those of his species, of his kind of being, of his realm of animal. To know these truths he needs little more than his brain, his blood, his eyes and hands. He listens overmuch to what does not speak to him, to what cannot speak to him. Within the boundaries of his own being, in that bright realm, let him claim the supremacy which is his; it will remain vacant, unless he seize upon it. It is his; he may take it or not. The choice is up to him. All else is the night and darkness. Music he will make among the stones and silence. He will sing for his own ears; the justification is himself and the song. To what must he be true, if not himself? To what else should he be true? He is born a hunter. Let him not forget the taste of meat.

It erupted from the water not a yard from the raft, hurtling upward, ten feet into the air, towering over the boards and T'Zshal, with a cry of rage, and joy, and I, too, screamed, thrust the lance deep into the body and it turned twisting in the air, jaws, teeth rows like hooks bent back, triangular the gills beneath the jaw, the pits in the side of the great head a yard, more, I could not tell, across; and then fell back into the water and twisted under the surface and circled away, the dorsal fin, sail-like, scarred from years before, tracing its angry circle.

'Greetings, Old One!' cried T'Zshal. He held the bloodied lance in his hand, fluid thick, black under the lamps, on the blade.

The Old One now again faced the raft. It scarcely moved in the water. It seemed to be watching us.

'It is not pleased,' said a man. 'You have angered it,' said another.

My heart pounded. I thought not then of our comrades of the day before, those slain by the monster in the water. I thought then rather of the beast, the foe, and the hunt. I feared then only that it might forsake the fray.

But I needed not fear, for it was the Old One with whom we dealt.

'Ah, Old One,' crooned T'Zshal, softly across the water, 'we meet again.'

I wondered that he had said this.

'Protect the lamps,' said T'Zshal, softly, to us. 'Cover them when the water is high.'

If the lamps were lost, and the torches unlit, I did not think it likely we would return to the salt dock.

I saw the water near the tail of the Old One begin to stir. It was moving its tail back and forth. Then it slipped beneath the surface.

'Hold to the salt tubs,' said T'Zshal.

We felt the great body of the Old One twist under the heavy beams of the raft. Then the raft lifted, to an almost forty-five degree angle as the monster humped beneath it, thrusting it upward. Men slipped, some fell, but none entered the water. Four times the Old One tried to turn the raft. Before we had left the salt docks we had filled the salt tubs with salt. He could not turn the raft. We retained the light on the poles. The Old One circled away and again lay out from us in the water, some fifty to sixty feet distant, seeming to watch.

Then he again slipped from sight. We did not see him for more than a quarter of an Ahn.

Then, suddenly, at the port side, aft, he erupted from the water a dozen feet away, and fell back, spattering torrents of water over the raft.

'Cover the torches,' cried T'Zshal. 'Protect the lamps!' The lamp at the aft, port corner of the raft, drenched, was extinguished. Men covered the torches with their bodies. The Old One had again disappeared.

'Perhaps he is gone now,' said one of the men.

'Perhaps,' said T'Zshal. The men laughed.

'Aiiii!' cried a man. The Old One rose, twisting, near him, near the forequarter on the port side. He leaped back. The Old One turned, its vast sicklelike tail snapping across the beams. It caught the man's leg between itself and the salt tub, breaking the leg, turning it suddenly, oddly inward below the knee. But it had not been the man, we surmised, that the Old One had wanted. The tail, like a twig, had struck loose the lamp pole, hurling it, spinning, flaming oil spilling, yards away into the circle of darkness outside the ring of lamplight on the dark, briny water.

'Bring the lamps to the center of the raft,' said T'Zshal.

'Stand within the frame of the salt tubs.'

Bits of oil burned briefly on the water, scattered from the struck lamp. Then they went out.

I saw the man whose leg was broken. He clung to the side of the salt tub, the salt on the side of his cheek, his arms and chest. He made no sound.

'You were clumsy,' said T'Zshal.

The Old One circled the raft four times, sometimes stopping, seeming to regard us.

'If you want us, you must come for us,' said T'Zshal, calling across the water. 'Come, little one. Come to T'Zshal. He waits for you.'

I saw the water begin to move about the tail of the Old One. The pits of its eyes seemed to rest even with the water.

'Beware,' I said to T'Zshal.

'He's coming!' cried one of the men.

The long, vast body hurtled through the water, tail switching. Almost at the edge of the raft the great body lifted in the water, turning to its side, jaws dropping open, lunging, falling, biting, onto the beams, thrashing. T'Zshal thrust the long lance, almost head-on, toward the monster, and it cut, slicing, a long wound, a yard in length, along its side. The teeth caught the wide cloth of the trouser, turning T'Zshal, spinning him, tearing away cloth to the hip. T'Zshal struck again with the lance, driving it into the tail of the monster as it twisted off the raft.

'Light a torch. Lift it high,' said T'Zshal.

He held the lance ready. On the left leg of T'Zshal, where the cloth had been torn away, I could see, white and wide, jagged, descending, a long, irregular scar. It almost encircled the leg and ranged from a half of an inch to two inches in width.

'We are old friends, Old One,' called T'Zshal, across the water. 'Come, call again.'

I had not seen the scar before. I then had no doubt that at some time in the past, T'Zshal and the Old One had become acquainted.

'Come, Old One,' whispered T'Zshal. 'Come, Old One.' He held the lance ready.

T'Zshal, and the Old One, as he had said, were old friends. I wondered how many men of T'Zshal had been killed by the Old One. I suspected it was not few.

In the lamplight, on the raft, on the dark water, among us, waiting, he held the lance ready.

We did not speak.

None of us suspected it. It came by surprise, from the back, from beneath the surface, then without warning, men screaming, wood splintering, among us seeing it, striking me, others too, tumbling, gone, then men crying out, arms in the water, one lamp only, tiny, alive in that blackness.

'Light torches,' I cried. From the lamp torches were lit. We saw the Old One emerge from the water, rising up, more than a dozen feet of that great, mighty body rearing upward, water streaming from it, in its jaws the body of T'Zshal.

I leaped from the raft, striking the surface of the water. I reached the side of the Old One before I realized fully the possibilities of my action. The teeth of the Old One, like that of the long-bodied sharks of Gor, and related marine species, as well as similarly evolved forms of Earth, bend rearward; each bite anchors the bitten material, which can be dislodged conveniently only in the direction of the throat. In short, the Old One could not easily release its quarry. Further, the reflex instinct of the beast would be to hold, not to release the quarry. Even for the Old One, in the black, almost barren waters, food would be scarce. In such an environment one would expect the holding instinct would be as near to inflexible as such an instinct could be. I seized the lateral fin on the right side of the beast. It dove, and rubbed itself, twisting, in the salt at the bottom of the pit. I did not release my hold. I thrust my hand toward the jaws. They were open, clenched on the body of T'Zshal. I could not reach into the jaws. Then the beast swept upward and I, clinging to the fin, erupted with it, eyes and nostrils stung with salt, half blinded, more than ten feet into the air. I was aware of the torches across the water on the raft, men crying out, then the fish, I clinging to it, fell into the water, thrashing. As the fish fell back into the water it rolled, lifting me into the air. I shook my head and released the fin, lunging for the jaws which were held open by T'Zshal's body. My arm entered the jaws. The fish rolled. I lost my grip. I seized T'Zshal's body. Again I reached my arm into the jaws, grasping. I got my hand on the hilt of the dagger. The fish leaped again from the water and I had the dagger free, plunging it, ripping, into the gill tissue below its jaw, one of the salt-adaptations of marine life in the pit. I did not know the number of its hearts or their location. These vary in Gorean sharks. Too, the heart is deep within the body. I did not think I could reach it with the blade at my disposal. But the gill tissue is delicate, like layers of petals, essential for drawing oxygen from the environment. Madly did the great marine beast thrash; its jaws distended, trying to disgorge its victim, but it was held by the teeth; it tried to bite through the body in its jaws but the body was wedged well within the jaws and it could exert little leverage. Then the thrashing grew weaker. The Old One was still alive when I was drawn away from it, pulled by Hassan and another man to the surface of the raft. I could not release the dagger. Hassan pried it from my fingers with his hands. I lay on my back on the beams of the raft. Near to me lay T'Zshal. I crawled on my hands and knees and went to him.

'You let the Old One seize you,' I told him.

'I was clumsy,' he smiled.

Flesh hung, ripped from his body. I tried to press together the wounds.

'The Old One?' asked T'Zshal.

'Dead,' I said.

The carcass lay in the water, whitish, buoyed by the salt. It was longer than the raft itself.

'Good,' said T'Zshal. Then he closed his eyes.

'He is dead,' said one of the men.

'Find the lance head,' said I, 'take the lacings from the blade. Bring me the dagger.'

'You cannot save him,' said Hassan. The beams beneath the body of the kennel master were drenched with blood. My forehead was drenched with sweat. I saw the wounds in the shifting torchlight above and behind me. There was salt on my hands, blood. I pressed together, as I could, the serrated flesh.

'I did not know there could be so much blood in a man,' said one of the men behind me.

'Bring me what I asked for,' I said.

The lance, shaft broken, was found floating near the raft. The lacings which had reinforced the head were removed. The dagger was thrust in the wood beside me.

'Help me,' I said, 'Hassan.'

'Be merciful,' said Hassan. 'Kill him.'

'Help me,' I said.

275

'There is no hope,' said he.

'We have shared salt,' I said.

'I will help you,' said Hassan.

Using the dagger as an awl, punching through the flesh, and the long lacing from the lance head, while Hassan held together the edges of the ripped furrows, I crudely sewed together the rent, bloodied meat before me.

Once T'Zshal opened his eyes. 'Let me die,' he begged.

'I thought you once made the march to Klima,' I said.

'I did,' said T'Zshal.

'March again to Klima,' I told him.

The fists of the kennel master clenched. A bit later he slept.

'I myself,' said Hassan, 'would not admit him to the leather workers.'

We laughed. T'Zshal slept.

'What of the Old One?' asked one of the men.

'Leave him,' I said. The lelts, as yet, had not even dared approach the shifting, buoyant carcass of the Old One. In time their hunger would bring them, nosing and nibbling, to its bulk, and the blind feast in the black waters would begin.

'Return to the salt docks,' I said.

The men picked up their poles. The great raft turned and began to make its way back toward the docks.

EIGHTEEN

I RETRIEVE A BIT OF SILK;
WE ENTER THE DESERT

'What would you have for saving my life?' asked T'Zshal.

'How is it,' I asked, 'that this interview takes place in the domicile of the Salt Master?'

I stood on cool tiles, blue and yellow, in a vaulted room, in the keep of the Salt Master. I stood before a draped couch, on which lay T'Zshal. Guards were about. Near me stood Hassan.

'I am the Slave Master,' said T'Zshal. Men of the caste of physicians, slave, too, at Klima, stood about the couch. 'What would you have?'

'My freedom,' said I, 'and water.' I regarded T'Zshal. He lay upon the couch, stripped to the waist, not deigning to hide the fierce, sewn wounds which encircled his body.

'There are no kaiila at Klima, said T'Zshal.

'I know,' I said.

'You would enter the desert afoot?' he asked.

'I have business away from Klima,' I said to him.

'You saved my life,' said T'Zshal. 'In return, you ask only for your own death?'

'No,' I said. 'I ask freedom and water.'

'You do not know the desert,' he said.

'I will accompany him,' said Hassan. 'I, too, ask freedom and water. I, too, have business away from Klima.'

'You know the desert,' he said.

'The desert is my mother, and my father,' said Hassan. It was a saying of the Tahari.

'And yet you would leave Klima afoot?'

'Furnish me kaiila,' said Hassan. 'And I will not refuse them.'

'I could place both of you high at Klima,' said T'Zshal.

'Our business lies elsewhere,' I said.

'You are determined?' asked T'Zshal.

'Yes,' I said.

'I, too,' said Hassan.

'Very well,' said T'Zshal, 'stake them out in the sun.'

We were seized from behind by guards. We struggled. 'I saved your life!' I cried.

'Stake him out in the sun,' said T'Zshal.

'Sleen!' cried Hassan.

'He, too,' said T'Zshal.

I pulled at the stake to which my right wrist was fastened.

'Lie still,' said the guard. I felt the point of his lance at my throat.

He retired to the canopy beneath which, with water, he sat, cross-legged, with his companion. Between them they had, in the crusts, scratched a board for Zar. This resembles the Kaissa board. Pieces, however, may be placed only on the intersections of lines either within or at the edges of the board. Each player has nine pieces of equal value which are originally placed on the intersections of the nine interior vertical lines with what would be the rear horizontal line, constituted by the back edge of the board, from each player's point of view. The corners are not used in the original placement, though they constitute legitimate move points after play begins. The pieces are commonly pebbles, or bits of verr dung, and stocks. The 'pebbles' move first. Pieces move one intersection at a time, unless jumping. One may jump either the opponent's pieces or one's own. A jump must be made to an unoccupied point. Multiple jumps are permissible. The object is to effect a complete change of original placements. The first player to fully occupy the opponent's initial position wins. Capturing, of course, does not occur. The game is one of strategy and maneuverability.

'Hassan,' I said.

'Lie still,' he said. 'Do not speak. Try to live.'

I was silent.

'Ah,' cried one of the guards. He had just made a move which pleased him.

I kept my eyes closed, that I be not blinded.

*

278

I was cold.

I moved the stake, to which my right wrist was fastened, a quarter of an inch.

'Hassan,' I said. 'Do you live?'

'Yes,' said he, from near me.

We had been staked out in the crusts.

The sun was now down.

Under the Tahari sun some men last as little as four hours, even those who have made the march to Klima.

Water had been nearby, but we had not been given any. We kept company with the stakes. One moves as little as possible. One must not sweat. Further, one shields, with one's body, the surface on which one lies. The surface temperature can reach one hundred and seventy-five degrees by late afternoon.

Oddly, I was now cold. It was the Tahari night. I could see the stars, the three moons.

The two guards had now gone.

'By noon tomorrow, we shall be dead,' said Hassan.

I moved the stake again, to which my right wrist was fastened, another quarter of an inch. Then, slowly, bit by bit, I drew it from the crusts.

Hassan's face was turned toward me.

'Do not speak,' I told him.

With the freed stake and my right hand, I rolled to my left and attacked the crusts about the stake that held my left wrist down. Then I had it free, and with my teeth and right hand, freed my left wrist of its impediment. Then I freed my ankles of the straps.

'Save yourself,' said Hassan. 'I cannot walk.'

I freed him of the restraints at his wrists, then of those which held his ankles. To my right wrist, dangling, hung the stake I had first drawn from the crusts.

'Leave,' said Hassan. 'I cannot walk!'

I bent down and lifted him to his feet. I supported him with my left arm about his waist. His right arm was about my shoulder.

We looked up.

About us, in a dark cloud, scimitars drawn, were more than a dozen men.

I seized the stake in my right fist, to do war with steel.

The men about us parted. I saw, among them, carried on a

279

sedan chair, the figure of T'Zshal. The chair was placed before us.

He regarded us, under the moons.

'Are you still determined to enter the desert?' he asked.

'We are,' I said.

'Your water is ready,' he said.

Two men, with yoke bags, falling before their bodies, on each side, stepped forward.

'We sewed together several talu bags,' said T'Zshal, 'to make these.'

I was stunned.

'I hoped,' said T'Zshal, 'to teach you the sun and the lack of water, that you might be dissuaded from your madness.'

'You have well taught us, T'Zshal,' said I, 'the lack of water and the meaning of the sun.'

He nodded his head. 'You will now, at least, with understanding,' said he, 'enter the desert.' He turned to a guard. 'Cut the stake from his wrist,' he said. It was done. Then he turned to another guard, one with a one-talu bag, who had been one of the men who had watched us, when he had been staked out. 'Give them water,' he said.

'You did not let me struggle in the straps,' I said to the guard. 'You saved the life of T'Zshal,' said the man. 'I did not wish you to die.' Then he gave Hassan and I to drink from the water he carried.

Before we finished the bag, we passed it about the men, and T'Zshal, that each of us, there together, might have tasted it, the water from the same bag. We had, thus, in this act, shared water.

'You will, of course,' said T'Zshal, 'remain at Klima for some days, to recover your strength.'

'We leave tonight,' I told him.

'What of him?' asked T'Zshal, indicating Hassan.

'I can walk,' said Hassan, straightening himself. 'I now have water.'

'Yes,' said T'Zshal. 'You are truly of the Tahari.'

A man handed me a bag of food. It contained dried fruit, biscuits, salt.

'My thanks,' I said. We had not expected food.

'It is nothing,' he said.

'Will you not,' I asked T'Zshal, 'in your turn, when your wounds heal, march from Klima?'

'No,' said T'Zshal.

'Why?' I asked.

I have not forgotten the answer he gave me.

'I would rather be first at Klima than second in Tor,' he said.

'I wish you well,' said I, 'T'Zshal, Salt Master of Klima.'

Hassan and I turned and, with the water, and our supplies, into the night desert, took our way.

We stopped outside the perimeter of Klima. From the place in the salt crusts, where I had hidden it, I took the faded, cracked bit of silk that had been thrust in my collar on the march to Klima. I held it to my face, and to the face of Hassan. 'A trace of the perfume lingers,' he said.

'Perhaps I should give it to those of Klima,' I smiled.

'No,' smiled Hassan. 'They would kill one another for it.'

But I had no wish to give it to any at Klima. Rather I wished to return it, personally, to a girl.

I tied the bit of silk about my left wrist.

Then together, under the Gorean moons, through the salt crusts, we began the trek from Klima.

We stopped once, on the height of the great shallow bowl which encloses Klima, to look back. We saw Klima white in the light of the three moons. Then we continued our journey.

NINETEEN

THE WIND BLOWS FROM THE EAST;
WE ENCOUNTER A KUR

I heard Hassan cry out.

Through the sand, I plunged toward him.

He stood on the side of a dune, in the moonlight. There was a flattish, large expanse of rock, exposed by the wind, below him.

'I saw it there!' he cried. 'I saw it.' He pointed to the flattish extent of rock. The wind swept across it. I saw nothing.

'It is madness,' said Hassan. 'There is nothing there. I am mad.'

'What did you see?' I asked.

'A beast,' he said. 'A large beast. It stood suddenly upright. Its arms were long. It looked at me. Then it was gone.' He shook his head. 'But it could not have been there. There is nowhere for it to have gone.'

'You describe a Kur,' I conjectured.

'I have heard of them,' said Hassan. 'Are they not mythical, creatures of stories?'

'Kurii exist,' I said to him.

'No such beast could live in the desert,' said Hassan.

'No,' I said, 'such a beast could not live in the desert.'

'Strange,' said Hassan, 'that I should imagine a Kur here, in the Tahari.'

I went to the rock, and examined it. I found no sign of a beast. The wind whipped the nearby sand. I could not discern footprints.

'Let us continue our trek,' said Hassan, 'before we both go mad.'

Shouldering again the water, I followed Hassan.

Yesterday we had finished the food. Yet we did have water.

Hassan saw five birds overhead in flight.

'Fall to your hands and knees,' he said. 'Put your head down.' He did so, and I followed his example. To my surprise the five birds began to circle. I looked up. They were wild vulos, tawny and broad-winged. In a short time they alighted, several yards from us. They watched us, their heads turned to one side. Hassan began to kiss rhythmically at the back of his hand, his head down, but moving so as to see the birds. The sound he made was not unlike that of an animal lapping water.

There was a squawk as he seized one of the birds which, curious, ventured too near. The other vulos took flight. Hassan broke the bird's neck between his fingers and began to pull out the feathers.

We fed on meat.

We had been twelve days on the desert, when I detected, suddenly, in a moving of the wind, the odor.

'Stop,' I said to Hassan. 'Do you smell it?'

'What?' he asked.

'It is gone now,' I said.

'What was it that you smelled?' he asked.

'Kur,' I said.

He laughed. 'You, too,' he said, 'are mad.'

I scanned the dunes about us, silvered in the light of the moons. I shifted the water bag slung over my shoulders. Hassan stood nearby. He moved the bag of water he carried to his left shoulder, it falling before and behind.

'There is nothing,' he said. 'Let us proceed.'

'It is with us,' I said. 'You were not mistaken, days ago, when you saw it.'

'No Kur can live in the desert,' he said.

I looked about. 'It is with us, somewhere, out there,' I said. 'Somewhere.'

'Come,' said Hassan. 'Soon it will be morning.'

'Very well,' I said to him.

'Why do you hesitate?' he asked.

I looked about. 'We do not trek alone,' I told him. 'There is another who treks with us.'

Hassan scanned the dunes. 'I see nothing,' he said.

'We are not alone,' I told him. 'Out there, somewhere, there is another, one who treks with us.'

We continued our march.

The march of Hassan had as its object not Red Rock, north-west of Klima, but Four Palms, a Kavar outpost known to him, which lay far to the south of Red Rock. Unfortunately Four Palms was farther from Klima than Red Rock. On the other hand, his decision seemed to be a sound one. Red Rock was a Tashid oasis under the hegemony of the Aretai, enemies of the Kavars. Furthermore, between Klima and Red Rock lay the regions patrolled by the men of Abdul, the Salt Ubar, who had been known to me as Ibn Saran. Beyond this, though Four Palms lay farther from Klima than the Red Rock, its route, it seemed, would bring one sooner out of the dune country than the route to Red Rock, and into the typical Tahari terrain of rock and scrub, where some game might be found, occasional water and possible nomadic groups not disposed to hostility toward Kavars. All things considered, the decision to attempt to reach Four Palms seemed the most rational decision in the circumstances. There was much risk, of course, attendant on either decision. We had no choice but to gamble. Hassan had gambled wisely; whether or not he had also gambled well would remain to be seen.

I followed Hassan, he orienting himself by the sun and the flights of certain birds, migrating. We had, of course, no instruments at our disposal, no marked trails, and we did not know the exact location of Klima with respect to either Red Rock or Four Palms.

We gambled. We continued to trek. The alternative to the gamble was not security but certain death.

A consequence of Hassan's plan was that we were actually moving, generally, south and west of Klima, in short, for a time, deeper into the most desolate, untravelled portions of the dune country, far even from the salt routes.

I realize now that this was why the beast was pacing us.

'We have water,' I said to Hassan, 'for only four more days.'

'Six,' he said. 'We may live two days without water.'

We had come to the edge of the dune country. I looked out on the rugged hills, the cuts, the rocks, the brush.

'How far is it now?' I asked.

'I do not know,' said Hassan. 'Perhaps five days, perhaps ten.' We did not know where we had emerged from the dunes.

'We have come far,' I said.

'Have you noticed the wind?' said Hassan.

'No,' I said. I had not thought of it.

'From what direction does it come?' asked Hassan.

'From the east,' I said.

'It is spring,' said Hassan.

'Is this meaningful?' I asked. The wind felt much the same as the constant, whipping Tahari wind to me, no different, save for its direction.

We had been fourteen days on the desert when the wind had shifted to the east.

'Yes,' said Hassan. 'It is meaningful.'

Two Ahn earlier the sun's rim had thrust over the horizon, illuminating the crests of the thinning dunes. An Ahn earlier Hassan had said, 'It is now time to dig the shelter trench.' On our hands and knees, with our hands, we dug in the parched earth. The trench was about four feet deep, narrow, not hard to dig. It is oriented in such a way that the passing sun bisects it. It affords shade in the morning and later afternoon; it is fully exposed only in the hours of high sun.

Hassan and I stood at the edge of the ditch, looking eastward. 'Yes,' said Hassan. 'It is meaningful.'

'I see nothing,' I said. Flecks of sand struck against my face.

'We had come so far,' said Hassan.

'Is there nothing we can do?' I asked.

'I will sleep,' said Hassan. 'I am weary.'

I watched, while Hassan slept. It began in the east, like a tiny line on the margin of the desert. It was only as it approached that I understood it to be hundreds of feet in height, perhaps a hundred pasangs in width; the sky above it was gray, then black like smoke; then I could watch it no longer that I might be blinded; I shielded my eyes with my hands; I turned my back to it; I crouched in the ditch; the wind tore past above me; there was sand imbedded in the backs of my hands; in places, where I dislodged it, there was blood. I looked up. The sky was black with sand; brush, like startled, bounding tabuk, leaped, driven, over my head; the wind howled. I sat in the ditch. I put my head on my arms, my head down, my arms on my knees. I listened to the storm. Then I slept.

Toward night Hassan and I awoke. We drank. The storm raged unabating. We could not see the stars.

'How long does such a storm last?' I asked.

285

'It is spring,' he said, shrugging, in the manner of the Tahari. 'Who knows?'

'Am I not your brother?' I asked.

He lifted his head. 'It is not known how long such a storm may last,' he said. 'It may last many days. It is spring,' he said. 'The wind is from the east.' Then he again put down his head.

He slept. In time, I, too, slept.

Suddenly, shortly before dawn, I awakened.

It was standing there, in the pelting sand, looming, looking down upon us.

'Hassan,' I cried.

He awakened immediately. We struggled to our feet, our feet buried in the sand, swept into the ditch, our backs suddenly cut by the lash of the storm.

It opened its great mouth, turning its head to the side. It was seven feet in height, bracing itself against the wind. Sand clung in its fur. It looked upon me. It raised one long arm. It pointed to the dune country.

'Run!' cried Hassan. We leaped from the ditch, rolling from it into the storm, scrambling to our feet. We crouched down, trying to keep our balance, the ditch between us and the standing beast. It swayed in the wind, leaning into it, but did not attempt to approach us. It regarded me. It pointed to the dune country.

'The water,' said Hassan. 'The water!'

He stood over the ditch, to protect me as he could. I slipped into the ditch and slowly, in order not to provoke the beast to attack, lifted the two bags to the surface. Hassan took them and, when I was clear of the ditch, we backed away from the beast, watching it. The wind and sand whipped about us. The beast did not move but remained, its eyes, half-shut, rimmed with sand, fixed upon me, its great arm pointing toward the dune country.

Hassan and I turned and, stumbling, carrying the water, fled into the desert. Once, briefly, I lost sight of Hassan, then again saw him, no more than a yard from me in the darkness, in the pelting, driven sand. Together we fled. The beast did not pursue us.

TWENTY

THE KUR WILL RE-ENTER
THE DUNE COUNTRY;
I ACCOMPANY HIM

'It is there,' said Hassan. 'But you are mad to approach it.'

'It could have killed us in the trench,' I said. 'It did not.'

The storm, surprisingly, had abated. It had lasted only a bit less than one day. The landscape seemed rearranged, but we had little difficulty in finding our way back to the trench. We had not been able to move far in the storm. We had gone perhaps less than a pasang when we fell, rolled from our feet, and lay in the sand, protecting our heads and the water. Almost as soon as it had come, it had, with a shifting of wind to the north, disappeared. 'There will be other such storms,' said Hassan. 'It was too short.' He looked at me. 'We must move while we can, before another, a longer, occurs.'

'I am returning to the trench,' I told him.

'I will go with you,' he said.

From a small rise, we saw the remains of the trench, filled with sand, to within six inches of its top. The sun was high. Beside the trench, on its back, half covered with sand, lay the Kur.

When we approached it, it turned its head toward us. 'It is not dead,' said Hassan.

'It seems weak,' I said.

'We, too, are weak,' said Hassan. 'We have scarcely the strength to carry the water.'

I walked about the Kur, which closed its eyes. Its fur was coated with sand.

I crouched down near it. It opened its eyes, and regarded me.

On its left forepaw, or hand, on one of the six digits, was a heavy ring, seemingly of gold.

I had not seen such an ornament on a Kur before. I had seen rings of the sort worn on arms and wrists, and earrings, but no ring of the sort which might encircle a digit. Many Kurii are vain beasts.

'I have seen this Kur before,' I said. I had seen it in a dungeon in the house of Samos. It had been apprehended months before apparently en route to the Tahari. Samos had bought it as a beast from hunters. Six men had died in its capture. The eyes, rimmed with sand, were black-pupiled; the corneas, usually yellow, seemed pale, flattishly colored; the leathery snout seemed dry, the lips were drawn back about the fangs; the tongue, black, seemed large; it seemed thin for a Kur, haggard; I realized then that its tissues reflected dehydration. That the Kur had been bound for the Tahari had been a portion of the mystery which had initiated my venture to the desert. What business had it in the Tahari?

'It will die soon,' said Hassan. 'Leave it.'

I remained near the Kur, looking upon it. 'It needs water,' I said.

'Do not approach it!' warned Hassan.

I suppose men had few enemies as terrible as the fearsome Kur, unless it be other men. Such beasts and Priest-Kings were locked in relentless war, two worlds, two planets, Gor and Earth lying at the stake. Men seemed puny allies to either species. Before me lay my enemy, helpless.

'Kill it,' said Hassan.

'It is a rational beast,' I said. 'It needs water.'

'Desist in this madness!' cried Hassan.

I lifted the shaggy head, more than a foot wide. Between the rows of fangs, the bag over my shoulder, I thrust the spike of the water bag.

The paws of the beast reached up, slowly, and placed themselves on the bag. I saw them indent the bag; the spread of the digits was more than fifteen inches in width. There were six digits, multiply jointed, furred. I saw the golden ring, heavy, strangely set, it seemed with a tiny square of silver, against the brown leather of the bag. It did not seem a normal ring. 'This morning,' I said, 'before dawn, it could have killed us and taken the water. It did not do so.'

Hassan did not speak.

Slowly the Kur rose to his feet. I closed the bag, twisting in the plug. There was only a gallon or so of water in the bag. It would last a human a day, then he must draw on his own tissues.

Hassan stood back.

The Kur turned away from us. Very slowly it lifted its head, as though literally feeling the water flowing through the vessels of his body. It was frightening in a way to see it. It was as though it was coming alive, and it was a Kur.

'You are insane,' whispered Hassan. 'The desert would have killed it for you.'

'It did not kill us when it could have done,' I said. 'It did not take the water.'

'So it was mad from the desert, the storm,' said Hassan. 'It will now be thinking clearly.'

I watched the Kur. It fell to all fours; then it rose to a half-crouched, shambling position, knuckles to the dirt, as a Kur most naturally moves. It suddenly rolled in the sand. Then it stood up. It reached out with one paw. The paw encircled the heavy, twisted interlacings of stems of a thick clump of narrow-leaved scrub brush. Like most desert plants it is deeply rooted. With one motion the Kur tore the brush from the ground and lifted it over his head, and threw it from him. It leaped in the sand, and struck the sand with its right fist. Then, exposing the claws on its right prehensile appendage, that heavy, six-digited hand, it tore down into the dirt, and threw dirt behind. Then it straightened its body and howled, and, dropping to all fours, turned toward us, observing us. Then, slowly, half-crouched, shambling, knuckles to the dirt, it approached us.

The corneas of its eyes were vivid yellow now. Its snout wore a sheen of sweat. Its tongue moved about its lips, which were wet.

It stopped a few feet from us. I had little doubt that it could kill two unarmed men in the desert.

But it did not attack. Instead, it looked at me. And it pointed back, toward the dune country.

It straightened up, perhaps to appear more like a man. I saw then that it had been wounded. In places its fur had been slashed away. Several cuts, as though from scimitars, half-healed, marked its body. It must, at one time, have lost much blood.

'I know this Kur,' I said. I regarded it. 'Can you understand me?' I asked.

It gave no sign that it could understand me.

'I had it freed from a dungeon in Port Kar,' I told Hassan. 'In Tor, in a courtyard, several men waited to slay me. Havoc and slaughter were wrought among them, such that only a Kur might accomplish. In prison in Nine Wells, though strangely I could not see it, a Kur came to my cell. It could have killed me, I helplessly chained. It did not. I think it might have tried to free me. It was surprised by Ibn Saran and his men. It was nearly killed, trapped in the cell. It was much wounded. Ibn Saran told me the beast had been killed. It had not been. This is he. This is that Kur. I know him, Hassan. He is, if only for this moment, my ally. I think, Hassan, strange though it may seem, that we hold a cause in common.'

'A man and a Kur!' protested Hassan. 'It is impossible!'

The Kur pointed to the dune country.

I turned to Hassan. 'I wish you well, Hassan,' I said.

'It is madness to enter the dune country again,' he said. 'The water is almost gone.'

'Try to reach Four Palms,' I said. 'Your first business lies with your tribe. There is soon to be war in the Tahari. When the Kavars ride, you must ride with them.'

'It is a hard choice you impose upon me,' said Hassan, 'to choose between my brother and my tribe.' Then he said, 'I am of the Tahari. I must choose my brother.'

'The water decides it,' I said. 'Your tribe awaits.'

Hassan looked at the Kur. Then he looked at me. 'I wish you well, my brother,' he said. He smiled. 'May your water bags be never empty. May you always have water.'

'May your water bags be never empty,' I said. 'May you have always water.'

Hassan turned away. I wished him well. It was my hope that he would reach Four Palms.

Already, loping, then turning back, then moving ahead again, the Kur moved before me, back toward the long ragged edge of dunes which lay on our left.

I followed him.

TWENTY-ONE

WHAT OCCURRED
IN THE DUNE COUNTRY

The Kur was an incredible animal. Without it I would not have survived.

The next day the water was gone.

To my surprise, though the Kur had pointed to the dune country, he led me in a path parallel to the dunes, through more normal Tahari terrain. I realized then that he had been pointing to his destination, whatever it might be, which lay within the dune country, as though I might know what it was, but that the route which he wisely selected would parallel the dune country, until he reached a given point, at which point he would strike out overland, into the forbidding dunes, to reach whatever objective it was within them which might concern him, or us.

'The water is gone,' I told him. I held the bag in such a way as to show him that no fluid remained within it. After his first drink, near the shelter trench, he had not had water.

The Kur watched the flight of birds. He followed them, for a day. He found their water. It was foul. We gratefully drank. I submerged the water bag I carried. We killed four birds and ate them raw. The Kur caught small rock tharlarion, and on this plenty, too, we feasted. Then we continued our journey. I drank much for the Kur seemed hurried. Surely he knew that one should move only at night, and yet the beast seemed tireless, and would press me on, as though I needed neither food nor sleep. Did he not know I was not a Kur? He, shielded by the fur, was less exposed to the sun. He would move day and night, but I could not. Impatiently, he would crouch near me when I fell to the sand, to sleep. He would, in an Ahn, awaken me, and point to the sun. Yet I did not think he wished to tell me the hour of the day, but call my attention to the passage of time. He seemed hurried. Surely even for this mighty body the heat, the sun, the scarcity of water, the scarcity of food, must have taken dreadful toll. At times his wounds must have tormented him. Twice I saw him lick crusts from their eruptions. Yet, slowly, as though by force of will, he moved on. I was sure he would kill us both. One does not tease the desert. It is implacable, like a stone or furnace.

'I need water,' I told him. It had been gone, for more than a day.

The Kur held up eight fingers, and pointed to the sun.

I did not understand his meaning.

We continued our journey. An Ahn later, nostrils distended, head to the ground, he became excited. He pointed to the ground. He looked at me, as though I must understand. I did not, of course, understand. He looked at the sun, and at me, as though weighing the values of alternative courses of action. Then he swiftly departed from his original direction. I realized, several Ahn later, that he was following an animal trail, the odors of which my senses were not keen enough to detect. We fell on our bellies before the foul water, stinking with excrement, and drank, and again filled the bag. There was a half-eaten tabuk by the water hole. The Kur warned me from certain pieces of meat, smelling it. Other pieces, farther from the eaten areas, more exposed to the sun, he gave me. He himself broke free a haunch and, with swift motions, with his teeth, holding it, ripped the dry meat from the bone.

The Kur motioned me to my feet. We must again proceed. Fed, watered, I followed him, though each step, because of my exhaustion, was torture.

He returned to his original trail, from which he made his detour, and continued his march.

The next morning he pointed to the sun, and held up seven fingers before me. But he let me sleep, in the shelter of a rock, while he watched. That night we again began the trek. The rest did me much good. The next morning he pointed to the sun, and held up six fingers before me. His rendezvous, I gathered, whatever it might be, must be accomplished within six days. It was for that reason that he had been driving us both.

Water became more scarce.

The Kur began to move more slowly, and drank more. I

think its wounds had begun to tell upon it. No longer did it seem willing to risk the trail to hunt for water. It was becoming a desperate beast. It feared, I gathered, missing its rendezvous. It had not counted on its own weakness. The leather I wore about my feet was in tatters, but in the footprints of the Kur there was blood. It moved on, indomitably.

Then the water was gone.

That morning the Kur had pointed to the sun and held up four fingers.

We went a day without water.

In a place, on the next day, we found flies, swarming, over parched earth. There, with his great paws, slowly, painfully, the Kur dug. More than four feet below the surface he found mud. We strained this through the silk I had had tied to my wrist, into his cupped paws. He gave me almost all of this water. He licked from his moistened palms only what I had left. In another place, that night, we found a narrow channel of baked mud, the dried bed of a tiny, vanished stream, of the sort which in the winter, should it rain, carries water for a few days. We followed this to a shallow, dried pool. Digging here we found dormant snails. In the moonlight we cracked the shells, sucking out the fluid. It stank. Only at first did I vomit. Again the Kur gave me almost the entire bounty of this find. Then we could find no more.

We retraced our steps to the point at which we had left the trail, and continued our journey.

The next morning the Kur pointed to the sun, and held up three fingers.

The water bag, in my hands, hung limp, dry.

'Let us rest,' I said to the Kur.

He pressed on. I followed the footprints. There was blood in them. I shut my eyes against the glare of the terrain.

I put one foot in front of the other, again and again. The Kur began to limp.

I felt weak, sleepy. I was not much interested in eating. I began to feel strangely hot. I felt my forehead. It was dry, and seemed unnaturally warm. I felt sick in my stomach, nauseous. That is strange, I thought. I have had little to eat. 'We must rest,' I told the Kur. But he continued to press ahead. I stumbled after him, the water bag in my hand. I looked at it. It had cracked in the sun. I clung to it, irrationally. I would not release it. When the sun was high, I fell. The Kur waited until

I regained my feet and then he limped on, ahead of me. 'I'm dizzy,' I told him. 'Wait!' I stood still, and waited for the dizziness to pass. The Kur waited. Then we went on again. I had a headache. I shook my head. The pain was severe. I put one foot before the other, continuing to follow the Kur. I began to itch. I scratched at my arms and body. I stumbled. The Kur moved on ahead of me. It was odd to feel no saliva in one's mouth. My eyes were dry. Bits of sand seemed to lie between the eye and the lid; I felt, too, the grit of sand in my mouth; I could not spit it out; my eyes would not form tears. My lips became sore and began to ache. My tongue felt large. I felt skin on my tongue peeling. I began to feel cramps in my stomach, and in my arms and legs. I looked about. There seemed much water here and there, in flat places, in the distance, rippling, stirring. Sometimes our path took us toward it, but when we reached it, it was sand, the air above it rippling and troubled in the desert's heat.

'I can go no further,' I told the Kur.

He turned to face me, crouched over. He pointed now to his right, for the first time. He pointed directly eastward, toward the dunes. It was at this point, I understood, that he would enter the dunes for his overland trek.

I looked at the dunes to my left, shimmering with heat, rippled in the wind, the tops like bright, tawny smoke in the light.

It would be madness and death to enter them.

He pointed to his right, with the long arm, to the dunes.

'I can go no further,' I told him.

He approached me. I regarded him. He took me by the arms and threw me to his feet in the dirt. I heard him take the water bag, and heard it being ripped. My hands were jerked behind me and tied. My ankles were crossed and tied. With portions of the water bag and shreds from it, the Kur bound his feet, to protect them from the sand. He twisted a rope from other strips of the bag. I felt this, as I lay in the sand and grit, knotted about my throat. With his teeth he severed the leather that had bound my ankles. I almost strangled. I was jerked to my feet. The Kur turned toward the dunes, the rope of twisted leather in his right paw. Then he led me, tethered behind him, his human prisoner, climbing, slipping, up the first long, sloping crest, into the dunes.

'You are mad, mad!' I wanted to scream at him. But I could

294

only whisper, and scarce could hear my own voice.

He continued on, and I, tethered, followed him.

The wind whipped across the sand.

I have marched to Klima, I told myself. I march again to Klima. I march again to Klima. But on the march to Klima I had had water, salt.

Sometime in the late afternoon I must have fallen unconscious in the sand. I dreamt of the baths of Ar and Turia.

I awakened in the night. No longer was I bound. I was carried in the arms of the Kur, over the silvered dunes. He moved slowly. He was lame in his right foot. I lay against wounds in his upper chest. They were open. But they did not bleed.

Again I fell asleep. The next time I awakened it was shortly before dawn. The Kur, near me, half covered with sand, stirred by the wind, slept. I rose to my feet, unsteadily. Then I fell. I could not stand.

I sat in the sand, my back against a dune. I watched the Kur. It had been an admirable, mighty beast. But now the desert, and its wounds, were killing it. It was now weak, and drawn. Its flesh seemed to hang upon its huge frame, a shrunken reminiscence of the former mightiness of the beast. I regretted, strangely, seeing its decline. I wondered at what drove it, why it strove so relentlessly in its mission, whatever that might be. It dared to pit itself against the desert. I noted its fur. No longer was it sleek, but now it seemed lifeless, brittle; it was dry; it was coated with sand. The leather of its snout, with the two nostrils, was cracked and, now, oddly gray. Its mouth and lips were dry, like paper. About the snout, the nostrils, the mouth and lips, were tiny fissures, broken open, filled with sand. Sand, too, rimmed the nostrils and eyes, and the mouth and lips. It lay in the sand, curled, its head facing away from the wind, like something discarded, needed no longer, cast aside. It, proud beast, had pitted itself against the desert. It had lost. What prize, I wondered, could be worth the risk the beast had been willing to take, the price it had been willing to pay, its own life. I wondered if it could rise again to its feet. I did not think either of us would survive the day.

The sun was rising.

The beast rolled to its feet, and shook the sand from its fur. It stood unsteadily.

'Go without me,' I said. 'I cannot walk. You can no longer carry me.'

295

The beast lifted its long arm and pointed to the sun. It lifted two fingers.

It approached me. 'I cannot go with you,' I said. 'What is so important?' I asked.

The beast, with one of his digits, rubbed about its lips and tongue. I thrust the finger against my lips. I tasted sand, and salt.

'I cannot swallow,' I said.

The beast regarded me for a long time. Its corneas were no longer yellow, but pale and whitish. There seemed no moisture in the eyes. At the corners the tiny cracks about the eyes were coated with sand. My own eyes stung. I no longer attempted to remove particles from them.

The beast turned away from me and bent his head over his cupped hands. When he again turned to face me I saw, in the black cup of its paws, a foul fluid. I thrust my face to his hands, and my own hands trembling, holding his cupped hands, drank. Four times did the beast do this. It was water from the last large hole we had visited, where the half-eaten tabuk had been found, held for days in the beast's storage stomach. It was water, in a sense, from its own tissues he gave me, releasing it now, into his own system, but yielding it to me, that I might not die. Again did the beast try to give me water, but then there was none left. He had given me the last of his water. Now again, from his mouth and lips and body, he scraped salt. He took it, too from the bloody crusts of his wounds. I took it, with the sand, licking at it, now able to swallow it. He had given me, it seemed an inexplicable gift, water and salt from his own body.

'I can trek again,' I told him. 'It will not be necessary to carry me, should you be able to do this, or to bind me, leading me as a prisoner. You have given me the water and salt from your own body. I do not know what you seek, or what your mission may be, but I shall accompany you. We shall go together.'

But the beast motioned now that I should rest. Then he stood between me and the sun and, in the shade of his body, as he moved from time to time, I slept.

I dreamed of the ring he wore about the second finger of his left hand.

When the moons were high I awakened. Then I followed the Kur. He moved slowly, being lame. His dessicated tissues, I did not think, would much longer support life. The water he

296

had been saving, perhaps for me, was gone.

I did not know what he sought. Yet I admired him that he should so indomitably seek it. I did not think it an ill or unworthy thing to die in the company of such a beast.

At his side I sensed the will and nobility of the Kur. They were indeed splendid foes for Priest-Kings and men. I wondered if either Priest-Kings or men could be worthy of them.

Thus, natural enemies, a human and a Kur, in a strange truce in the desert, side by side, trekked. I knew not toward what. I did not question, nor had I questioned, did I think my companion could have responded to me. I accompanied him.

Many times during the night he fell. He grew visibly weaker. I waited for him to regain his feet. Then we would again take up our march.

Near morning we rested. In an Ahn he tried to rise, but could not. He looked at the sun. In the sand, with one digit, he drew a single mark. He curled the great clawed right fist, and struck the sand once with it, hopelessly. Then he fell into the sand.

I thought that he would die then, but he did not. At times during the day, when I lay in the shadow of his body, I thought him dead but, putting my ear to his chest, I detected the beating of the large heart, slow, irregular, sporadic, fitful, like the clenching of a weakening fist.

In the night I prepared to bury the Kur. I dug a trench in the sand. I waited for it to die.

I regretted that there would be no stone with which to mark the grave.

When the moons were full, he put back his head and I saw the rows of fangs. To my horror he struggled again to his feet, and, shaking the sand from his body, took up again the march. In awe I followed it.

In the morning he did not stop to rest. He pointed again to the sun, and this time lifted a closed fist.

I did not understand his meaning. Then the hair rose upon the back of my neck. He had indicated time, by pointing to the sun, and days, by lifting his fingers. He had now pointed to the sun, and lifted only the great, dry fist, obdurate, closed.

I then understood, in horror, suddenly, the meaning of his mission. There were no more days left. It was the last day. It was a world's last day.

'Surrender Gor,' had been the message to the Sardar, from

the Kurii ships. It had been an ultimatum. The Priest-Kings, of course, had been only puzzled; their response had been curiosity, inquiry; it had never occurred to them, rational creatures, what might be the enormity of the plan of Kurii. I sensed there might be different parties among them, creatures so menacing, so fierce, so aggressive, so proud, so imperialistic, so uncompromising, factional and belligerent. After the failure of the major probe in Torvaldsland, it seemed not unlikely a given party or tribe might have fallen from power. I did not think it would be desirable, among Kurii, to be among a party which had fallen from power. It seemed clear to me then that a new force had come to power among the enemies of the Sardar, one willing, if necessary, to sacrifice one world to gain another.

The Kur had held up a closed fist. There were no more days. I found myself struggling to keep up with the beast.

The slave runs had been stopped. Doubtless key operatives, particularly those who spoke languages of Earth, had been evacuated from Gor. Others, ignorant of the horrifying strategy of interplanetary warfare, would remain. Even Ibn Saran, with all his brilliance, did not, I supposed, conjecture his role as dupe in this plan, precipitating tribal warfare, thus effectively, for almost all practical purposes, closing the desert to intruders, strangers, agents either of Priest-Kings or even of alternative Kurii parties. Kurii, I suspected, were as little united as men, for they, too, are jealous, proud, territorial beasts.

Gor, I understood, was to be destroyed. This would eliminate a world, but, with it, Priest-Kings, and leave Earth unsheltered, vulnerable, to the attack fleets of the steel worlds. Better one world than none.

Though it was in the heat of the Tahari noon the beast did not pause. The Kur, like the great cats, hunts when hungry, but it is a beautifully night-adapted animal. Its night vision is perhaps a hundred times keener than that of humans. It can see even by starlight. It would be blind only in total darkness, as in a brine pit at Klima. The pupils of its eyes, like those of the cat, can shrink to pinpoints and expand to wide, dark, light-sensitive moons, capable of minute discriminations in what to a human being would seem pitch darkness. The Kur, commonly, emerges from its lair with the falling of darkness. It is then that its nostrils distend and its ears lift, listening, and that it begins its hunt. I had no doubt that the destruction of the world, as would seem fitting to a Kur, would occur with the coming of night. It is then that the Kur, commonly, chooses to hunt.

In the late afternoon the Kur cried out with rage. It stood on the crest of a dune, sand almost to its knees, sand sweeping about it. The wind had picked up. I saw its fur blown.

The wind had shifted again to the east.

Within moments the storm fell. The Kur pressed on, through the pelting sand. The sky was dark. I held to the fur at its arm, fighting to keep my balance. Suddenly the Kur stopped, and stood, leaning against the wind. I opened my eyes, and saw, briefly, before me, not more than a hundred yards away, in a fleeting gap in the storm, swiftly closed again by the hastened, stinging sand, crooked, leaning to one side, half buried in the sand, a cylinder of steel; it was perhaps twelve feet in diameter, perhaps forty feet of it exposed; at its apex I saw clustered thrust chambers; it was a ship; it had been crashed into the sand.

I felt the hand of the Kur close on my arm.

It is difficult to speak of what I then saw. The Kur, near me, removed his hand from my arm. With his right hand he took the ring on his left hand, that on his second finger, and turned the bezel inward, so that the silvered plate set in the gold faced inward. On the exposed side of the ring there was a circular switch, which he then depressed. For a moment in the sand, he seemed to shimmer and then I saw only the sand, the whipping, pelting sand. I was alone.

I knew then it hunted, in the vicinity of the tower. On my hands and knees I crawled a few yards in the direction of the ship. I saw it again, once, briefly, in a break in the storm. It seemed to me of primitive design. The thrust chambers suggested a liquid-propellant rocket. It was not disklike. I supposed it might have been an obsolete ship, perhaps a derelict, even an ancient ship, little more now than the fuselage for housing a bomb.

I shuddered when I thought of the power concealed in that casing of steel.

I wanted to run, into the storm, away from it. But I knew that nowhere on Gor would there be escape from that inert ship. 'Beware the steel tower,' had been written on the rock. It was a weapon, pressed to the temple of a world, set to be discharged with the falling of darkness.

I thought I heard, wild, though it was hard to tell in the wind, the screams of men. Then I heard the howling of a Kur, and four sudden, swift explosions.

Then I heard only the wind.

I waited, for more than a quarter of an Ahn. Then I sensed it near me. The air shimmered. It stood unsteadily. The Kur was before me. Its paws were red. In its left thigh was one, and across its chest, were three holes, three-quarters of an inch in diameter. Its eyes could not focus. It turned its back to me. In its back, where the force had burst loose of its body, were holes corresponding to those in his leg and chest. I smelled burned flesh. A white smoke, tiny, in wisps, like the smoke of dry ice, rose from the holes, then was whipped away by the wind. The Kur sank to the sand. I knelt over it. It opened its eyes. They focused on me.

'It is accomplished?' I asked. 'Is the work done?'

With its bloodied paw the animal pulled the ring from its finger. It thrust it toward me. It was covered with blood, that I assumed of men it had slain. The circle of the ring was not made for a human finger. It was an inch and a quarter in diameter. It pressed the ring into my hands. With a bit of leather string, from the wrappings on my feet, I tied it about my neck.

The beast lay in the sand. It bled slowly. I suppose it had little blood to bleed. Too, the force that had penetrated its body had, apparently, searing, half-sealed the wounds it inflicted. It was as though a hot poker, chemically active, had been thrust through the body. The sand beneath the beast grew red. I took wrappings from my feet, to thrust into the wounds. The beast pushed me away. He lifted his arm to where the sun must be, could it be seen.

I stood unsteadily beside it. Then, I started for the ship, through the storm.

Beside the ship I found the remains of a shelter of stones and tarpaulins. Scattered about were men. I did not think they were alive. I froze, as I saw, through the wind and sand, another Kur. It was armed. In its right paw it held a small device. It was hunched over, it peered through the storm.

I was startled that there would be a Kur at the ship. I think, too, the Kur with whom I had trekked had not anticipated this development. Kurii, no more than men, willfully commit themselves to destruction. Yet there was a Kur here, guarding the ship. I knew it would be a determined, desperate beast. It was willing to die, apparently, that the success of the plan of its superiors be fulfilled. I supposed many Kurii had competed for this honor. Kurii do not believe in immortality. They do believe, however, in glory. This Kur, of all, in the cruel selections of the steel ships, had survived. He would be the most dangerous of all. He turned toward me.

I saw the paw lift and I threw myself to the side. A large, square rock, near me, one of those which had held the tarpaulin, leaped upward, split in two, burnt black, and the slightest instant, almost simultaneous, afterward I heard the atmospheric concussion of the weapon.

I think the Kur was startled to see me. It did not expect to find a human at the ship. Perhaps it was this which, in his startled reflex, spoiled his aim. Then the sand closed between us. I crawled from the area of the shelter. I saw him, twice, through gaps in the sand. But he did not see me. The next time I saw him, he turned toward me, hunched down. I backed away. He approached, through the sand. He did not fire. He held the weapon outward from him, toward me. He tried to hold his balance. I conjectured that his weapon held a limited number of charges. It did not fire like a ray, but rather on the analogy of a cartridge weapon. Suddenly I felt the steel of the ship at my back. The beast emerged from the sand. I saw its lips draw back; it steadied the weapon in the whipping wind with both paws; I thrust at the circular switch on the ring about my neck. Suddenly I saw the Kur as though in red light, and the sand, too, darkly red to black. To my amazement, it seemed startled; it hesitated; I leapt to the side. A blast from the hand-held weapon struck the steel of the ship. In its side there was a blackened hole, as though drilled; metal ran in droplets down the side of the ship.

I suddenly realized, with elation, that the Kur could not see me.

The ring concealed a light-diversion device, encircling the orbit of its wearer with a field. We see in virtue of light waves reflected from variously textured surfaces, which waves impinge on the visual sensors. We see in virtue of the patterns of these waves. The field about me, I conjectured, diverted and reconstituted these waves in their original patterns; thus, a given wave of light in the normal visual spectrum which might strike me and be reflected to the visual sensor of another organism

301

did not now strike me but was diverted; similarly patterns of light from objects behind me were diverted about my field and reconstituted beyond it, to impinge, as though I were not there, on the visual sensor of an observing organism. The light in virtue of which I saw was shifted in its spectrum; it was, I suspect, originally in the nonvisible portion of the spectrum, perhaps in the infrared portion of the spectrum, which could penetrate the field, but was shifted in such a way by the diversion field that I, within the orbit of the field, experienced it in a range visible to myself. It was thus, I conjecture, that I could not be seen by those outside the field and yet that I, within the field, could experience the world visually which lay beyond it. Such a device would have been useless among Priest-Kings, for they do not much depend on their visual sensors. Among Kurii I was not certain how effective it would be. Kurii, like men, are visually oriented organisms, but their hearing and their sense of smell is incomparably more acute.

I did not know how many charges the weapon of the Kur held. Further, I was unarmed. I slipped back into the whipping sand. I crouched down.

The howling of the wind screened the sounds of my movements; its swift, lacerating blasts must have torn the atmosphere of my scent to pieces, scattering it wildly about, affording the Kur only suddenly, misleading, fleeting, confused sensations. He could not at the moment locate me. I saw him, red in the twisting, howling sand, moving about, weapon ready, hunting me.

I was puzzled that the Kur with whom I had trekked, who had worn the ring, had been hit four times, accurately, with the weapon of the Kur who stalked me. Furthermore, he had been struck, as nearly as I could determine, head-on. It was not as though the Kur with the weapon had located him at the throat of a man, and then fired.

It seemed likely then that the Kur must have been struck as it had framed itself, perhaps in an opening, the other Kur, smelling it, hearing it, firing when it had tried to enter. The Kur with the weapon had then come out, hunting for it, to finish it.

He had not counted on there being an ally, and one who was human.

Similar thoughts must have coursed through the brain of

the Kur and I, but I did not know the position or nature of the portal.

I saw him turn toward the ship, abandoning his hunt, recollecting his principal objective.

He thus led me to the portal. He reached it before I did. He scrambled, claws slipping on the leaning steel, and then crouched in it. The opening must once have been the outer opening of a lock; it was rectangular; the exterior hatch was missing; there was twisted metal at the side of the opening, as though it had been wrenched away from rusted hinges; the beast crouched in the lock, peering into the storm. Then it disappeared within.

My heart sank; time was on its side; it would soon be night; it needed only wait.

I made my way to the stones and tarpaulin; there, feeling about, I located one of the bodies, which was mostly whole. Some were missing arms and heads.

I carried the body toward the side of the ship. Though the Kur had not used them, there were cuts in the side of the ship, probably used by the humans in entering and leaving it. A steel ladder, twisted, fitted the rounded side of the ship. Given the attitude of the ship, however, the ladder was roughly at a twenty-degree angle to the ground, and some twenty feet from the sand; it was useless to me. I would use the cuts. I made no effort to conceal sound. I scraped the side of the steel. I made certain that the Kur within, if he could hear aught, would be able to tell that someone ascended the side of the ship, dragging an inert weight, presumably a body.

I knew the Kur must be cunning, if not brilliant. It could be no accident that this Kur and not another had received this dreadful assignment, to protect the device of a planet's destruction until its detonation.

But also it would be under stress. And in the storm it could not see clearly beyond the portal. It would assume that I would not relinquish the shield of the ring's invisibility. A diversion would be ineffective, for what could draw the Kur from his position? If the blood of the slaughtered humans about had not been sufficient to override his obedience to the dark imperative of the steel worlds, I did not think anything I might contrive could lure him forth. He had resisted blood; the will of this Kur, restraining its instincts of feasting and carnival, must be mighty indeed. He would assume, perhaps,

I might attempt to draw fire with a decoy, thus slipping into the ship. The only likely object to use in such a plan would be the body of one of the humans about, victims of the Kur with whom I had shared the march in the desert. I made no attempt to conceal my sounds. I let it be clear that I was outside the portal, that I had ascended the side of the ship, that with me, dragged, was an inert weight, presumably a body.

A likely plan, it seemed to me, would be to thrust the inert body into the portal, and draw the fire of the Kur within. Perhaps then, in the sudden moment of confusion, one might slip within, behind it, invisible.

It would be an elementary decoy strategy.

This was a likely plan. I did not adopt it. The Kur waited within. I did not think I played Kaissa with a fool.

But I would use a decoy strategy. Only I, myself, would be the decoy. Behind the decoy there would be nothing. One thing the Kur would not expect would be that I would surrender the shield of invisibility; one thing he would not expect would be that it would be I, myself, who would present myself to his weapon.

I clung to the side of the portal. I propped the body beside me, holding it that it not be swept from the side of the ship.

I counted slowly, five thousand Ihn, that the reflexes of the Kur within be drawn to a hair-trigger alertness, that the whole nervous might of the beast be balanced on a razor's edge of response, that every instinct and fiber in his body would scream to press the trigger at what first might move. But I counted, too, on its intelligence, its control, that it would not fire on what first might move, particularly if it were visible.

The wind howled and the sand swirled about the ship. I pressed the circular switch on the ring tied about my neck. I again saw in the normal range of the spectrum. I now realized I saw in the light of the moons; I broke out in a sweat; it was night. Limply, as though thrust from behind, I pushed myself, awkwardly, sagging, into the opening, and fell forward. Scarcely had I fallen into the lock than I heard, loud, over me, the concussions of the weapon, firing five times; almost simultaneously the Kur leaped from somewhere within, from a nest of piping, and scrambled past me; its foot pressed on my shoulder; it peered out into the storm; it spied the body below, which had slipped from the side of the ship when I had entered the ship, no longer holding it; it seemed momentarily puzzled;

it fired into the body twice more; it scrambled from the opening, turning, slipping on the steel, and slid down to the sand at the side of the ship.

I came alive, crawling through the interior hatch, which was hanging back open, fastened back, so that the Kur could have his clean shot. I slipped inside, and nearly fell, my feet scraping for a hold. I found it. I heard the Kur outside howl with rage. I tried to swing the hatch shut, to lock it, but it hung crooked on its hinges and would not close. Perhaps it had been damaged in the crash of the ship. Perhaps the Kur with whom I had trekked had, with the frenzy of a Kur's strength, wrenched it aside, before meeting the four charges of the other Kur's weapons. I heard the Kur's claws swift on the steel outside, scraping, climbing. I reached for the ring at my neck. It was gone! The bit of leather, brittle, worn from the sun, had separated. I heard the snap of the hand weapon. I looked up. It was not more than eighteen inches from my face. It snapped again. I dropped into the darkness of the ship. It was empty. The Kur howled with rage. I fell, dropping, striking objects, sliding for perhaps forty or fifty feet, until stopped by a compartment wall. I looked up. The interior of the ship was suddenly illuminated. In the cylinder above me, in the portal, his paw at the disk, stood the Kur. He looked down at me. His lips drew back. He had discarded the weapon. I looked about myself, wildly. The interior of the ship, given its attitude, seemed oddly askew. Beyond this it was not as compact as I would have expected, as filled with devices, panels and storage cabinets. It had been muchly stripped, apparently, presumably, to lighten it. I saw the Kur easily, gracefully for its bulk, with its long arms, pipe to pipe, swing down toward me. When it reached my level I tried to climb upward, clinging to piping at the ship's side. Its hand closed about my ankle and I felt myself torn from the piping. I was lifted in the air and hurled against the wall of the ship, and I fell back from the wall, falling some ten feet to the remains of a twisted, ruptured bulkhead, slipped from it and fell another five feet into a debris of scrap and wire. I crawled on my hands and knees. I heard the Kur approach. Under some pipes, below me, suddenly, I saw the ring. I fell to my stomach, my arm clawing downward. I could not reach it. I scrambled to my feet. The Kur looked down, he, too, seeing the ring. I backed away, stumbling a bit, back in the debris and wire. I looked upward, in the inclining cylinder of the ship. High above me, some sixty or seventy feet, I saw six dials. The Kur reached down with its long arm. I bent to the pile of debris and wire. The Kur's arm was long enough to reach the ring, as mine was not, but the piping beneath which it had fallen was too closely set to accommodate the large arm of the Kur. I began to climb upward, on projections, on spaced piping, on the remains of sundered bulkheads, toward the dials. The Kur took the pipes in his hands, to bend them apart. He had separated them some five inches when he looked up. He saw me. He howled with rage. No longer did he concern himself with the ring. Instantly he began to climb toward me. He climbed swiftly, purposefully.

I crouched on a steel beam athwart the cylinder, opposite the six dials. The first four dials were motionless. The last two were still in motion. Each dial had a single sweep. Each dial was divided into twelve divisions. The sweeps in the first four dials were vertical. I could not read the numerals on the dials. I surmised the vertical position was equivalent to twelve or zero. It was the position, at any rate, it seemed clear, in which the devices stopped. The movement of the sweeps was counterclockwise.

The Kur was climbing toward me.

The first dial, I surmised, registered something equivalent to months, the second to weeks, the third to days, the fourth to hours. I did not know the rate of revolution of the Kurii's original planet, nor the rate of its rotation. I had little doubt that these measurements, however, were calibrated on the movements of a world, presumably vanished, destroyed in their wars. They had destroyed one world; they now desired another.

With my teeth I tore the insulation from a part of the wire I had taken from the pile of debris and wire, coiled and, in my teeth, carried with me in my climb.

I looped the noose where the wire was naked. As the Kur climbed near me, his back to me. I caught its great shaggy head in the loop and drew it tight. It tore at the fine wire with its thick digits but they could not slip beneath it. I flung myself backward off the beam and the wire pulled the Kur from the side of the ship until it hung, struggling, I hanging a few feet below it. It flung out its paws but could grasp on nothing. It tried to hold the wire, and climb on it, or relieve the pressure on its throat, but its great paws slipped on the slender strand; then its weight began to pull me upward; I, hands knotted in the insulated portion of the wire, kicked the Kur back as it reached for me; then I was above it, being drawn by its weight to the height of the beam; the shoulders of the Kur were mantled in red; blood ran heavily from its throat, in throbbing, gigantic glots; I braced myself, head down, feet pressed up against the beam, to hold the Kur in place; then, without warning, the wire parted; when the wire parted I was almost horizontal to the beam, trying to keep from being pulled over it, trying to hold the Kur; the force of my legs, relieved suddenly of the counter tension of the Kur's weight, flung me back, almost to the other side of the ship, and I slid down a few feet and caught some piping. The Kur, striking four times, fell some sixty or seventy feet, to the lowest level of the ship, past the door, well below the level of the sand outside.

I looked to the dials. The fifth sweep, on the fifth dial, was almost vertical.

Outside I knew it was night. The storm still raged.

There was heavy glass over the faces of the dials. I climbed to the beam from whence I had snared the Kur. I could not reach the dials.

I cast about wildly. I could not stop them.

Below me, to my horror, I saw the Kur, a mass of blood, struggle to its feet. It was still bleeding, heavily, from the throat. I had little doubt that the great vessel of its throat had been opened, if not severed.

The beast seemed indomitable. Its strength was almost inconceivable.

It climbed slowly. I saw its uplifted face, its terrible eyes, the fangs, the ears laid back against its head. Hand over hand, not swiftly now, not easily, but foot by tortuous foot, it climbed.

I seized a narrow pipe over my head, jerking at it. It contained wire. In a frenzy I tried to free it of the side of the ship. I could not loosen it.

The beast was nearer now, and still climbing. I saw its eyes. It moved another six inches toward me.

I tore loose the pipe. The sweep on the fifth dial, suddenly, stopped. The sweep on the sixth dial began to move toward the vertical, swiftly, counterclockwise. I did not think its journey would take more than a few seconds. I struck at the sixth dial with the pipe, again and again, shattering the glass. I saw the Kur not a foot below me. It tried to lift its head, to seize me. Blood no longer ran from its throat. It was dead. It tumbled back from the piping on the side of the ship, and fell to the lower level.

I jammed the thin pipe, like a spear from the beam, into the face of the dial. The sixth sweep, a moment later, struck against this obstacle, stopping short of the vertical mark.

I lay on the beam and wept, and feared that I would fall.

When I dared to move, I left the ship. Outside the storm had abated. I found the Kur in the sand, with whom I had trekked.

'The task is accomplished,' I told him. 'It is done.'

But he was already dead.

His lips were drawn back from his teeth, which, in the Kur, as I understand it, is analogous to a smile. I think he died not unhappily.

I returned to the ship, in which I found much food and water. In the next days, carefully as I could, disconnecting them, I dismantled and destroyed components within the ship. In time, Priest-Kings would find the ship and more adequately disarm it. I buried the men who had died near the ship. Though I removed the one Kur from the ship, I did not bury either of them. I exposed them for the scavengers of the desert, for they were only beasts.

TWENTY-TWO

I OBTAIN KAIILA

I crouched between thrust chambers, some seventy feet from the ground, on the height of the tall ship, half buried in the Tahari sand. The chambers, facing the sky, were filled with sand. Between them I had rigged a shelter from the sun. I reached the height of the ship's stern by a rope. I sipped water, watching the two riders approach. From the vantage of the ship's height I could see several pasangs on all sides. The desert was clear.

As I had surmised, there was contact between the ship and the nearest agents of Kurii, the men of Abdul, Ibn Saran, the Salt Ubar. The food and water, the provisions, must have been brought in by kaiila. Presumably there would be routine provisionings, or communications, with Kurii agents, though not by radio or any similar device which might attract the attention of listening stations on the Sardar. The suppliers would have their schedules prepared weeks in advance. The schedules would have been designed to carry through and beyond the date set for the planet's destruction, in order not to arouse curiosity or suspicion among the Kurii's human agents. The men approaching, leading four pack kaiila, were ignorant. They approached slowly, in the leisurely fashion of the Tahari. There was nothing unusual, as far as they knew, concerning the delivery or the date on which it was occurring. I smiled. The planet could have blown apart beneath their feet. Yet they came in placid caravan.

I was satisfied to see them. I had considered walking out of the desert. There was ample food and water at the ship. I could have rigged a flat travois, with shoulder harness, to slip over the sand, loaded with water and food, and could have traveled at night, but I had decided against this. I did not know the distances nor directions to oases. I might have wandered in the desert for weeks, until even such large stores were exhausted. I might have encountered unfriendly riders. I would be afoot. I did not know how long the energy of the ring would last. I assumed it could generate its field for only a finite period. If I met several riders I might, with the ring, escape, but I might, too, loose the stores. I needed a kaiila; I needed direction. In a day on a kaiila, if it was well-watered and strong, I might cover the ground which, afoot, might take weeks. Too, the kaiila, given its head, is excellent in locating water.

It seemed not improbable to me that there might be a recognition signal, to be given by the approaching riders in the vicinity of the ship, to be answered by a countersignal, before they would bring the kaiila in. Not receiving it I had little doubt that they would investigate most warily, or, possibly, simply withdraw. I did not know what their standing order might be. I was not prepared to risk the second alternative. I threw the shelter which I had rigged down to the sand, behind the ship. I tossed the steel flask of water down, slowly, handhold by handhold. I did not know how observant might be the riders. Even though I might stand, unseen, in the shelter of the ring's field, the sand, disturbed, might reveal my movements, my presence. If I attacked one rider, invisible, the other, alarmed, might simply flee, panic-stricken and terrified. At the level, where the sand ringed the fuselage of the ship, I drank deeply, then I threw aside the flask. I then went into the desert.

'Water!' I cried. 'Water!'

The riders stopped, a hundred yards from me. I did not approach them from the direction of the ship.

'Water!' I cried. I stumbled toward them. I staggered, and fell, repeatedly.

They let me approach. I saw them exchange glances. I fell to one knee, again struggled to my feet. I extended my right hand to them. There was sand in my hair, on my body. I moved as though in pain, as though suffering from abdominal and muscular cramps, as though I were dizzy. I stood unsteadily. 'Water!' I cried to them. 'Please, water!' I stopped some fifty yards from them. I saw them loosen their lances.

I fell in the sand, on my stomach. I kept my head down.

310

In the sand, I smiled. I knew these men. I had seen them ride. They were truly agents of Kurii, minions of Ibn Saran, Abdul, the Salt Ubar. They had been among the herders of the wretches on the chain to Klima.

'On your feet!' called one of them. He was some forty yards away.

I struggled to stand upright in the sand, the sand about my ankles. I swayed, unsteadily. I stood looking at them, stupidly. The sun was at my back. I had seen to this in my approach.

He who was called Baram, the most skillful, would make the first pass.

'Water!' I cried out to them. 'Please, water!'

He was right-handed. He would pass on my right. I noted the lance. It was long, slim, some eight foot Gorean in length; it was marked with red and yellow swirling stripes; it terminated in an extremely narrow point, razored, steel, some eleven inches in length, lanceolate, as the leaf of the flahdah tree. It was no mistake that I stood where I did. The sand between us was smooth. I wanted the gait of his kaiila to be even. I judged the angle of the lance. His thrust would be to the head; I assumed it would be to the right ear. It would be easy enough to judge that when the point sped toward me. One often feints with the point, dropping it, or lifting it, or moving it to the one side or the other, dropping or lifting, or horizontally, in war; but in sport accuracy and not deception is paramount; I observed the rider; I saw him smile, I saw the kaiila rear up; I saw the lance fall into position; he lanced in sport; I faced him in war.

He was unwary; his attention was fully focused on his target; did he think I was a slave girl on the plains of the Wagon Peoples, standing, a tospit on my mouth for his lance sport?

I moved to the side and, with both hands, a yard behind the point, turning, caught the lance; the rider, crying out, was torn from the saddle and fell rolling in the sand as the kaiila sped by; the lance strap broke; I lifted the lance and, as he rolled onto his back, eyes looking up, horrified, thrust it through his body, pinning him to the sand; I jerked the lance from his body, holding it down with my left foot and swirled to meet the charge of the next man. I was startled. He had not charged. He had missed his chance. He was not skillful.

I motioned him to charge.

311

He remained in his position, not moving. There was fear in his face.

I motioned him again to charge. He lifted his lance; he lowered it; then he did not charge; he backed his kaiila away.

I turned my back to him and, slowly, insolently, walked to fetch the kaiila with the empty saddle. If he had approached, I would have heard him.

I caught the rein of the other animal. The pack kaiila were near the other man, untended.

I put my foot in the stirrup and swung into the saddle. The other rider turned his kaiila about, and fled. He neglected the pack animals.

I rode my kaiila to the other animals and brought them back to the slain warrior.

It would not be difficult to follow the trail of the other man. I would do so at my leisure. I took what I needed, weapons and boots and clothing from the fallen rider. I did not take the shirt but threw it aside, for it was bloodied. Then, on my kaiila, leading the other animals, I returned to the ship, to sort through the packs, and, from them, and the stores of the ship, to choose my supplies.

It would not be necessary to follow the backtrail of the two riders who had approached the ship. There would be a fresher trail to follow. I would let the fleeing man lead me from the desert. He could not have had more than a one-talu water bag at his saddle.

I slept during the late afternoon, and then, when it was night, and cool, the kaiila fed from their pack supplies, and watered from the stores at the ship, I set forth. In the light of the moons, the trail was not difficult to follow.

TWENTY-THREE

I MAKE THE ACQUAINTANCE
OF HAROUN,
HIGH PASHA OF THE KAVARS

I could hear the drums of war.

'For whom do you ride?' challenged the man.

'I ride with the Kavars,' I told him. I moved the kaiila, with the string of pack animals, over the crest of the hill. The wretch, stripped, wrists crossed, and bound on a tether to my pommel, stumbled behind me and to the side. I had taken even his boots. He was almost lame; his feet were bloody; his legs were covered with dust and sweat, and marked with blood, where he had followed, tethered, through brush. I had followed him for four days, using his trail, and then, when I had found him in the sand, delirious and weak, trembling, thirsting, unable even to move, I had stripped and bound him. I then revived him with water and salt. I then climbed again to my saddle.

'Do not leave me!' he wept.

'I no longer need your trail,' I told him. 'I can find Red Rock now,' I told him.

'Do not leave me!' he cried out. He knelt naked in the hot sand, his ankles bound, his wrists tied behind his back.

I moved the kaiila, and the pack animals, slowly from him. When I had gone a few yards, I turned in the saddle.

'There is to be war,' I said. 'The Kavars, and the Aretai, and their attendant vassal tribes, gather.'

'Do not leave me!' cried the man. He could not rise to his feet.

'Do you know where will be the field of their war?' I asked him.

'Yes! Yes!' he cried.

I regarded him.

'Yes,' he said, '– Master.'

'Can you lead me there?' I asked.

'Yes, Master!' he cried. 'Yes, Master!'

His own kaiila was gone, wandered away. The pack kaiila were tied together, the long, lead rein of the first animal looped about my pommel. I redistributed the burdens of the animals. I untied the ankles of the man and put him, hands still tied together behind his back, on the lead animal. His ankles I then tied together beneath the belly of the animal.

'Lead me,' I told him.

'Yes,' he said.

I unsheathed the scimitar I carried.

He tensed himself. 'Yes, Master!' he said.

I resheathed the scimitar.

Two days later we arrived in the vicinity of the field. Some five hours from the field, I slashed the ropes that tied his ankles beneath the kaiila and, thrusting up on his left foot, sprawled him in the gravel, turning him then to his stomach.

'Do not kill me now!' he wept.

I tied together his ankles. I redistributed the burdens again on the pack animals.

'Do you wish to fight me to the death!' I asked him.

'No! No, Master!' he said.

I then crossed and tied his hands together before his body, and ran a tether from his hands to the pommel of my saddle.

I could hear the drums of war.

'For whom do you ride?' challenged the man.

'I ride with the Kavars,' I told him. I moved the kaiila to the crest of the hill.

It was a splendid sight.

In the field below, on the plain, there might have been some ten thousand riders. They were stretched out for pasangs, several deep. I could hear the drums. I saw the pennons, the standards. They were separated by some four hundred yards. Lances bristled in the ranks. Behind each of the arrangements of lines were hundreds of tents, striped in different colors.

My kaiila shifted on the crest of the hill. The blood of the warrior in me raced.

'Are you Kavar, come late to the formations?' asked the man.

'No,' I said.

314

'Of what vassal tribe are you?' asked the man.

'Of no vassal tribe,' I said. 'But it is with the Kavars that I choose to ride.'

'Welcome,' said the man, delightedly, lifting his lance. The others, too, behind him, lifted their lances. 'It should be a magnificent battle,' said the man.

I stood in the stirrups. I could see the Kavar center, white. On the left flank were the pennons of the Ta'Kara and the purple of the Bakahs. On the right flank were the golden Char and the diverse reds and bright yellows of the Kashani.

'By what name are you known?' asked the man.

'Hakim of Tor,' I said.

'Will you ride to battle leading pack kaiila?' asked the man.

'I think not,' I said. 'I give them to you.'

The man gestured and one of those with him led away the kaiila, making a great circuit that would lead him behind the Kavar lines, to the tents. There were hundreds of pack kaiila in evidence among the tents.

'Who is this?' asked the man, pointing to the wretch tethered at my pommel.

I addressed myself to the wretch. 'Do you wish to fight me to the death?' I asked.

He put down his head. 'No, Master,' he said.

'He is a slave,' I said to the man. 'I have no further use for him. I give him to you.'

'We can use him,' said the man. 'Such are useful in hoeing vegetables at remote oases.'

I threw the wretch's tether to one of the riders, one indicated by the man with whom I spoke.

'Come, Slave,' said the rider, he who now held the tether.

'Yes, Master!' said the man. Only too pleased was he that his tether no longer was looped about my pommel. The rider moved his kaiila away. He did not spare the wretch, who struggled to keep his pace. Behind the Kavar lines, among the tents, with the kaiila and other goods, the man would be chained, to await his disposition among masters.

To my right were the lines of the Aretai. The Aretai themselves, of course, with black kaffiyeh and white agal cording, held their center. Their right flank was held by the Luraz and the Tashid. Their left flank was held by the Raviri, and four minor tribes, the Ti, the Zevar, the Arani and the Tajuks. The Tajuks are not actually a vassal tribe of the Aretai, though they ride with them. More than two hundred years ago a wandering Tajuk had been rescued in the desert by Aretai riders, who had treated him well, and had given him water and a kaiila. The man had found his way back to his own tents. Since that time the Tajuks had, whenever they heard the Aretai were gathering, and summoning tribes, come to ride with them. They had never been summoned by the Aretai, who had no right to do this, but they had never failed to come. Usually an Aretai merchant, selling small goods, would visit the tents of the Khan of the Tajuks, the black kaffiyeh and white agal cording guaranteeing him safe passage, and, at the campfire of the Khan, after his trading, while drinking tea, would say, 'I have heard that the Aretai are gathering for war.'

'At what place,' would inquire the Tajuk Kahn, as had his father, and his father before him.

The Khan would then be told the place.

'We will be there,' the Khan would then say.

I could see that there was trouble on the left flank of the Aretai. The Tajuk riders were forcing their way to the front of the lines, between the Zevar and the Arani. Tajuks were accustomed to this position. They had held the front lines of the Aretai left flank for two hundred years. The left flank, incidentally, is the critical flank in this form of warfare. The reason for this is interesting and simple. The primary engagement weapons are lance and scimitar, and the primary defense is a small round buckler. There is a tendency, after the lines are engaged for each force to drift to its right. In a Gorean engagement on foot, incidentally, assuming uniform lines, this drift is almost inevitable, because each man, in fighting tends to shelter himself partially, as he can, behind the shield of the man on his right. This causes the infantry lines to drift. A result of this is that it is common for each left flank to be outflanked by the opponent's right flank. There are various ways to counter this. One might deepen ranks in the left flank, if one has the men to do this. One might use tharlarion on the left flank. One might, if one has the men, use clouds of archers and slingers to hold back the enemy. One might choose his terrain in such a way as to impede the advancement of the enemy's right flank. One might abandon uniform lines, etc. This drift is much less pronounced, but still exists, in cavalry engagements. It probably has to do with the tendency of the fighters to move the buckler to the right, in shielding themselves. These considerations, of course, presuppose that some semblance of lines is maintained. This is much more difficult to do in a cavalry engagement than in a foot engagement. Tahari battles, at some time or another, almost always, the forces deeply interpenetrating one another, turn into mêlée of individual combats. The left flank of the Aretai, in two hundred years, it was said, had not been turned. It had been held by the fierce Tajuks, a culturally united but mixed-race people, many of whom were characterized by the epicanthic fold. Now, I gathered, the Zevar and Arani had prevailed upon the Aretai command to defend the front lines of the left flank, or perhaps the Tajuks had merely come late, to discover their position occupied by others. There was not good feeling between the Tajuks and the Zevar and Arani. 'They are not even vassal to the Aretai,' it had been charged. 'Yet they are given prominences in the left flank!'

I could see a small group of riders hurrying from the Aretai center to their left flank.

It would scarcely do for the Tajuks and the Zevar and Arani to begin fighting among themselves. I realized, however, as must have the hurrying riders, that this was not at all impossible. The Tajuks had come for a war; at a word from their Kahn they would, without a second thought, with good cheer, initiate this enterprise against the Zevar and Arani tribesmen. The Tajuks were a touchy people, arrogant, proud, generous, capricious. If offended, and not deeming it honorable to attack the allies of the Aretai, they might simply withdraw their forces and return to their own land, more than a thousand pasangs away. It was not impossible, in order to demonstrate their displeasure, that they would choose to go over to the Kavar side, assuming that they would be given prominence in the Kavar left flank. I respected the Tajuks, but I, like most others, did not profess to understand them.

One of the riders going to the left flank from the Aretai center was tied in his saddle. His body was stiff with pain. I recognized him. I was pleased. I saw that Suleiman, Pasha of Nine Wells, master of a thousand lances, lived. Rising from his couch, his wound, inflicted by Hamid, the would-be assassin, not yet healed, he had taken saddle. Beside him, held in the hand of Shakar, captain of the Aretai, was a tall lance, surmounted by the pennon of command.

Before the Kavar center I saw another figure, robed in white, bearded. Near him a rider held the Kavar pennon of command. Another held the pennon of the vizier. That man, I knew, must be Baram, a not uncommon name in the Tahari, Sheik of Bezhad, vizier to Haroun, high Pasha of the Kavars. Nowhere did I see the pennon of the high Pasha himself. I did not know even if there were such a man.

About my neck, on a leather string, I wore the ring of the Kur, it containing the light-diversion device. I fingered the ring, looking down on the lines.

There was still much disturbance on the left flank of the Aretai, hundreds of riders angrily milling about, Tajuks with Zevar and Arani mixed in. Suleiman, with his immediate retinue, was with them, doubtless expostulating.

I saw motion among the ranks of the Kavars and their vassal tribes. I heard the drums change their beat; I saw the lines of riders ordering themselves; I saw pennons, the pennons of preparation, lifted; I assumed that when they were lowered the pennons of the charge would be lifted on their lances, and then that the lances would drop, and with them the lance of every rider in the Kavar host and that, drums rolling, the lines would then, in sweeping, almost regular parallels, charge.

It seemed a not inopportune time for Baram to commit his forces.

Thanks to the Tajuks, Suleiman was not in the center, and thanks, too, to them, the Aretai left flank, instead of being ready for action, swarmed and broiled like the crowds in a bazaar.

I saw Baram, vizier to Haroun, high Pasha of the Kavars, extend his arm before his body, and then lift it. I saw the pennons of the charge, with his arm, raised.

Suleiman, in the midst of the Tajuks, and Zevar and Arani, turned, stricken.

But the arm of Baram, the vizier, did not strike forward, the lances with it. Instead, suddenly, he turned in the saddle, lifting both arms, signaling to the lines, 'Stop!' The lances of readiness and of the charge slipped to the stirrup boots.

Slowly, not hurrying, between the lines, came a single rider, in swirling Kavar white. In his right hand he held a high lance, from which fluttered a broad and mighty pennon, scarlet and white, that of Haroun, high Pasha of the Kavars. Behind him and to the side staggered four stripped wretches, their wrists

318

crossed and bound, each on his own tether to the pommel of the saddle.

Baram, swiftly, with his guard, rode to meet the rider. The lines on each side, shifted, but did not move. Suleiman hurried to the Aretai center.

I saw the lance with its mighty pennon of the rider in white, veiled, dip and circle, and then dip and circle again. Riders, from both sides, moved their kaiila slowly toward the figure, their guards hanging behind them. There came to that parley in the center of the field of the pashas of the Ta'Kara and Bakahs, and of the Char and Kashani; and, too, riding deliberately, strapped in the saddle, there came Suleiman, high Pasha of the Aretai. With him, Shakar, captain of the Aretai, and their guard, and, with them as well, the pashas of the Luraz, Tashid and Raviri, with their guards. Then, I saw the pasha of the Ti, with his guard, join them. Lastly, riding abreast, swiftly across the field, I saw the pashas of the Zevar and the Arani, and the young kahn of the Tajuks, join the group. Behind the pashas of the Zevar and Arani, strung out behind each, in single lines, came their guard. No one rode behind the young khan of the Tajuks. He came alone. He disdained a guard.

I had no one to represent me but myself, and I was curious. I urged my kaiila down the slope. I would mix in with the parleying group. I had little doubt that each there would assume I had business there, and was legitimate party to some group not their own.

In a few moments, crowding my kaiila in, moving with courtesy but resolution through the guards, I found myself near the center of the parleying group, in the line behind the pashas and the khan.

'Mighty Haroun,' said Baram, Sheik of Bezhad, 'the command is yours! The Kavars await!'

'The Bakahs, too!' cried the pasha of the Bakahs. 'The Ta'Kara!' 'The Char!' 'The Kashani!' Each of the pashas lifted their lances.

The veiled figure, robed in white, with the lance and pennon, nodded his head, accepting the command of these thousands of fierce warriors.

Haroun then turned in his robes. 'Greetings, Suleiman,' said he.

'Greetings, Haroun, high Pasha of the Kavars,' said Suleiman.

'I heard your wound was grievous,' said Haroun to Suleiman. 'Why have you taken to the saddle?'

'Why of course to do war with you,' said Suleiman.

'On grounds, or for sport?' asked Haroun.

'On grounds,' said Suleiman, angrily. 'Kavar raids on Aretai communities, the breaking of wells!'

'Remember Red Rock!' cried a Tashid guard.

'Remember Two Scimitars!' cried a man in the retinue of the pasha of the Bakahs.

'No mercy is shown to he who destroys water!' cried a man, one of the Luraz.

Scimitars were loosened. I shifted my wind veil about my face. There were Aretai present. They paid me little attention. I saw Shakar look at me once, and then look troubled, then look away.

'Look!' said Haroun. He pointed to the nude, tethered wretches, bound to his pommel. 'Lift your arms, Sleen,' he said to them.

The men lifted their arms, their wrists crossed, bound, over their heads.

'See?' asked Haroun.

'Kavars!' cried one of the Raviri.

'No!' cried Suleiman. 'The scimitar on the forearm! The point does not face out from the body!' He looked at Haroun. 'These men are not Kavars,' he said.

'No,' said Haroun.

'Aretai raided Kavar oases,' cried a man, a guard among the Ta'Kara. 'They broke wells!'

'Suleiman's hand clenched on the hilt of his scimitar. 'No!' he cried. 'That is not true!'

There was angry shouting among the Kavars and their cohorts.

Haroun held up his hand. 'Suleiman speaks the truth,' said he. 'No Aretai raided in this season, and had they done so, they would not destroy wells. They are of the Tahari.'

It was the highest compliment one tribesman could pay to another.

'The Kavars, too,' said Suleiman, slowly, clearly, 'are of the Tahari.'

The men subsided.

'We have a common enemy, who would put us at one another's throats,' said Haroun.

320

'Who?' asked Suleiman.

Haroun turned to the tethered wretches. They lowered their arms and fell to their knees in the gravel and sand of the field. They put down their heads.

'For whom do you ride?' demanded Haroun.

One of the men, miserable, lifted his head. 'For Tarna,' he said.

'And whose minion is she?' asked Haroun.

'The minion of Abdul, the Salt Ubar,' said the man. Then he put down his head.

'I understand little of this,' said the young khan of the Tajuks. He carried a leather, black, lacquered buckler on his left arm, a slim, black, tem-wood lance in his right hand. At his side hung a scimitar. He wore a turban, and a burnoose, with the hood thrown back over his shoulders. His eyes, sharp and black, bore the epicanthic fold. At his saddle hung a conical steel helmet, oddly fashioned with a rim of fur encircling it, bespeaking a tradition in armory whose origin did not seem likely to be the Tahari. The young khan looked about, from face to face. He was angry. 'I have come for a war,' he said. 'Is there to be no war?'

Haroun regarded him. 'You shall have your war,' he said. Haroun looked at Suleiman. 'I speak in good faith,' he said. 'The Kavars, and all their vassal tribes, are yours to command.'

'I am weak,' said Suleiman. 'I am not yet recovered from my wound. Command the Aretai, and those who ride with them.'

Haroun looked at the young Tajuk khan. 'And you?' he asked.

'Do you lead me to war?' asked the Tajuk.

'Yes,' said Haroun.

'Then I will follow you,' he said. The young khan spun his kaiila about. Then he turned again, and looked over his shoulder. 'Who holds your left flank?' he asked.

'The Tajuks,' said Haroun.

'Aiii!' cried the young khan, rising in his stirrups, lifting his lance. Then he sped upon his kaiila to his men.

'Should you not return to Nine Wells?' asked Haroun of Suleiman.

'No,' said Suleiman. Then he said, 'I go to marshal my men.'

The pashas and their guards who had surrounded us re-

321

turned to their forces. Haroun, high Pasha of the Kavars, handed the lance and pennon of his office to one of the men with Baram, his vizier.

'Shall we kill these sleen?' asked Baram, indicating the kneeling, groveling wretches tethered to the pommel of Haroun's saddle. They put their heads to the gravel and sand, trembling.

'No,' said Haroun. 'Take them to the tents and chain them there as slaves. There will be more later. They will bring a high price in Tor.'

The tethers of the wretches were given to a rider. They were taken from the field.

Orders were given. In a short time, great lines, strung out, began to move across the desert. In the center were the Kavars and the Aretai. On the right flank, riding together, were the Ta'Kara and the Luraz, the Bakahs and the Tashid, the Char, the Kashani and the Raviri. On the left were the Ti, the Arani, and the Zevar, and, holding the extremity of the flank, forty deep, the Tajuks.

Behind us, behind Haroun and myself, who rode alone, we leading, strung out, were the long lines of riders, the gathered tribesmen of the Tahari.

'How did things go in the dune country?' asked Haroun.

'Well,' I told him.

He dropped the wind veil about his shoulders. 'I see you still wear about your left wrist a bit of silk,' he said.

'Yes,' I said.

'You must, in the march, inform me of what occurred in the dune country,' he said.

'I shall be pleased to do so,' I said. 'By what name should I address you?'

'By the name by which you know me best,' he said.

'Excellent,' said I, 'Hassan.'

TWENTY-FOUR

I BIND A GIRL,
RESERVING HER FOR MYSELF,
I THEN ADDRESS MYSELF
TO THE DUTIES OF STEEL

The outcome of the battle, some twenty pasangs from the kasbah of the Salt Ubar, had never been in doubt. That Ibn Saran met us at all, with the twenty-five hundred mercenaries he could muster does him much credit.

He was swiftly enveloped. Many of his men, I believe, did not understand the nature of the forces they faced until we swept over the hills upon them. We outnumbered them four or five to one. Many of the mercenaries, unable to escape, discarded their bucklers and dismounted, thrusting their lances and scimitars into the ground. There was hard fighting, however, in the vicinity of Ibn Saran's own men, those of the Salt Ubar and his allies, those who had fought with Tarna. I came once within one hundred and fifty yards of Ibn Saran; Hassan, or Haroun, high Pasha of the Kavars, came within twenty yards of him, fighting like a wild animal, but was turned back at last by a wall of bucklers, a hedge of lances. I did not see Tarna in the battle. I did see her men, but they fought under Ibn Saran. I gathered she had been relieved of her command.

Late in the afternoon, Ibn Saran, with four hundred riders, broke through our lines and fled northwest.

We did not pursue him but consolidated our victory.

'He will take refuge in his kasbah,' said Hassan. 'It will be difficult to take the kasbah.'

That was true. If it could not be taken swiftly, it might not be possible to take it at all. We did not have enough water to maintain our men in the field. At best we might be able, failing to take the kasbah, to invest it with a smaller force that it would be practical to supply with water from Red Rock. Such a siege might last for months. Our extended, thinned lines would invite attack; it would be difficult, too, even if our investing lines were not broken in force, to prevent the escape of small parties at night.

'Ibn Saran,' I said, 'may slip through your fingers.'

'We must take the kasbah,' said Hassan.

'Perhaps I can help you,' I said. I fingered the ring of the Kurii, which hung about my neck on its leather string.

The girl knelt before the low vanity, with the natural, insolent grace of the trained slave. She combed, with a broad, curved comb of kailiauk horn, her long, dark hair. The comb was yellow. She wore a bit of yellow slave silk, her collar. She was beautiful in the mirror. How like a fool I felt that I had ever surrendered her. She knelt on broad, smooth scarlet tiles. About her left ankle, looped, were several golden slave bangles. The light in the room was from two tharlarion-oil lamps, one on each side of the mirror.

She had not yet noticed the bit of silk I had left to the side.

I regarded the slave, as she combed her hair. She, in a dungeon, in a holding somewhere of agents of Kurii, had betrayed Priest-Kings. Chained nude in a dungeon, in the darkness, among the urts, she had screamed for mercy. She had revealed all she knew of the Sardar, the plans of the Priest-Kings, their practices and devices, the weakness of the Nest. If she fell into the hands of Samos I had little doubt he would have her bound and thrown to the urts, among the garbage, in the canals of Port Kar. Emptied of information she had been brought by Ibn Saran to the Tahari. Here she had, for him, identified me, when I entered the Tahari. I remembered her as one of the slaves who, bangled, in the high, tight vest of red silk, the sashed, diaphanous chalwar, had served wine in the palace of Suleiman at Nine Wells. She had been in the audience chamber when Suleiman had been struck. She had testified that it had been I who had attacked him. I had seen her smile, when taken from the rack, after her testimony. Once she had served Priest-Kings; then, later, she had well served others, the Kurii and their agents; I watched her comb her hair; now I suspected she was for most practical purposes useless in the politics of planets; but she had been spared; I watched her movements; I smiled; I, too, would have spared her; surely she was not now completely without use; she retained, I noted, doubtless the reason for which she had been spared, the general utilities of any charming, pretty slave girl. Her flesh would bring a high price. To see her was to wish to own her. Pretty Vella.

She put down the comb and reached for a tiny bottle of perfume. She touched her neck, below the ears, and her body, about the shoulders, with the scent. I knew the scent.

I had carried it with me to Klima. I had not forgotten it.

Her eye, as she put aside the tiny bottle of perfume, was caught by the bit of silk, lying to one side on the vanity.

She looked at it, puzzled, curious.

I recalled the morning I had, in chains, waited to be herded with other wretches to Klima. I had looked up. In a narrow window in the wall of the kasbah, high over my head, there had stood a woman, a slave girl, veiled and robed in yellow, a slave master behind her. With the permission of the slave master she had removed her veil. With what contempt, and scorn, and triumph she had looked upon me, a mere male slave, chained and bound for Klima, below her. She had thrown me a token, a square of silk, slave silk, red, some eighteen inches square, redolent with the perfume fitted by some perfumer, on the order of her master, to her slave personality, her slave nature and slave body. It was something by which I might remember her at Klima. I had vowed to return from Klima. She had wished to see me hooded and led away. This treat, as useful discipline, despite her pleas, had been denied her by the slave master. She had thrown me a kiss, and then, before the slave master, hurried from the window.

I stood back in the room. I flicked the switch on the ring I wore, that I might be visible to her.

She picked up the bit of silk. She opened it. It was tattered, faded, almost white. She held it open before her, looking at it. She took it in her hands and held it to her face, inhaling it. Suddenly she cried out in joy 'Tarl!' She turned, springing to her feet. 'Tarl!' she cried. 'Tarl!' She ran to me, with a clash of bangles, and took me in her arms, her head at my chest, weeping. 'Tarl!' she wept. 'Tarl! Tarl! I love you! I love you!'

I took her wrists, and forced them, slowly, from my body. I held them. She struggled to reach me, to press her lips to my body. I did not permit this. She threw her head, in frustration, from side to side. Her face was stained with tears. She wept. 'Let me touch you,' she cried. 'Let me hold you! I love you! I love you!'

I held her, by the upper arms, from me. She looked up into my eyes. 'Oh, Tarl,' she wept. 'Can you ever forgive me? Can you ever forgive me?'

'Kneel,' I told her.

Slowly, humbly, the beauty slipped to her knees before me. 'Tarl?' she said.

I drew from my garment a rag. It was thin, brief, tattered, much torn; it was cheap rep-cloth, brown and coarse; it was stained with dirt, with grease. I had found it in the kitchens of Ibn Saran.

I threw it against her body. 'Put it on,' I told her.

'I am a high slave,' she said.

'Put it on,' I told her.

She parted the bit of yellow silk she wore, dropping it to one side. She reached for the bit of rep-cloth.

'Remove first the bangles,' I told her. She sat on the tiles and, one by one, slipped the bangles from her left ankle. Then she stood up, and pulled the rag over her head. Her body involuntarily shuddered as the grease-thick rag slipped over her beauty and clung snug, revealingly, about it; I examined her, walking about her; I tore the neckline down, to better expose the beauty of her breasts; I ripped away a strip from the garment's hem, shortening it; she must now walk with exquisite care; I ripped the left side of the garment a bit more, to better reveal the delicious line from her left breast to her left hip.

I backed away a few feet from her.

She faced me. 'The gown much reveals me,' she said, 'Tarl.'

'Cross and extend your wrists,' I told her. She did so. With a strip of leather binding fiber, I fastened them together. The strip was long and enough was left to lead her, serving as tether.

'We do not have a great deal of time,' I told her. 'There will soon be fighting in the kasbah.'

'I love you,' she said.

I looked at her with fury.

She was startled at my anger. 'I am sorry I have so offended you,' she whispered. 'I have suffered much for it. You cannot know how I have suffered, weeping in the nights. I am so sorry, Tarl!'

I did not speak.

'I was cruel, and terrible,' she said, 'and petty.' She looked down, miserably. 'I can never forgive myself,' she whispered. She looked up. 'Can you forgive me, Tarl, ever?' she asked.

I looked about. I could use one of those tharlarion-oil lamps by the large mirror.

'I testified against you at Nine Wells,' she said. 'I lied. I spoke falsehood.'

'You did as you were told, Slave Girl,' I told her.

'Oh, Tarl!' she wept. She looked at me, fearlessly. 'For Lydius,' she said, 'I wanted to send you to Klima!'

'Your wishes are not of interest to me,' I told her.

She looked at me with horror. She wept then, and put down her head. 'I identified you for Ibn Saran,' she said.

I shrugged.

'Are you not angry!' she cried.

'A slave girl,' I said to her, 'owes her master absolute obedience.'

She looked aside, angrily. 'I dare not even speak to you what else I did,' she said.

'You betrayed Priest-Kings,' I told her, 'fully, and to the best of your ability.'

She turned white. 'Will it make a difference?' she said.

'I do not know,' I told her. 'It could mean the loss of Earth and Gor, the ultimate victory of the Kurii.'

She shuddered. 'I was weak,' she said. 'There was a dungeon. I was stripped, chained. It was dark. There were urts. I was terrified. I could not help myself. They told me I would be freed.'

By the leather strap I yanked her wrists, indicating to her that they were well tied. 'You will not be freed,' I told her.

'Oh, Tarl,' she wept. Then she asked, 'Will what I did make a difference?'

'I do not know,' I told her. 'Perhaps those on the steel worlds will not believe your protestations. They may believe you only spoke sincerely what you believed to be true, not what, necessarily, was true.'

She shuddered miserably.

'There are many who know of your treachery,' I said. 'Doubtless some will be captured, or fall into the hands of

327

agents of Priest-Kings. Soon your life will be worth little among the agents of Priest-Kings,' I thought of Samos. He was not a patient man.

She lifted her eyes to me. 'I could be tortured and impaled,' she said.

'You are a slave girl,' I told her. 'No such honorable death would be yours. You would be given one of the deaths of a slave girl, who has not been pleasing. In Port Kar, doubtless, you would be given the Garbage Death – bound naked and hurled to the urts in the canals.'

She sank to her knees in horror. I looked at her. In time she again lifted her head.

'Can you forgive me,' she asked, 'for what I have done?'

'What seems to concern you,' I said, 'does not to me seem to require forgiveness. You are a slave girl. You were simply obedient to your master. No man objects to a girl obeying her master.'

'Then,' she said, softly, 'you will not even have the kindness to be cruel to me?'

'I am not lenient,' said I, 'Girl, certain other gratifications you permitted yourself, which were not commanded of you.'

She looked at me. 'What?' she asked.

'At Nine Wells,' I said, 'following your testimony, falsely accusing me, when removed from the rack, you looked upon me, and smiled.'

'So tiny a thing?' she said. 'I'm sorry Tarl.'

'And when I was chained, and bound for Klima,' I said, 'again you smiled upon me. You cast me a token, a bit of silk. You blew me a kiss.'

'I hated you!' she cried, from her knees.

I smiled.

'I acted like a slave girl,' she said, her head down.

'Do you know why you acted like a slave girl?' I asked.

'No,' she said.

I looked upon her, in the brief garment, bound, kneeling before me, looking up at me. 'Because you are a slave girl,' I told her.

'Tarl!' she cried.

There was a sudden pounding on the door. I slipped instantly behind the girl, my hand over her mouth, my dagger across her throat. She could feel its edge.

'You will not cry out or give the alarm,' I told her.

She nodded, miserably. I removed my hand from her mouth.
'Vella! Vella!' called a voice. There was more pounding.
'Do you not trust me, Tarl?' she asked, softly.
'You are a slave girl,' I whispered. 'Answer.' The knife was still at her throat.
'Yes, Master!' called the girl.
'You know that at the twentieth hour you are to give pleasure to the guards at the north tower!' called the man.
'I am applying my cosmetics,' she called. 'I shall hurry!'
'If you are late by so much as five Ehn,' he called, 'you will be caressed by the five fingers of leather.' This was an allusion to the Gorean five-strap slave whip, commonly used on girls because of the softness and width of its lashes. It punishes severly but, because of its construction, does not permanently mark the girl.
'I hurry, Master! I hurry!' cried Vella.
The man left.
'You are in great danger,' said Vella. 'You must flee.' I sheathed the dagger I had held her in obedience with.
'Those in the kasbah are in greater danger than I,' I smiled.
'How did you get in?' she said. 'Is there a secret entrance?'
I shrugged. 'I entered unobserved,' I said. I looked at her. 'Curiosity is not becoming in a Kajira,' I said.
She stiffened.
I had waited near one of the gates of the kasbah, in the shelter of the ring's invisibility. When a reconnoitering party left the kasbah I had simply slipped unseen within. I had stopped in the kitchens of the kasbah to find a suitable garment for Vella. Then I had examined various areas, until I found her, in a room in which girls, who are to be summoned to the pleasure of men, may prepare themselves.
I looked to the lamps at the side of the mirror. One of them would do well.
Soon, Vella closely before me, her wrists bound, the tether looped about her forearm, I entered one of the long, tiled halls, carrying one of the lamps.
We passed only one or two men. I wore garments of the men of the Salt Ubar, taken from a prisoner. There were new mercenaries in the kasbah. No notice was taken of me, though much notice was taken of the luscious slave who, so briefly and shamefully clad, preceded me. I saw Vella, the vain wench, lift her body, instinctually, beautifully, brazenly, as the eyes of

each man fell upon her. She, a slave girl, found much pleasure in being well displayed before masters.

I chuckled. She tossed her head, angrily.

When I came to one of the narrow windows, not wide enough to admit the body of a man, facing the desert on the north, I lifted and lowered the lamp, and then did this once again. I blew out the lamp. I put it down. We stood in darkness, save for the moonlight at the window.

We heard the sentry's bar, on the wall, striking the twentieth hour.

'They will want me, Tarl, in the north tower,' said Vella. 'It is the twentieth Hour.'

'I think not,' I said. I looked out over the desert. We heard the sentry's bar.

'When I do not appear, they will come for me. They may find you. Escape while you can.'

I saw the men, riders, pouring out of the desert.

'They await me in the north tower,' she said.

'I think, in the north tower,' I said, 'they have other things now on their mind than a slave girl.'

'I do not understand,' she said.

I had paid a visit to the north tower, which commanded the north gate.

'The kasbah,' I said, 'will fall.'

'The kasbah will never fall,' said the girl. 'There are water and supplies here for months. One man on the walls is worth ten in the desert. No force sufficient to invest the kasbah can be long maintained in its vincinity.'

At the north gate, in the gate room, at the foot of the tower, ten guards struggled, come recently again to consciousness, finding themselves bound and gagged. Above the gate, in the tower itself, lay another ten.

We heard the last stroke of the bar. It was the twentieth Hour.

'Flee!' whispered Vella. 'Flee!'

The north gate, deplorably, perhaps, from the point of view of those within the kasbah, and surely from the point of view of the guards, had been left ajar.

'Flee!' said Vella.

'Look,' I told her. I put my hand over her mouth, and held her to the window. I heard her gasp, and struggle. She squirmed. A girl within the kasbah, she was terrified at what she saw. Like any beautiful female, slave or free, she knew what it might portend for her. She tried to cry out. She could not do so. 'Cry out, Slave Girl,' I whispered. 'Give the alarm.' Her voice, beneath my large, heavy hand, was muffled. She moaned in misery. She was helpless. Her eyes were wild over my hand.

Riders streamed toward the kasbah. I saw the white burnoose of Hassan, swelling behind him, in their lead.

In a moment someone on the walls had seen the riders. There were shouts. The alarm bar, struck by its great hammer, began to ring madly. Men began to appear in the yard below. Men swarmed to the walls. But to their horror riders were already within the yard, fighting with defenders. Men leaped from their kaiila, climbing, scimitars flashing, up the narrow stairs, toward the walls. The enemy was within. The enemy was behind them. Riders streamed in through the gate, and, too, men afoot, running over the sand. The north gate had fallen. The north tower was theirs. More men entered, flooding within the walls of the kasbah. Defenders rushed forth. Everywhere there was sword-play, the ringing of steel, on bucklers. I saw torches. There was much shouting. I heard the crying out of men. I stepped back. I removed my hand from the mouth of the slave girl. Vella looked at me, her eyes wide with horror.

'Cry out now, Slave Girl,' I said. 'Give the alarm.'

'Why did you not let me cry out?' she asked. 'They will kill us all!'

She had a girl's instinctive fear of riders of the desert.

I turned her about, and thrust her before me, down the hall. 'I am one of them,' I told her. She moaned.

I could hear shouting in the kasbah. By the arm I thrust her again into the room where I had first found her, where there were the broad, scarlet tiles, the vanity, the mirror, now a single tharlarion-oil lamp at the side of the mirror.

'You have returned for me,' she said, pressing her body to mine, lifting her head. 'I wanted you to come back for me. I dreamed that you would!'

I thrust her back. I could hear shouting outside. 'I have come back for you,' I told her.

'You love me!' she cried.

She cried out with misery when she saw my eyes.

'Then why?' she begged, piteously.

'I want you,' I told her.

'You love me,' she whispered.

331

'No,' I said.

'I do not understand,' she whispered.

'Foolish female of Earth,' I laughed, 'do you still understand so little of your incredible desirability? Do you not yet know that it drives men mad with desire to look upon you? Have you no sense, foolish woman, of the madness of passion the very sight of you inspires in men?'

She turned away. 'I know that I am attractive,' she said. Her voice was uncertain, frightened.

'You are an ignorant female,' I said. 'You do not know what the very sight of you does to men.'

She spun to face me, her eyes flashing. 'What does it do?' she demanded.

'To see you is to want you,' I told her, 'and to want you is to want to own you.'

'Own!' she cried, in horror.

'Yes,' I said. 'Every man wants to own his woman, completely. He wants to have her in his absolute power. He wants to have absolute control over her, in every respect, however minute. Dominance is genetically dispositional in his nature. Males are divided into those who satisfy their nature and those who do not. Males who satisfy their nature are vital and joyful, and, statistically, live long; those who deny their nature are miserable and, statistically, shorter lived, their tortured body chemistry falling prey frequently to hideous diseases.'

'Men want women to be free!' said Vella.

'Men, sometimes,' I said, 'will accord small freedoms to women, thinking that these will make them more pleasing. Surely you are familiar with the master who, at certain moments, permits the girl to speak her mind. And at these moments she does so, well and boldly. But she knows that these permissions may, at his whim, be withdrawn. This torments her with joy, and she revels in his strength. He gives her what she most deeply desires, in the female genetic depth of her, the delicious feeling of her own domination, the subjection of her beauty and weakness to the will of a strong male.'

'Men on Earth,' she cried, 'will be dethroned by law!'

'Earth has a complex and intricate political history,' I said. 'Policies and institutions, over hundreds of years, may have consquences unforseen by their authors, consequences which would have horrified them. On Earth men have succeeded in building a complicated trap from which they may perhaps be unable to escape. Perhaps they can shatter its bars. Perhaps, in the cage they themselves have built, they will merely languish and die.'

Vella said nothing.

'Do you feel,' I asked, 'that the women of Earth are happier than those of Gor.'

'No,' she said, 'No, no.'

'Kneel,' I said.

She knelt.

'On Gor,' I asked, 'who have been the happiest women you have known.'

'Many of the happiest women I have known on Gor,' she whispered, 'have been mere slave girls.'

'Man has a genetic disposition to dominance,' I said. 'This is doubted by no one qualified to form an opinion on the matter. It may, in certain circumstances, be politically expedient to deny this truth, but that is a separate question and involves separate issues.'

'I do not doubt men have a disposition to dominate,' said Vella. 'But they must control this disposition.'

'Tell a man not to breathe,' I told her. 'Tell his heart not to beat.' I looked at her. 'Tell a man not to be himself.'

Vella looked at me, stricken.

'I know little of rights,' I said, 'for I am more accustomed to attending to realities, but permit me to ask you this question? Does a man have the right to be a man?'

'Of course,' said Vella.

'What if,' I asked, 'in being a man, it was necessary to exercise the disposition for dominance?'

'Then,' said Vella, 'no man has the right to be a man.'

'What if,' I asked, 'in order to fulfill oneself as a woman, it was necessary, at least at crucial times, to be subject to the total domination of a male?'

'Then,' said Vella, 'no woman would have the right to be a woman.'

'Under these circumstances outlined then,' I said, 'neither a man nor a woman would have the right to be themselves.'

'Yes,' said Vella.

'The circumstances I have outlined,' I told her, 'are reality. It is undeniable men have a genetic disposition to domination. Does it seem likely to you that this disposition could have been selected in isolation?'

She looked at me, kneeling, not answering.

'Does it not seem likely that men and women, together, in a complementary fashion, forming a race, a kind of animal, were conjointly shaped by the long, harsh application of evolutionary forces? Does it seem likely to you that biology would have shaped the man and neglected the woman?'

'No,' said Vella. 'It does not.' She put her head down.

'Nature, in teaching man to dominate, has not failed to provide his victim.'

Vella looked up, angrily.

'Luscious and beautiful women,' I said. 'And what must be the genetic dispositions of these women, beneath the overlays, the encrustations, the conditionings of impersonal, mechanistic, industrial societies, to which sex is an embarrassment and human beings a puzzle?'

'I do not know,' she said.

'There is in them, perhaps,' I suggested, 'a disposition to respond to dominance, to yearn for it, to seek it out, to, by their behavior, beg for it. They try to control, but in their hearts, they yearn to be controlled, totally, for they are females.'

'What you say goes against much of what I have been taught,' said Vella.

'Do females,' I asked, 'wish to relate to strong or weak males?'

'Strong males,' she said.

'Why would this be?' I asked.

She looked down, not answering. 'What if, Tarl,' she asked, 'I should have these feelings, these terrible, unworthy feelings? What if I should, in my heart, desire domination by men?'

'A healthy society,' I said, 'would make provision for the satisfaction of these feelings.'

She looked up at me.

'Gorean society,' I said, 'makes provision for them. Surely you have heard of the relation of master and slave?'

'I have heard of it,' she snapped.

'The most complete and perfect institution for the total domination of a woman is that of female slavery,' I said. 'How could a woman be more perfectly and completely dominated, more helpless, more dependent on a male, more vulnerable, more subject to a man's will, more at a man's mercy than to be literally his, an owned slave?' I looked at her. 'Pretty Vella,' I said, 'to look at you is to want you, to want you is to want to own you, completely, every bit of you, to have you completely at one's mercy – completely.'

'It is such lust,' she wept. 'It is such a complete and uncompromising desire. What could compare with it? I had not known such passion, such desire, could exist. It overwhelms me. I can scarcely breathe. And I am to be its helpless victim.'

I heard men shouting, in the halls, not far from the door.

'No!' she wept, rising to her feet, trying to turn and run. I was on her in an instant and, taking her in my arms, put her on the floor, sitting. I took her wrists and, with the length of the tether, bent her forward and tied her wrists to her ankles. The end of the tether I knotted in and about the leather on her wrists, so that she would be unable to reach it, even with the fingers of one of her hands. I looked upon her. She sat, bound, the rag I had given her high about her thighs. She was incredibly desirable. She saw herself in the mirror. She could not rise, tied as she was, so she could not reach the other tharlarion-oil lamp, high, hanging from a chain, at the side of the mirror.

'Free me!' she wept. 'Free me!'

I checked the knots. They were satisfactory. She would be held perfectly.

There was the sound of scimitars clashing down the hall. 'Am I not to be freed?' she asked.

On her left thigh, rather high, small and deep, was the sign of the four bosk horns. I fingered it. She recoiled. 'Kamchak branded me,' she said.

'What does it mean that you have bound me?' she asked.

I decided that I would have her rebranded.

She looked at me. I took a long strand of her dark hair, some inch and a half in thickness. I loosely knotted them at the right side of her cheek.

'The bondage knot,' she whispered.

'This will mark you as having been taken,' I said.

'Taken?' she asked. I stood up. She struggled. I strode from her, going toward the door.

'Tarl!' she cried.

I turned to face her.

'I love you!' she cried.

'You are a consummate actress,' I told her.

'No!' she cried. 'It is true!'

'It is of no interest to me whether it is true or not,' I told her.

She looked at me, tears in her eyes, sitting, bound, the loosely looped bondage knot at the side of her face, at the right cheek.

'Does it not matter to you?' she cried.

'No,' I said.

'Do you not love me!' she wept.

'No,' I said.

'But you have come here,' she said. She struggled. 'You have risked much.' She wept. 'What is it then you want of me?' she asked.

I laughed. 'I want to own you,' I said.

'You are a man of Earth!' she protested.

'No,' I told her. 'I am of Gor.'

She shuddered in her bonds. 'You are,' she whispered. 'I see it in your eyes. I am at the mercy of a man of Gor.' Her beauty, helpless in its leather bonds, shuddered with the comprehension of what this might mean.

I turned away.

'Tarl!' she cried.

I turned again, angry.

'Am I to be kept as a slave?' she asked.

'Yes,' I told her.

'Under full discipline?' she said, disbelievingly.

'Yes,' I said.

'To the whip?' she asked.

'Yes,' I said.

'Could you, Tarl,' she asked, 'whip me? Could you be capable of that, if I displeased you? Could you, once of Earth, be so strong?'

'You have already much displeased me,' I told her. I recalled Nine Wells, when she had smiled. I remembered the window in the wall of the kasbah, the kiss she had flung me, the token of silk.

'Am I to be whipped now?' she asked. It would have been easy, parting the back of the rag she wore, she tied as she was, to whip her then. She knew that.

'No,' I said.

I went to her and took the bit of faded silk, which I had carried to Klima and back. She looked at it, in misery. I tied it about her left wrist, above the binding fiber. She wore it as I had worn it.

336

'When will you whip me?' she asked.

'When it is to my convenience,' I said.

The door burst open and two men, back to me, backing through the door, embattled, fighting, others outside the door, entered the room. Scimitars clashed. One of them turned wildly. I unsheathed my scimitar. He knew me then for an enemy. We engaged. He fell back from my blade. The other fellow was cut down by the door. I threw aside the robes of the man of the Salt Ubar. Those outside the door lifted their scimitars to me.

'I shall join you presently,' I told them.

With my boots I rolled the two fallen men from the room, closed the large double door and again turned to face Vella. We were then again alone in the room, in the light of the single tharlarion-oil lamp.

I turned again to face her. She sat on the floor, bent forward, her wrists tied to her ankles; the rag she wore was well up her thighs; the pleasures of her breasts were not much concealed, as I had torn the garment; the calves of her legs, drawn up, were marvelous; her face, her hair, was beautiful.

'You are an exquisitely beautiful slave, Vella,' I said.

'One men wish to own?' she said.

'Yes,' I said.

'And on this world,' she wept, 'I can be owned!'

'You are owned,' I told her.

'Yes,' she wept. 'I know. I know that I am owned.'

'I think,' I said, 'that I will give you to Hakim of Tor.'

She suddenly looked at me. 'No! No!' she wept. 'No, please, no!'

'I can do what I wish,' I informed her.

'Oh, no, no, no!' she wept. She knew then the true misery of the slave girl.

I went to her and pulled down the rag from her right shoulder. With a lipstick, from one of the tiny drawers in the vanity, I inscribed Taharic script on her shoulder.

'What does it say?' she wept.

'It says,' I said, ' "I am the slave girl of Hakim of Tor." '

She looked at the writing in horror upon her body. 'No, Tarl, please, no!' she cried.

I stood up. She looked up at me.

'Tarl!' she wept.

'Be silent,' I said, 'Slave Girl.'

She put her head down. 'Yes,' she said.

'Yes?' I asked

She looked up. There were tears in her eyes. 'Yes,' she whispered, '– Master.'

I strode from her, and closed the door behind me. There was slaughter to be done in the halls. It was the work of men. There was a time for work, and a time for the pleasures of slave girls. It was now the time for work. I strode toward the sound of metal clashing in the distance.

TWENTY FIVE

THE SECOND KASBAH FALLS;
WHAT WAS DONE TO TARNA

'Where is Ibn Saran!' demanded Haroun, in the flowing white of the high Pasha of the Kavars.

The man kneeling before him, wrists bound behind his back, cried out, 'I do not know! I do not know!'

'The kasbah is invested,' said another man. 'It is ours. He is not within the kasbah. He did not escape.'

'He must be still within!' cried another man.

Haroun, or Hassan, as I continued to think of him, with his boot, spurned the bound prisoner.

'He must be still within the kasbah!' cried he who had shouted before.

'Burn the kasbah,' shouted another.

'No,' said Haroun. The kasbah was too valuable to burn. He wanted it, for Kavars.

I looked at the bound prisoners in the great room, kneeling. Ibn Saran was clearly not among them.

Outside, in the shadow of the kasbah wall, there were many other prisoners. Ibn Saran was not among them either.

Ibn Saran was not the only man missing. I did not detect, among the prisoners or the fallen, the small Abdul, the water carrier and henchman of the great Abdul, Ibn Saran, the Salt Ubar, nor Hamid, traitor to the Aretai, who had struck Suleiman Pasha.

Haroun spun about, his burnoose swirling, and, angrily, leaped to the dias of the Salt Ubar, and strode upon it, like a frustrated larl.

'Let us assume, Pasha,' said I to Hassan, 'that Ibn Saran entered this kasbah.'

'He did,' cried a man.

339

'Let us assume further that our search has been most thorough and our lines resisted penetration.'

'These seem reasonable assumptions,' said Haroun, 'but how is it possible they can all be true and yet Ibn Saran neither fallen nor in chains?'

'There is another kasbah nearby, that of his confederate, Tarna,' I said.

'It could not be reached across the desert,' said a man.

'Yes! Yes!' cried Haroun. 'Come with me!' Followed by many men, carrying lamps, he descended to the pits and dungeons and storage areas below the kasbah. An hour later, beneath a trap door, and behind what appeared to be shelving in a small underground storage room, we found the door.

Broken open, it proved to lead to a dark tunnel. This tunnel provided a communication, under the desert, with the neighboring but small kasbah of Tarna, the desert chieftainess.

'Ibn Saran,' said a man, 'is doubtless in the kasbah of Tarna.'

'But we have not invested that kasbah,' moaned a man.

'Thus,' cried another, 'Ibn Saran has slipped through our lines. He will then flee from the kasbah of Tarna. We have lost him.'

'I think not,' smiled Haroun.

The men were silent. Then his vizier, Baram, Sheik of Bezhad, spoke. 'How can it be that we have not lost him, Pasha?' he asked.

'Because,' said Haroun, 'the kasbah of Tarna is invested.'

'That is impossible,' said Suleiman Pasha, leaning on a man, a scimitar still in his hand. 'No Aretai are there.' Other pashas, too, spoke. The Char had not invested it, nor the Luraz, nor the Tajuks or the Arani, or the others.

'By whom, Pasha,' asked Saleiman, 'if not by Kavars, and not by the Aretai, and not by we others, is the kasbah of Tarna invested?'

'By a thousand lances, a thousand riders of the kaiila,' said Haroun.

'And whence did you procure these thousand lances?' asked Suleiman.

Haroun smiled. 'Let us discuss these matters over small cups of Bazi tea at the end of the day,' he suggested. 'There are more important matters to attend to at the moment.'

Suleiman grinned. 'Lead on, sleen of a Kavar,' he said. 'You have the audacity of Hassan the bandit, to whom you bear a striking resemblance.'

'I have been told that,' said Haroun. 'He must be a dashing, handsome fellow.'

'That matter may be discussed over small cups of Bazi tea at the end of the day,' said Suleiman, looking narrowly at Haroun.

'True,' said Haroun.

Hassan then turned and led the way into the tunnel. Hundreds of men, including myself, followed him, many bearing lamps.

It was on the height of the highest tower of the kasbah of Tarna that Hassan, I close behind him, cornered Ibn Saran.

'Comrades!' said Ibn Saran. Then he lifted his scimitar.

'He is mine,' said Hassan.

'Beware,' I said.

Immediately the men engaged. Seldom had I witnessed more brilliant play of the scimitar.

Then the two men stepped back from one another. 'You fight well,' said Ibn Saran. He stood unsteadily. 'I could always beat you,' he said.

'That was years ago,' said Hassan.

'Yes,' said Ibn Saran, 'that was years ago.' Ibn Saran lifted his scimitar to me in salute.

'One gains a victory,' I said. 'One loses an enemy.'

Ibn Saran inclined his head to me, in Taharic courtesy. Then his face went white, and he turned, and staggered to the parapet of the tower. He fell to the desert below.

Hassan sheathed his sword. 'I had two brothers,' he said. 'One fought for Priest-Kings. He died in the desert. The other fought for Kurii. He died on the tower of Tarna's kasbah.'

'And you?' I asked.

'I thought to remain neutral,' he said. 'I discovered I could not do so.'

'There is no neutrality,' I said.

'No,' he said. Then he looked at me. 'Once,' he said, 'I had two brothers.' He clasped me about the shoulders. There were tears in his eyes. 'Now,' he said, 'now I have only one.'

We had shared salt at Red Rock, on a burning roof.

'My brother,' I said.

'My brother,' he said.

Hassan shook himself. 'There is work to do,' he said. We

hurried down from the tower, to the wall below. There I saw, from the wall, on the desert below, prisoners being herded back to the kasbah, men who had attempted to flee the walls and escape into the desert.

Herded at the point of a lance, bound, was Abdul, the water carrier. At the point of another lance, too, herded, ropes on his neck, between two kaiila, staggering, bloody, was Hamid, who had been the lieutenant to Shakar, captain of the Aretai. Shakar himself rushed forth from the kasbah to take charge of the miserable Hamid. Hamid, whatever might be his guilt in the matter of the striking of Suleiman Pasha, had obviously fought with the men of the Salt Ubar, and had raised his blade against his own tribe, the Aretai.

Other prisoners, too, were being brought back from the desert. Haroun's lances had well invested the kasbah.

Hassan and I went down to the yard of the kasbah.

Startled was I to discover in the courtyard, mounted in the high saddle of the kaiila, the leader of Hassan's mystery lancers, who had invested the kasbah of Tarna. He swept aside his wind veil.

'T'Zshal!' I cried.

He, bearded, grinned down at me from the saddle, a lance in his hand.

'I sent,' said Hassan, Haroun, high Pasha of Kavars, 'a thousand kaiila, a thousand lances, supplies, to Klima. I thought such men might prove useful.'

T'Zshal raised the lance. The kaiila reared. 'We shall not forget the Kavars, Pasha,' said T'Zshal.

I feared that Hassan had made a terrible mistake. Who would dare to arm such men?

T'Zshal turned the kaiila expertly. He had once been of the Tahari. And then, with a scattering of sand, men following him, returned to the desert, again to supervise his men in their encircling ring of will, steel and kaiila flesh.

Hamid and Abdul knelt in the sand, bound.

Hassan held his blade to the throat of Hamid. 'Who struck Suleiman Pasha?' he inquired. Hamid looked up at him. Suleiman and Shakar stood near. 'It was I,' said Hamid.

'Take him away,' said Suleiman Pasha. Hamid was dragged away.

'How did you know it was he who struck me?' asked Suleiman.

342

'I was there,' said Hassan. 'I saw it.'

'Haroun, high Pasha of the Kavars!' cried Shakar.

Hassan smiled.

'No!' he cried. 'There were none there but Aretai, Ibn Saran, Hakim of Tor and –' Shakar stopped.

'And Hassan the bandit,' said Hassan.

'You!' cried Suleiman, laughing.

'Surely you did not think there could be two such handsome, dashing fellows?' asked Hassan.

'Kavar sleen!' laughed Suleiman.

'Do not be too broadcast with my additional identity,' requested Hassan. 'It is useful at times, particularly when the duties of the pasha become too oppressive.'

'I know what you mean,' said Suleiman. 'Your secret is safe with me.'

'I, too, will guard its nature,' said Shakar.

'You are Hakim of Tor, are you not?' asked Suleiman, turning to me.

'Yes, Pasha,' I said stepping forward.

'Grievously did we wrong you,' he said.

I shrugged. 'There are still pockets of resistance to be cleared up in the kasbah,' I said. 'I beg your indulgence that I may be excused.'

'May your eye be keen, your steel swift,' said Suleiman Pasha.

I bowed.

'And what of this small sleen?' asked Shakar, indicating the small Abdul, who knelt, cowering, in the sand.

'He, too,' said Suleiman Pasha, 'let him be taken away.' A rope was put on the throat of Abdul, and he was dragged whimpering from our presence.

I looked to the central building of the kasbah. Within it, here and there, in rooms, men still fought.

'Find me Tarna,' said Suleiman Pasha. 'Bring her to me.' Men rushed from his side. I did not envy the woman. She was free. She had broken wells. Prolonged and hideous tortures awaited her, culminating in her public impalement, nude, upon the walls of the great kasbah at Nine Wells.

The men of the Tahari are not patient with those who break wells. They look not leniently upon this crime.

I slipped to one side, and left the group.

*

343

Tarna, in her quarters, spun to face me. She was startled. She had not known I was there. I had touched the ring. A moment later, she turning, saw me, standing in the room.

'You!' she cried.

Her eyes were wild. She was distraught. She wore the manish garb of the Tahari, save that she did not wear the wind veil nor the kaffiyeh and agal. Her face and head, proud and beautiful, were bare. Her hair was wild, long, loose behind her, behind the thrown-back hood of the burnoose. The garments she wore were torn, and stained. The left trouser leg had been slashed. There were long scimitar slashes at the left sleeve, which hung in tatters. I did not think she had been wounded. There was dirt at the left side of her face.

'You have come to take me!' she cried. She carried a scimitar.

'Your war is lost,' I told her. 'It is done.'

She looked upon me in fury. For an instant there were tears in her eyes, bright and hot. I saw that she was a woman. Then again she was Tarna.

'Never!' she cried.

'It is true,' I told her.

'No!' she cried.

We could hear men fighting in the distance, somewhere in the corridors beyond.

'The kasbah has fallen,' I told her. 'Ibn Saran is dead. Haroun, high Pasha of the Kavars and Suleiman, high Pasha of the Aretai, are already within the walls.'

'I know,' she said, miserably. 'I know.'

'You were relieved of your command,' I told her. 'You were no longer of use. Even those men who once served you fight now, decimated, for their lives.' I regarded her. 'The kasbah has fallen,' I said.

She looked at me.

'You are alone,' I said. 'It is over.'

'I know,' she said. Then she lifted her head, angrily, proudly. 'How did you know where to find me?' she asked.

'I am not unfamiliar with the quarters of Tarna,' I said.

'Of course,' she said. She smiled. 'And now you have come to take me,' she laughed.

'Yes,' I told her.

'Doubtless for he who brings me in, his rope on my neck, before the noble Pashas Haroun and Suleiman, there will be a high reward,' she said.

'I would suppose that would be the case,' I said.

'Fool!' she said. 'Sleen! I am Tarna!' She lifted the scimitar. 'I am more than a match for any man!' she cried.

I met her charge. She was not unskillful. I fended her blows. I did not lay the weight of my own steel on hers, that I not tire her arm. I let her strike, and slash, and feint and thrust. Twice she drew back suddenly in fear, almost a wince, or reflex, realizing she had exposed herself to my blade, but I had not struck her.

'You are not a match for a warrior,' I told her. It was true. I had crossed steel with hundreds of men, in practice and in the fierce games of war, who could have finished her, swiftly and with ease, had they chosen to do so.

In fury, again, she attacked.

Again I met her attack, toying with the beauty.

She wept, striking wildly. I was within her guard, the blade at her belly.

She stepped back. Again she fought. This time I moved toward her, letting her feel the weight of the steel, the weight of a man's arm. Suddenly she found herself backed against a pillar. Her guard was down. She could scarcely lift her arm. My blade was at her breast. I stepped back. She stumbled from the pillar, wild. Again she lifted the scimitar; again she tried to attack. I met her blade, high, forcing it down; she slipped to one knee, looking up, trying to keep the blade away; she wept; she had no leverage, her strength was gone; I thrust her back, and she fell on her back before me on the tiles; my left boot, heavy, was on her right wrist; the small hand opened and the scimitar slipped to the tiles; the point of the blade was at her throat.

'Stand up,' I told her.

I broke her scimitar at the hilt and flung it to a corner of the room.

She stood in the center of the room. 'Put your rope on my neck,' she said. 'You have taken me, Warrior.'

I walked about her, examining her. She stood, angrily, inspected.

With the blade of my scimitar I brushed back the slashed, left leg of her trousers. She had an excellent leg within.

'Please,' she said.

'Remove your boots,' I told her. In fury, she removed them.

345

She then stood, barefoot, on the tiles in the center of the room.

'You will lead me barefoot before the Pashas?' she asked. 'Is your vengeance not sweet enough, that you will so degrade me?'

'Are you not my prisoner?' I asked.

'Yes,' she said.

'Then I will do with you as I please,' I told her.

'Oh, no!' she wept.

In a moment I told her to kneel. She knelt on the tiles, her head down, her head in her hands. She was stripped completely, by my scimitar.

'What have we here?' asked Hassan, entering the room. To my interest he had changed his garments. He no longer wore the white of the high Pasha of the Kavars but simpler garments, those which might have befitted Hassan, the outlaw of the Tahari.

'Lift your head, Beauty,' said I, gently putting the point of the scimitar beneath her chin, lifting it.

She looked at Hassan, incredibly beautiful, her cheeks stained with tears.

'This is Tarna,' I said.

'So beautiful?' he asked.

'Yes,' I said.

'The capture is yours,' said Hassan. 'Put a rope on her neck. Haroun, high Pasha of the Kavars, and Suleiman, high Pasha of the Aretai, are eager to see her.'

I smiled. From within my sash I found a length of prisoner rope. It was coarse rope.

'Doubtless,' said Hassan, 'Haroun, high Pasha of the Kavars, and Suleiman, high Pasha of the Aretai, will pay a high reward to the man who brings Tarna before them.'

'Doubtless,' I said.

'I have heard them crying out for her,' said Hassan.

I knotted the rope about the beauty's neck. She was mine.

Hassan looked down upon the stripped, tethered beauty.

'I do not want to die,' she suddenly cried. 'I do not want to die!' She put her head down, in her hands. She wept.

'The punishment for breaking a well,' said Hassan, 'is not light.'

Tarna, shuddering, wept, her head to the floor, my rope on her neck.

'Come, Female,' I said. I jerked her head up, by the rope.

346

'We must go to see the Pashas.'

'Is there no escape?' she wept.

'There is no escape for you,' I said. 'You have been taken.'

'Yes,' she said, numbly, 'I have been taken.'

'Are you thinking, Hassan,' I asked, 'what I am? That there might be one hope for her life?'

'Perhaps,' grinned Hassan.

'What?' cried Tarna. 'What!'

'No,' I said. 'It is too horrifying.'

'What!' she cried.

'Forget it,' I said.

'Forget it,' agreed Hassan. 'You would never approve. You are too proud, too noble and fine.'

I jerked on the rope, as though to draw Tarna to her feet, in order to lead her to the presence of the Pashas.

'What!' she cried.

'Better torture and impalement on the walls of the kasbah at Nine Wells,' said Hassan.

'What?' wept Tarna.

'It is too horrifying, too terrible, too utterly degrading, too sensual,' I said.

'What?' wept the tethered beauty. 'Oh, what?'

'On the lower levels,' said Hassan, 'I understand that slave girls are kept.'

'Yes,' said Tarna, 'for the pleasures of my men.'

'You no longer have men,' I reminded her.

'I see!' cried Tarna. 'I might be slipped among them!'

'It is a chance,' admitted Hassan.

'But I am not branded!' wept Tarna.

'That can be arranged,' said Hassan.

She looked at him with horror. 'But then,' she said, 'I would truly be a slave.'

'I knew you would not approve,' said Hassan.

I jerked at the rope on the beauty's neck. Her chin was pulled up. The knot was under the jaw on the right, turning her head to the left. 'No,' she said. 'No!'

We looked at her.

'Make me a slave,' she whispered. 'Please! Please!'

'There will be much risk,' said Hassan. 'If Haroun, high Pasha of the Kavars, should hear of this, he might skin me alive.'

'Please!' wept Tarna.

347

'It will not be easy,' I said.

'Please, Please!' she wept.

'How should we go about this?' I asked.

'One thing,' said Hassan, 'prisoner rope is not appropriate. She must be put on a wrist tether.'

'I see little problem in this,' I said.

'A more serious problem,' he said, 'will occur in leading her through the halls.'

'I can walk with my head down, as a slave,' said Tarna.

'Most female slaves,' said Hassan, 'walk very proudly. They are proud of their slavery, and their mastery by men. They have learned their womanhood. It has been taught to them. In their way, though imbonded, totally, I suppose they are the truest and freest of women. They are closest, perhaps, to the essentials of the female, those of subservience to the masculine will, obedience, service and pleasure. In being most themselves, utter slave, they are most free. This is paradoxical, to be sure. Most girls, verbally, will object to slavery, but this half-hearted, pouting ineffectual rhetoric is belied by the joy of their behavior. No girl who has not been a slave can understand the joy of it, the profundity and freedom. The objections of the girls to slavery, I have noted, are usually not objections to the institution which, in the sweet heat of their bodies, they love dearly, and fear only to lose, but to a given master. Given the proper master they are quite content. In the proper collar a woman is serene and joyful.'

'Are slave girls truly proud?' asked Tarna.

'Most,' said Hassan. 'You may think only of girls you have dominated, or seraglio mistresses, presiding over male weaklings. But have you seen girls, truly, before men?'

'In a café, once,' she said, 'I saw a girl dance before men. She was scandalous! And the girls, too, who served in the café! Shameful! Scandalous!'

'Speak with care, girl,' said Hassan. 'For someday you, too, may so dance and serve.'

Tarna turned white.

'Did the girls seem proud?' asked Hassan.

'Yes,' said Tarna, sullenly. 'But why should they have been proud?'

'They were proud of their bodies, their feelings, their desirability,' said Hassan, 'and proud, too, of their masters, who had the will and power to put them in a collar and keep them there,

348

because it pleased him to do so.'

'How strong such men must be,' whispered Tarna.

'Too,' said Hassan, 'undeniable females, secure in their sexuality, it was difficult not for them to be proud. Too, joy can make girls proud.'

'But why, why,' wept Tarna, 'should they be proud?'

Hassan shrugged. 'Because they knew themselves to be the most perfect and profound of women,' he said. 'That is why they are proud.' Hassan laughed. 'Sometimes,' he said, 'girls grow so proud it is necessary to whip them, to remind them that they are only slaves.'

'I can walk proudly,' said Tarna. 'Lead me through the halls.' She rose to her feet, and stood before us.

'There is a difference,' laughed Hassan, 'between the pride of a free woman and the pride of the slave girl. The pride of a free woman is the pride of a woman who feels herself to be the equal of a man. The pride of the slave girl is the pride of the girl who knows that no other woman is the equal of herself.'

Tarna suddenly shuddered, inadvertently, with pleasure. I could see that this insight had thrilled her to the quick.

'You are no longer competing with men,' said Hassan. 'You are now something different.'

'Yes, yes!' suddenly whispered Tarna. 'I see! I am different! I am not the same!' She looked at us. 'Suddenly,' she said, 'for the first time I love the thought of not being the same.'

'It is a start,' said Hassan.

'Do you think she is fit to be led through the halls?' I asked. I could hear men shouting outside. There was singing, the sounds of carousing.

'She cannot yet walk like, or truly seem a slave girl,' said Hassan, 'for she is not yet a slave girl, but if little attention is paid, we may have a chance.' He turned to the captive. 'How do you look upon men, Wench?' he asked. 'How do you meet their eyes?'

Tarna gazed upon him.

Hassan moaned. 'We shall lose our heads,' he said.

I dragged Tarna by the rope to her vast couch, and flung her to the yellow cushions. At the head of the couch I tied the rope which was knotted on her neck. She could not rise more than a foot from the cushions. She twisted on the cushions, turning to look at me. 'What are you going to do with me?' she asked, horrified.

Hassan grinned. 'She is your capture,' he said. 'First capture rights are yours.'

Tarna cried out with misery.

In a short time, we led Tarna through the halls of the kasbah. We had taken the prisoner rope from her neck, to conceal the fact that she was a free prisoner. I led her by a wrist tether, her wrists crossed and bound, and the tether running to my hand. Sometimes I pulled her abruptly, making her stumble, or run or fall. I did this for three reasons; it concealed her awkwardness; I was in a hurry; and it pleased me. The wrist tether was from the cords holding the hangings in her room. The cords were not such that they could be easily identified.

'Are these cords such that they are unique to your quarters?' I had asked her.

'No,' she had said. 'No.' I had then bound her with them.

'Is she not much too clean?' asked Hassan.

I looked at the bound girl. 'Yes,' I said. Then I said to the girl, 'Down, down on the floor, on your belly and back, roll.'

She looked down at us angrily, but then complied. When she stood again before us, Hassan took soot from one of the tharlarion-oil lamps and rubbed it, here and there, on her body. He then took some tharlarion-oil and, as she shuddered, poured and rubbed it on her left shoulder.

'Of great danger to us now,' said Hassan, 'is her lack of a brand.'

'Unless you have an iron with you,' I said, 'there is not much helping that at the moment.'

Still the problem was serious. Girls are branded prominently, usually on the left or right thigh. The brand on a slave girl is not something for which, when the wench is stripped, one must hunt. If it were noted, in our journey to the lower levels, that the woman we led was unmarked, it would be assumed that she was free. This would excite curiosity, and would be sure to be later recalled. Tarna, of course, would be unmarked. Indeed, she would be likely to be the only unmarked female in the kasbah.

I tore down one of the hangings, a yellow one, and ripped a narrow strip from it. I wound this about the girl's thighs, low, to reveal her navel. It is called the slave belly. On Gor it is only slave girls who expose their navels. But the cloth would cover the area, on either hip, which be the likely site of the

350

incised slave mark.

'It might be better,' said Hassan, studying the beauty, 'if she were completely stripped.'

'Not without a brand,' I said.

'You are right,' said Hassan. 'We cannot risk it.'

'Let them assume,' I suggested, 'that we are leading her to someone to whom we are giving her, and that we wish to tear off her last veil, to her horror, only before her new master.'

'Excellent,' said Hassan. 'It is at least plausible.'

'It will have to do,' I said.

'Please,' said Tarna. 'Lift the cloth to cover my navel.'

I thrust the cloth down, another inch on her hips. She shook with anger, but was silent. She did not much approve either when Hassan cleaned his hands on the cloth about her hips. This dirtied the cloth, making it more fitting to be worn about the hips of a slave; too, of course, it removed the soot from his hands, from the tharlarion-oil lamp.

As we had led her through carousing soldiers, many of them reached for the girl, whom they assumed, as we had intended, was slave. 'Oh,' she cried. 'Oh!' She found herself much caressed, with the rude familiarity with which a slave girl is handled.

'Hurry, Slave,' I barked at her. She did not even know enough to say, 'Yes, Master.' I did not lead her gently. At last, to my relief, we reached the door leading to the lower levels.

'Did you see them look at me?' she asked. 'Is this what it is to be a slave girl?'

We did not respond to her. Hassan threw back the heavy door. I removed the bonds from the girl, and threw them aside. I took her by the arm and, Hassan preceding us, I conducted her down the curving, narrow, worn stairs, deep below the kasbah.

We had brought her safely through the halls. This pleased me.

I have little doubt that our success in this matter was largely to be attributed to what Tarna, stripped and roped back by the neck, had learned on her own couch. There is a great deal of difference in the way that various sorts of women relate to men and look upon them. These differences tend often to be functions of what their experiences have been with men. For example, do they regard themselves as the equals of men, or their superiors? Or, have they been taught, forcibly and clearly, that they are not the dominant organism? Have they been put, helpless, beneath the will of a male? Have they learned their delicious vulnerability, that they are the male's victim and prey, his pleasure and delight? And have they learned, to their helpless horror and joy, the fantastic things he can do to their body?

'How do you look upon men, Wench?' Hassan had asked. 'How do you meet their eyes?' he had asked.

And Tarna had gazed upon him.

He had moaned. 'We shall lose our heads,' he had said.

I had then dragged her by the neck to her own couch, that swift instruction be administered to her.

She had thousands of pasangs to go, but we had made a start with her, enough to get her through the halls.

I had seen her react as we had dragged her through the soldiers. She was not then the Tarna of old. She was a woman who had been taught what men could do with her.

I heard singing, shouting, from below, too. We descended four levels, until we reached the bottom level. Tarna looked sick.

'The smell,' she said. A drunken soldier, carrying a bottle, brushed against us. I let her throw up, twice, in the hall. Then I pushed her ahead of me, holding her by the arm, stumbling through the straw and slime down the corridor. She cried out, miserably, as an urt scurried past, brushing her ankle. We looked through one cell door, swung open. It led into a large, long, narrow room. Against the far wall, chained by the neck, on straw, were more than a hundred slave girls. Soldiers, many drunken, sported with them. Some, holding the slaves in their left arm, forced wine from bottles down their throats. Some of the girls squirmed, eagerly, their hands on the bottles. Others, at the end of their chain and collar, on their knees, held out their hands. 'Wine, Master, please!' they cried. They did not bargain, as might have a desperate free woman, 'Anything for a sip of wine, Noble Sir!' for they were slave girls. Anything could, and would, be demanded of them, and for nothing. They were slave.

'How horrid men are,' moaned Tarna.

'Speak with care,' warned Hassan, 'for soon, as much as any slut at the wall, you will belong to them.'

Tarna threw back her head, and moaned.

'It is here,' said Hassan. He moved back the heavy iron door and we entered the room. I looked about, at the chains

352

and devices. Tarna shrank back. She could not run, for my hand was on her arm. She seemed faint. I steadied her. It was dark in the room, except for a small tharlarion-oil lamp on a chain in one corner, and a brazier, glowing, near the branding rack. Hassan stirred the coals in the brazier. In a large kasbah irons are kept always hot. The slaves know this.

I ripped the bit of cloth away from her hips and threw her against the rack. I swung shut the two heavy bands and with the two twist handles, tightened them on her thigh. She turned, trying to pound at the metal that held her. I took her wrists and pulled them forward, to the two posts, some six inches apart, part of the branding rack, putting them in the snap bracelets which dangled there, one from each post. These are simple mechanisms. It is quite easy to open and shut them, and it may be done with a snap of the finger, one for each bracelet. As the bracelets are situated, some inches apart, of course, and as the snap is on each bracelet itself, at the wrist, the girl herself cannot get a finger, of either hand, on the mechanism. Others may open them easily; she, on the other hand, is perfectly held. I took again the twist handles. I turned them extremely tightly. 'Oh, oh,' she cried. She pulled futilely at the snap bracelets. Then I again turned the twist handles. 'Please!' she cried. 'Be quiet,' I told her. She bit her lip. I tightened the handles more and put in the locking device, that they might not slip back. Her thigh was absolutely immobile.

'I see you like a left-thigh-branded girl,' said Hassan.

The girl can writhe in the rack or squirm, or scream, but the held thigh will not move. It is held for the kiss of the iron.

With a heavy glove, Hassan pulled an iron from the brazier. 'What do you think of this brand?' he asked.

It was the Taharic slave mark.

'It is beautiful,' I said. 'But let us assure ourselves that this will be a common slave, one fit to sell north.'

'A good idea,' said Hassan. He returned the one iron to the brazier and reached for another. It glowed red. It was a fine iron, clean and precise. At its tip, bright red, was the common Kajira slave mark of Gor. Tarna looked upon it with horror.

'It is not yet hot enough, my pretty,' said Hassan. He returned it to the brazier.

We heard shouting, as though from far away. Hassan looked at me. 'I shall investigate,' I said. I left the room and ascended

353

to the third level. The noise was coming from the level above, the second. A soldier was stumbling by. 'What is going on?' I asked. 'On the level above?'

'They are searching for Tarna,' he laughed. He then stumbled away.

I saw two slave girls led past me, on wrist chains, in the grip of another soldier.

I returned to the fourth level. I returned to the room where Hassan waited.

'They are searching for Tarna,' I said.

'On what level are they?' asked Hassan.

'The second,' I said.

'Ah,' said Hassan, 'then we have plenty of time.' In a few Ehn he removed the iron from the coals, and examined it. He then again replaced it. Shortly thereafter, however, for it must have been almost ready, he drew it forth again. It glowed white.

'You may scream and cry out, my pretty,' said Hassan, not unkindly.

She struggled in the bracelets, she watched the iron. Then she screamed. For five long Ihn Hassan held the iron, pressing it in. I saw it sink in her thigh, smoking and hissing. Then he, cleanly, withdrew it. Tarna was marked.

She sobbed, wildly. We did not rebuke her. I freed her thigh of the rack. She fell on her knees at the posts, sobbing. I freed her wrists of the snap bracelets. I lifted her, sobbing, in my arms.

I, Hassan, leading, carried Tarna to an empty cell on the fourth level. Hassan pushed back the door, tying it open. There was dim light in the cell, from the hall outside. I put Tarna, still sobbing, on the dank straw at the back wall of the cell.

'I'm a slave girl,' she whispered. 'I am a slave girl.'

We found the chain and collar, and I fastened it about the girl's neck, locking it.

We looked at her.

She was chained to the wall.

'I am a slave girl,' she whispered to us, disbelievingly, through her tears.

We heard sounds, from the level above.

'They are searching the third level, that above us,' said Hassan. 'They will soon be here.'

'I am a slave girl,' she said.

'If it is discovered that you were Tarna,' said Hassan, 'it

will not go easy with you.'

She looked at him, numbly, comprehending his import. Tarna had been spoken of in the past tense. No longer was she Tarna. Tarna was gone. Tarna no longer existed. In her place now, there was only a slave girl, nameless as a kaiila or verr.

'If it is discovered that you were Tarna,' said Hassan sternly, 'it will not go easy with you. No longer would you be entitled to certain forms of torture, suitable for free persons, culminating in your honorable impalement. Your death would surely be one of the deaths of a slave girl, who has not been pleasing.'

'What can I do?' she wept. 'What can I do?'

'You are a slave,' said Hassan, cruelly. 'Please us.'

And in that foul cell, on the stinking straw, in the feeble light of the lamp outside, the once proud Tarna, now only a nameless slave girl, chained by masters, struggled to please us. We were not easy with her. We were harsh, and hard, and cruel. Often she wept and despaired of her ability to please us, but she was cuffed and kicked and set again about her duties.

At last Hassan and I rose to our feet.

'The slave hopes that she has pleased her masters,' whispered the girl.

Hassan looked at me. 'She has much to learn,' he said, 'but I think, in time, she may be satisfactory.'

I nodded, concurring in his judgment. We then stepped outside. We were encountered in the hall by a soldier, with a lifted lamp. 'I search for Tarna,' he said.

'Tarna is not here,' I said. 'In the cell there is only a female slave.'

The soldier looked into the cell, and lifted the lamp. The girl lay on the straw, curled up, the collar and chain leading to her throat. She shielded her eyes from the lamp. It was not bright, but, in the dimness of the cell, it hurt her eyes.

She was beautifully curled on the straw. She lifted her head, shielding her eyes.

'Master?' she asked.

'What is your name, Girl?' asked the soldier.

'Whatever master wishes,' she said.

He held the lamp up, examining her beauty. With a sinuous movement, with a rustle of chain, she sat upright, her back straight. She extended her right leg, looking at him over her right shoulder; her toes were pointed; her leg was flexed, revealing to its best, delicious advantage, the curve of her calf.

I felt like raping her.

'What is the name of your master?' asked the soldier.

'I do not know,' she said. 'I belonged to Tarna. Now I hear from soldiers that Tarna has fallen. I do not know who will be my master.' She looked at him. 'You seem strong,' she said.

She, sitting, as she was, thrust forward her breasts, accentuating the line of her beauty.

'Slut,' he laughed.

She put her head down, chastened.

He laughed. 'Be as you were before,' he said. She obeyed. 'More so,' said he. She obeyed.

'I search for Tarna,' he said.

'Do not search for her,' begged the girl. 'Stay with me.'

'You are dirty,' he said. 'And you stink.'

'Bring slave perfume,' she said to him. 'Rub it on my body.'

He turned from the door. She fled to the length of her chain, kneeling, her hands outstretched to him. 'The fourth level is deep,' she said. 'I am in a cell to myself. Many men do not even know I am here. The kasbah has fallen and only two soldiers have entered my cell. Stay with me!'

'I must search for Tarna,' said the man.

'When you have finished your search,' said the girl, arms outstretched, 'return to me.'

'I will,' said the soldier. He laughed brutally.

'Thank you,' she cried, 'beloved Master!'

He turned to go.

'Beloved Master,' she whispered. She knelt. She put her head down. 'If I were a bold free woman,' she said, 'and not a bond girl, I would ask that you bring with you on your return a bottle of wine for your pleasure, that you would enjoy me more.'

'Little she-sleen!' he laughed. He entered the cell and, putting down his lamp, kicked and cuffed the girl, until she rolled in the straw, tangled in the chain, covering her head, her body half covered with straw, at the wall. He then again took up the lamp, and went to the door. 'I shall return,' he said, 'and when I do, I shall bring wine.'

She rolled to a sitting position. 'Thank you, Master!' she cried. 'And I will bring slave perfume, too,' he said, 'to souse you with, you stinking little slut of a slave.'

'Thank you, Master!' she cried.

Laughing he left the cell, to continue his search for Tarna.

'Let us go upstairs,' said Hassan. 'Doubtless there are those who wonder as to the whereabouts of Haroun, high Pasha of the Kavars.'

'Doubtless,' I said.

I looked into the girl's cell. 'You are an excellent actress,' I said.

She looked at me, puzzled.

'The soldier,' I said, 'I wager he will return.'

She broke a bit of straw between her fingers. 'I hope so,' she said.

I looked at her. 'You want him to return?' I asked.

'Yes,' she said. Her head had lifted, in the chain and collar. 'Why?'

'Did he not seem strong to you?' she asked. 'Did you not see the ease, the audacity, the authority with which he handled me?'

'Yes,' I said.

'I want to be had by him,' she said. 'I want him to have me.'

'Are you serious?' I asked.

'Yes,' she said. 'I want to serve him as a female slave.'

Hassan stood behind me. 'I wish you well, Girl,' he said. 'I, too, wish you well, Slave Girl,' I said.

'A slave girl gives you her gratitude,' she said. As we turned and left, she said, 'I wish you well, Masters.'

TWENTY-SIX

THE MARCH

It was early morning.

I could hear the drums. The march was soon to begin. The kaiila shifted in the sand. Leather was looped and loosely knotted about the high pommel of my desert saddle. My boots were in the stirrups. The scimitar was at my side. I held the light lance of the Tahari, its butt in the stirrup sheath on my right.

I saw Haroun, high Pasha of the Kavars, in swirling white, ride past. At his side, in the black kaffiyeh and white agal cording of the Aretai, rode Suleiman, high Pasha of that tribe, holder of the great kasbah at Nine Wells, master of a thousand lances. Behind Haroun rode Baram, sheik of Bezhad, his vizier. Behind Suleiman, on a swift kaiila, rode Shakar, with silver-tipped lance, a high captain of the Aretai.

I looked behind me, at the long lines of men. The sun was now striking the south wall of what had been the kasbah of Abdul, Ibn Saran, who had been the Salt Ubar. The line of march extended from this kasbah, across the desert, to the kasbah which had once been the holding of Tarna, once a beautiful and proud desert chieftainess. It was at that kasbah that could be found the head of the march.

I saw the young khan of the Tajuks, in white turban, ride by, going to the rear of the columns. He was accompanied by twenty riders.

The march would proceed to Red Rock, thence to Two Scimitars, thence to Nine Wells, thence, by a major caravan route, to Tor. Different bodies of men would leave the march at various points, as tribesmen returned to their lands. Only some few hundred would journey as far as Tor, and those largely to conduct herded slaves to the fine markets of that

358

city, which is the Tahari clearing house for slaves to be sold north. Already word had been sent ahead to Tor that preparations be made. Cages must be scheduled, chains forged, slave meal garnered. For the female slaves cosmetics and perfumes must be anticipated. Arrangements must be made for auction houses. Dates must be set. Advance publicity is particularly important. The sale must be widely and thoroughly advertised, in many cities. Before the first girl, barefoot, nude, ascends the block, to be sold, much must be done. A great deal of planning, and organization and hard work must take place before she lifts her head to the buyers, looking out upon them, one of whom will own her, and she hears the first call of the auctioneer, he lifting his coiled whip behind her. 'What am I bid?'

In the march were Kavars, Ta'Kara, Bakahs, Char, Kashani, Aretai, Luraz, Tashid, Raviri, Ti, Zevar, Arani and, holding the position of the rear guard, with black lances, Tajuks.

In the march were hundreds of pack kaiila, many carrying water.

The tempo of the drums increased, indicating that the time for the beginning of the march would be soon.

The sun was now full on the south wall of what had been the kasbah of Abdul, Ibn Saran, the Salt Ubar.

A dozen kaiila moved past in stately line, laden with water.

Some six hundred women had been taken in the two kasbahs, all female slaves.

Some fifteen hundred men, who had surrendered, now wore the chains of slaves.

The men would march toward the rear of the columns, before the rear guard. The women, for there were insufficient wagons or kaiila for them, would march, in separate groups of fifty, within the columns and toward their center. They were more valuable than the men. Each female slave group was a fifty bracelet coffle.

I moved the kaiila over to regard the female slave groups, which stood at the wall, not yet herded to their places in the columns. Each girl was fastened by the left wrist, in wrist coffle in her group. Each girl was separated by some five feet of light, gleaming chain. It was not a heavy chain to carry. As I moved the kaiila slowly along the line of chained girls, to examine them, the leather, looped and knotted about the pommel of my saddle, grew taut. It led to the crossed, bound wrists of the girl I had tethered to the pommel. She had ten feet of tether. She followed.

The feet of the women had been bound in leather. They stood ankle deep in the sand. Later, when the sun was high, sheets would be thrown over them, to protect their eyes from the glare, their bodies from the sun. The sheet is placed over the head, completely, so that the girl cannot see. Then, with a piece of string, looped twice about her neck and tied snugly, it is held in place. This is inferior, of course, to moving a woman in a sheltered slave wagon or in a kurdah.

The sheets, of course, had not yet been placed.

The girls stood straight, proud under the gaze of a warrior. 'Tal, Master,' said many of them, as I rode slowly by. 'Buy me in Tor, Master,' called another. One girl, in the fourth group, pressed out from the others, her left wrist behind her, held by the chain. She pressed her face against the left forequarter of my kaiila and, turning looked up at me, her face tear-stained. It was Tafa. I recalled her in the dungeon in what had been the kasbah of Ibn Saran, the morning before I had begun the march to Klima. She was a good wench. I moved the kaiila on. Zina, who had been taken with Tafa in a caravan raid by Hassan, the bandit, had not been at the two kasbahs in the desert. We did not know to whom she had been sold. We did not know at whose feet she knelt.

Toward the beginning of the fourth group I saw another girl I remembered. She turned away, trying to hide her face. I stoped the kaiila. Sensing that I had stopped, she fell to her knees and faced me, her head down. 'Forgive me, Master,' she whispered. 'Look at me, Slave Girl,' I told her. She looked up, frightened. It was Zaya, the red-haired girl, who had served sugars with the black wine in the palace of Suleiman Pasha. She had testified against me at Nine Wells.

'Do you recall,' I asked, 'who it was who struck Suleiman Pasha?'

'Hamid!' she wept. 'Hamid, lieutenant to Shakar, captain of the Aretai!'

'Your memory has improved,' I congratulated her. From my saddlebags I threw her a candy.

'Are you not angry with me, Master?' she asked. 'No,' I said. She thrust the candy in her mouth. I moved the kaiila on.

Hamid was not chained with the male prisoners. He had been taken to a remote Aretai oasis. There, in this exile, he would be a slave.

In the second group from the front I passed two women I had earlier met, Lana, the tall girl, who had been the seraglio mistress in the kasbah of Tarna, and the other girl, who had served with her, in charge of the oils of the bath. They stood proudly, as chained slave girls. Their utility in the seraglio terminated by myself and Hassan, Tarna had, in fury, sent them to the lowest levels of her kasbah, to serve there as wench sport for her soldiers. Little did they know but their proud mistress, whom they had never seen, had recently, as they had, now, too, served men, a rightless slave girl, she herself richly yielding rude soldiers delicious wench sport.

'Tal, Master,' they said to me.

'Tal, Slave Girls,' I said to them.

I moved the kaiila on. The male slaves of the seraglio had been freed. They were to be given money and safe conduct to Tor. They, though afoot, joined the march. One exception had Haroun, high Pasha of the Kavars, made. 'That one,' he had said, sitting in court, in the audience chamber of what had been the kasbah of Ibn Saran, indicating the silken fellow who had worn the ruby necklace, who had tried to betray us to the guards of Tarna, 'that one sell in Tor – sell him to a woman.' The fellow had been dragged away. He was with the male slaves toward the rear of the column; he alone among them was not stripped; he wore his seraglio silk, the ruby necklace; they did not look pleasantly upon him.

At the first group of fifty girls, nude, waiting in wrist coffle, I stopped. She was the twenty-third girl from the first girl on the line.

Her left wrist behind her, held by the chain to her sisters in bondage, she stepped forth. She put her head to my stirrup, not looking up. I felt her press her lips deeply, fervently, to my boot.

She looked up then, tears in her eyes.

'My thanks,' she whispered, 'Master.'

'You are in the first group, twenty-third girl,' I said. 'I hear among the men that you are quite good.'

'A girl is grateful,' she said, 'if men should find her pleasing.'

I made as though to ride from her. Her small right hand was at the stirrup. Her left hand was behind her, locked in its bracelet.

'I am not the same as a man,' she said, looking up.

361

'Obviously' I said, looking on her stripped slave beauty.

'I am different,' she said. She looked up. 'I love being different,' she whispered.

I nodded.

'I love men,' she said. 'They are so strong, so magnificent. I love being commanded by them. I love obeying them. I love knowing that if I displease them in the slightest, I will be whipped or slain. I had not known such feelings were possible.'

I regarded the girl in her rapture. How thrilled she was to discover the deliciousness of her own domination by men. Women desire male domination. Not receiving it they become petty, frustrated, competitive, hostile, and vicious, a function of this basic need having failed to be satisfied. The institution of female slavery in a society provides a vehicle for the expression and satisfaction of this basic need. The slave girl, of course, is completely and totally at the mercy of men. She is the most dominated of women. Further, her domination is supported by her civilization; it is legally binding and culturally sanctioned; it is complete; she sees it in the eyes of all who look upon her; it is complete; she is slave.

'I love being a slave,' said the girl, looking up at me.

'Kneel,' I told her.

'Yes, Master,' she said. She knelt. I lifted the single rein of the kaiila. I set my heels to touch its flanks, to move ahead in the line of march.

'Master,' said the girl.

'Yes,' I said.

'May I speak?' she asked.

'Yes,' I said.

'Will I be sold in Tor,' she asked.

'Yes,' I told her. 'You will be sold nude in Tor, from a slave block.'

'To whom will I be sold?' she asked.

'A Master,' I said. Then I kicked the kaiila in the flanks and moved ahead. The leather at the pommel of my saddle grew taut as I pulled with me, stumbling, the girl I had tethered there. Behind me, kneeling in the sand, in wrist coffle, fastened to others, on each side of her, I left a nameless slave beauty, who once had been Tarna.

It would be time enough in Tor, for her to have a name. She would receive it from her master. It would be whatever he wished. It is useful for a slave to have a name. It makes it easier to summon and command her.

I looked at the girl tethered to my saddle. Of all the slave girls about, save one in a white kurdah, near the head of the march, she was the only one who was clothed. Her neck was encircled by a band of steel, the slave collar. It was no longer that of Ibn Saran; it wore the name of Hakim of Tor. That was who the girl belonged to. Tight leather bound her wrists; her tether led to my saddle. The garment she wore was incredibly brief, a rag; it was of brown rep-cloth, stained with grease and dirt; I had found it in the kitchens of Ibn Saran; it had been used in the cleaning of pans; I had ripped it at the neck; I had torn it, lengthily, on the left side, to reveal the marvelous curve from her left breast to her left hip; let men look upon her beauty; it would be as public as I cared to make it, for she was my slave.

After she had falsely testified against me at Nine Wells, she had smiled, slyly, in triumph, pleased with her work, pleased that I would be sent to the brine pits of Klima; I had escaped from Nine Wells, but, recaptured, was enchained, destined for Klima; I well recalled her elation, her contempt, her scorn, as she had looked down upon me, helpless in the chain; she had flung me a token, something by which to remember her, a bit of slave silk, redolent with slave perfume; she had flung me a kiss, laughing, before being ordered back to her barred alcove by the slave master who at that time was supervising her.

I would not forget pretty Vella. Now I owned her. She had begged me to forgive her, as though a word from me would make all things right. When she had been flung to the feet of Hakim of Tor, she had looked up, in terror, then joy, seeing then who was Hakim of Tor, the master to whom I had consigned her, myself.

'Do not rise, Slave Girl,' I told her.

'Am I forgiven, Tarl?' she had begged. 'Am I forgiven?'

'Fetch the whip,' I told her.

I saw T'Zshal, who was riding past, leading his thousand lances. He reined in, and his men behind him.

'We are returning to Klima,' he said.

'But you have kaiila,' I said.

'We are slaves of the salt, slaves of the desert,' he said. 'We return to Klima.'

'The Salt Ubar is gone,' I said.

'We will negotiate with local pashas and regulate the desert, and discuss the prices of the varieties of salt,' said T'Zshal.

'The price of salt will soon rise,' I suggested.

'It is not impossible,' said T'Zshal.

I wondered if it were wise to have armed the men of Klima and put them in the saddles of kaiila. They were not typical men. There was none there who had not survived the march to Klima.

'Should you ever need aid,' said T'Zshal, 'send word to Klima. The slaves of the salt will ride.'

'My thanks,' I said. They would be fierce allies. They were desperate and mighty men. Each there had made the march to Klima. 'Things, now,' I said, 'I conjecture, will change at Klima.' I recalled that Hassan had warned me against taking a bit of silk, perfumed, into Klima. I had hidden it in the crusts. 'Men would kill you for it,' he said.

T'Zshal looked about himself. Slave girls, in coffle, shrank back.

'We will need taverns, cafes, at Klima,' he said. 'The men have been too long without recreation.'

'With control of much salt,' I said, 'you may have much what you wish.'

'We shall confederate the salt districts,' said T'Zshal.

'You are indeed ambitious,' I said. T'Zshal, I saw, was a leader. Haroun, sitting in court, in what had been the audience room of the kasbah of Ibn Saran, had invited T'Zshal, and his lances, to join his service. T'Zshal and the others had refused. 'We will return to Klima,' said he, 'Master.' T'Zshal, I knew, would serve under no man. 'I would rather be first at Klima than second in Tor,' he had said. He was a slave, true, but of no man, only of the salt, and the desert.

'I wish you well,' said T'Zshal.

'I wish you well,' I said.

His kaiila, with a scattering of sand, sped from me. He was followed by a thousand riders.

I rode, slowly, toward the head of the columns, across the desert between the two kasbahs.

Some two hundred yards from the head of the column, I passed the small Abdul, who had been a water carrier in Tor, and an agent of Ibn Saran. It was not impossible, through his work with Ibn Saran, that he knew matters of importance pertaining to the wars of Priest-Kings and Kurii. Two chains

364

ran to his metal collar, on opposite sides, leading, respectively, to the stirrup of a mounted rider on each side of him. His hands were manacled to a loop of chain about his waist. He did not raise his head. He feared to look me in the face. 'Let him be sent to Tor,' I had suggested. 'I will have agents of Samos, of Port Kar, sent to that city.' 'It will be done,' had said Haroun, high Pasha of the Kavars. The agents of Samos have interesting techniques of interrogation. I had no doubt that they would learn all that small Abdul had to tell them. After that, no longer of use to the agents of Priest-Kings, he could be sold south, into the Tahari.

Some hundred yards from the head of the column, I passed a large white kurdah, on a large, black kaiila. I did not brush aside the curtain. It did not contain a girl I owned. It contained a slave girl, an exquisitely feminine girl, blond-haired and blue-eyed; she was richly veiled and bejeweled; it was said she was the preferred slave of the great Haroun himself, high Pasha of the Kavars; it was said her name was Alyena; she was of high station; she wore silks, and veils, and jewels; but the collar on her throat was of steel.

In what had been the kasbah of Ibn Saran she had been thrown naked to the foot of the dais on which, cross-legged, sat the great Haroun himself. She had not dared to raise her head. 'I will keep this slave,' he had said. She had been dragged away, weeping. 'I am the slave of Hassan,' she had wept. 'I love only him!' That night, sent to his quarters, she had knelt before her veiled master.

'Do you love another, Girl?' he had asked, sternly.

'Yes,' she said, 'Master. Forgive me. Slay me, if you must.'

'And who is he?' asked her veiled master.

'Hassan,' she wept. 'Hassan, the bandit.'

'A most splendid fellow,' said her master.

The girl looked up, startled. His veil was about his shoulders.

'Hassan!' she wept. 'Hassan!' She threw herself to his feet, covering them with kisses as a slave girl.

When she looked up, he commanded her to the couch. She ran eagerly to it, tearing the slave silks with which she had been adorned from her body, and knelt upon it, small, her head down, awaiting her master. He joined her, discarding his robes. Then he seized her by the hair and pulled her head up and flung her on her back to the depth of the luscious silk, and then, with the cruel exploitativeness of the Tahari master, he claimed her – as his own.

Toward morning he reminded her that she must be whipped three times. First, she had called out his name at Red Rock, among the flames, during the raid of Tarna's men; secondly, she had fled from his riders, to return to Red Rock, to seek him out, when she had been captured; third, she had, that very evening, upon discovering who might be her master, cried out his name, 'Hassan! Hassan!'

'Whip me, Master,' she said, lying in his arms. 'I love you.'

'Am I forgiven, Tarl?' Vella had begged. 'Am I forgiven?'

'Fetch the whip,' I had told her.

She looked at me, dumbfounded. Women of Earth are always forgiven. They are never punished, no matter what they do. They, of course, are not slave girls. They lack the legalities, and the collar.

'You cannot be serious,' she said.

'Did I not speak of this to you when I first bound you as a slave girl?' I asked. I referred to our conversation in the room of preparation, when I had first surprised and captured her, making her mine.

'I asked when you would whip me,' she said, numbly. 'You responded, when it was to your convenience.' She looked at me, miserably.

'It is now convenient,' I told her.

She sprang wildly to her feet. 'I hate you!' she cried. 'I hate you!'

Her small fists were clenched. She was, wild with rage, quite beautiful in the brief, stained rag I had given her to wear.

'I hate you!' she cried. 'I hate all of you!' she cried, turning to look at the many warriors in the great room. 'I hate men!' she cried. She was barefoot on the tiles. She was the only woman in the room, and she was slave. 'I hate all men!' she cried. 'I hate them! I hate them!' She spun to face me. 'And I hate Priest-Kings, too!' she cried. 'I hate you all!'

No one responded to her, but gazed impassively upon her.

'I betrayed Priest-Kings!' she cried. 'Yes! I served Kurii! Yes! And I am glad I did, glad! Yes, glad! Glad! Glad!' Her eyes blazed. 'Punish me!' she demanded.

'You are not to be punished because you betrayed Priest-Kings,' I told her.

'You left me in a paga tavern in Lydius,' she cried out, 'a chained paga slave!'

'You chose to flee the Sardar,' I told her. 'It was a brave act. It did not turn out well for you. You fell slave. On Gor, as not on Earth, a girl bears the consequences of her actions.'

'You could have purchased me!' she cried.

'Yes,' I said, 'you were within my means.'

'But you did not do so!' she cried.

'It did not seem convenient to me, at that time,' I said, 'to purchase you, to keep you as a slave.'

'As a slave!' she cried. 'You should have freed me!'

'As I recall,' I said, 'you begged to be freed.'

'Yes!' she cried.

The men in the room looked at one another.

'I had not known, until that time,' I said, 'that you were, in the belly of you, a true slave girl.'

She looked at me, angrily. She turned red.

On Gor it is said that only a true slave begs to be freed. That act, incontrovertibly, on Gor, more deeply than a brand and a collar, marks the individual as a true slave. Who but such a true slave would beg to be freed? Such individuals, of course, are never freed, but, commonly, their nature now being made undeniably clear, are put under heavier restraints and treated more harshly. When Talena, the daughter of Marlenus of Ar, Ubar of Ar, had, in a missive to him, begged her freedom, he had, on his sword and on the medallion of Ar, sworn against her the oath of disownment. As a consequence, she was no longer of high birth, no longer his daughter. I had had Samos free her and transmit her to Ar. There she lived, free but of no status; she was no longer recognized, in the sight of its Home Stone, as a citizen of Ar; she had not even the collar of a slave girl for her identity; she was kept sequestered by Marlenus in the central cylinder, that his shame not be publicly displayed upon the high bridges of the city.

'No!' cried the girl. 'You should have freed me!'

I looked at her, in her rage. I did not suppose she had acted much differently than would have many women. The Goreans believe, of course, that in the belly of every woman there is a slave girl, waiting to be revealed by the right master.

'You should have freed me!' she cried. 'You should have freed me!'

I looked at her, in her rage, her beauty, her clenched fists, the brief, revealing rag.

'You are too beautiful to be free,' I told her.

367

She reacted as though struck.

She looked about, at the men in the room, clad in the garb of the Tahari. They looked upon her. She shuddered, knowing that among them she was too beautiful to be free.

She turned again to face me. She drew herself up. 'I am pleased I identified you for Ibn Saran,' she said. 'I am pleased that I testified against you at Nine Wells. Punish me.'

'You are not to be punished because you identified me for Ibn Saran,' I said, 'nor because you testified against me at Nine Wells.'

She looked at me, furious.

'Were you not commnded by your Master, Ibn Saran, to so testify?' I said.

'Yes,' she said.

'You are a good slave girl. You are to be commended,' I said. 'Throw her a candy,' I said to one of the men.

He did so.

'Eat it,' I told Vella.

She did so.

'You are to be punished,' I said, 'and punished only, because you, a slave girl, have not been found pleasing.'

She looked at me with horror.

'For so little? she said.

I gestured to man, an Aretai, in white burnoose, with black kaffiyeh and white agal cording, who stood nearby. He tossed a Gorean slave whip to the tiles, some twenty feet from the girl.

She looked at the whip in disbelief. Earth women, no matter what they do, are never punished. She could not believe that she was to be treated as a Gorean slave girl.

'Fetch the whip,' I told her.

She stood straight. 'Never!' she cried. 'Never! Never!'

'Bring a sand glass,' I said, 'of one Ehn's sand.' It was brought. The Gorean day consists of twenty Ahn; the Gorean Ahn, or hour, of forty Ehn, or minutes; the Ehn consists of eighty Ihn, or seconds. An Ihn is slightly less than an Earth second.

The glass was inverted.

She looked at it. 'You can never make me do this,' she said, 'Tarl.'

She watched the sand slip through the glass. She turned to face me. 'I'm pleased that I betrayed Priest-Kings. I'm pleased

368

that I served Kurii. I'm pleased that I identified you for Ibn Saran. I'm pleased that I testified against you at Nine Wells! Do you understand? Pleased!'

A quarter of the sand had slipped through the glass.

'You did not free me in Lydius. You kept me a slave!' She cried petulantly.

The sand had now slipped half through the glass. She looked about, from face to face, finding in them no sign of emotion, and then again she faced me.

'Of course I smiled at Nine Wells,' she cried. 'I wanted you sent to Klima! I wanted you sent there! Vengeance was sweet! Only you escaped! Of course I mocked you from the window of the kasbah of Ibn Saran! There would be no women at Klima! Of course in insolence I hurled you a bit of perfumed silk, to torment you in the march and, later, at Klima. Of course I lightly blew you a kiss of farewell, delighted in my triumph over you! Of course! Of course! Yes, yes, I mocked you when you were helpless! It gave me much pleasure to do so!'

There was only a quarter of the sand remaining. She looked at it miserably.

She turned to me again. 'I was cruel and petty, Tarl,' she said. 'Forgive me!'

The sand was almost slipped from the glass.

'I am a woman of Earth,' she cried. 'Of Earth!' Such women, of course, were never punished, no matter what they did. They were always forgiven. 'Forgive me, Tarl!' she cried. 'Forgive me!'

But she was a Gorean slave girl.

'Never will I fetch the whip!' she cried.

Then, crying out with misery, frightened, a moment before the sand slipped from the glass, she turned toward the whip.

'In the fashion of the Tahari,' I told her.

She moaned, and fell to her hands and knees. The men, impassively, watched her go to the whip and pick it up, in her teeth.

'Put the whip down,' I told her.

She put the whip down, dropping it from her teeth. She looked at me, joyfully. 'Kneel,' I told her. She did so, puzzled. 'Strip,' I told her, 'without rising to your feet.' She did so angrily, slipping the tiny, torn rag over her head and putting it to one side. She shook her hair; she straightened her body. A murmur of appreciation coursed through the men in the room. Then one, in Gorean fashion, struck his left shoulder, and then the others. She knelt, straight, while men applauded the beauty of her. How proud she was! How fantastically beautiful are women! And I owned her.

'Tie your garment about your right ankle,' I told her. She did this, sitting, and then, again, knelt.

'Now pick up the whip again,' I said, '– in your teeth.' She did so.

She did not wear a collar. I had had that of Ibn Saran removed. I would put her in one of mine later. She was naked except that about her right ankle, was tied a rag, and strangely perhaps, about her left wrist was knotted bit of bleached slave silk.

She looked at me, the whip in her teeth.

'Now go to your former slave alcove to be beaten,' I told her. She left the room, a slave girl on her way to discipline.

I turned to one of the men nearby. 'Be as her caller and guard,' I said to him.

He nodded, and, bending down, picked up a strap which lay nearby. 'I shall come presently,' I told him. He acknowledged this. He left the room, following the girl.

A guard is not used in such cases to prevent the escape of the girl, for, in such a situation, in a house or kasbah, there is no escape for her. He serves to protect her, interestingly, from other slave girls. The strap or coiled rope he carries is used less often to hasten, in a humiliating fashion, a girl who might otherwise dally on the way to discipline, though it may serve this purpose, than it is to drive other girls from her. Such a strap or rope, of course, can sting hotly through slave silk. She is very vulnerable, you see, the girl who is to be punished, on the way to discipline. She is naked; she is not permitted to rise; she may not even speak, for the whip must be held between her teeth; to drop it is twenty extra lashes. Resentments, jealousies, petty feuds, enmities, are common among the female slaves. Particularly is there jealousy and hatred for the most beautiful slaves, or for the highest slaves. Such a girl, on her way to discipline, is a delight to those who hate and envy her, and who would be only too pleased to take this opportunity to jeer and abuse her, sometimes cruelly and physically. Although many girls in the kasbah were chained here and there for the pleasures of men, most were freed of impediments, that they might fetch and serve, and be seized when and wherever the men might want them. These, in the halls, would constitute a genuine danger to Vella, who, a high slave, had been the object of much envy. How pleased they would be to see proud Vella crawling in the halls to her discipline. The second reason a man accompanies the girl is to be the caller. He performs what is spoken of sometimes as the whip song, though it is not a song, but rather a series of calls or announcements. These summon other girls to witness one of their sisters on the way to discipline. 'Here is a girl who has not been fully pleasing,' cries the man. 'Look upon her. She is going to discipline. She was not completely pleasing. See her! Come, witness a girl who has not been fully pleasing!' These cries bring the other girls, with their burdens, and such, to watch the progress through the halls of the girl who is to be punished. Soon a derisive, moving gauntlet is formed, through which, constantly, the miserable, whip-bearing girl crawls. She is spat upon, and struck, with hands and straps, and kicked, and much abused, but, of course, only within those limits set by the caller and guard. This sort of thing is thought desirable in the Tahari, in encouraging the whipbearing girl to be more dutiful in the future, and the girls of the gauntlet to resolve, too, to be more dutiful, that it not be they, next, at the mercy of their enemies and rivals, who carries the whip. The actual whipping in the Tahari, incidentally, is usually a matter between the girl and the master, or he and his men. Other girls are seldom permitted to watch one of their sisters being whipped. All they know, when the doors close, is that she will be whipped.

I found the girl kneeling before the small iron gate of her former slave alcove. The guard, having accompanied her to the quarters for female slaves, which were now empty, the girls being elsewhere, serving men, had left her there. We were alone in the large, beautiful, tiled, pillared room. She looked at me. I took the whip from her teeth and thrust it in my sash.

'Remove the rag from your right ankle,' I told her. She did this, and put it to one side.

She had come through the corridors from the audience chamber on her hands and knees, carrying the whip, head down, in her teeth, between two lines, moving with her, of slave girls, girls running, when she had crawled by them, to be again at the head of the line, to have again their lashing stroke, their cry or jeer.

I threw her a towel that she might wipe her body and long,

swirling dark hair, cleaning it. She did so, gratefully. I saw that she had been much struck and abused. The girls had had much sport with her as she had crawled, helpless, to her discipline. Vella was obviously the object of much hostility among the other slave girls. She was apparently much resented and hated. Vella was too beautiful, I supposed, to be popular with women. The very beauty which made her prized among men would make her an object of hostility and loathing among women. A beauty like Vella on Gor had little choice but to relate to men, and, of course, she a slave, on their terms. Too, she had been a high slave, much above the other girls, now fallen far below them, now a fit object for their abuse and scorn, to be tempered only to the degree to which they were willing to feel the flash of the guard's strap through their silk. She looked at me, tears in her eyes.

'Tarl?' she asked.

She moved toward me, and slipped to her feet, encircling my body with her small arms. About her left wrist, knotted, was the bleached silk from Klima. She put her head against my shoulder, and then lifted it, softly kissing me. She was a very delicious and beautiful naked slave. 'I love you, Tarl,' she said.

'Give me your wrist,' I said.

She extended her left wrist to me. I removed from it the silk from Klima. I put it in my sash.

'I did not realize until now your plan,' she said, 'to pretend to make me your slave, to fool the others.' She looked about. 'We are alone,' she smiled.

I opened the small square gate in the alcove, set in the bars, some ten inches from the floor. The opening is about eighteen inches square.

'What are you doing?' she asked.

I would use a standard Tahari tie.

'Tarl?' she asked.

The door is opened that the girl's beauty not be hurt against the closed bars of the tiny gate.

'Oh!' she cried. I thrust her, holding her by her arms from behind, on her knees, belly tight, against the flat iron piece over which the door swings, in closing. Her knees were thus through the bars, on the inside of the cell. With a length of binding fiber, about her knees and behind and over the bars I secured her in position. She could not fall backwards. I then took her wrists up, one at time, she, startled, not resisting, and tied them, on the outside, each to a separate bar, on either side of the small iron gate. 'Tarl!' she said. She can grasp the bar with her small hand.

I regarded her.

'Tarl,' she said, 'you need not carry your plan so far. We shall not be surprised. Girls will not be permitted to return here until the earliest hours of the morning. We shall not be surprised. It is not necessary to fasten me like this, so help-lessly.'

I said nothing. How foolish I thought her. But she was, of course, a woman of Earth.

'Enough of this joke,' she said, irritably. 'Release me, now! Now!'

But she did not find herself released.

'Tarl,' she said. The right side of her face was pressed against the flat iron bar, some two inches high, at the top of the open-ing, against which the gate, when closed, rests. 'Do you realize what you have done?'

'What?' I asked.

'You have put me in Tahari whipping position,' she said.

'Oh?' I said.

'It is degrading,' she said. 'Release me, immediately!' She squirmed. She was helpless, warrior-tied. 'Immediately!' she said. 'Immediately!'

But she was not released.

I took the whip from my sash.

'You will not truly strike me with the whip, will you?' she asked. She spoke to me, her head turned, over her left shoulder. 'I am a woman of Earth,' she said. 'You cannot treat me like a mere Gorean slave girl. You know you cannot do it.'

I opened the whip, letting the broad, soft leather fall loose.

'We are alone here,' she said. 'None will know whether you strike me or not. You need not strike me. You may simply say that you did. I shall, in the deception, corroborate your story. The charade that you would keep me as a slave need not now be prolonged.' She tried to turn her head, to look at me. But she could not see me. 'Surely you have no intention of making me a true slave, for you are only of Earth,' she laughed. 'Only of Earth!' Then she said, 'Release me, now! I demand it! You are only of Earth! Only of Earth! I simply demand to be released, Tarl! Now! Now!'

I said nothing.

She did not find herself released.

'None will know if you do not whip me,' she said.

'I will know,' I told her. 'And one other, too, will know.'

'Who?' she asked.

'The pretty little she-animal and slave, Vella,' I said.

Her fists clenched in the bindings.

'You may call me Elizabeth,' she said.

'Who is she?' I asked.

'Oh, Tarl,' she scolded.

I smiled. Did she not know there was no Elizabeth unless a master chose to call her by that name?

She spoke more confidently now. 'I am a woman of Earth,' she said. 'It is not necessary to beat a woman of Earth, to teach her a lesson, should that be perhaps, amusing and preposterous uiough it is, what is in your mind. She, Tarl, is not an animal who must be whipped. She is a person. She is not a mere Gorean girl, a simple, vital, half-animal thing. She is a person! A true person! I have learned my lesson, Tarl. I am truly sorry. I was cruel and petty. I know! I am sorry. I have learned my lesson. It will not be necessary to beat me.' She smiled. 'Untie me, Tarl,' she said. 'Untie me now.'

I stepped to the bars.

'Thank you, Tarl,' she said. But I did not untie her. I held the bit of bleached slave silk, removed from my sash, over her nose and mouth. She could breathe easily through it, and speak through it. But she could not breathe or speak without feeling it, without inhaling and taking into her very body the faint, lingering traces of slave perfume, hers, which yet clung to it. Suddenly her voice, her lips moving beneath the silk, became less certain. 'I am not a Gorean girl,' she said, 'fit for physical discipline. I am not one of those animals who understands only the whip.'

I replaced the bit of silk in my sash. I stepped back.

'I am a woman of Earth!' she cried. Her small hands, wrists warrior-tied to the bars, clenched the bars in terror. She turned her head again, desperately, trying to look at me. She could not see me. 'Tarl!' she cried. 'Tarl?'

I swung back the whip.

'You will not punish me as a Gorean slave girl!' she cried.

'You have not been pleasing,' I said.

After the fourth stroke she screamed out, weeping, 'I have been punished! Stop! Stop! A girl has been punished! Stop!'

After the sixth stroke she cried out, 'Please stop, I beg of you, Master!'

Twenty strokes did I give the slave girl. Then I untied her from the bars. She fell to the tiles before me, reaching for my ankles, pressing her lips, hot and wet, to my boots, her tears hot on the leather. 'What are you?' I asked. 'A Gorean slave girl at the feet of her master,' she said.

'I have not begun to punish you,' I told her. She looked at me with fear, and wonder. I tied her small garment, which I picked up from the floor, about her neck, and her hands behind her back. I strode through the halls, she, stumbling, running, following me. Outside, I untied her, and then retied her, belly up, head down, over the saddle of a kaiila, and took her to the nearby kasbah, which had once been that of Tarna. There I took her down to the fourth level, the lowest level, and, throwing the tiny garment into a cell, whence it would be retrieved later, I took her to the branding chamber, threw her into the device, and locked it on her thigh. Hassan was there and the iron was already hot. It was the same iron with which he had, the night before, marked the proud Tarna. It had been cleaned, with a solvent. One iron, properly cared for, can mark thousands of women. 'No, Master,' she said, 'please!' 'Do you wish to mark her?' asked Hassan. 'Yes,' I said. I would place the mark on her left thigh, above that of the four bosk horns. It would be the common Gorean female slave mark, fitting for a low girl, such as she, one who had not been fully pleasing.

I held up the iron, white hot, for the girl's inspection.

'You will soon be branded, Girl,' I told her.

'Don't brand me!' she cried. 'Please don't brand me!' She wept.

Hassan regarded her with interest.

'We are now ready,' I told her.

She looked at me, then at the glowing, white-hot marking surface of the iron. She watched it with horror, as it approached her.

I held it poised at her thigh.

'Don't!' she cried. 'Don't!'

'You are now to be branded, Slave Girl,' I told her. 'No,' she screamed. Then I branded her. For five long Ihn I held the iron, pressing it in. I watched it sink in her thigh, smoking and crackling and hissing. It was a larger brand than that of the four bosk horns; I made sure it marked her more deeply. We three, Hassan, I and the girl, smelled the marked, burned slave flesh of her. Then, swiftly, cleanly, I withdrew it. Her head was back. She was screaming and weeping. 'A perfect brand,' said Hassan, looking on. 'Perfect!' I was pleased. Such a brand would be envied by other girls. It would improve the sleek little animal's value.

I removed the locking device, and spun loose the twist handles, releasing her thigh. I freed her of the snap bracelets. I carried her, naked, branded, weeping, to the small cell where I had thrown her tiny garment to be retrieved later. I put her down on the straw. Her throat was bare, for I had had, the preceding night, the collar of Ibn Saran removed from her throat.

'Assume the posture of female submission,' I told her. She did so, kneeling back on her heels, her arms extended, wrists crossed, her head between them, down. She was weeping.

'Repeat after me,' I told her, ' "I, once Miss Elizabeth Cardwell, of the planet Earth —" '

'I, once Miss Elizabeth Cardwell of the planet Earth —' she said.

' "— herewith submit myself, completely and totally, in all things —" '

'— herewith submit myself, completely and totally, in all things —' she said.

' "— to he who is now known here as Hakim of Tor —" '

'— to he who is now known here as Hakim of Tor —' she said.

' "— his girl, his slave, an article of his property, his to do with as he pleases —" '

'— his girl, his slave, an article of his property, his to do with as he pleases,' she said.

Hassan handed me the collar. It was inscribed 'I am the property of Hakim of Tor'. I showed it to the girl. She could not read Taharic script. I read it to her. I put it about her neck. I snapped it shut.

' "I am yours, Master," ' I said to the girl.

She looked up at me, tears in her eyes, her neck in my locked collar. 'I am yours, Master,' she said.

'Congratulations on your slave!' said Hassan. 'She is lovely meat. Now I must attend to my own slave.' He laughed, and left.

376

The girl sank to the straw, and looked up at me. Her eyes were soft with tears. She whispered. 'I am yours now, Tarl,' she said. 'You own me. You truly own me.'

'What is your name?' I asked.

'What ever master wishes,' she whispered.

'I will call you "Vella",' I said.

'I am Vella,' she said, her head down. After a time she lifted her head. 'May I call you Tarl?' she asked.

'Only if given permission,' I told her. This was normal Gorean slave custom. Generally, of course, such permission is not even asked, and, if asked, would be denied. Sometimes a girl is whipped for even daring to ask this permission.

'A girl asks permission to call her Master by his name,' she said.

'It is denied,' I said.

'Yes, Master,' she said. I would not permit the slave girl to speak my name. It is not fitting that the name of the master be soiled by being touched by the lips of a slave girl.

I looked at her in the straw. 'You were displeasing,' I told her.

'A girl has been punished by her master,' she said.

I took the chain and collar in the cell, and locked it on her throat, over her close-fitting steel collar, that identifying her as mine. She was, thus, chained to the wall.

'I have not begun to punish you,' I told her, looking down at her.

'I hate you,' she said, sullenly. 'I hate you!' She looked up at me. 'You caused me much pain,' she said. 'You whipped me. You branded me.' She turned her head to one side. 'I am confused,' she said. 'I do not know what to think.'

'How is that?' I asked.

'It hurt terribly to be whipped, and branded,' she said.

'Yes?' I said.

'And yet, because of these things, I stand wonderfully and vulnerably in awe of you, and of men in general,' she said.

'What thrills you,' I said, 'is not the whip, not the iron, not pain, but masculine domination. It is that to which you, unknown to yourself, are responding. What is important is not whether the master whips you or not, but that you know he is fully capable of whipping you, and will, if you are not pleasing.'

'Yes,' she said, 'that is it – not the pain – but my weakness, and the strength of men, and that I am under their will, and that, if I am not pleasing, I know that he is man enough and powerful enough to put me under harsh discipline, and, should I not be pleasing, will, without a thought, do so.'

'Your body is now hot, Slave Girl,' I said.

'No!' she said.

I touched her and she writhed in the straw, turning away from me, pulling her legs up. I touched her on the shoulder, and she shuddered. Every inch of her was alive. 'Slave Girl,' I sneered.

'Yes, Slave Girl!' she cried, turning on her back, throwing her body brazenly open to me.

'You seem little of Earth now,' I laughed.

She spread her hair back on the straw. 'I am only a slut of a slave,' she laughed. 'Treat me as such. I love you, Master!'

We heard soldiers in the hall outside.

'Will you give me to others?' she asked.

'If it pleases me,' I said.

'Yes,' she said, 'you will – if it pleases you.' She turned her head to the side. 'How vulnerable I am!' She looked up at me. Her head was back in the straw. 'For the first time in my life,' she said, 'I know that I am a slave girl, only a slave girl. It is such a strange, helpless feeling. No longer am I a woman of Earth. I am now only a Gorean slave girl.'

I lifted her by the arms. 'I do not know if I love or hate,' she said. 'I know only I am a slave girl, and that I am helpless, and that I am in the arms of my master.'

I lifted her toward my lips, to claim her. 'Have you forgotten Earth?' she asked.

'I have never heard of that place,' I told her.

She lifted her lips, timidly, delicately, to mine. 'Nor have I,' she said. She whispered, very softly, 'I love you, Master.' I did not let her kiss me. Rather, I suddenly, with a larl's ferocity, thrust my lips to hers, cruelly, in the raping kiss of the master, and pressed her savagely back into the straw, against the very stones of the dungeon cell in which she lay slave, chained, beneath me. She squirmed and then, held, cried out, a scream that must have carried to every cell, through every corridor, of that grim level, startling the enslaved beauties chained there, amusing the soldiers in whose arms they lay, a scream at once of wild love and of a helpless slave girl's total submission.

Near the front of the march I joined Hassan.

'One thing puzzles me,' I told him. 'One thing I do not yet understand.'

'What is that?' he asked.

'In the house of Samos, at Port Kar,' I said, 'there was a girl, Veema, a message girl. The message she bore was "Beware Abdul." Mistakenly I took the Abdul of this message to be Abdul, the carrier of water, in Tor.'

'That is not a mistake which one of the Tahari would have made,' said Hassan. He looked at me. 'Was not Ibn Saran at that time in the house of Samos?'

'Yes,' I said.

'The timing is interesting,' said Hassan. 'Perhaps he who sent the message assumed that the information of the agents of Priest-Kings was sufficient to identify Ibn Saran with Abdul, the Salt Ubar, or, at least, to link him with that villain.'

'At that time, it was not,' I said. Since the time of the Nest War the intelligence and surveillance networks of the Priest-Kings had been severely impaired. Even had they not been, their information, they, seldom leaving the Sardar, not being as humans, was little better than that of their human agents, widely separated in space and time.

'But who sent the message girl, Veema, to the house of Samos?' I asked.

'I did,' said Hassan. 'My brother told me to do this. He had had the message placed months before. I merely transmitted her. He then entered the desert to investigate rumors of a tower of steel. He must have been captured by men of Ibn Saran. He was released in the desert with insufficient water.'

'He made it very far,' I said.

'He was very strong,' said Hassan.

'The Priest-Kings are fortunate,' I said, 'that such men fight for them.'

'I knew another,' said Hassan, 'quite as strong, who fought for Kurii.'

I nodded. I would not forget Ibn Saran, lithe, like a silken panther. He had been a worthy foe. One gains a victory; one loses an enemy.

I lifted my head to the sky, wide and blue, with no clouds. Somewhere up there, beyond atmospheres, beyond the orbits of Gor, and Earth and Mars, in a boulder-strewn, enigmatic blackness of space, in the silence of the fragments of the asteroid belt, were the steel worlds, the lairs and domiciles of Kurii. A Kur had fought by my side to save the Gorean world. It was desired not only by men. It was desired, too, by Kurii. I did not think that Kurii, again, would be willing to sacrifice this world, to achieve another. Already, in their remote past, they had lost one world, their own. The political ascendancy of the party which had been willing to destroy Gor, to secure the Earth, had, with the failure of their project, doubtless been brief. That a Kur had been sent to foil them was doubtless significant. Further, Gor was the true prize of the planets rotating about the sun, not the Earth, for, in the name of rights and liberty, and business, the fools of Earth, confused by the rhetoric of law and morality, shielding short-sighted greed and madness, had stood aside, permitting the poisoning of the air they breathed, the water they drank, the food they ate. That the poisoners will die with the poisoned will perhaps yield them some comfort. Priest-Kings, of course, who are accustomed to think directly in terms of realities and consequences, not words, had not permitted this same insane duplicity to be practiced upon their gullibility. They do not shrivel before the moral fervor of fanatics; rather they seek to look behind words, discarding them as largely meaningless, to discover what is truly meant, what is wanted, what is being striven for, and, if these programs and policies are implemented, what will be the nature of the resultant world, and is that world acceptable or not. To exploitation, to waste, to pollution, Priest-Kings had simply, in their technological abridgments imposed on man, said, 'No.' It is, in defense of their tyranny, their despotism, you see, after all, lest you think too badly of them, their habitat as well.

I looked up at the sky. The Kurii, I suspected, did not want Earth, but Gor. Earth might be useful as a slave planet, but the true prize, the object of their predation, would be Gor.

What then could be the next step? The uprising of native Kurii had been foiled in Torvaldsland. I had been in Torvaldsland at the time. The destruction of Gor, to rid themselves of the opposition of Priest-Kings, had been foiled. When this had occurred I had been at the steel tower in the Tahari, the half-burried ship which had housed the destructive device. I gazed at the placid sky.

Surely Kurii must, by now, sense the weakness of the Nest. The ship, for example, which had housed the destructive device had penetrated the weakened defenses of the Priest-Kings. But the Priest-Kings, after the Nest War, would be rebuilding their power.

It might well seem to Kurii that they must strike soon. There was not a cloud in the wide, bright Tahari sky. The invasion, I surmised, must be impending.

The drums of the march increased their beat. I turned on the kaiila, looking behind me, at the long columns of riders, of kaiila, of slaves. I saw the desert, the pennons. I saw the two kasbahs, which had been those of Abdul, Ibn Saran, the Salt Ubar, and Tarna, once a proud desert chieftainess.

I felt the cheek of the girl tethered to my saddle press softly against the side of my left boot. I looked down, and she looked up at me. 'Master?' she asked.

'The march will be long,' I told her. 'If you cannot make it,' I said, 'you will be dragged.'

She smiled up at me. She kissed the side of my boot. 'A girl knows,' she said, 'Master.' She again kissed the side of my boot, in the stirrup, and again looked up at me. 'I know I deserve to be whipped,' she said, and she looked at me in awe, and admiration, 'and you whipped me.' She again kissed my boot, and again regarded me, eyes smiling. 'I was proud,' she said, 'and arrogant, and insolent, and contemptuous, and, when you were helpless, mocked you to my delight from safety. You did not approve of this. You returned from Klima. You burned me with the iron and made me your slave.' Her eyes shone. 'You are magnificent!' she said. With the back of my left hand I cuffed her from the side of the saddle.

I saw pennons on the lances. I listened to the drums. I was eager to begin the march.

Hassan, in swirling white, lifted his hand. The drums stopped. I rode between Hassan, Haroun, high Pasha of the Kavars, and, in the black kaffiyeh with white agal cording, Suleiman, high Pasha of the Aretai. Near us were Baram, sheik of Bezhad, vizier to Haroun, high Pasha of the Kavars, and Shakar, with silver-tipped lance, a captain of the Aretai. With us, too, were other pashas. In the march were Kavars, and Aretai, Ta'Kara, Bakahs, Char, Kashani, Luraz, Tashid, Raviri, Ti, Zevar, Arani and, holding the position of the rear guard, with their black lances, Tajuks.

I looked back at the kasbahs which had been those of Abdul, Ibn Saran, the Salt Ubar, and Tarna, once a proud desert chieftainess. Their walls were bright, hot and white in the morning sun.

Hassan lowered his hand. Pennons dipped and straightened. The drums began the beat of the march. There was a jangling of kaiila harness, the movement of weapons.

I began the march. Beside me, at my stirrup, my slave, was Vella.

SCIENCE FICTION
STAR

Joanna Russ
| 0352398655 | **Picnic on Paradise** | 50p* |

Kilgore Trout
| 0352398469 | **Venus on the Half Shell** | 50p* |

SCIENCE FANTASY
STAR

W.W.
| 0352398523 | **Qhe: Prophets of Evil** | 50p |

SCIENCE FANTASY
TANDEM

Edgar Rice Burroughs
| 0426148401 | **Out of Time's Abyss** | 35p* |

THE FANTASTIC GOR SERIES
John Norman
0426144961	**Assassin of Gor**	45p*
0426167821	**Captive of Gor**	60p*
0426147952	**Hunters of Gor**	45p*
042617531X	**Marauders of Gor**	60p*
0426144880	**Nomads of Gor**	45p*
0426167740	**Priest-Kings of Gor**	50p*
0426124235	**Raiders of Gor**	40p*
0426143736	**Tarnsman of Gor**	35p*

PLANET OF THE APES
David Gerrold
| 0426147448 | **Battle for the Planet of the Apes** | 35p* |

John Jakes
| 0426147529 | **Conquest of the Planet of the Apes** | 35p* |

Jerry Pournelle
| 042614760X | **Escape From the Planet of the Apes** | 35p* |

George Alec Effinger
0426156757	**Escape to Tomorrow**	35p*
0426160371	**Journey into Terror**	35p*
0426151739	**Man the Fugitive**	35p*

Jane Gaskell
0426159667	**Atlan**	60p
0426164326	**The City**	45p
0426159586	**The Dragon**	45p
0426159314	**The Serpent**	60p

John Jakes
0426167074	**Brak the Barbarian**	45p*
0426167236	**Mark of the Demons**	45p*
0426167155	**The Sorceress**	45p*

*Not for sale in Canada

Wyndham Books are obtainable from many booksellers and newsagents. If you have any difficulty please send purchase price plus postage on the scale below to:

Wyndham Cash Sales,
123 King Street,
London W6 9JG

OR

Star Book Service,
G.P.O. Box 29,
Douglas,
Isle of Man,
British Isles

While every effort is made to keep prices low, it is some-times necessary to increase prices at short notice. Wyndham Books reserve the right to show new retail prices on covers which may differ from those advertised in the text or elsewhere.

U.K. & Eire
One book 15p plus 7p per copy for each additional book ordered to a maximum charge of 57p.

Other Countries
Rates available on request.

These charges are subject to Post Office charge fluctuations.